MIDNIGHT FIRE

He came in quietly, expecting her to be asleep. She didn't tell him she wasn't. He laid his pistols on the table, along with his riding gauntlets—and a weighted purse. He quietly brought the fire back to life, and took off his greatcoat.

Jane regarded him in a way she hadn't consciously done before: he was heavy, but favorably proportioned. And undeniably handsome. His hair was black as the midnight sky. His rough-hewn features were alive with willfulness and character. There was a smooth, brawny strength in his shoulders, and his thighs were sleek and powerful.

He moved a chair before the fire. He seemed tired. He pulled his sword from its scabbard and examined the blade. The glow from the flames glanced off the bright metal.

After a moment, he stood up and peeled off his black shirt. Jane had never seen him shirtless. Now she did. Her eyes saw all too distinctly. He was well made, broad of shoulder, narrow of hip, muscles well defined by his labor with axe and pistols. He sat down again to pull off his boots. His legs were long, strongly molded by horsemanship. His bare feet were narrow. He stood again to take off his drawers, his breeches.

When he was done, Jane said quietly, "Keith."

NADINE CRENSHAW

THE HIGHWAYMAN

PINNACLE BOOKS
WINDSOR PUBLISHING CORP.

PINNACLE BOOKS are published by

Windsor Publishing Corp
475 Park Avenue South
New York, NY 10016

Pinnacle and the P logo are trademarks of Windsor Publishing Corp.

First Printing: November, 1993

Printed in the United States of America

I've fallen in love at least a hundred times, always with the same man. That is why so many of my books, including this one, are dedicated to my husband, Robert.

The wind was a torrent of darkness
            among the gusty trees,
The moon was a ghostly galleon
            tossed upon cloudy seas,
The road was a ribbon of moonlight
            over the purple moor,
And the highwayman came riding
            up to the old inn-door.
Alfred Noyes: "The Highwayman"

Chapter One

The Face of Jane Fitzpatrick

Midnight. A dusty crossroads in the dead vast middle of the night, a place that had about it a feeling of utter remoteness, a spot where the silence was as real and as substantial as sound. The moon threw down the sharp shadows of an upright and crossbeam from which hung a rope, and at the end of the rope the shape of a man with his head tilted severely to one side.

Another shadow moved from a nearby wood into the open. A horseman cloaked in purpose, covered with stealth. A pair of heavy pistols, their butts jutting from their leather cases, were slung over the pommel of his black stallion's saddle. When the animal's hooves met the road there came a *cloppa-cloppa* sound, muffled by the dust, hardly enough to disturb the night.

The moving shadow went directly to that other, unmoving shape. The living regarded the dead. The corpse's head sagged sideways on the noose, which had bitten deep into the neck. The wide-open, empty eyes were distended, thrust bulbously out of their sockets. The moon was caught in them; they glittered gold and green, as hard and unseeing as precious gems. The mouth gaped, the jaw was spilled over to one side. Over the lips, like a gigantically swollen slug, the tongue poured onto the chin.

" 'O villain, villain, smiling, damned villain.' "

The highwayman sat studying the corpse for another minute. If he felt any qualm of horror or disgust, if his hair prickled on his skull beneath his tricorn hat, he didn't show it.

"Here is the end you deserved, Georgie, and no more than any of us expect. Still, it's enough to be hung, and vile business—don't you think—to leave a man dangling when he should be decently in his grave?"

He pulled the leather gauntlet off his left hand. An opal ring set in silver gleamed as he reached for his side-arm sword. As he swung the blade, it became a bright, thin streak of light. He cut the rope from which hung the frightful remains of George Moraga. The body dropped to the whitened dust of the crossroads.

With patrician easiness, the highwayman dismounted. His midnight eyes narrowed, as if against the moon—though in reality against the noisome smell of his dead mentor as he heaved the body over the saddle of his mount. The corpse in place, he turned away and gave an openmouthed gasp.

He led his burdened stallion back to the woods, holding his face in a mask of stretched revulsion. "I came all the way from Derbyshire to do you this favor, Georgie, because we were friends of a sort. And in the hope that someone will do it for me one day. I don't mind hanging for my sins, but I have a finicky objection to rotting in public. I warrant I'll make no lovelier a corpse than you do—and no lovelier a stench."

He led the horse beneath dark branches that were laced with a tracery of silver moonlight. No single leaf moved on its stem. The oaks crowded thicker and

8

higher and blacker overhead. Shadows merged with shadows. The highwayman and his cargo disappeared beyond a jut of stone, leaving the moonlight to lay like ashes upon the landscape, to fall silently upon the crossroads, upon the dust, to cast a dark, sharp-angled shadow of an empty gallows.

The moon set, and rose again. One night older it shed its light on the magnificent country villa of the present Baron of Murdock, Robert Hamilton. The first frost of the season dusted the avenue of trees and glistened on the landscaped lawns. The only evidence of life in the house was the threads of smoke escaping from the square, stone bedchamber chimneys. Some of the villa's windows were shuttered—but not those of the morning room. There the white light drizzled and sifted unchecked into the interior.

The silence in that room seemed impenetrable. Though heavy with shadow, it was decorated in the highest style. On the table, elaborately inlaid in the French manner, stood dark purple wine in a glinting glass decanter. Sugar wafers lay in a sterling dish. The prisms of the chandelier winked blue in the moonlight. The coals in the small fireplace were banked in gray ash. The moonlight barely illuminated the antique smiles of the many blackening paintings on the walls. The largest portrait was new, however, a full-length canvas set in a gilt frame that itself was six inches broad.

Within that frame the likeness of a young woman stood alone in the dark near a garden bench. Walls of white roses surrounded her. Her face tilted up as her hand cupped one of the blooms to inhale its scent. She wore the barest hint of a smile, as if musing on some pleasing secret. Against the somber background,

9

she stood out like porcelain. A tiny-waisted, bare-shouldered beauty amidst the midnight roses. The full skirt of her white gown was worn over a hooped petticoat that spread out sideways, extending the line of her hips in the current fashion. Her hems ended just above the toes of her white taffeta slippers. Her cheeks and shoulders and hands had that pale, soft roundness which comes from having plenty to eat and little to do. A young lady, tranquil with ease and courtesy.

The author of this portrait was none other than the current Lord Murdock himself. A man of modest ability, he had been inspired by his model. The little, stooped, pot-bellied baron had been offered impressive sums for this work; but perhaps knowing it was the best he would ever do (a disturbing thought since he was not terribly old) he found he couldn't part with it. However, he had agreed to let it be copied by a York etche.)

Hence reproductions of "The Rose of Midnight" were at the moment displayed widely, even in public ordinaries where all persons were welcome to spend their money, including many a misbegotten wretch and many a coarse buffoon.

Including tonight a certain man who had traveled to the north on an errand of decency, a man of the midnight, of pitch black vices, the sort who would come to naught soon enough, most likely on a gibbet or a gallows at a lonely crossroads where he would rot all-too publicly.

A fire-opal set in silver flashed from the rogue's left hand as he sat in a roadhouse outside the city of York. With the taproom's firelight playing on his face, he stared up from beneath dark brows at a cheaply framed etching of a Madonna-faced woman surrounded by roses. She stood in a shadowy garden, dressed in silk, her oval face framed with luxurious hair, her white shoulders and round bosom more exposed than not. And for a moment she seemed more real to the highwayman than reality. His senses opened; a certain scent seemed to waft over him, a faint rose-sweetness.

Her potent serenity held him in an eddy of silence amidst the tavern's merrymakers. The noisy hobnails of the yeomen, the smelly tobacco of the draymen, the foaming punch of the local topers and drunken coachmen, all arguing about the German king upon the throne and the Whig politicians who tolerated the religious free-thinkers with which the country was rife—none of this touched the highwayman. He heard their voices as if from a great way off.

That face . . . her eyes were exotic in shape, with just the merest hint of blue in that midnight-and-moonlight color scheme. She had a sensual, full-lipped mouth, the corners tucked in ever so slightly and the petal of the lower lip curled out ever so richly. Her hair, uncapped, was bound back only by a ribbon. Long and dark and thick and splendid, it poured over her shoulders. A beautiful woman, fair of skin, who seemed to have some mysterious joy hidden just beneath her secret expression. Looking at her, the highwayman knew exactly how her skin might feel to the palm of his rough hand, how her hair might smell.

A great whiplash of presentiment caught him. He blinked like a fool, then closed his eyes, realizing they were burning.

Where the frost fell, the moonlight fell. It fell over the past that still littered the region, a past of castles and ruined abbeys and strange stones left by the Druids. It fell over farmhouses that sat resembling afterthoughts along the roads, and over the rolling, empty

11

moors behind them. It fell over the city of York, on paupers' holes and through the grand stained glass of Minster Cathedral. It fell on a handsome, three-storied house, through the upper window of the garret chamber, and across a maidservant's narrow bed.

Jane Fitzpatrick slept deeply, remote from fine gowns and elegant morning rooms, innocent of noisy public houses and the shadowy doings of highwaymen and the stark manner of their deaths. Hers was a life of humble usefulness, of hard work and deep sleep.

Her days began at five A.M., when she lit the fires in the kitchen for Mrs. Galbraith, the cook. Jane then tied up her overskirt, covering it with her apron, and protected her indoor shoes with a pair of wooden pattens while she went out to the street pump to bring back buckets of water. She then gathered her broom and set about sweeping away the debris dropped by the pair of clipped yews that guarded the front steps. Next came lighting the fire in the dining room and laying the table for her master's breakfast. Her own breakfast was taken quickly, before she lit the fire in Mr. Welby's chamber, waking him at the same time by calling through his bed curtains, "Here is your tea, master."

"Thank you, Jane."

Downstairs again to light the fire in the parlor, then on to her daily duties of cleaning, sweeping, dusting, and shopping for the household.

Dinner broke the day neatly in half.

In the afternoon, she "turned out" one room thoroughly, moving in sequence from parlor, to library, to dining room, to halls and stairs, to Mr. Welby's chamber, to the guest chamber. Six rooms, six days. On the Sabbath the household attended church.

After the daily turn-out, Jane took her brief teatime with Mrs. Galbraith, who was fat and plain but good enough company. Then came the ironing and mend-ing. (A laundress came once a week, so blessedly Jane had not that labor to attend to.) Then Mr. Welby's supper and the last cleaning of the kitchen, including a serious scrubbing of the pine table. Lastly, while the cook enjoyed an hour to herself before bed, Jane had her lesson.

This was the only particular of her day that made her life any different from the lives of a hundred, a thousand, other maidservants. Her master, who in his youth had been to Pembroke College, Oxford, had undertaken to be her teacher. In his library she sat on a leather stool while he strode about telling her of ancient Rome, or leaning over her as she read aloud from John Donne's poems, or sitting behind his desk as she recited the names of the rivers of the world. He worked her unrelentingly on grammar, and was even teaching her to speak well, like a lady, or in his words, "a speech adequate to all design of use or elegance."

By the time her lesson was finished, it was nine o'clock and she was so weary it was all she could do to climb the stairs to her chamber, put on her smock and nightcap, and fall into the deep and guiltless sleep in which she was now smothered.

She had followed this routine since her mother's death two years ago, when she'd found herself on her own at the age of sixteen. She was grateful for her place here, for this narrow bed (she had never had her own bedchamber before), for Mrs. Galbraith's good food, and yes, for Mr. Welby's lessons. Her life had not always been so regular. It had not always been lived with so little hunger, so few quarrels, so little disorder.

Order ran though this tidy brick house. No clutter existed, no crowded nooks or dirty corners. The kitchen shone. The library was a library through and through. The dining room, with its round table, was used to eat in, thrice daily, and the meals were ever punctual. The small parlor, though rarely used, enchanted Jane, the tiny couch backed against the bow window, with pillows at each end, the seashell that served as the doorstop, the several pieces of hand-painted china that glowed on the mantelpiece, the rug that showed a small flowered pattern, the cabinet that had marquetry design. Seldom used yet always ready for use.

Everything was ordered and complete: napkins were rolled in napkin rings; plants grew in ornamental bowls; a spare blanket lay at the foot of every bed. Doilies protected tables; platters and sauce boats and strawberry dishes and different-shaped glasses and quarter-moon-shaped bone dishes and cups and cake plates lay in the china cabinet. A brightly polished pewter card-receiver lay on the hall table. Nearby stood a hat rack.

In the kitchen were black iron pots and black tin bread pans, a cauldron, a big wooden mixing bowl, pudding cups, pie tins. Mrs. Galbraith often made a single large pie for supper. Jane found the sight of this on the kitchen table, with sauce oozing from the pattern cut in its brown crust, the most beautiful thing in the world.

She loved this house; she loved the way the sunlight came in so strongly on fair days and cast strong shadows all through it. She could distinguish the time of day and the season of the year from the way the shadows pitched back from certain table and chair legs.

She loved it because disorder was never allowed.

The shaft of moonlight moved in its slow and imperceptible way, picking out details of her life: the water jug sitting in the hand basin, the covered slop jar, her two dark work dresses and her two cheaper but more colorful personal gowns. Her heavy, hooded, scarlet cloak. Her leather shoes and the wooden pattens that clattered as she walked the cobbled streets of York in wet weather.

The diagonal of moonlight crept on. A corner of it fell over her pillow, over her white nightcap. She turned in her sleep. Now the dusky light lay full on her face.

It was a startling face for such a simple maidservant, and had caused her no small measure of concern. She was well known about the district, a situation she had not sought and would erase if she but knew how. She had never set out to attract such attention, yet she had attracted it. It all began when she'd undertaken an errand for Mr. Welby to the watchmaker's last spring. Coming home under a waiting, rain-gray sky, she was stopped by a stooped and pot-bellied stranger, dressed all in black and silver. He said, startlingly, "I must paint you."

Britain was alive with painters and engravers and drawing masters, all of them poor, but one look at this man and she could see that he was wealthy, not only because of his dress and manner, but by his asthma and gout, rich men's diseases both of them.

She edged away, doing her best to escape without actually giving offense. After all, what had she to do with aging cavaliers in silk stockings and silver lace? He let her go, but got into his coach and followed her all the way home. Within a half hour of her hurrying to the side entrance, Mr. Welby rang his bell. She went into the library—and there sat the wheezy gentleman in silver and black. He had his gouty foot propped on the leather stool, quite at home.

Mr. Welby stood behind his desk. He was wearing his favorite full-bottomed periwig. "Jane, this gentleman is Robert Hamilton, Baron Murdock."

She curtsied, her eyes safely lowered to the brass-capped andirons of the hearth.

The man said nothing, only looked at her with scavenging eyes.

"Lord Murdock is an artist of some note in our dis-

15

trict, Jane." Mr. Welby always spoke in the measured, exact prose of his books. "He wishes to paint you, and he has generously offered to pay for your time."

"I have no time, master," she said humbly, stating nothing but the truth: she regularly put in sixteen-to-seventeen hour days, with hardly a minute to visit the pine-seated privy over the cesspit in the basement. In fact her thoughts at the moment were more concerned with the table that had yet to be laid for dinner than with this outrageous idea that an important man wanted to immortalize her.

Not looking at her, but adjusting the flare of his black, long-waisted coat, the great lord himself spoke. "Your master tells me you get a half-holiday every Sunday, Betty."

"Yes, my lord." The hair prickled on her head. "Betty" was a stock name given to female servants. It also could connote female promiscuity. There was many a risqué ballad praising the charms of maidservants named Betty. "But . . ."

"But?" The idle voice of one used to being indulged.

"But I don't—begging your pardon, my lord—I don't care to be painted."

He looked at Mr. Welby. "One must admire the girl's spirit, though I fear she is headstrong and willful." His irritation was barely hidden.

Jane threw Mr. Welby a frightened glance. He failed to defend her. "My lord, perhaps I have pampered her."

"Hmm, yes, no doubt. Such a handsome wench to have in the house."

Mr. Welby blushed violently.

The baron considered her again, his face screwed up as if he were looking at a dazzling light. At last he said, "Nay, maid, I cannot let you turn me down. One look

16

at such a face and any disheartened man would take courage and go on trying to be the kind of fellow he was intended to be. Such a face should have been born to a lady, but as it was not, I feel it is my calling to paint it so." He mustered a smile, albeit with clenched teeth. "As your master says, I will pay you. Shall we say . . . forty guineas?"

Pot-bellied though he was, and middle-aged, he was a lord indeed, and used to personal authority. He wanted to paint her and he could guess to within a shilling what her wages were. Forty guineas to someone of her station was a fortune. Stunned, she looked to her shy and mannerly master, suddenly fearful now that he would chide Lord Murdock for being too generous, that five guineas would secure her agreement quite as easily.

He did not, however, and soon the great lord took his leave. Jane and Mr. Welby stood together at the door as the coach drove away. The sun was setting; a russet flush lay over the walls of York. "Jane," said her master, "this is a great honor for you. Lord Murdock is a man of ancestry and fortune, known by the king. His family is among the first and oldest about the district; and he, though not the most moneyed, is one of the most powerful. He knows everyone, and is known to everyone."

She made a curtsy. An agreement came mechanically to her lips. "Yes, master."

When she had time to think about it, she decided it might not be honor so much as opportunity. Forty guineas! She'd been saving all her earnings toward a dream she had, an ambition nursed by Mr. Welby's lessons in geography. The future had seemed closed down to one narrow corridor for someone like her until she'd learned how big the world was. That was when she'd got the idea that she might venture out into it. She'd never dared mention her design aloud to anyone for fear of being ridiculed. She could hardly form it into words for herself even, yet from her point of view it had a great deal to recommend it. And with forty guineas—perhaps she could really make it happen.

And so she sat for Lord Murdock. She was collected by a fine carriage and horses and driven through the settled fair weather of May to Hockness Hall three Sabbaths in a row. There she was treated with utmost courtesy. A girl helped her put on a white sack-back gown such as she'd never worn before. She felt exposed by the wide neckline and silly in the awkward side-hoops—though even she could appreciate how the width enhanced the long sweeping folds of the fabric that fell from the back of the neck in a train, displaying the beauty of the silk to its full.

She was utterly relieved when from the first the baron treated her as coldly as he'd done in Mr. Welby's library. She'd been afraid he might want to seduce her. There could be no arguing with him, of course, though he was such a little man, a mere boy in height. A maid of her class was considered the rightful prey of such men as he. Yet her luck held in that Robert Hamilton was not a sensuous man. Bored and haughty, certainly. But reasonably virtuous.

When the painting was complete, she examined it with some misgivings. She had no idea if it was good; she saw a girl with a face somewhat like hers, a girl of marble, stillness personified. She was content that he had finished with her, and glad to have her half-holidays to herself again. She accepted her forty guineas gratefully and dismissed the experience from her mind.

She was surprised when, as summer came on, she began to be pointed at on the street. She learned that

18

an engraver was making reproductions of the baron's painting. At first she was only unsettled—and amazed that people should think her likeness worth the price being charged! It was not long, however, before dismay and amazement gave way to sharp regret, for as the fury of her fame rose, she learned that forty guineas was hardly enough for what she suffered.

"The Rose of Midnight" got more and more widely known—that gentlewoman in her rose garden, that tender maid whose face held a special inner smile, that face which was recognizably Jane Fitzpatrick's. She was often acknowledged on the street, awarded the sidelong flick of a look, or less subtly, a horse laugh and a shout: "Hullo, Rosie!" There were fearful occasions when her way was blocked by strange men who asked, "Are ye 't one then?" (How she hated that age-old stance of masculine superiority, that assumption of the right to stop her and ask her questions!)

She'd been asked to join a cry of players. And twice tourists had called upon Mr. Welby and asked if they might see "The Rose." She was not much good at meeting people. She never knew what to say or how to act. Yet on both occasions she had to go into the parlor and be exclaimed over as if she were an object: "How blue and guileless her eyes are . . . what pretty hands, especially for a mere servant . . . how unaffected she seems for all this heed."

Last week an Irishman with a dreadful accent had offered her a half-guinea to go to an inn house with him.

And the stories! People believed everything they heard. Rumors sprang up like weeds, untruths that offended her deep sense of exactness. Many of them touched upon her character, which caused her especial anguish. Those who believed she was gentleborn and a great lady had it that she was married to Mr. Welby,

19

a match beneath her, which had caused to her to be cast out of her rightful position. Those who knew she was a servant said she'd posed for the painting in order to support a secret lover. Others said she was Lord Murdock's mistress, someone he'd found in a ditch by the roadside.

She'd been unprepared for any of this, particularly the malice, and she resented it with a bitterness beyond expression. She would rather have never posed or made a penny than have one one-hundredth of such lies about her noised abroad.

Amidst all this, she did her best to continue as before, working, learning, and sleeping deeply. She tried to be unchanged by it—though inevitably she grew more profoundly reserved than ever, and more highly suspicious of people who might want to use her, and necessarily more protective of her reputation and her person.

Her master was not exceedingly amused with the predicament, no more than she was. He was a restrained, fragile man, courteous in manner and locution, with a decided preference for ascetic studies. He led an almost hermetic, unsophisticated life, a life defined entirely by books and scholarship. He, too, had heard the rumors, and he was mortified.

From the first, he had taken a benevolent interest in Jane, an orphan of sixteen years, and so comely—how could he not? And when he discovered she had a lively and inquisitive mind to go with her sedate manner (and her beauty), he'd impulsively determined to teach her whatever she could learn. She had already attended lessons in the village of Dulwych whither she'd been reared. The humble dame school there was operated by a Huguenot refugee, Madame Marisot, whose slight education had been enough to teach Jane her letters and numbers. Mr. Welby built upon this, rapidly introducing her to poetry, geography, and history.

Their relationship was most unusual, he knew, and so, except for that last hour of the day, he was careful to keep their connection closely proscribed: master and maid, employer and employee, lord and servant.

But during that last hour, ah, Welby came to life. With Jane, he could be the man he felt he truly was: erudite, exciting, arousing. His conversation was filled with allusions to Homer and Chaucer, to Greek mythology and French roundelays. Far from finding him dull, as many of his own class did, Jane seemed to thrive on the ideas he threw down about her like gauntlets to be taken up.

Hence, after two years under his roof, Jane Fitzpatrick knew just about all there was to know about Gage Welby. But it is safe to say that Welby knew nothing at all about Jane Fitzpatrick. It wasn't that she deliberately concealed herself; it was just that a certain secrecy was bound into her nature. She'd learned it from her mother, who had gone about her life with an aura of great secrecy and remained much alone. Mr. Welby thought Jane quiet, and so she was, externally. Yet she had a truculent spirit under her stillness, and was full of shrewdness in her submission, and could measure the whole stature of those who looked down on her and correctly ascertain their weight and caliber.

Mrs. Galbraith, the cook, hugged her fat arms across her bosoms and hinted that if Jane played her tune right, Mr. Welby might be brought to the point of asking her to marry him. Jane considered this. She'd been pursued by men, of course, but she'd displayed so little patience with would-be suitors that they soon were discouraged, perhaps by her behavior, perhaps by feelings of self-doubt when faced with both beauty and a strong, calculating nature. At thirty-four years her senior, most certainly Mr. Welby would be a temperate husband. Hers would be a temperate life. The blunt and unshakable frankness in her view of herself recognized that she was a servant and it would be a crowning achievement for her to marry her master.

But Jane had her own ambition, her own plan, her own thrill of hope, which did not include a gentle life of books in York.

The shaft of moonlight in the dark attic chamber moved from her face to the wall by her bed. The light narrowed, narrowed, and finally left the chamber in darkness again.

But the moon was not finished with shining upon the face of Jane Fitzpatrick.

Chapter Two

A Large Lichened Stone

Sunday dawned cold and clear and windy. Mr. Welby, with his cook and maidservant, attended the weekly summons of Christendom, that vast pulpit which worked so extensively on the popular intellect to admonish, to warn, to alarm. The household attended the Minister, England's largest medieval cathedral, famous for its west front and its magnificent stained-glass windows. It had taken two and a half centuries, from 1220 to 1470, to complete this ballad in sandstone. Within its walls, kaleidoscopes of light exploded from the windows that were among the art treasures of the world.

The subject of the sermon, delivered by a curate this morning, concerned marriage.

"A woman chooses her own husband," the cleric said, paraphrasing an essay by John Winthrop, "yet once chosen, he is her king and she is subject to his rule." Sweat streamed from under his periwig. He looked up constantly at his congregation, as if unsure of the soundness of his message and eager to locate someone in accord with it.

"His yoke is as sweet to her as her bridal ornaments; and if through audaciousness or wantonness, she shakes this yoke off, her spirit is at no rest until she accepts it again; and whether her lord smiles on her and clasps her in his arms, or whether he frowns or chides or smites her, she appreciates the sweetness of his devotion in all, and is refreshed, braced, and instructed by every measure of his authority over her."

Jane had trouble keeping her mind on the sermon, first because the message made her feel uncomfortably rebellious, and second because, though Mr. Welby had chosen seats close to the rear, she was being stared at. She knew it without looking around; her back felt it. She tried to take the weight of these stares as the man behind the pulpit was saying a wife should take the yoke of her husband's authority. She sat with her hands clasped in her lap and her eyes fixed on Mr. Welby's shoe buckles.

As the crowd made their way out of the cathedral, someone pinched Jane's buttocks. She didn't yelp, didn't give any sign she'd even felt it. It was too shameful a thing.

Once that weekly ordeal was got through, she had the whole afternoon to look forward to, hours of freedom. She quickly changed from her best dress into the one she kept specially for her half-holiday outings. It was a pretty masquerade purple stuff gown with a black quilted petticoat. She put on blue stockings with red clocks, and her black leather shoes, a white shaving hat with a green ribbon, and white handkerchief and apron. During the week she had to wear the sedate black dress Mr. Welby provided, but when her time was her own, she liked color. She arranged a white bonnet over the shaving hat, slung her scarlet cloak around her shoulders, and she was ready.

Downstairs, she tapped at the library door. "Come

in." Mr. Welby was sitting behind his desk, writing a letter in his spiky vertical hand. "Going for your walk, Jane?"

"Yes, master."

"Very good. The history of our times is written on the landscape hereabouts." He leaned back in his chair. "I should get out myself. Maybe before winter comes I'll go fishing. I haven't been fishing for years. I used to be pretty good with a trout on the end of a line." He paused, stout with good feeling, well satisfied with himself and his world. But at last he seemed to realized what she had come for. "I suppose you want your pay."

"Yes, master."

She was paid semiannually, and this was the day. She watched him closely as he took out the limp vellum-covered account book in which he recorded the household expenditures. (Such blessed order in all things!) After making a notation, he took ten shiny gold guineas from his desk. "There you are. Be careful with that now."

She deposited the coins deep in the pocket of her skirt. The wind rattled the windows behind her like knocking hands, like children calling a mate out to play.

He said suddenly, unexpectedly, "What do you do with your money, Jane? You never seem to spend any."

She regarded him with dismay. He'd never asked such a personal question. She dropped her eyes away from his face. "I save it, master."

"For what?"

Her throat dried.

"Well!" he said curtly, aware that he had transgressed. "Saving is always wise. Very wise."

Dismissed, she went through the kitchen, saying goodbye to Mrs. Galbraith. "Spiced mutton for supper," the cook called, "don't thee be late, Jane Fitz-patrick."

A moment later, in something of a pother, she was out on the street, her back to the little, tidy brick house. She wished wholeheartedly that Mr. Welby hadn't asked about her money. Once he did, of course she'd had to tell the truth. But she hadn't liked to. It was her private business, the existence of her little cache.

The more she considered it, the angrier she got. She felt her emotions rise with unprecedented fierceness: Mr. Welby had betrayed her twice now, first to Lord Murdock, and now with this intrusion into—

No, she wouldn't think that way. He was a kind and good master, as good as a maid could hope for, and she would not think a bad thought about him.

Yet her emotions remained high. Among all her faults, she thanked heaven that no one could accuse her of poking into the affairs of others.

Autumn had arrived; she smelled it and felt its wind on her face. Although the houses of York stood securely fixed to the ground, the rest of the city was wild and blowing about the streets. Smoke streamed from the chimneys, leaves pulled from the trees and rushed and blew against carts and people. From high in the sky the sun shone brilliantly down everywhere. Children were blown along past Jane, shouting and running. They blew up the paths to their homes, or through the orchards between the houses to catch fruit in their aprons.

The Romans had chosen this dry location beside the Ouse River for a fortress. Constantine was proclaimed emperor here. Later the Danes founded a settlement, and later still the Normans built fortifications—all long before prosperity finally came with the medieval wool trade.

As Mr. Welby said, history was written on the landscape round about, and the city's history was written in its streets. Four medieval gates led through the walls, which were built upon the old Roman foundations. They girded the ancient city for three miles, and could be followed by a rampart walk. From atop them one could see curious and often glorious towers, and always the awe-inspiring spectacle of the Minster. The Ouse coursed right through the city, and was bridged by the narrow Shambles. Antique timber-framed houses leaned toward each other. Cramped streets such as High and Low Petergate connected quaint and crooked squares.

Jane's path passed through one of these market squares, quiet on this breezy Sunday. The rattle of a carriage and some talk and laughter between a pair of couples passing the time beside a fountain came to her, sounding almost transparent across the cobbles. At intervals a long swell of bells from the Minster or from one of the smaller churches washed over the rooftops above.

As she left the square and rounded a corner, a fresh blast of wind struck her; and at the same instant a trio of young men coming along the street spied her. As the distance between them closed, they grinned and cheered boisterously at the spectacle of ''The Rose of Midnight'' herself approaching them: ''Will ye meet me at midnight, Rose, eh?''

''Not him, me!''

She kept her head down, trying not to give them the least provocation. Nonetheless, one of them bent down to leer right into her face. ''Gi' me a kiss, Rosie.'' He was perhaps nineteen, small and haggard, with a face blackened by unshaved whiskers and grease and covered with pustules.

Blushing, seething, she passed through them with-

27

out a word, and strode on, out of the fading sound of their mocking laughter, into the very fringes of the town.

Jane felt the sharpening of her awareness. Here was York's seamy side. While silks and splendor might abound among some quarters, there were always rags and dirt closeby. How ugly some of these people were! Both men and women carried ugly scars of skin diseases and boils and carbuncles. She could pick out which children were afflicted with scrofula by their disfigured jaws and poor eyesight. The very young, who should have been taut and ruddy, were often scarecrow thin—or monstrously bloated.

It disturbed Jane to think how unfortunate most children were. Generation after generation, their lot never changed. As for their parents, she was not always convinced that their poverty wasn't their own fault. It seemed there was work to be done and not enough people willing to do it. She felt, a bit smugly perhaps, that she herself had proved there was no such thing as involuntary unemployment for the able-bodied.

She was stopped by a sudden, violent jerk on her cloak. A woman sitting on the cobbles, dressed in amazingly dirty castoffs, glared up into her face. Long, coarse black hair hung over the hag's squinting eyes. She had no hat.

"Ye're her! Ye're the Rose! Gi' us a wee pence, miss."

"Miss" was another word that had two meanings. It was a term of honor for a young girl of high caliber, or it might be applied to a strumpet. The woman's face was mottled purple from drink, her mouth was stretched across blackened gums in a hollow, angry smile. All Jane's poise deserted her. The woman read the disgust in her expression. "Nay so pretty as ye, am

28

I?'' She smiled wider and her eyes fixed Jane with a hard-boiled stare. "Gi' us a pence now."

"I'm sorry." Jane wrenched her cloak from the hag's grasp. "I work for my money. You might try doing the same."

"Work! Aye and sure ye do, ye damned whore! Ye've got more work than ye need, what wi' all the fancy lords ye service! Gi' us a farthing, whore!"

Jane was already walking on, staring ahead glassily as the woman berated her with filthy epithets, delivered in an indifferent monotone now. Jane was appalled at this free language. She looked even more narrowly at this section of town. The close, fetid streets and alleys suited as refuges to thieves and pickpockets and whores, and harbored the maimed whose only method of survival was to beg. It was the meanest, the dirtiest, the ugliest and most vicious part of York—for such were the people who lived here. Such were the poor.

Once she'd thought her own life was sure to be a journey from the squalor which had characterized her childhood to another squalor probably as vile and verminous as that endured by these residents of York's stinking alleyways. As little as two years ago, she'd expected nothing better. But look what she'd accomplished! All her present good fortune, her place with Mr. Welby, her lessons, her cache, her plan.

She felt a superstitious twinge, as if allowing herself to gloat might cause everything to vanish before her eyes. It was best to be conservative in one's hopes, and certainly never giddy.

Any tendency toward giddiness had been early murdered in young Jane Fitzpatrick. Days, months, and years of endless and unchanging poverty had led her to a kind of resignation. It was a wonder she'd found the motivation to make her plan—though Mr. Welby had opened her mind to thoughts she would never have thought elsewise. She had simply taken for granted that it was impossible to escape the fate of her birth. Then one day, as she was cleaning the hearth in the parlor, she suddenly found herself working out the details of her own escape with care and precision.

Her mother had not been so lucky. Alexandra Fitzpatrick had lived and died poor. Though from a prosperous Welsh family, she'd grown up as a struggling poor cousin, trained to mend and wash ladies' ribbon-trimmed headdresses. Perchance she might have ended as such girls often did, as a person of ill-fame, with two or three fatherless children to her credit. But she'd been spirited, and stunningly pretty, and having had enough of headdresses and linen, of gloves and ribbons, she ran away to marry Rip Fitzpatrick, a darkly moody young man. It was not a happy match. The two flung themselves into long years of joint misery. Most of what Jane knew of her father she'd pieced together from her mother's muttered complaints. It seemed that among Rip's several defects was a dreadfully explosive temperament. His ill-treatment of his wife had caused her several miscarriages before she'd managed to provide him with a child in her forty-first year.

Just two years later, Rip abandoned both wife and toddling daughter to become a sailor on a ship bound for the African slave trade. He went without a word, leaving Alexandra and Jane to scrattle on as best they could without him, and without the year's shearing money, which he'd taken with him.

Jane could remember patches of happiness in her youth, one or two days that seemed to flash with dragonflies in her recollection, yet there were few truly sweet memories, little that could be called a real childhood. Alexandria eventually became a dried up, emaciated woman with a barbed nose and ferret eyes—a small horror. It had been hard for Jane to realize that her mother was once hailed as a beauty. When she died following a sudden paralytic stroke, the burden of poverty which she had partially held off her daughter fell suddenly and squarely onto Jane's shoulders.

After Alexandra's burial, there was the decision of what to do with the farm. Though Jane was young and her energy was in full flood, she couldn't do the work alone, nor could she expect help, for her mother's gloom—and that peculiar secrecy she owned, along with a certain hardness of heart—had estranged their neighbors over the years. Jane tried to sell the place, but she was frustrated by the fact that it was still owned by her father, who was presumably alive.

In the end, she'd simply abandoned the three fields and poor cottage and come to town. Ragged and pinched with hunger, she'd had the good fortune to find Mr. Welby.

Debts left by her mother had taken all but a few pence of her first six months' wages. After that, however, she'd owed not a penny.

She forced her mind to set these musings aside. She would not have her half-day spoiled with things that were long done and past.

Steady walking had brought her beyond the walls of the city. She leaped across a ditch flooded with autumn yellow wildflowers and struck out across some low meadows used for pastures. Sheep grazed beside her path, each animal solemnly set upon the task which filled its every waking hour. The flock ignored her— and she felt the blessed relief of it, of being left alone, of not having to bend herself to other people's needs, to their demands. Though she was a placid person, it would be difficult to describe the terrific excitement produced in her by a simple afternoon of solitude.

She loved the open moors, the beautiful blankness,

the cold, bright wind which forced her to hold her cloak with one hand on her shoulder in the manner of a play actor.

Beyond the long pastures, she came to a field fenced with rock. She skirted it, her footsteps slashing through the long grass with quickened purpose. A mile on, she entered a copse of beech and hazel and ash. Beyond the first trees, she left the common path.

She left it at a different place each time, always taking a slightly different route, going around and about so as to leave no track. But always she came to the same end, a remnant of shoulder-high wall, all that was left of an old dry-set stone fence built out of boulders from the nearby fields. It had been used ages ago for pigs. In the one corner still standing was a certain large, lichened stone.

As far as she could tell, no one else ever came here. Yet she stood quietly for a long while, her hands on the wall, striking an attitude of doing nothing more than looking out beyond the trees toward the sunny moorlands. About her on the floor of the windy copse was a scattering of dark and bright, shadow and sunlight.

Only after a full twenty minutes of patient caution was she completely certain that she had not been followed and was not being observed. She knelt down and pulled out the big lichened stone.

Beneath it was a leather pouch, and in the pouch was all her money, her earnings from Mr. Welby, and the sitting fee from Lord Murdock. She emptied it into her lap, marveling at the spilling coins. She added those from her pocket. The total was . . . seventy guineas, six shillings, and four pence! For a moment she lifted her face to the swaying boughs overhead and closed her eyes and smiled.

She replaced the pouch and restored the stone, careful not to rub off any of its mossy covering. She stood up deliberately, looking about her for the least sign of change, of hazard.

All was as it should be. Now she could go back out into the full sun.

A discreet distance from her secret, she sat in the long grass of the fellside and watched the east wind blow across the dale. Voices came from a field away where a horse stood between the shafts of a cart with its head lowered and its ears twitching. Haymakers were loading the cart to the sky. Down in the pastures a shepherd caught a sheep, rolled it, and held it quiet with its forelegs up while he pared back the horn from its hooves with a sharp, curved knife. The rind fell from his blade.

The day was a work of beauty, full of harvest-ripeness. The City of York stood shiny bright to Jane's left, with here and there a pennant pulled almost stiff in the powerful blast. Paint sparkled on the walls. The more-distant views of the moors were clean, with nothing to stay the eye from sweeping from one naked rise to another.

Looking through the day, through the distance, Jane's heart filled to overflowing. Oh, why are the works of nature so perfect?

"It's because nature works according to a plan—and never departs from it."

She smiled at herself for speaking aloud. She, too, had a plan. From Mr. Welby she'd learned about the Crown Colony of Georgia, in North America, located between the Savannah and Altamaha rivers. King George had great hopes that the place would supply semitropical fruits, silk, and wines, all much desired in England. To that end, a Mr. Oglethorpe, with one hundred thirty-five settlers, had founded the city of Savannah in 1733. A regiment of troops had also been supplied.

Jane's plan was to emigrate to Georgia.

She didn't think it too outrageous an idea. Mr. Welby said the roughest pioneer labor was done in the colonies by now. And the element of danger had largely evaporated with the establishment of political and fiscal organization. Success was practically assured the man or woman who arrived with even a modest amount of capital and ability. Vast tracts of land were to be had almost for the asking: rivers swarmed with fish; primeval woods awaited the ax.

Jane wasn't quite sure what she would do when she got there—except that she wasn't going to be poor. She could always go as a maidservant; arrangements were regularly offered to transport domestics across the sea for an agreed-upon term—at a salary of as much as thirty-five pounds a year, nearly twice what she was earning now! But even as she thought this her back stiffened. She wasn't going to have a master when she got to the New World. She would never again be forced to sit up and beg (as her mother would have put it) for her daily keep. As much as she respected Mr. Welby, she hated being his servant.

She believed she must have enough money now for her passage, but just to be sure she was going to wait until she had an even one hundred guineas. Another year and a half, if she saved every penny. Not so long. Yet more and more now she felt a terrible pulling in her veins.

As the time grew nearer, she would confide in Mr. Welby and ask him to help her obtain passage on a ship. She knew that many ships came and went out of Liverpool, which was closer than either London or Bristol. She would hire transportation to Liverpool and there get on a ship and sail across the great Atlantic

Ocean—and when she stepped off that ship, she would not be Jane Fitzpatrick, maidservant; she would be someone new: Jane Fitzpatrick, British colonist.

The thought touched something in her heart and gave her a melting feeling, a sense of things divinely fair and immeasurably vast . . . and somehow immeasurably sad.

It was dark and whistling cold as Jane made her way home. She'd never returned so late before. She'd fallen asleep—slept in the blazing sun like a lazy cat for hours! Frightened, she found her way back along the edge of the woods, around the fenced field, through the pastures, and across the weedy ditch. It was that darkening hour before full night descended. She walked quickly, in a daze of spinning thoughts:

The wind's died down . . . how could I have fallen asleep? . . . it's so late, they'll be worried . . . Mrs. Galbraith's supper . . . . what's that?

She glanced around wildly at some faint noise.

Nothing, it's nothing, I'm not afraid, there's nothing to be afraid of . . . here's the town . . . how could I have fallen asleep like that?

Last Sunday she'd spent her afternoon reading a fashionable, picaresque novel, *The Fair Jilt,* in which the heroine was forced to journey through the night at great peril to her virtue. She saw now that it was much more entertaining to read about than to experience.

You're such a very perfect idiot, Jane Fitzpatrick.

At last she was hurrying through the streets of York, between the candlelit windows. The night breeze lifted the tendrils at the back of her neck and she shivered. The moon hadn't risen yet; her way was dark. She almost stepped into the kennel—the channel that ran down the middle of the street, full of noisome filth.

The gleam of lamplight from the windows of Mr. Welby's house was a welcome sight. She hastened along the path that led to the side entrance. As she shut the door against the rim of the rising moon, and began to take off her gloves and bonnet and cloak in the tiled passage, Mrs. Galbraith appeared and started right in on her. "Well, here thee are, and not a minute too early! I was that worried, Jane!" Her words nipped like bird pecks, but what truly alarmed Jane was: "Master says he wants to see thee directly as soon as thee comes in."

Jane took no time to warm herself by the fine fire in the kitchen. She went directly to the library. Mr. Welby was seated in the high-backed settle which stood close to the hearth. He rose when she came in, holding two sides of a book closed over his index finger to mark his place. He looked surprisingly stern; his pallid blue eyes seemed agitated and his wig was slightly askew. He delivered his reproof in a dry, crisp tone she'd seldom heard: "Jane, you must be more mindful of the hour."

"Yes, master, I'm sorry."

"There are men about, loutish, wicked men, the sort you wouldn't like to meet in the dark, men who are all your nightmares come to life. Do you understand me?"

"Yes, master." She turned her face into the firelight. She was not naive. Did he think she didn't know what men could stoop to? A scolding like this made her feel instantly defiant. Her mother had showered her with a wearying drizzle of such cautions, all concerning her chastity and the means men would try to use to relieve her of it. Jane was tempted to answer back, but of course she didn't, couldn't; meanwhile Mr. Welby went on with his own line of thought.

"They hunt best by moonlight, that kind. A high-

36

wayman was hanged only a few weeks ago for carrying a milkmaid off into the moors. They say he plucked her eyes out, Jane, after he . . . er, molested her.''

She hadn't heard of the incident; what struck her was that the word "molested" caused Mr. Welby's cheeks to redden. She felt aware of the way he was looking at her, and of the fact that she was not wearing her working dress but her prettiest purple stuff gown. Warmth flooded her veins. She lowered her eyes from his homey features and struggled to address him as always. "You are right to scold me."

"Yes, well." He moved away from the fiercely burning fire, came a few steps nearer to her. "I have been remiss. Your age and your situation, and with that portrait everywhere, strangers noticing you . . ."

Beneath his words, beneath his deliberate exterior, she sensed a sharpened hunger. Other men had found her beautiful; she had never been able to make herself be concerned. But this was her master, her own Mr. Welby.

He'd fallen silent. His eyes roamed over her; he seemed balanced on the brink of some feeling. She muttered another apology; he continued to stare at her. She had an odd feeling that they had entered a new relationship.

"Will you be wanting anything else, master?" Her voice was soft and careful.

He didn't answer her question, just stood there with his lips pressed together as if he feared the least sound might reveal some secret thudding of passion. She found herself willing him to make some move, to come a step nearer, to break through the barrier. But he didn't. The silence stretched in all directions.

"Well," she said, losing hope, "good night then."

She paused outside the door, just to gather herself

together before she had to face Mrs. Galbraith again. And so she heard Mr. Welby's exclamation of disgust from within the room behind her. What did that sound mean? That he was revolted at himself because he had not come forth with what was in his heart? Or was it because the object of his affection was only a lowly maidservant and hence forever beneath his reach?

Chapter Three

'T Sweet-scented Miss

Unaware that her civilized, orderly life was about to fall apart, Jane went back into the kitchen, where she was allowed to have her supper—no spiced mutton, for Mrs. Galbraith was piqued with her—but some bread and a bowl of thick soup made from dried peas and onions. All the time it took her to eat, Mrs. Galbraith's mouth kept pursing as if she were sucking something sour. Jane's mind remained full of the meeting with Mr. Welby. There would be no lessons with him tonight since it was Sunday; still, she vaguely hoped he might call her back into the library on some excuse, any excuse.

The library bell didn't sound. She had no choice but to take her night candle and light her way to her chamber.

The boards and nails of the familiar stairs murmured under her feet. The intimacy of Mr. Welby's warnings spoke on in her mind, warnings about her person, her chastity, her most private self. He'd been beside himself with worry of what some highwayman might do to her—and to think she'd considered him too anemic to have those kind of thoughts!

But that sound he'd made when he'd believed himself alone again. Was he revolted by his attraction to her?

She stopped on the second floor, and after a moment's hesitation, tip-toed down the hall to peek into his chamber.

There was the curtained bed behind which he greeted her so blandly every morning. It was huge, three times the width of any bed she had ever slept in. The oak base stood half her height, and there was a feather mattress atop that. The draperies all around kept out the cold. Looking at it, she felt aflutter. What if he should propose to her, as Mrs. Galbraith hinted he might? Would she give up her plan?

She crept nearer and parted the curtains.

It looked the same as when she'd made it up before church this morning. She'd expected to experience some new excitement, some thrill. But no. She didn't know whether to feel relieved or disappointed.

She left the chamber and quietly returned to the stairs. At the very top of the house, a sudden yawn overtook her. Blinking, she crossed the landing and went into the small, slope-ceilinged chamber under the roof.

It was there that the downward sweep of fortune's turning caught her off balance.

She shut the door, turned around, and at first all she saw in her candle's fitful light was the alarming disorder.

I left the window open and the wind has got in here.

Then she saw the man, and the scene became a frozen glare, held suspended as in a flash of lightning. Her breath hitched. Her throat made a toneless sound. He gave her such a shock that she lost sight of the room entirely. She stood stock-still, trying desperately to

40

make sense of who he was and why he was in her chamber and how he had gotten there.

The answers to two of these questions came to her quickly enough: Instinct told her that he was her father, Steven Fitzpatrick, known as Rip, a fitting nickname for such a mean and vulgar man as her mother had led her to believe he was. He'd obviously come in by way of the window. That must have been rather difficult, her mind reasoned; he would have to climb up onto the coach house roof, step over to the kitchen roof . . .

The answer to the third question, what he wanted, would be answered soon enough.

She watched him with wary eyes. She remembered very little about him, except that she used to be afraid of him when she was small. Or was that fear something Alexandra had taught her later, with her constant bitter mutterings? No, Jane had some personal memory of fear, however vague. And she was still afraid of him, though he must be sixty-four years old now, and looked it, despite the fact that his long, unclubbed hair was all black, with no gray yet. So were his stubbly whiskers black. His coarse fists were rough-haired and blotched with some ancient ailment of the skin. His nose was the port-red of a drinker.

As for his tarpaulin naval coat and soiled shirt and breeches, they were only weeks from being rags. The way he sat on her bed, with one ankle resting on the other knee, she could see the extra piece of leather he'd put inside the sole of his worn-through shoe. His tricorn lay beside him, old and misshapen.

His eyes, however, shone like something brand new. They were enough to make Jane's flesh crawl.

She stood looking at him. He sat looking back at her, resting against the wall, at his ease. She felt no kindness toward him, no tenderness at all. Nor did she see the least flare of tenderness in him.

She put her candle on the washstand. His first words were, "Ain't ye 't sweet-scented miss now?" His voice was flat and somehow threatening. "Clean mattress, looking glass on 't wall, piece 'o carpet on 't floor. I ne'er seen such a daughter, so full 'o frills. But then yer mother was like that. Aye," he said, examining Jane, "ye're 't image 'o Alexandra. Same looks, more or less—more, I'd say. She were always a bit skinny."

His voice was thick with age, worn down at the edges by time. "Ne'er thought to look upon my like again, eh Janey?" His eyes narrowed. "By 't time ye'd turned a year old I'd learned ye to fear 't rod—and to bawl softly when ye felt it. I bet I could take some 'o them frills out 'o ye yet. Why, there's no end to yer airs! Look at that dress! They said ye was rich, aye, rich and full 'o pride, they said."

He scratched his chin; his expression was almost waggish. "I'm back in Liverpool just two days and it outs that ye're some 'Rose 'o 't Midnight,' sassy to 't lords and taking their money without giving 'em full value for it."

"Where did you hear such things?"

"In a bawdy-house in Bingley, that's where. They had yer picture on 't wall right in 't parlor. I thought it were yer mother till I realized she'd be—what? near sixty by now? Nay, it had to be my Janey, all grown up." He paused; his expression changed. "Ye got money, they say. Give it to me. I want it."

Her blood ran hot, then very cool. "I haven't got any money." She gestured to the mess he'd made of her chamber. "You've looked. What did you find?"

He stood all in one motion and loomed over her so suddenly that she was forced back against the door. The candle flame flickered on the washstand. Rip's

42

hand was raised. "Look careful how ye talk to me! Don't think ye can sass *me* in yer ladyish way o' speaking, Mistress Rose o' Twelve O'clock! I won't stand for it!" He backed away a step. "Turn out your pockets."

She did.

His shiny eyes slid from side to side. His greed seemed a sort of derangement. In a voice to stab her heart, he said, "Where is it? Ye got it hid somewhere."

"I don't."

He swung so abruptly she hardly saw the hand coming. She fell sideways. One instant she was standing, the next she was crumpled on the floor beside her bed. She clutched her cheek in dumb surprise. There was no pain yet; the cheek was numb. He towered over her so that she could not lift herself. His hand grabbed her shaving cap—it came unpinned and he tossed it aside with a curse. He caught her plaited hair and dragged her head back. Her eyes were oddly affected by the blow he'd dealt her; she saw him blurrily, as through a rainy window.

"Where is it?"

"Mr. Welby," she gasped. Her heart was pounding and she thought she was going to be sick. "He keeps it for me."

That gave him a moment's pause. He released her and stood straight, alert, calm again—yet there was something grisly about his calm. "All right then," he said, "I'll just have a talk with him."

She could almost see his mind calculating: he couldn't go downstairs, not without explaining how he'd gotten into the house. "It's late," she said. "Master's in bed." That might keep him from going around to the front door tonight.

"First thing in t' morning then." He found his hat

43

and put it on at a self-pleased tilt. "I'll make him give it to me or I'll know t' reason why."

She forced herself to be blank. "Really, it's not worth your bothering about. D'ye . . . do you really think I make enough here to—"

"Don't lie to me!" The deep line of anger was back between his eyes. "They say ye ne'er spend a penny though ye make ten guinea ever' six months. Ten guinea! Why, 'tis disgraceful. And that lord who did t' painting, he paid ye a sackful 'o money."

Cautiously she got to her feet. She felt dizzy and half sick. Even in her distress, however, it offended her that strangers should know so much about her, that her name was bandied about, that anyone at all could find out the most private information about her, that her picture was displayed in bawdy houses and public houses for all manner of men to gape at.

She said, "Ye've been listening to gossips." She inadvertently lapsed back into the dialect of her youth. "Aye, I sat for Lord Murdock—but since when have the nobles ever paid the likes 'o us for anything? I'm still owed what he promised and not likely to ever see a shilling o' it."

All of Rip was intent on her, seeing nothing but her. He shook his head imperceptibly. Seeing how he was weakening, she pressed harder. "And the reason I ne'er spend a pence is because ever'thing I've made has gone to pay the debts Mother left when she died— did ye even know she was dead? D'ye care?"

His eyes tightened at the contempt in her voice. For an instant she thought he might fly into another rage and rush for her and punch at her with all the strength in his hoary old fists. But he only said, quietly, "That's right, sass me some more, Mistress Rose. Ye'll learn better soon enough. Ye might make the lords and the dandies dance to yer tune—a maiden, they say, and at yer age! Why, 'twould be a crime against nature if I believed it for a minute! But ye'll see I'm not impressed by yer pretty face. Yer mother had a pretty face—that same white, white skin—and I got so's I hated the sight o' it. Had to go to Guinea and purge my eyes with the blackest hides on earth.

"And don't ye be looking at me like that. I'll take that sulky look off yer face, my girl." Malice vibrated from him, blistering and tangible as a forge fire, alighting an indistinct memory in Jane—what was it?

He left the way he came, through the window. She stood without moving for a long minute, then jerked into action, closing the window with a bang. If only it had a lock!

She felt everything she'd worked toward was tottering beneath her. She had not imagined that the fruits of her labors could suddenly be wiped away like this—by him! He had no right to come back into her life now.

She examined her face in the tiny looking glass on the wall. Though her cheek bore the burning red imprint of his hand, there would be no lasting mark. At least she prayed there wouldn't. She couldn't bear the shame of Mr. Welby, or even Mrs. Galbraith, seeing her soiled by such a bruise.

She blew out her candle, but feeling frightened and wide-eyed and close to weeping with shock, she lacked the strength and purpose to ready herself for bed. For some time she was afraid even to take off her shoes. The wind outside continued to softly jiggle the window casement, but no grizzled face appeared there.

At last she took off her clothes in the dark. She hardly noticed the smell of the sunshine caught between the folds of her skirts as she hung them on their peg. Her fingers were clumsy with the front and back strings of her faded blue damask stays, but at last the close, narrow linen-lined boning fell away and she could breath deeply again. She changed into her smock, found her white nightcap in the dark, and crawled into bed.

She had not thought to put her room back into order, and she was aware now, under everything else, of its disarrangement.

Perhaps she should go tell Mr. Welby what had happened.

But it was so late; he was in bed, surely. There would be time enough in the morning.

Oh God, I just want this to not be so, none of it.

She tried to pray. But her prayers were empty. She had fallen into an inattention to religion, or an indifference to it. Without noticing, she had lost all her faith. Well, no great calamity; she doubted it would do her any good anyway. It never had before.

No more than would the law, which as far as she could tell, protected few and punished anyone who came within its shadow. The law had kept Jane from selling the farm, though she was starving—because her father was not proven dead. Alexandra had applied to the law once to get her marriage to Rip annulled, in order to be absolved from paying his debts. The court decided they were indeed husband and wife, even if they were married by a Fleet parson in a distiller's house.

Jane was surprised to find herself so frantically afraid of this appearance of her father. It humiliated her. She had been so superior and carefree just an hour ago.

As she closed her eyes, the memory Rip had stirred in her, the one she hadn't been able to remember earlier, came back: a forgotten scene of violence. She was a very little child, lying in a small bed with high sides, probably a basket. The ceiling above her was candlelit; strong shadows moved against it. Her mother was crying—then a sudden quiet ensued—then Alexandra

46

screeched. Jane's father was there, too, somewhere among those shadows. He grumbled drunkenly, "Ye damned harridan! Ye shitten trollop!"

Then her mother was over her, catching her up and carrying her out of the place. They were fleeing, running for their lives it seemed. It was a scene of the utmost terror. They were being chased . . .

Jane remembered no more. The rest was blank. What had happened? What had she seen? Experienced? Why couldn't she drive these feathers out of her head and *remember?*

What kind of man was Rip Fitzpatrick?

The second minute past midnight. The wind had died away. The world was coming to the season of naked trees and dreams. Leaf smoke hung in the air. A white owl flew over the harvested, empty cornfields around Hockness Hall. The bird's ghostly call was the only sound in the deep rural peace, its shape the only object moving in the landscape so mysteriously pearled by the autumn moon. The bird landed atop a wall surrounding a bench in an el of the garden. The plantings about the villa were fading toward October, but in this sheltered spot a few white roses still bloomed.

Inside the oak-timbered Hall, "The Rose of Midnight" hung in darkness. The house was still, the fire in the morning room had collapsed to a dull glow. No horse had sounded along the tree-lined avenue or on the cobblestone drive, yet the shape of a large man in a black greatcoat stood at the mullioned windows. Soon, with a minimum of noise, the casement opened.

The highwayman stepped over the low still onto a cedarwood chest, and hence entered the hall. He seldom did such a thing. Housebreaking was not his specialty. Even so, as he stood in this place that would

47

normally be forbidden to him, he was giddy with that familiar joy which dwells at the heart of terror.

The walls were hung with various dark paintings. Which was her? The air about him almost rippled with impatience.

His black, thigh-high jackboots were soundless on the rich carpet. His fingertips skimmed over a small wooden writing desk, feeling the fragile marquetry and ivory inlay. He touched a wooden box with small compartments which probably contained fishing lines, hooks and flies, perhaps a penknife and some pens swaddled in silk.

He went to the hearth, to the banked fire, and knelt down. Soon a candle stub lighted in his left hand. The opal ring on his smallest finger glimmered. The light picked out glints in the dark hair showing beneath his hat, and in the depths of his dark eyes.

As he stood, the rich, hushed room broke into soft gleams. He stepped around a high-backed chair that was like a small bishop's throne and went directly to the full-length portrait of the young lady in her rose bower.

The blob of light from the candle shone on her white white face. There was a shudder in the core of him. Something broke in his expression: he permitted himself a thin smile. He'd come from Derbyshire to bury a fellow thief, but then he'd seen her and he found he couldn't leave without *really* seeing her. She, more than Georgie Moraga, had become the purpose of his journey north.

He'd heard a few of the rumors about her, but no one could convince him that she'd ever worn a servant's mob or had her arms covered with flour and dough up to her elbows or strained her back over a butter churn. No, she was a lady through and through.

A ravishingly beautiful young lady, tender of complexion, small, supple, and alluring.

She could be in this very house. Perhaps earlier she'd sat in this fine room—by the fire there, matching floss for her needlework or sipping a cup of purple wine from the glinting decanter on the table. She might be upstairs this minute, in a deeply feathered bed, asleep, vulnerable.

He smiled with terrible gentleness.

A sound—and cold walked down his spine. He cupped the flame of his candle and stood immobile, alert, every inch of him listening.

But it was only the house creaking. Switching the candle to his right hand, he lowered his left to touch the cool smooth butt of the pistol thrust into his belt. This was madness, madness. His teeth flashed again in a grin that held as much danger as humor.

He pulled the bishop's chair about and sat down, stretching his long legs out before him. He poured some wine into one of the small silver cups. He ate a sugar wafer, then a second one, then dusted the crumbs from his greatcoat. He moved restlessly. Damn this chair, he wasn't built properly for it. A man needed to have withered buttocks to be comfortable in such a piece of furniture.

He stared at the portrait as he had in the roadhouse last night. He'd fallen in love. "The Rose of Midnight" was a dream of bliss, a dream that couldn't come true. He stared down into the delicate silver cup in his big hand. Madness. A dream, and not even a dream of what could be, but of what could never be. The woman might not even be real, as love is often not real but only everything we wish were real.

He sighed from the bottom of his deep chest. Dear God, dear unmerciful God. What am I doing here?

At five and twenty minutes after midnight, the

49

morning room of Hockness Hall was empty once more. "The Rose of Midnight" stood on in her rose bower, her secret expression giving away nothing, nothing.

Jane opened her eyes to the blurred twilight of a foggy morning. Between midnight and dawn the sky had become all smoked with mist. She'd had no solid sleep, but many dreams and stirrings. The events of last night seemed clouded now. She sat on the edge of her narrow cot to plait her hair and wind it about her head. She covered it with a small round-eared cap that tied with a pink ribbon, and put on her daily black uniform with its black gauze neckerchief and clean white apron, which also tied with pink ribbons.

She went about her early morning chores in a haze of apprehension. It was all she could do when she woke Mr. Welby not to cry through his bed curtains, "Master, I'm so afraid!" Fearing she might say exactly that, she daren't speak to him at all, though she'd planned to tell him immediately that her father was coming. It was all simply too humiliating.

The trouble she anticipated didn't keep her waiting long. A terrible knock came at the front door while Mr. Welby was at his breakfast. Jane felt like a lark caught in a hunter's net. She didn't want to answer that knock. She hesitated, fingering the white cuffs of her black sleeves. She hated to think of her father's filthy, worn-through boots standing on her freshly swept front step. She hated to think she must open the door and let him come inside. Life was turning over on her, getting terrible suddenly.

He was dressed exactly as he'd been the night before, in a rusty tricorn, tarpaulin coat, wide belt. This time he had a sack slung over his shoulder. He put it down on the doorstep. His face confronted her smugly as he stepped into the hall. She noticed nothing except his eyes, those glittering, greedy eyes; they were afire, brimming with light. He didn't say a word, but walked a little down the hall without being asked. She refused to show him into the tidy parlor, but left him waiting where he was, his misshapen hat in his hand. Her head bowed, she went into the dining room like a shadow of herself, dark, silent.

"Who has come, Jane?" Mr. Welby dabbed at his lips with the end of his neckcloth. "Why . . . what is it, child?" He was dressed for a day at home, wearing his oldest gray bob wig, the one that looked as though moths had tasted it once and decided to leave it alone. His breeches were unbuttoned at the knee.

She smoothed her white apron. "My father is here to see you, master." Her voice sounded thin to her ears. She fought to control her face. "He wants to see you about"—as Mr. Welby rose, she finished swiftly, nearly choking with shame—"about my money. I told him a lie, master, and you mustn't—that is, please, *please,* say it is the truth."

"A lie? Why, Jane!" He stretched out a hand, but then it fell back without reaching her. "I feel as if you've told *me* a lie! I can't recall exactly what you said when you applied for your position, but I do know that I have been under the impression that your father was not alive."

"Oh, he's alive. God that he wasn't."

"Jane!"

It had been a wicked thing to say, but she couldn't take the words back now. There was no time. If she had more time she might be able to explain everything in a way he could understand.

Yet she'd already had two years and she hadn't found a way. Or hadn't felt the need, because in her youth and her pride she'd felt safe from this disaster.

51

She would still be safe but for that hateful portrait. In any case, there wasn't any time left now. Mr. Welby was heading toward the hall. She heard her father greet him: "How d'ye do, sir. Steven Fitzpatrick is the name."

Her master took him into the library. Jane found she couldn't stand; her knees were like water. Her face, she suspected, was white and peaked. She sat down in one of the dining room chairs—something she'd never done before. For two years she'd cleaned this room, every square inch of it, and laid the fire, and laid the table, and served Mrs. Galbraith's food and cleared it away, and never once had she simply sat here for a moment. It struck her that as well as she knew this room, much better, much more intimately in fact than he who owned it, it was not *her* room.

She could hear her father's voice from across the hall, and her master's voice in return. Though she couldn't make out their exact words, she sat listening, dumb as a frightened dog. She didn't dare budge from her chair. A quarter of an hour passed. Sitting hunched like an invalid, she remembered her father's brawny old body, his fierce and battered face with its port wine-colored nose, his ragged, unshaved beard, the sound of his hand meeting her face.

She shook herself. Mr. Welby would make everything all right. She trusted him. He loved her—even if he couldn't confess it. He would find some way to protect her, to make this terrible thing come out all right.

Chapter Four

Simple Greed

Jane heard the library door open. Mr. Welby came across the hall. She sat up very straight, stationing her hands in her lap.

"Jane, come in here, please."

She rose slowly. Slowly she went into the library.

There sat the shameful ugliness of her father. Her hopes lifted, however, for Rip, sitting on the settle, looked stooped and tired. He had his naval coat thrown over his lap. His face was not the face Jane had seen last night, which had burned like a brand all through her dreams. This was a weary face, rather pathetic. Mr. Welby has saved me! The pang was unendurably sweet.

Mr. Welby took a seat in the carved armchair opposite the settle. Only Jane was left to stand. After a moment, he began to speak:

"Jane, it is your father's wish that you leave your position here and go with him back to your family farm. He needs you there. He's going to work it again, and—"

"Go? Leave here?" The words stood up in her

mind. She heard herself say them with disbelief. "No!" She looked at Mr. Welby with all her heart in her eyes, wanting, *demanding* the reassurance of his fine valor.

"Jane." He was unhappy, but he was going to do his duty. "You know how fond I am of you. I will— that is, Mrs. Galbraith and I will sorely miss you. But if your father needs you I have no choice but to discharge you."

The room was getting darker.

"I do need ye, Janey," Rip said. "I'm going to the farm, like he says, and I need ye there. There's a lot o' work that I need ye for."

She couldn't bring herself to look at him.

Mr. Welby went on, "He has told me how he abandoned you and your mother, but now it seems he is making the effort to resettle himself, as a man and as the head of his family."

Jane remained imprisoned in a darkening silence. Mr. Welby knew only what Rip had told him, because she had told him nothing. She'd pretended not to have a childhood behind her, she'd pretended it even to herself. It is an act of will to have a memory.

Mr. Welby stirred uncomfortably. "He is your father. He has authority over you which even I may not disregard. Now, as for your pay, you must tell him the truth, that I have not been keeping it for you."

Her pay, her savings! She'd almost forgotten what her father really wanted. She saw the slight pivot of his head that told her he was as alert as a falcon. She spoke out of panic. "I spent it. I gave it to someone. A man. The rumors, they're true, there's a man."

"But Jane, just yesterday—!" Mr. Welby was nearly too dumbfounded too speak. The firelight shadows flicked across his face as he went white, and then scarlet. "Just yesterday, right here in this room, you told me you'd been saving it."

Rip sat with his ears akimbo, listening to every word. Jane was frantic that Mr. Welby couldn't see what she was doing—trying to protect what she'd worked so hard for from her father's rum-drinking and going to whores. *Mr. Welby, help me!* "I lied," she said. "I spent it, every farthing."

He gave her a look of pained disillusionment. "That's all right, sir." Rip sat looking weary and pathetic. He touched his brow to Mr. Welby. "She's got it hid somewheres. She'll tell me where when she gets to knowing me again."

Jane felt a tremor of new fear. Could it really happen? Would she have to go with him? She looked desperately at her master. Mr. Welby's wig had slipped back from his forehead. He was often forgetful of his appearance. But she could hardly believe his years of scholarship had left him so blind to the facts of real life, to the wretchedness and villainy which abounded among his fellow creatures, among men like Rip Fitzpatrick, that he could believe the man wanted to take up farming again! A growing panic hovered in her mind, as if her whole life was sliding into a chasm. "What he means is if you send me away with him, he'll beat me."

That had not the effect she'd hoped for. Instead of igniting a fire, the words seemed to settle as quiet as embers around her master. He said, "I'm afraid it is his right to chastise you if you refuse to obey him. He is your *father,* Jane."

She looked him straight in the eye, and did not let her gaze waver for a fraction of a second. "He'll take my money, and then he'll leave again. My money's all he wants. He took the money from our spring shearing when he left before—and left my mother and me to starve."

Her father, behind her, sighed. He stooped forward

over his knees, his hand holding his head in an attitude of most plaintive remorse. "Haven't ye forgiven me for that, Janey? What must I do to—" His voice broke. He glanced up at her. Somehow he screwed up his face into a hundred wrinkles, as if he were about to weep. Jane looked away; she stared into the blazing logs on the hearth.

Mr. Welby said, "He's an old man, Jane. You mustn't hold on to spite. Everyone deserves a second chance."

"I worked for two years for that money. He'll take it and leave me with nothing, just like he did before."

Her father's face sagged and all the corrugations on it crumpled up. He said in a whining voice, "I didn't *mean* to do it! Don't ye understand, Janey? I didn't *mean* to." To Mr. Welby he said, "It was the drinking, sir."

"He broke into your house last night, master."

"Janey! Ah, what's this now?"

"He came through my window and went through my things—and it wasn't rum that made him do it, but simple greed."

"I ask ye, sir, d'ye believe this?"

"He wants my money, that's all. He has no intention of taking up life on the farm. He always hated it there. He—" She stopped. Her pride reached its sticking point when it came to confessing that he had struck her. Why humiliate herself that far when she'd already seen it would do no good? Mr. Welby shared the common belief that a father had every right to "chastise" a daughter in any way he saw fit.

" 'Tis all a wild lie, sir. Her mother had the habit o' slipping in a little lie now and then, whenever it suited her purpose."

Jane was so outraged she couldn't even look at him, or at Mr. Welby. She waited to see if her master was

56

going to come to her defense—but no; it seemed that in a half hour's time he'd lost all his care for her. He was sitting stiffly, as if holding his breath against some unpleasant smell. Whatever illusions he'd held about her were sullied forever by this ugly exposure of her private past.

The log cracked as it burned in the hearth. Jane couldn't bear the humiliation any longer. "Very well," she said. She felt remarkably in control of herself again. "If you are discharging me, then I suppose I must go."

Mr. Welby stirred himself; relief freed him from his stiff posture. "I think that would be best. And," he added, "you must give him your earnings, Jane. He needs them to buy stock and seed." His cheeks were flushed in hectic spots, as if he had a fever. "With your help, he will be successful. And if he is successful, then so shall you be." He nodded, well content with that last remark. He looked at her father. "I assume your days of irresponsibility and debauchery are a thing of the past, Mr. Fitzpatrick. The dangers of drink are fully contemplated in many pamphlets. I believe I have a copy of Thomas Wilson's *Distilled Spiritous Liquors, the Bane of the Nation,* if you'd like to borrow it."

"Can't read, sir."

"Oh, but Jane can. She could read it aloud to you." He glanced up at her and condescended to smile. "You'll find her a great asset to you now, Mr. Fitzpatrick. I have taught her everything I can. She absorbs learning like a sponge. Her powers of concentration are exceptional for a woman. Why, she's learned some things which cost even gentlemen hours of anguish."

That smile. That self-satisfaction. Jane had never been tempted to spit on anyone in her life before, yet now she felt saliva well in her mouth.

There was silence except for the snapping of the fire and the rustle of her blood in her ears. Mr. Welby rose. "Well." The motion and the word were signals; the conversation was ended. Rip also stood up. Both were looking at Jane. She swallowed hard, and said very clearly, "You may dismiss me, master, but he'll never get a tuppence of my money. Nay, I'd rather die first."

Mr. Welby's mouth opened; but before he could respond, she turned to face her father squarely. "Aye, I'd rather die—or better, see you dead!"

Rip's eyes, so oddly bright and shining, held hers. The challenge was accepted.

Mr. Welby sighed. "Jane, I am very sorry to hear you speak so. I can only recommend, in the most earnest fashion, that you consider seriously your attitude. You will only come to a bad end if you do not."

"Don't ye fret on it, sir. I'll see she comes to her senses and learns to respect me proper again. I'm going to live to a ripe old age." He gave Mr. Welby a pathetic little smile. "There's no worry that she'll end on the gallows for the murder 'o her poor father."

"Indeed, I should hope not." Mr. Welby's eyes looked out at Jane as though from a great distance within himself. He was betraying her, abandoning her, washing his hands of her. She could hardly believe it. Why, just yesterday . . . just last evening . . .

She barely comprehended the final exchange between him and her father. Their voices were noise, empty wind. She was alone on the far shore of shock.

They were both staring at her. Rip scratched his stubbly face then reached out to touch her arm. "Get your things now, Janey."

She wrenched away from his touch and was suddenly awake again to the crisis that was upon her.

" 'Tis time to go." Rip's head was still sunk down

58

on his shoulders, but his eyes—they were iridescent, gathering the light from all directions. And now his lips drew back. It was by no means a smile. It made her whole body go rigid.

"Jane . . ."

She threw a savage glance at Mr. Welby. If he said anything more, she couldn't promise that she would remember all the fine things he'd taught her, things about being well-spoken and agreeable. She turned on her heels and left the room before she did something she would always regret.

Encased in a hard shell which kept all feeling at bay, and all thought, and all care, she climbed to her chamber and changed from her servant's dress to the purple stuff gown she'd worn yesterday. She was making a roll of her other garments and personal odds and ends, the small accumulation of her two years' residence here, when she heard a heavy step on the attic stairs. She stood quite still, like a cat listening. Was that Mrs. Galbraith? Never had the cook condescended to come up here before. The landing creaked as she came into the small chamber. Jane didn't want to look at her. She was afraid she might feel something, and if there was one thing that would break her altogether now it was emotion.

Though Mrs. Galbraith was not a person of lavish gestures, she came forward and took Jane into her fat arms and pressed her lips against the top of her bent head. Jane stood stiffly in that amply fleshed embrace, too rigidly contained to appreciate the affection it showed.

"I'll not worry about thee too much, Jane Fitzpatrick. Thou'rt one who never did accept gentlelike her condition."

The stairs creaked with her descent.

There was nothing more for Jane to do. Her hands

59

quivered so that she couldn't tie her bonnet strings. She left them dangling. As she faced the door, the shell encompassing her cracked minutely; her skin crawled with insects of fear. She looked at the window. Could she make it out the way her father had come in? The fog had slicked the steep roofs, but . . .

That would be too shameful. She couldn't bear for Mr. Welby to see her reduced to such an undignified leave-taking. She had no intention of returning to Dulwych with Rip Fitzpatrick, but she would wait until she was out of her master's house to make her escape.

She went downstairs. *Go through the kitchen and let yourself out the side door. You can flee down the alley. Mrs. Galbraith won't say anything—at least not until it's too late.*

She tamped down the urge. Wait, wait, when we're clear of York, then I'll get away from him, and no one need see that I'm afraid.

The door to the library stood closed. Mr. Welby was not going to wish her farewell. He was disabused of his former opinion of her. Rip had soiled her in his eyes. She shouldn't feel bad—but she did.

Then she almost smiled (her mind was moving close to the edges of hysteria now); she should have asked Mrs. Galbraith, "I suppose there is no possibility of marriage to him now, would you say?"

The near-smile faltered. Despite everything, she wished he would at least say goodbye to her. Last evening he'd looked at her so soulfully. He'd nearly spoken aloud what he felt.

She almost broke then. She caught herself once again. Her father must be waiting outside. She stopped at the front door to look back along the hall. This was not her home. The knowledge clenched her deep within. She had called it home, but . . .

She went out and shut the door softly behind her.

She hadn't thought the October damp would be so

chilly or she would have worn a pair of drawers under her petticoats. She was going to get cold even before she made it outside the city walls.

Rip was at the bottom of the stoop, beside one of the clipped yews. He smiled when he saw her, not a pleasant smile. "Ah, but ye're yer mother's image!" He said it a little too loudly, as if he suspected Mr. Welby might be watching from the parlor window. Jane knew he wasn't, she knew he had locked himself in his library. Rip's eyes were slits of anger as he took her arm. His touch revolted her, and she tried to shake it off, but he wouldn't release her.

He pulled her along into the cobblestoned streets. Though it was a Monday, the city was quiet, the fog keeping everyone inside who did not absolutely have to be out. As they passed a public house, a frightened female squeal came from an upper room.

A soldier passed. He bestowed a brief, arid smile upon Jane. Her eyes followed him beseechingly. Rip's hand on her arm tightened. He hissed a blood-curdling threat.

They came upon an almost silent funeral procession for a woman of some wealth. Four women passed, casting sweet herbs and flowers on the damp cobbles. They were followed by two beadles with their staves covered with cypress. Next came a pair of ministers and a clerk. The pall was supported by six ladies of obvious good standing, led by their well-dressed husbands.

They all passed in the fog without even looking at Jane. Could no one see what was happening to her? Would no one help her? No, that would be too much to expect of a fine officer of the King's Army, or the members of the local gentry, or the prominent citizens of the town, men and women of breeding one and all, men of education, of judgment. It would be too much to expect them to care what might befall anyone not so gently born as they.

Nor would the people of the quiet lanes and farms along the road that led toward the village of Dulwych care. They probably wouldn't even note the pair's passing, for fog was everywhere. It lay on the dismal and frightening bogs, on the heights. It was in Jane's eyes and throat.

Beads of moisture gathered on her cloak. She would have lifted its capacious hood over her head, but her right arm was burdened with the roll of her belongings, and Rip's hand had her left arm. He carried his bulging cloth sack over his shoulder whilst she trudged along at his side with the overwhelming and flooding sensation that this was all just a dream. Part of her was still confident that all would be well. Nothing so terrible could happen, even if she didn't escape him. He was her father, after all. And she was a grown woman now and not a child to be pushed around and beaten. Why, if he tried to lay a hand on her, she would fight back with all her considerable strength.

Outside the city, the country quickly became thin of houses and people. The road was bad. Mr. Welby complained that even the best roads in England were vile. Jane believed him, though she lived in a time when a woman might go through her whole life and never travel farther than the closest market village.

After a walk of three or four miles, they passed an ancient church and a jumbled parish graveyard. "Mother is buried here," Jane said absently, peering through the fog at the moss-stained headstones. An ancient rosebush grew by the gate. Petals blown from the last flowers lay over the long, dewy, unkempt grass. The air was so still a candle flame would have stood as upright as a sentinel.

Rip said nothing, only maintained his iron grip on

62

her arm and that same odious expression of self-satisfaction and smugness on his face.

Jane knew the fog was to her advantage, and that her escape must be accomplished before they arrived at the farm, but Rip didn't relax his hold for an instant. The pressure was rising, however; the moment had come.

Though she couldn't see it, she knew the hamlet of Dulwych lay ahead, with small farms clustering about it. Before entering it, however, they left the road by way of a footpath of beaten earth. It looked dark and narrow, this path, winding out of sight among high bracken. Jane felt goose pimples lifting on her arms. She had not walked this way in two years, and had not thought to walk it ever again. What was she doing here? What was this waking dream through which she seemed to be treading?

As they left the public thoroughfare for this piddling footpath, a flock of blackbirds startled and lifted themselves into anxious flight. They disappeared into the heavy fog. This was an eerie place, imbued with spectral figures and shapes misrepresented by the clouded air. The path, slick with rotted leaves, descended step-by-step. Once, when Jane slipped, Rip gave her a spiteful push. He still had hold of her arm, but Jane decided she would have no better opportunity of escape.

Suddenly, with a spasm of release, she tore free of his hand. He caught her by her sleeve, though, and by some means, she wasn't quite sure how exactly, she lost her balance and fell heavily, face down on the slanted path. Her roll of possessions was crushed beneath her.

She was not hurt; the leaf mold from the coarse, weedy ferns was deep here, and gave up a soft, acrid smell. She got to her hands and knees—and for an instant had a close and minute view of some lovely, seed-shedding stalks of grass, crystaled with drops of moisture—but before she could even spit the dirt off her tongue, Rip was slipping something rough and stickery over her head.

"What—?" Rising up on her knees, she raised her hands to find it was a noose. As she pulled at it, he slipped other loops of the rope about her wrists. This was the spring of a trap! "What are you doing!"

He pulled an end of the rope and her hands were jerked up beneath her chin, causing her teeth to click. When she tried to pull them free, the rough hemp rope cut into the back of her neck.

Panic seized her, and for a long instant she struggled to unfetter herself. She spun around on her knees, and fell back and twisted her wrists, all in unbelieving outrage. Like the nursery rhyme, her thoughts ran up and down in a crazy way, striking noon, striking midnight. Shock suffocated her, strangled her, so that the whole appalled clanging of her nervous system could achieve no outlet.

She fell sideways onto her hip and shoulder. Still, she couldn't get free. She went a little wild, kicking uselessly, writhing in the dirt, soiling her cloak and skirts and making sounds such as she'd never made before. Her hair came undone. The delicate skin of her wrists and neck became hot and chaffed.

At length, she realized Rip was laughing at her. She gathered herself together, and took a deep breath. He was almost dancing with glee. "Got ye, ye impudent slut, ye wanton bawd! Think ye can sass me and get away with it? Go ahead, sass me now; ye sinful strumpet!"

She had never felt she was a particularly stupid person, but she felt incredibly stupid now. That she had come so far with him without trying to break free earlier! She should have kicked and screamed every inch of the way and *damn* the humiliation and the indignity and the shame. Damn Mr. Welby and the upright citizens of York.

With effort, she got her feet beneath her. Her struggles had accomplished nothing but to burn and abrade the skin of her wrists and neck. He had the long end of the rope in his hand, and he grinned at her like a hungry fox at the sight of a cornered hen. Her heartbeat filled her ears. Frenzy lay just behind a curtain in her mind. She tried hard to follow what was happening, what he was saying.

"That there, Madam Rose, is what's called a slave coffle.'Tis what we use down in Guinea to march the black savages out o' their jungle to the coast."

Her horror of him increased until she was afraid her imagination could not hold anymore. Her throat nearly closed. She sucked in a long breath. The frenzy bulged behind that curtain in her mind; her sanity shivered. Her knees felt so unsteady she was afraid they might not hold her up.

He bent down and with his free hand shook out her roll of clothing and personal items. His mouth was like a puckered scar as he felt the hems and seams of her spare dress, perversely smashed a box that held her hairpins, and in frustration, when he couldn't immediately find anything of value, kicked everything—her clean smock and linen bedwrap, her long winter drawers and her heavy mittens—down into the leaf mold.

"Where is it!" he snapped over his shoulder. He turned, giving her a cold ophidian stare.

Her body tightened and shrank together, she curled into herself, bracing for the blow. There was no sound in the fog, not even the soft, low wind that came in clearer weather over the moors and whispered through the ferns, that immense quiet sound she had lived with most of her life. In this absolute silence, a dreadful sense of their solitude entered her. He could do anything to her.

Rip's eyes narrowed. His fists clenched. She was completely helpless to protect herself with her hands bound up to her throat.

He didn't hit her. Instead, a smile cut across his seamed face. He came close. "Just ye wait, Janey. Soon now," he whispered, right into her ear.

Stepping back, he wound the end of the rope around his fist and towed on it so suddenly and so hard that she nearly sprawled again. Without mercy, he dragged her forward, saying, "In Guinea, if any o' the savages hold us up, we take 'em behind a bush and cut their throats. So mind me when I say don't try to drag your feet, Madam Rose."

The footpath wound about in the bracken for perhaps five miles before it came out from under the dark overhang of a rock into a tiny dale marked by a trio of rock-fenced fields, all without a sign of ownership, all utterly deserted. The shallow gully of a seeping beck wandered from one end of the dale through the largest enclosure, which was perhaps an acre in size. The second, much smaller, was bordered on one side by a thorned hedge. The beck oozed beside the third, which was smaller yet. There sagged a splintered fence of woven reeds once meant to protect the meager garden of vegetables that Jane and her mother had attempted to grow.

It was hard for Jane in her present state to equate these scrubby fields with herself. It seemed that by making a short seven-mile journey, she had stepped into a different world, back into a former life, a grittier life, a life without order, without hope.

The furrows of that garden, which had provided peas, broad beans, and a few turnips and parsnips, were overgrown with weeds now. The enclosure was as nasty as a pigpen. Animals had rooted all through it. Jane thought of her mother's dry, bony hands sowing precious seeds, one by one, and dragging buckets of water to make the furrows sprout.

The grapevine at the far end, which had produced a few precious purple grapes each year, had produced nothing this season. Jane remembered her mother caring for the half-dozen clusters the vine usually spawned, protecting them from birds and insects and animals until they were ready for picking. Now the vine, so long fussed over, was all but eaten up.

Close by, under a gnarled and nearly leafless apple tree, stood their old beehive. And the stake where they'd tied their goose. They'd somehow managed to have a goose each year, which they fattened as best they could for their Michaelmas feast.

Alone, they'd herded their seven or eight sheep, sheared them, cleaned and carded the wool. They'd gone up onto the fells for heather each year in order to restuff their pillows and mattresses. They'd collected marsh grasses to weave baskets for sale—anything to earn a penny, a halfpenny, a farthing. Anything to be able to eat, to ward off starvation, to buy a sack of barley flour, the staple of their diet, which provided them with the coarse black bread, oatcakes, porridges, and gruels that got them through the long, cruel northern winters.

Alexandra insisted Jane must go to the local dame school, a four-mile trek each way. Yet her schooling didn't excuse her from spinning wool from the age of five years, or minding the sheep, or hiring out to aid with land-clearance and other rough field labor the minute she was old enough.

The path nearly disappeared in grass that was high and thick and tangled. They were at the place where the seeping beck took its leave of the dale. The only sound was the fog in Jane's ears, the lonely, solitary fog of the moors.

Rip pulled her across the stones that served as a crossing for the meager flow of water. And once on the other side, at last she looked at what her eyes had been avoiding: the stone cottage in which she'd been born.

Even when lived in and cared for it hadn't been much. It was at least two hundred years old and looked now as though a heavy rain would collapse its roof. If only Mr. Welby could see it, he would take back all he'd said about Rip being a success. This cottage, this farm, was past saving. Someone had broken in the door. The single window stared like an eye without a lid. The shutters that had closed it against the January gales were missing. The ancient thatched roof sagged sadly in the middle.

Rip threw his sack down outside the door-opening and hauled Jane inside.

Chapter Five

When Necessity Is Upon Us,
Then We Must Suffer

Had the cottage always looked as dark as an animal's hole? And so quiet? Spiderwebs had formed sticky, menacing traps in the corners and over the window hole. When Jane had lived here, she hadn't noticed how black with hearth smoke the thatched ceiling was, or how small the room was, or how poor. She and her mother had picked savin and rue to scatter on the packed earth floor to sweeten the air and keep away lice. The present fetid air sickened her. Something had died in here recently.

The main ceiling beam was so low that Rip could reach up and tie the end of the coffle rope around it. This blackened oak beam was the cause for the sag in the low roof. It was rotted and splintering; Jane had a vision of it coming down, and the moldering thatch with it. Tethered as she was, she saw herself smothered, helpless to escape.

Rip knocked about through the clutter of discarded junk littering the floor, cursing, until he found the dead thing, a rat, among the debris collected in the hearth at one end of the room. Jane recalled fires in that hearth, the smoke rising into the thatch before it wandered out through the smoke hole. She recalled a cat sitting on the flat stones—Juniper, his name was. And she recalled her mother sitting on a bench with her skirts raised above her knees, her feet extended to the warmth.

Once there had been a rugged trestle table, made by a younger Rip Fitzpatrick from planed pieces of wood and burnished clean with sand. There had been a tureen the young husband had carved, which his wife kept stored along with the earthenware plates in a cupboard. An old hogshead had been cut down for stools.

The couple's bed had been their major possession, being of an elaborate wooden design, complete with doors and hangings to stop the cold. Alexandra had sold this soon after Rip's abandonment. The money had kept her and Jane through that first year, for Rip had left the day the baskets of spring wool went to market. Instead of bringing back the vital proceeds, they'd learned he'd used the money to equip himself for a position on a ship called the *Richard L.* So the bed had to be forfeited, along with a valuable ironbound chest. For the next seven years, Alexandra and Jane slept on planks set by the hearth.

It seemed so long ago. Jane had escaped all this—hadn't she? She'd labored, and saved, and dreamed a dream. How could she lose all of that? How could she see it sacrificed to the ignorance and misery of this desperate, unawakened being who called himself her father? There was more than her present fear at stake here, or even her hate, and far more than mere obstinacy.

He held up the dead rat by its horrible tail. For amusement, he swung its bloated body near Jane's face. She winced back, pulling the coffle rope taut; the

70

beam above her creaked. "Untie me!" she shouted, looking up. "It's going to come down!"

He squinted up at the beam. "It might. It might at that." Clearly he was pleased to know he'd given her one more thing to worry about.

He went to the door and threw the rat's carcass off into the bracken and gorse that had grown right up into the dooryard. He followed it out, and disappeared from Jane's sight, though she could hear him still. He was rummaging in his sack.

With the dead rat gone, the pervading smell inside the cottage was of mildew. It filled her like the breath of sickness—of hopelessness, of desperation. A wave of despair seized her. She didn't dare struggle against her rope. He had her strung up so that she couldn't move more than a foot or two in any direction without pulling against the rotten beam. She heard him outside humming a tune. Oh God, to realize that just yesterday she'd been fool enough to think herself happy. She'd been nothing but a girl, a child without sense, living on passion and air.

Rip reappeared carrying a knife in a plain sheath and leather-covered rod. From the end of this rod sprouted several knotted leathern cords which he held coiled back in his hand. She regarded him as she would any dangerous beast of prey. As she watched, he shook the coils of leather out, and the object became a whip, what she believed was called a cat-o'-nine-tails. Her senses leaped outward in new fright. As he jiggled the whip to untangle the cords, he said, "This is what we use aboard the *Richard*. This here lovely has cut many a black back—but it'll do just as nicely against white skin."

Her heart chilled. There came a taste of her tongue like cool steel. She twisted as he tried to step behind her. "Father!" She forgot about the condition of the

71

beam overhead, she forgot about the moldered, smothering thatch. All she could think was: is he really this brutal and capricious? Is he really nothing but a savage beast?

" 'Father' is it now? Then I'll give ye one more chance. Where's that money?"

She was helpless, with her hands held in an attitude of prayer beneath her chin, the rope of the coffle chaffing her neck. Her lips opened, her tongue formed the first words of surrender. *There's an old rock pigpen, just outside York, along the pasture path into the woods. I'll take you there.*

But she couldn't say it aloud. A proverb came to her, one of her mother's favorites: when necessity is upon us, then we must suffer.

Cursing, he fumbled at the strings of her cloak, and tugged it from her shoulders and flung it aside. His old, strong hands took hold of the back of her purple bodice. He ripped it to her waist, muttering, "Did yer Mr. Welby teach ye to be so stupid? Now ye'll learn what yer old father can teach ye. Bunch o' city manners, eh? So ye don't even sound like ye should no more. Ye forget yer place. Nay, that gormless lout can't teach ye nothing! Not like *I'm* about to teach ye!"

He used his knife to cut open her stays. Above her jangling tension, she felt the coolness of the damp air rushing over her flesh as her split dress was pushed forward over her shoulders by those coarse hands. Her back was laid bare. *Cre-eak.* Even as she struggled, she looked up at the beam uneasily.

And then came the whip.

It came down hard, and expletives came out of Rip's mouth. The leather cords struck her bare skin with a sharp slap, snatching her breath away. The force behind the blow drove her forward and left a burning sensation that made her eyes water. She cried out in

72

defiance. But just as the Africans' defiance did them no good, neither did hers.

Twisting, she saw him over her shoulder. The sight of his face added to her pain. She choked herself as her arms strained backward in a gesture of self-protection.

But there was no altering her vulnerability to the whip, which even now lifted again, and sliced through the air. With its second impact her whole body jerked upward. Her cry was of slashing pain. It flamed out, like shine from a turned blade. Rip was warming to his work. Jane forgot all about the Crown Colony of Georgia, the red earth she'd read of and found hard to envision, the freedom, the dignity of helping to create a new place in a new world.

While she was still recovering from that second shockingly painful blow, the third came. The fingers of her coffled hands clawed the air. Reflexively, her body turned. Rip cursed and moved to stay behind her. "Where is it? Tell me!"

Would she have spoken? She was still just catching her breath when the fourth blow fell. She wailed; her knees buckled. Her lips moved wordlessly as she fought to digest this new pain, this sensation of the skin being torn from her bones. Hence she was unprepared for number five.

Again she was driven forward. Something liquid ran down her back. Despite this dampness, her flesh burned as though he were holding a torch to it. Her breath caught in her throat; she strangled on her own saliva, her helpless fingers clutched at nothing.

What—what was that sound? The whip lifting again? But she wasn't braced yet! Out the corner of her watering eyes she saw Rip angling his body into the whip's slant, she heard the whir, the snap—

Her mind was filled with the pain that flailed and cut her. She couldn't bear it. And whilst she contem-

73

plated her inability to bear it, she suffered the next blow.

Her head fell forward. A veil of darkness dropped across her eyes. Her legs gave way. She choked—the coffle was like a noose. Her whole being slackened. Her tongue lolled helplessly in her mouth, its thickness prohibiting either speech or complaint.

She stumbled to get her feet beneath her, to suck in breath. The whip. Her fear of that *whoosh*-ing sound was as great as the lash itself. Yet the lash followed, again fell furiously. Her mind reeled, the very knobs of her spine felt exposed. She wanted to be dead, to wake from this bad dream. She wanted to fall unconscious. God take me in Your mercy. As from far away she heard a woman scream. Oh, the terrible pitch of that scream.

The next blow came, cruelly. Instead of pushing her past the edge into blessed unconsciousness, it revived her. She rose out of the whirlpool of a dissolving dream. She locked her knees, thus relieving her neck. She caught two shallow breaths in her lungs. Her eyes even cleared.

But Rip flailed her again in grim earnest. His grin had long since gone wild. He was muttering something: ". . . till ye beg my pardon for yer wicked manners." He seemed more bent on inflicting pain than on extracting the information which had led them to this juncture.

His mind had lost its original direction. Just as Jane's distracted mind had lost count of the whip strokes. At five, hearing a gruff voice suggesting that she give in, she might have told him everything he wanted to know. Perhaps even at six she could have followed the trail of some remembrance and recalled enough words to save her. But as the whip continued to flog her, she knew only forgetfulness, an awful dissociation in her bowels,

74

in her flesh, and in the bones beneath her flesh. Tears ran openly down her cheeks. She forgot why she was suffering this pain. She even made anguished cries for her mother, dead now for over two years.

Jane's body swung limp. Her breathing was a noisy intake requiring hard labor from her lungs. Her mind walked in a still, quiet place. She came back to herself when she heard the whip whistle upward again. Opening her eyes with a start, she got her feet beneath her. She looked frantically right and left over her shoulder. Fear twisted in her heart.

But she was alone. By slow degrees her heart quit hammering. Her throat burned, crying for water. Her back . . . the feel of her back frightened her. She'd seen animals hung up and skinned. She imagined something much worse. Her back felt as if something with sharp claws had ripped and torn and left her mauled.

She closed her eyes again, gratefully, for just a moment. She flexed her wrists in their bonds. She must lock her knees and stay awake, for if she let herself lose awareness, she knew her legs would give out again and then she would slowly strangle.

And so there she stood.

How long she remained there, she wasn't sure. Her brain seemed to veer beneath blurred confusion and a race of vivid, alert thoughts. Thoughts that broke up and dissolved as fast as they formed. There had been screaming before; she recalled that much distinctly. But it was stopped now. Very slowly she comprehended that it had been she who had screamed. That was why her throat was so dry.

Oh, for a drink of water.

Though she couldn't have said how she did it, she

75

remained standing, with the coffle binding her hands beneath her chin and circling her throat. Once—or was it twice?—she nearly fainted again: she began to droop and at the same time, all at once, her vision enlarged. She saw the Atlantic Ocean, as she imagined it, and Georgia, the red earth, the green, silent, wooded hills. But then she heard the whip once more—or was it a groan from the splintery beam over her head? She even imagined she felt a few straws of rotted thatch sift down about her.

Rip had been outside. Now he came in. She saw him through a reddish haze of pain and fatigue. He came toward her with his knife out again. Though her eyes sharpened, she was too numb to flinch. She could not make the required effort. If he meant to murder her . . . but no, he only fumbled at the nape of her neck, carelessly brushing against her raw back so that she whimpered. Her hands suddenly fell: he'd cut the coffle. The freedom hurt. Roughly he pulled her about to face him. His breath, newly sweetened with alcohol, fanned her face. He cut her wrists free. She was so unsteady she almost fell against him. She had a horror of touching him, however, and put out a hand, groping for balance. She staggered, yet remained on her feet.

They exchanged haggard looks. He said, "I found some wood." He gestured toward the meager pile he'd thrown down inside the door. "Start a fire, warm this place up. I got a tinderbox in my sack. There's some bread and cheese and a bit o'capon in there, too, but ye leave that alone. Ye'll get naught to eat till I have that money."

This was a new mood. He seemed tired. Was it because he'd never expected her to withstand such a beating? A wisp of pride rose in her.

But she hadn't really defeated him, only exhausted

him. He would rest, and then . . . could she bear another attack?

"Make yourself decent," he growled, moving away.

She looked down at herself. He'd pushed her bodice off her shoulders when he'd torn it to bare her back. With her arms now down, it had fallen further, revealing the upper slopes of her breasts. Mewling with misery, she reached inside and pulled away her useless stays, then she pushed the dress back, covering her shoulders. She felt every ragged thread where it touched her back. Her cloak was on the floor. She risked bending to retrieve it, not allowing herself to consider her aching muscles, her cramping limbs. She cautiously swung the cloak behind her shoulders. It settled cruelly against her open wounds. She felt the fabric stick in places where the blood was still wet. But it gave her a sense of security to have that awful mauled flesh covered.

What had he bid her do? She felt bewildered, as if something totally incomprehensible had happened. Warm the place? Moving with extreme care, she picked up some of the wood. She laid a clumsy fire. She felt very vague and unclear, as if she were in a dream within a dream. In his sack she found a flask of gin— she needed a drink of water—and there was a packet of food, which didn't interest her at all, and that dread thing, the cat-o'-nine-tails, and finally she found his tinderbox.

She was not handy with flint and steel, especially not now; her hands were unsteady. As she knelt beside the hearth, Rip tried to prop up the broken door. It wouldn't cooperate. His frustration heated to a quiet, simmering rage. She got a spark, and blew softly on the tinder, but no thread of smoke curled up. She felt a sobbing, puling anxiety that any little thing would set him to beating her again. Light, light, oh, please, light! Tired he might be, but he would spare her neither pity nor mercy.

A single tentative strand of smoke wafted up into her nostrils as Rip stopped cursing the door. "Stupid hussy!"

His voice froze her with fear. She'd had the frailest of flames begun, but now she couldn't even breathe on it.

"Can't ye even light a fire!" He used his knee to knock her over—not difficult since she was so giddy. The sudden movement made her back screech. A dozen places stung instantly, and she felt more wetness and knew she had broken open many of the places where the blood had been trying to scab. The pain brought tears to her eyes. Whilst she huddled on the floor, trembling, he cursed her over and over, without looking at her, half demented it seemed. He himself struck up the beginnings of a fire. His shoulders hunched over his efforts. He looked like an ox, a big, slow beast, blind and deaf to pain.

Her condition seemed so unreal she could hardly bring herself to believe it. Her eyes were wide, fixed on him. She didn't know him. Yet she knew that if she had something heavy at hand, she would strike him with all her might. If she had a gun, she would shoot him. If—

The overhead beam groaned . . . and abruptly cracked. Jane had had plenty of time to think about what that sound meant, hours of time whilst she had been strung up to it, struggling to keep her footing, struggling not to lose consciousness, not to give in to the unbelievable pain and faintness. Now, moving faster than she'd thought possible considering her condition, she staggered to her feet and took the few steps that separated her from the propped door. She moved quickly, though she would remember each footfall forever afterward, as if each one had taken an age to accomplish. The door needed no more than a weak pull to bring it down. Then she was out of the cottage.

There she sagged with relief with her hands over her heart, which continued to flutter bird-swift.

Rip, blowing to keep his start of a fire going, had looked up as the beam cracked. Slower to react—he was not quick either of vision or of conception and conceivably he'd forgotten all about how rotted the roof beam was—he didn't start to rise until the last frail splinters of wood that held the weight of the rotten thatch gave way.

There was no hideous splintering din. It all happened very quietly. He straightened, flexing his heavy shoulders, twisted toward the door, toward Jane—she saw his leathery face, white with fear, his merciless, calculating eyes consumed now by blind frantic fear— then the beam caught him. Jane saw it strike the back of his head; she heard the ugly thump of wood against skull bone, she saw his eyes become an ox's eyes, full of nothing but opaque brute endurance—and then he was lost from her sight. The ancient roof came down on him with a gentle *whoosh*. The stone walls of the cottage remained standing, though several stones crumbled away.

Jane swayed on her feet just beyond this scene of this all but silent mayhem. She couldn't see Rip now. She didn't call out to him.

Let him be dead.

She backed away, slowly, slowly. By the time she reached the edge of the dooryard, she saw smoke rising above the standing walls. She recalled the tender wisps of smoke rising from the clumsy fire.

Still no sound indicated that he was alive. More smoke, blue and bitter, lapped up through the crumbled thatch. It stung her lungs. She coughed painfully.

Someone had to do something. She should call to him at least. He might just be unconscious.

Let him be dead.

She took a few steps toward the door, then stopped and stood trembling. Part of the thatch was caught on the left wall. It now fell in with the rest. She was amazed by the billow of smoke and the blast of heat. Tall orange flames leaped higher than the top of the walls. Jane felt a double shattering inside her: relief and horror. She drew her cloak about her and turned her face into her own shoulder. The light was so bright it blazed through her eyelids.

Wait, what was that noise, that whisper?

Jane.

It couldn't be. It was just the rustle of the fire in her ears. The pump of her heart in her chest. The thatch settling more heavily. Smoke in clouds boiled over the walls along with the flames.

Jane.

She stood stock-still. Flames licked out the window and door holes. Red flames as thick as beech trunks roared and lapped over the walls. There was a faint smell of flesh scorching. Jane's eyes frosted over.

The heat brought her out of her daze. The smell was stronger now. A lurch in her throat told her she was about to be sick. Abruptly she turned and wobbled toward the seeping beck. She forgot how thirsty she was. She crossed the water without stopping, and broke into an ungainly trot. Stiff, slow, she ran.

She ran up the fellside, following no footpath, looking back often as if afraid something was after her. She ran until the ferns began to seem like a maze, a labyrinth of somber aisles among which she was lost. The smoke seemed to follow her, and that smell. In her nostrils was the stench of burning flesh.

But that couldn't be. It was fog, fog, not smoke.

She ran too swiftly down a hill, hardly seeing the clumps of ling and spur-heeled whin before she had to leap over them. All her sense of direction was gone. She was all but blind with pain. Her breath burned in her lungs. She stumbled and swerved from a tree in her path as if she were drunk. She plunged between more trunks; leaves and branches lashed her face and arms.

She reached the bottom of the ghyll and started up the far side. She lost her momentum; her pace became more and more lumbering. She was concentrating entirely on the next few steps when she slipped and fell against the bulwark of a half-rotted toppled tree. Her breath was knocked from her. She cowered there, lying against the fallen log, struggling to breathe, to fill her lungs with one breath after another. The world skidded and whitened around her.

When her vision steadied, when the hurt in her chest lessened, she made a sobbing noise, hardly louder than the pounding of her heart. Just yesterday . . . just yesterday . . .

She'd felt mighty and big, like a river that needed a broad bed. Just yesterday. And now she was dwindled to a tiny, ebbing trickle.

She heard a voiceless whisper: *Jane*.

The stink of burning thatch—and something more terrible than burning thatch—made her stomach clench. She made a queer, stifled noise and lifted onto her hands and knees. The vomit came spilling out of her, stinging her nose and mouth. Another convulsion came, violently. She couldn't catch her breath, gagged, retched again. She vomited until she was weak and drenched with sweat, until she was shivering uncontrollably. It left a sour taste in her mouth.

She inched away from her own filth. A remnant of vomit dribbled from her lip. She untied her apron and wiped her face with it. She shuddered from the cold and damp.

She'd seen the beam strike him; he'd probably died then. And she couldn't have pulled him out, even if she'd tried, not from beneath that matted mess, not in her condition—which he'd caused.

Still, she kept trembling and making queer noises. She felt amazingly queer. Her very mind ached. Her mouth tasted sour with bile and exhaustion. The smell of vomit hung on the bitter cold. She gave in to her weakness and lay face forward in the deep loamy leaffall of the ages, and closed her eyes. She didn't want to think anymore. She wanted to forget everything. Having reached the farther shore of hysteria, she longed for sleep with every cell in her body. The horror and disgust were transformed into an inexorable soporific. She closed her eyes.

The woods she rested in were quiet, a small copse in the bottom of a ghyll in the midst of the rutted, matted moors, with neither cottage nor beast within hailing distance. While Jane wandered in a dim, curious dream, the clouded afternoon cleared; a feeble sun came out, shone fitfully through the solid greenery above her for a while. Bits of sun fell over her. Later, the day, which had begun so damp and so gray, closed with a sort of splendor. She lay inert through it all, even the last slanted pink evening light as the sun vanished beneath the horizon.

Bells sounded briefly, fairylike, from a long way off, as a shepherd passed within a mile of her, taking his flock toward home for the night. The boy kept thinking he smelled smoke. The only place in the area was the old Fitzpatrick farm, abandoned for two years now. Out of curiosity, he herded his sheep in that direction, just to have a little look down into the dale.

He reported to his parents that night that the fire

had burned down into a heap of cold ashes within the cottage walls. Over their supper, the three of them wondered how the old place could have caught fire on such a damp day. Perhaps a tramp had got inside, the boy suggested. His parents nodded. It bore looking into. The father would have a look-see tomorrow, or the next day, or soon, anyway.

Chapter Six

"Tempt not a desperate man."
William Shakespeare: *Romeo and Juliet*

Jane came up from a memory of her father whispering, *Just you wait, Janey.*

She didn't know how long she listened for more. The copse in which she lay with her cheek cradled on her arm was utterly quiet. One could suffocate in that quiet.

She was stiff and miserable. It hurt to make the slightest movement, not just in her back, though that was by far the worst, but in all her body. She had strained in every nerve and fiber against the whip, and now she ached in the very marrow of her bones.

Where was she? She'd run several miles, she supposed. The last light told her that to her left was the west. Thus she regained her sense of direction. But as soon as it became full dark she would lose it again. She must get up and try to find herself more specifically.

Easier said than done. Just rising took an awful act of will. Her head whirled. Her legs were shaky with all she'd done and withstood today—the walk from York, the flogging, remaining on her feet beneath the beam, running through the bracken over the moors. Now she was jittery and dumb with fatigue.

Her forearm was scraped. Fear had so dominated and immersed her that she couldn't remember how it had happened. And of course there were red rings about her wrists. She touched her neck and found another ring of burnt, chaffed skin. She shuddered to think of the nooselike coffle that had caused these marks. However, these small injuries hardly mattered when compared to the condition of her back.

If she moved cautiously she could manage. Fortune gave her a small chance at this point: she soon discovered an overgrown but familiar trail, remembered from her youth. It would eventually lead her to the road to York.

Her mind kept touching the image of the farm cottage, the fallen roof, the threads of smoke rising from amongst the tinder-dry straw of the thatch. For some reason, she looked back along the path. Her heart pounded as she set out again, walking as fast as her pain would allow her.

The bracken was very thick; she was more aware than ever of the multitude of shapes and the mesh of the fronds. Her path was walled by branches, leaves. A tunnel. And always the strong, ferny odor. The landscape listened; shadows held their breath. She tried to walk silently. She told herself that nothing could hear her, nothing would notice her or rise up to block the path.

She came to the road. Darkness had fallen. For a moment she considered going back to where she'd lost her belongings, where Rip had taken out his ire on her things. But her spare clothes and little oddments seemed unimportant at the moment.

She gave not even a glance in the direction of the village of Dulwych. No one there would help her. Her mother's unfriendliness had made the Fitzpatrick women unpopular with their neighbors. Jane started in the opposite direction, toward the city.

The road was worn deep by the centuries. She met no one. She moved in a half-dream of steady walking. Her mind became occupied with thoughts so dragging and slow that they couldn't even be set into words, for there weren't words long enough.

When she saw the first lighted houses at the outskirts of York, she automatically hastened—but then stopped, suddenly, in the darkness just beyond the walls of the town.

Where was she intending to go? Back to Mr. Welby? A startling thought shot arrowlike into her mind: he'd been relieved to give her over to her father. She recalled that sound she'd heard him make—was it just yesterday? That sound of disgust. He'd been disgusted by his attraction for a common maidservant. That was why he'd been so easily persuaded by Rip. It must have come as a great deliverance to him to have her father show up in such a timely way and want to take her off. Off of his conscience. And out of his reach.

The idea knifed into her stomach. He'd all but ordered her out of his house, right into her father's cruel hands. He'd betrayed her to save himself from the indignity of admitting he was attracted to a servant woman. She reached compulsively for her throat, as if feeling the coffle tightening about her windpipe like a noose again. She swayed; her eyes dimmed.

He certainly wouldn't welcome her back now. His disgust would be multiplied tenfold by what had been done to her, because he would know that he was responsible, as much as Rip was.

Hot beads of liquid formed at the corners of her eyes.

None of that now.

She looked about her, more than ever aware of the

night. She had nowhere to go. The shadows shifted, towered, reached.

She left the open road and skirted several fields, eventually finding the path into the copse where her cache was hidden. For once, she took the straightest route to the rock pen.

But there old habits took over. She paused. She stood as immobile as a figure carved of wood. She listened. And because of her motionlessness, she became aware of her pain again. It seemed to radiate through her whole body.

She wavered. If she left her money where it was and instead went to Mr. Welby . . . he wasn't so hard that he would not let her in the door. Mrs. Galbraith would help her out of her ruined, blood-stiffened dress and bathe her back with cold, soothing water, all the while clucking and sympathizing. Jane could weep then. She wanted to weep so badly. Tears rose in her eyes. She jerked with a sob.

Go to Mr. Welby. Throw yourself on his mercy.

It seemed such a sensible plan that she started out of the copse again. She paused under the last trees, in the high grass at the edge of the fields. From the pastures a sheep bleated plaintively. Jane saw the city.

But it looked different somehow, as if it lay under the shadow of a long cloud. York, the candlelight in Mr. Welby's windows, the blaze on the kitchen hearth, her own attic chamber warm as a burrow. But her chamber was empty. She'd been cast out, betrayed, gotten rid of.

Her decision solidified into pride. She would never go back, never let him know what his urge to protect himself had caused her. She would leave Yorkshire, it was time to go to Georgia. Liverpool would be the closest port. She would walk until she found a place where she could inquire about a coach, or even a cart.

And if the price for transportation was too high, then she would walk all the way to Liverpool.

How far would that be? How many days would it take? It had taken Mr. Welby a week to travel from York to London last year, and he had gone by coach. She tried to make clearer her memory of the map of England he'd shown her. It seemed to her Liverpool was closer than London. But she was afoot . . . that might not make much difference, though; Mr. Welby had said he could have walked to London faster, which had led into a lesson about the bad state of the nation's roads and how isolated towns were from one another.

Could she do it, hurt as she was?

She must. She couldn't bear the shame of returning where she wasn't wanted. Her throat ached with all she couldn't share with anyone.

Meanwhile, time was drawing on. The sky said it was nearly midnight. Not the most advantageous time to start such a jaunt. But truly there was no advantageous time.

She turned from the warm yellow window lights of York and went back to the stone pen, awed by the wild chances she was about to take. She took out the big, lichened stone, found the leather pouch. She tore a long strip from her petticoat. The moon was not risen yet, and though the night was blazing with stars, the light coming down through the trees above her was barely enough for her to work by. She sat in the dense high grass and took the coins one by one, careful not to drop any and lose it in the dark. She wrapped and knotted each piece of gold securely into the long strip of cloth.

When she was finished she had an odd-looking money belt. She stood, painfully, and unfastened her skirts. They fell to her feet and, except for her stockings and her cloak, she was naked from the hips down. All this movement hurt her back terribly. The stinging warned her of scabs breaking open again. But somehow she wrapped the long money belt around her hips, twice, three times, tying it so that it rode a little below her waist. That way it would not be detectable beneath the gathered folds of her skirts.

She pulled her clothes back up and took a few steps. The weight felt secure; it would neither give itself away nor slip down. She'd never thought much about her figure, but now she was glad she had curves.

So far so good. No one seeing her would realize that her mind was clawing and scratching along a steep surface and holding on tight with ragged fingers.

Unexpectedly, her stomach growled. She didn't feel hungry, but she hadn't eaten anything since a skimpy and nervous breakfast.

What am I going to eat? Where will I sleep at night?

She refused to think about these things. She couldn't think about them or she would lose her fragile courage, which was all that was keeping her from running into York and throwing herself on Mr. Welby's pity. It angered her all over again, and stiffened her resolve, to realize that her master, her hero, was unequipped for any problem outside his cloistered, literary domain. He'd known he couldn't withstand his own passions, so he'd sacrificed her.

She would eat when she could and sleep where she could, and if she should die of starvation or exposure— well, so be it, and to hell with the Honorable Mr. Gage Welby!

Now she must find her way to the highway which led west to Liverpool. The further she got tonight, the less likely she would give in to misery and self-pity and creep back to a place where she wasn't wanted.

She started out. Her mind shouted, 'Tis a crazy idea,

this! But she went on. There was no home behind her; there was no return to that old tranquility of yesterday, that contentment, that feeling of largeness and invincibility. The thread upon which she had strung that part of her life was tied off.

But she had her plan yet, and she would stay with it, for she had already given so much for it.

The road from York was deserted, a lonely stretch heading into even lonelier moors. As the round moon rode torpidly up the sky from the horizon, a dark horse walked slowly, its rider slumped in his saddle. They traveled beneath a copse of black trees growing under the looming crag of dark fell. The highwayman had just pulled off one gauntlet and taken out a roll, hard and grainy but with a pleasant flavor, and with it a lump of goat's milk cheese. He carried with him a strip of smoked mutton as well, but he would save that for later. The night was long.

As he ate, the silver and fire-opal ring blazed on the little finger of his bare left hand.

He had lingered in Yorkshire to see a lady in a rose garden. He knew himself to be a fool. His attachments to females were always brief and unimportant. It was no doubt this necessary friendlessness of his life which had driven him to fall half in love with a portrait.

But, ah, she was fair, his Rose of Midnight! She seemed timeless, the woman in that painting, a study in black-and-white and shadow.

He'd reined that madness in, however, and now he was going home—to what he called home.

Though he was outside his personal territory, his senses were those of a highwayman always, and by habit he kept his mount off the road. There had been no traffic tonight, save a single horse pulling a gig.

That had passed by him earlier, when there was still some dusky pink in the sky. Most people stayed off the roads after dark, knowing that men like himself were about their business in the midnight hours. The few travelers that found themselves abroad so late were either too weary or too drunk to be wise, or too urgent to heed sober wisdom. All of which made them especially good prey.

He glanced upward. He could tell the time to a quarter hour by the angle at which Arcturus rose above the autumn horizon to do his early morning plowing of the stars. Midnight. This was the highwayman's hour.

Though he was tall and powerfully built, few who passed under his watchful eye ever saw him. He wore black—black greatcoat, black waistcoat, black shirt, black breeches, black jackboots. He tied back his dark shoulder-length hair with a thick black ribbon and hid it further with a black tricorn. His glossy stallion's trappings were black as well, with no foolish vanity of silver decoration.

A pair of heavy double-barreled pistols, their butts jutting from leather cases, were slung over the pommel of his saddle. Each weapon was as heavy as a small piece of artillery; it took a full man's strength to load and prime them, to level them accurately, and to sustain the impact of their discharge.

He was expert at his work. His highwayman's ears were practiced at hearing the least noise. Still, he hadn't heard the woman coming. The instant he saw her, he snapped erect in his saddle and pulled his horse to a halt. She moved so softly—afoot! Most unusual, especially at this time of night. He was immediately intrigued.

His stallion had been bred right here in vast Yorkshire, where the world's finest horses were made. Eclipse was his name, and though he was swift and strong, he had been well trained by his master. Both had certain patterns of stealth fixed in their muscles. Neither made a sound now; the highwayman sat motionless, holding the stallion's reins in one hand, his roll and cheese in the other. He watched the woman with a steady, predator's stare.

Traveling afoot, unguarded, unattended. She was demented, surely, and believed herself one of the gods' protected. Who else would tread on so thin a sword's edge between life and death?

Though he couldn't quite put his finger on why, it seemed to him that she was walking oddly. Her cloak was dark, but she wore a head-fitting bonnet, the kind that could be fastened beneath her chin. It shone out in the newly risen moon like a white star, making the air around her head light. She probably didn't even realize how it gave her away. She hadn't considered that on the highroad at night she ought to pull the hood of her cloak up to conceal it.

But that was the least of her foolishness. She also must not realize that there were cutthroats and ruffians and frosty-spirited rogues abroad on the mantling night, men who would fix on such a spot of brightness as moths on a candle's blaze. It was dangerous enough for a man to be out; a woman alone couldn't possibly hope to survive.

He looked down his nose at her as if sniffing bad fish. An escapee from some asylum? A distinct possibility. But no timorous gray-headed beldam; no, young she was.

A runaway then? Rejected in love, perhaps, and in a daze, filled with enough romantic nonsense to curse ten lives?

Or perhaps seduced by a master who had introduced her to the crasser pleasures of the flesh and now, addicted to them, off to seek employment at some road-side inn.

Or mayhap a daughter pressed to marry where she didn't wish to marry. Spoiled to the core. And stubborn. Stubbornness was a bad quality in a woman.

He smiled thinly, the merest feeble glimmer of white teeth. His humor was directed at himself. Leading such a lonely life, his imagination was fully developed. More likely the girl was naught but a thief, just like himself, carrying gold from her master's cashbox in her pockets. Tsk, tsk. Maybe he should have a look into those pockets.

He made up his mind—but then she stopped. Simply stopped in the road where she was bathed in bright moonlight and vulnerable to every fate. She took in a deep breath, very slowly, as if it caused her some pain. Then she lifted the heel of her hand to her bowed forehead. It was an attitude of abject despair.

As she straightened and began to walk again, the highwayman sensed even more strongly that something was wrong with her. She did not move with the assurance of a maid with a pocketful of neatly stolen guineas. She was under some kind of physical duress.

His several theories of who she was and what she was dissolved into a much more interesting enigma. He let her pass, more out of curiosity than because his own youth had largely been one of hindrance and bitterness and poverty—and sometimes abject despair. Or so he told himself. After all, he could stop her any time. The contents of her pockets, whatever she might have there, he already considered his. She herself was nothing to him, she was prey. But she promised to make the night interesting.

When she was at some distance, he turned his horse to follow her. At the same time he swallowed the last of his roll and crammed the cheese into his mouth to be eaten in his silent and somber manner. His stare was both narrow and guarded in the shadow of the hat that hid his face.

Where do you go, maid? What brings you to such a wild road, so far to the south of safety?

There was little enough else to entertain him on such a quiet night. And she was young. And very possibly fair. And desperation had its uses.

And the night was often long for a man of such fierce intensity, often endless, timeless, minute after minute hanging dead and adding up to nothing.

He kept far enough behind her to let the rise and fall of the land hide him, then, as the next hour passed, he followed her into a vast expanse of scrub and harsh woodland. The road became no broader than the width of a cart, with the luxuriant growth of summer dying between the oaks that lined it. And still he followed her with his alert, voracious eyes.

Jane was no longer certain whether she was conscious or not; this could be one of those weary dreams where you walk and walk and walk, not sure where you're going, not sure where you are, yet strangely unable to rest for fear of some vague menace.

Why couldn't she stop? Oh yes, because she might be tempted to crawl back to Mr. Welby and beg for aid he didn't care to give. That fear was conscious enough, alive enough to bite her. Even thinking about it tantalized her with the ache to turn back, go home— and she had to forcefully remind herself that what she'd thought of as her home was not.

She heard her father's voice inside her head. It admonished her: *Jane.* She felt a pang, centered below her throat, that made it hard to swallow. She touched the place, and felt again the circle of chafed skin that

94

the coffle noose had left. Her whole neck felt bruised. She lifted her head, lifted her eyes above her feet and the next yard of the highroad.

The stars were all but hidden behind the tree limbs overhead. She was in wild country now. There must be animals in these woods. Raised on the moors, she wasn't unduly afraid of wild animals. Not ordinarily.

At least she didn't have to be afraid of getting lost, for the road was definite enough, though it seemed to go on and on.

What—? In sudden rabbit terror she froze, every sense abruptly alert. She'd heard a noise like a hoof-beat. She suffered one of those quiet instants that clutch the heart. A hoofbeat, a horse? Could it be an outlaw? A highwayman? Some mounted and masked despera-do? She realized with a slam to her heart that she hadn't even considered the danger of that. She'd had so much to think about that she'd overlooked the one fear that was among the worst of any considered by a person set upon traveling. Everyone talked about high-waymen, and the darker the rumors were the more they were accepted for their pessimism.

She stood unmoving, in a hard knot of nerves.

He was tiring of simply following her. He wasn't sorry when Eclipse crossed a patch of bare, hard earth so that his hoof made a sound and startled her out of her daze. Her breath caught, a gasp, soft but distinct in the silence. The wet glint of her eyes betrayed her stark terror. Well and good. Time to unnerve her a little.

He almost smiled, watching her from behind some trees. His head tilted as if in reflection; his eyes nar-rowed. He prided himself for owning none of that sym-pathy the persecuted felt for each other which sucked

95

men down into pity. For an hour or more he'd watched her trod her line as thin as a sword edge, and it annoyed him that she stood so steady on it yet. He wanted to see her waver a little. Maybe she would do something more interesting now. Maybe grab for her pockets and give away more than she meant to. He bent his head sidewise and inspected her unfeelingly.

The full moon floated directly above her now, showing how battered her cloak was, how stained. He could even make out that it was scarlet, and that her skirts were purple. Curiosity gnawed at him, he could hardly resist spurring his horse out into the open and ending the game at once. He sat still in his saddle another moment, however. And he knew exactly when she decided that the noise she'd heard was nothing. She rubbed her forehead again, and for a moment her eyes fell shut. She lowered her hand and lifted her face to the moon. Her eyes opened. Something about her . . . she seemed familiar.

He gave Eclipse the barest signal. The stallion moved forward cautiously so that the highwayman could see his prey more clearly. That face . . .

A terrible certainty loosened and shifted. He knew that face. God's blood, it was her, it was her. Hadn't he broken into Hockness Hall and stared at her directly, wondering about her lips, that exquisite skin under her chin, wondering about her heart? She was his dream. His soul's shape made flesh. His love. (He could admit it, in the darkness that was the center of him. He had fallen in love with a woman in a portrait.) And here she was, flesh and blood, alive.

For a few seconds at least he lost all will and wit. "Ah God," he whispered on the merest breath. "She's real. 'The beauty of heaven walking by itself on the world.' " He could swing down from Eclipse and in twenty paces touch her. A half step more and he could have her in his arms.

As "The Rose of Midnight," she'd been dressed in a fine gown the cool, pale color of a winter field; but tonight she wore the plain, ill-fitting, gaudy clothes of a maidservant. Why would she disguise herself thus, why would she risk the road and the reavers on the road and the night? A thief—ha! She was no thief! That notion and all his imagination had built upon it dissolved in his mind.

What else did women let drive them to foolishness? Romance? Could the rumors of lovers be true? Baron Murdock? Old enough to be her father? She wouldn't be that stupid.

But halt! Beauty was no proof she wasn't a stupid, ignorant wench, disorderly in heart and head.

She swayed on her feet, and opened her eyes, and looked about her. Despite his certainty that she couldn't see him, he shrank back in his saddle. His confidence was unsettled. When she started out on the road again, he cast his eye here and there, with an especially sharp sense of the moment, of the hour. He felt angry. Didn't she know what kind of danger she'd placed herself in? What kind of men were abroad in the night—and not one of them who could claim an absence of villainy in their purposes?

No, not even one.

Chapter Seven

The Whip Cuts Were Fresh, Laid Neatly in a Basket
Weave Pattern That Crisscrossed Her Flesh.

For some time Jane hadn't looked up. She saw only
the toes of her shoes moving forward, one and then the
other, saw only the road she set them down on—which
seemed more a path now, wide enough only for a horse.
Was the sky lightening? The moon was still up, but it
had risen late. As she looked upward, she stumbled.
Her ankle gave and she fell to her hands and knees.
She gave out a cry.

When she got up, her legs were like stakes of pain
propping up that larger pain, her back. She couldn't
go any further. If she didn't get some rest, she would
fall again, for she was increasingly lost in a trance,
unaware of herself, of where she was, of where she was
putting her feet. She feared she might simply lose consciousness, faint on the road, and then she would be
vulnerable indeed.

But where to rest? There was no sign of any village
or farm. Nothing but the deep silence of the moors.
The road did not seem wide enough to be the main
road from York to Liverpool. Had she made a wrong

turn in the dark? She couldn't remember, she couldn't think back.

She had for some time heard a rill of water off to her left. She was very thirsty, and so very very tired. She made up her mind. Wearily she turned from the path toward the open fells and the sound of water.

There were no markings here. This was a solitary spot. The fact reassured rather than alarmed her. She could rest for an hour or so.

Her steps led down into a hollow, then turned sharply and rose. Down again through a copse, and then she found the beck. It gleamed and glanced and quarreled with every boulder in its bed. The sound heartened her, if only minutely. She was not coffled and at her father's mercy. She was not smothered or burned to death. Things she had thought could not befall her had befallen, yes, but things she had thought she could not bear she was bearing.

The highwayman had watched her mindlessly take the wrong fork and lose the highroad. And now he watched her move awkwardly toward the beck. She spent a while lowering herself down so that she could scoop some water to her mouth. She drank for a long time.

Leaning over the water, Jane inhaled the scent of the small ferns and water plants crushed beneath her hands and knees. Suddenly she had a peculiar feeling. Someone was watching her. The unnatural awareness of being under scrutiny was so powerful that she turned and looked back.

She'd come through a stand of round-leaved, pale-trunked trees to get to the water's edge. It was pitch dark under those close, shadowy trees. For a moment she saw eyes shining bright in that formless dark behind her. She started up wildly, with a gasp. But then they were gone; only two leaves were there, reflecting the moonlight off the water. She was awash with relief, her limbs felt weak, her vitals felt watery.

It was several minutes before her heart calmed, before she could really believe that she was still alone, unwatched, unobserved. She bent to the water again and now washed her face, sloshing off soil and salt. Though the cold sliced through the very bones of her hands, she opened her cloak and pulled up her sleeves and sluiced water up her wrists and over the back of her chaffed neck. It roused her a little, though her mind still felt dull and cloudy.

She rested a moment, stored up her strength—for she'd begun to suffer a profound fatigue of will. At last, slowly, she removed her cloak and pulled her dress forward.

Since the night he'd first seen "The Rose of Midnight," the woman in that portrait had lived in the highwayman's mind at the continual point of perfection caught by the artist. She lived there, but she didn't vary. She existed somehow beyond simple mortal needs, beyond hunger and thirst, outside of loneliness and weariness, below joy and above despair. She didn't speak, she didn't breathe—she didn't need breath. He'd assigned to her that flawless expression and near-smile by which he'd initially come to know her, and he had steadfastly refused to consider her capable of anything less.

Hence it confounded him to find her walking on the highroad in the dark hours of the night, very much alive and in need of human breath. He found that her obvious mortality made him feel disdainful and bold.

Now he stood unmoving among a grouping of gray boulders and arching ferns, balanced on his own muscled legs (his horse was tethered behind him for the moment), unconscious of the morning chill and wholly absorbed as he watched her sluice water over marks that were clearly rope burns on her wrists and neck. When she began to remove her cloak, he was annoyed at the thumping in his chest.

She shed it and, with a sting of alarm, he saw that her dress was ripped open down the back. As she pulled it forward over her shoulders, he was for several heartbeats unable to think or feel anything at all. Yet his eyes recorded what they saw: the whip cuts and welts were fresh, laid neatly in a basket-weave pattern which crisscrossed her flesh. The deed had been done by someone with expertise. It was all the more shocking to see because of the pale ivory-and-pink of the rest of her; ivory shoulders, ivory, pink-tipped breasts . . . she was like a piece of good china that had been wantonly scored. He had seen men, full grown and brutish, who had been whipped that cruelly. They acquired a look, the survivors of such savagery.

When his faculties began to trickle back, he felt a sense of loss. He felt as if something had been taken from him, pulled from his very body. His rose maiden, she of the painting, was gentle yet, and kind yet, and perfect. But she was wholly a thing of his imagination. He had lost her to reality.

As for this girl . . . she was a puzzle. He knew nothing whatever about her; she was a stranger (an impostor!) She was utterly human, absolutely mortal. If she had ever been his Rose . . . what was she now? What would she be as the marks on her ivory back became scars?

Jane's eyes squinted nearly shut. The water was burning cold on her back, yet it numbed the pain a little. After she'd done what she could to cleanse herself, which was not much, she took another drink. It ran over her chin, down the sides of her throat. A thin fog was beginning to rise from the beck. She hadn't been able to keep her dress from getting wet while splashing water over her shoulders, and she shivered now. She pulled up her gown and got to her feet—laboriously, wincing as she moved.

She held her stained cloak around her shoulders while she found a likely spot to rest, a place between two tree roots, deeply cushioned with old leaves and ferns and moss. She wrapped her cloak tight around her, remembering at last to raise the hood over her bonnet. She sat down cautiously. Then her body gave slightly, just a bowing of her head to begin with, then came the softest of collapses.

She listened to the slip and murmur of the beck. Briefly she thought of the new life that beckoned from a new land. Then her mind dissolved into a jumble of impressions, glaring fragments of the last two nights and the day between. They jostled together like little pieces of colored glass inside a child's kaleidoscope. Finally all thought and all emotion stood in abeyance. An hour, a mere hour of rest, of peace—oh please, God.

Anger had made the highwayman's hands curl, had cut off his breath. She was a stranger to him, yet he felt full of a primitive desire to get his hands on the man who had done such a thing to her. He wanted to batter him senseless.

What could have been her crime? What conceivable mischief could such a beautiful woman cause to license a flogging like that?

Once at Tyburn he'd witnessed the hanging of a young mother for the theft of a loaf of bread. Her ten-year-old son was brought to the gallows with her, first to witness her death, then to be half hung himself. The hangman had stood the boy on a barrel next to his dangling mother, and put a noose over the lad's head, a noose not knotted to break his neck. When the barrel was kicked out from beneath him, he spent several long minutes wrestling his wrists against the hemp rope that bound them behind his back and simply strangling. When he stopped writhing, he was cut down and revived. But his torment was not over.

He was tied to the back of the cart in which his mother's body had been thrown, and he was flogged all the way back to London. This to teach him not to follow in the dastardly life of crime his poor mother had followed. A hard lesson for a pauper child who all his ten years had understood only killingly hard labor and drained sleep and daily striving for every mite to merely exist.

Had this woman been half hanged and flogged? That's what it looked like. But why? She didn't look to be starving, like the boy and his mother, who had both been as lean as skeletons. Women were often flogged for fornication in the smaller villages, especially where the people were under the sway of some fanatical hedgerow preacher. He'd heard of women receiving up to forty lashes for nothing more than "malice of the tongue." But half hanging was rare.

What had she done? There were no answers, only the horror of what had been done to her.

Suddenly the highwayman did not want any of this to be true. He had fantasized about stepping forward

103

and making himself known to her and bowing and kissing her fingers, saying, "My lady." But he had no desire to confront her now. He didn't even want to be here. A sickness had settled in his stomach.

Yet he could not make himself go elsewhere. He rubbed his hands over his face. Weak and hurt and vulnerable as she was, she still had some power over him. He watched her fall asleep. He stepped right out into the open, crossed to her, and looked down at her for an unendurable, immeasurable time. The morning mist rose through the little stand of woods. It settled like dew on her face and formed drops in the mesh of her hair around the edge of her hood. She was a living creature, no dream, no moonlight fancy.

The vapors condensed into a low-lying mist. It penetrated his woolen greatcoat. He stayed until dawn began to lavender the sky. He turned away from her then, to step back through the knee-deep, mossy fog toward his horse. As he disappeared into the trees, he wasn't sure what he was going to do next—or if he was going to do anything at all.

Leave her! a voice warned. Leave her to her fate.

He would. It was the wisest thing to do. She was nothing to him, nothing. He galloped swiftly away over the slanting moor ahead of the dawn.

Jane slept a sleep that was deeper than dreams, deeper than nightmares, a sleep as dark and resistless as the current of a deep river. The hour she'd prayed for passed, and another, and another. She slept through the morning, through the noon, through the late day and early evening. An hour or so before sunset, she sat up suddenly, struggling out of the tight wrap of her cloak as though someone had shaken her, saying "Wake up!"

104

For a time she sat where she was, huddled, hunched, still sleep-drugged, fighting against the various insistent chimeras that swirled though her mind. So many outrageous things had happened, all so quickly, that she could hardly trust herself to believe what she remembered of them. Except that her back felt stiff and sore and lacerated. That was proof that she wasn't mad.

She looked about her, at the ferns, the beck, the trees, the colored sky. Her whole body hurt. It seemed this pain had been with her forever, something she had always endured, always known.

She was also hungry.

And she'd slept through the daylight and now must face traveling by night again.

Eventually she crawled over to the water, to where the current rilled over a large gray stone. She crouched there to drink. She washed her face, and her back again. That cleared her mind. Carefully she fingered the wounds, where she could reach them. Mostly they were scabbed over now. She felt the ridges tenderly. They pulled her skin tight and she was certain that when she started to move, they would sting again.

She adjusted her loose, ripped bodice over her shoulders as well as she could. And ran her hands around her middle, feeling the heavy belt of her money. There was one thing at least to give her some comfort; she had not lost quite everything. That and the hope of Georgia.

The road beckoned. But not yet. Not quite yet.

Getting to her feet was the hardest thing she'd ever done. "Come *on,*" she said aloud, hauling herself up. She moved cautiously for a while; she just shuffled back and forth there beside the constant music of the beck, working the soreness out of her legs. She lingered among the ferns, the boulders, the glimmer of the water, the steady branches of the trees while the sun set.

105

As she made her way back to the highroad in the twilight, she found a few dried berries on a bush. The fruit did nothing to satisfy her appetite, which was by now almost as demanding of her attention as the stiffness and stinging and deeply bruised soreness that gripped her body.

She must stop at the first cottage, the first hamlet, and buy food. And a bed to rest in, even if it was nothing more than a pile of hay in a byre.

Even as she planned all this, she wondered what strangers would make of her, of the marks on her neck and wrists, anyway. (Her back she would not show to anyone.) Experimentally, she pulled her hood close about her chin. She knew well enough how suspicious country people could be. They might demand to know what had happened to her; they might shun her.

Well, that was something she'd worry about when the time came.

She regained the road she'd traveled last night—which was not the road to Liverpool, she was sure of it now. There were no trees. She came upon an ancient milestone, too faint and ageworn to read. Once, while it was still light enough to see, she went back to the beck. She felt a craving for water, felt soothed by the coolness and clarity of it. Opposite the stream a large flock of sheep suddenly crested the fell. She struggled to her feet. That was when she saw on a boulder, hard by where she stood, a shepherd, sitting, staring ahead. She hadn't seen him when she came, and no wonder, since he sat boulder-still himself. And mysteriously, he seemed not to see her, either, even now.

He was an old man, with ragged silvery hair and beard. He sat with his crook against his legs. He had a sack from which he took a packet. He unwrapped bread and cheese. Jane's mouth flooded with saliva. The universe contracted; at its exact geometric heart floated those hunks of dark bread and pallid cheese. Her fingers felt the food, her tongue tasted it. A shudder passed over her famished body.

Suddenly the shepherd shouted a sharp command. The flock was gathered by three yelping dogs and driven across the beck. They did the shepherd's bidding at once. While he went back to his dinner. But then the dog nearest to Jane broke from its work to look at her. Though the beck separated them, the animal lifted its muzzle to sniff the air. The dog went back to work, yet its momentary silence was enough to alert the shepherd. He turned toward Jane. She started forward, pulling her hood around her throat and lifting one hand in greeting.

Leaning on his crook, the old man got to his feet and peered in her direction—but queerly. The words Jane had thought to use died on her tongue. She halted. He stood staring blindly toward her for a full half minute. His face was empty, as were his white, empty eyes. He lifted his nose and sniffed the air, a smooth, canine gesture. Jane felt a creeping chill. At last his attention slid back to his flock. He called out another command to the dogs—but then turned his face roughly in Jane's direction again. She had started to back away; now she halted once more. His milky eyes seemed to stare over the top of her head.

Eventually he shouted to the dogs again. They had almost completed herding the sheep over the bridge. The shepherd broke his bread and cheese and left half of each on the boulder where he'd been sitting. He followed his flock, wading the beck with a blind man's grace. He walked behind them, very near to where Jane stood. His blank eyes gazed in her direction.

Eventually the bleating of the sheep and the yelping of the dogs faded away over the crest of the next fell. Jane splashed across the beck and rushed to the food and tore at it, chewing and swallowing quickly. All the while she looked about her. A blind shepherd? Could he have been real? He'd seemed ghostlike, so much so that she'd been frightened speechless.

But his food was real enough. It restored her somewhat. However, the eerie encounter had left her more aware of the falling night. She felt a morbid fear.

Yet she must go on. She questioned the wisdom of following the path she was on. Could it be the road to Liverpool? It was too narrow, there were too many obstacles, too many things to stumble over. Common sense told her that carts and coaches couldn't come this way on a regular basis. No, she'd made a wrong turning somewhere last night and now she must go back. It disheartened her, but she knew it was the wisest thing to do.

While she was being wise, she considered the food in her stomach. It was solid and real. The shepherd who had shared it with had not been a specter. She should have spoken to him. He could have advised her, he might have offered her shelter for the night. She felt stupid for her speechless fear now. Perhaps it wasn't too late. She could go after him. She left the path and climbed a fellside, thinking that from its height she could see him, or hear his sheep and dogs.

The white stars were opening above. At the top of the fell she saw and heard nothing. She climbed the next. No sign of a shack, or even a campfire. No sound of sheep or dogs. She stopped. She must go back to the path before she got hopelessly lost.

Too late. Darkness had fallen in earnest. The moon wouldn't rise for hours. She couldn't find any sign of the path. She was lost in country she knew nothing about.

The moors rose to greater heights and fell more precipitously than any she'd grown up with. After one especially trying ascent, she stopped to catch her breath. It seemed she must be on top the world, up where the earth and sky met. On all sides she sensed the bleak moorland that surrounded her, the desolation of gorse and bracken rolling away. To her right, the fellside broke sharply down through dark bracken to where a beck was squeezed into a narrow, snowy white cataract that rushed between black slabs of slate. She was learning firsthand that York and its environs were really quite small; she was gaining a firsthand and sickening awareness of the muchness of the world.

Though her back hurt less tonight, she was more sore all over. As she traveled along a stretch of track where there had been a minor landslip, her footing was unsure. Every step jolted her frame.

The moon rose. Midnight came and went. Now she was in a narrow valley set in craggy hillsides. She walked on more and more slowly, growing dazed once more, and feeling herself drifting. She wanted to sit down, to give up.

Then her body carefully, but without any notice, brought her to a halt on a slope of sheer blue shale. Not until she was standing stock-still did her mind ask: what was that?

The noise came again, ahead of her. Horse hooves ringing clear on stone. There! her tardy reflexes screamed. Ahead—there!

In the full moon's light, a man on horseback sat looking at her. Her breath snagged, as if on something sharp. The black-as-night horse reared beneath its rider and then raced forward. She turned and rushed blindly for some refuge. She heard the horse galloping toward her. She crouched down behind some bracken. Horse and rider went past her, bounding like shadows.

She stayed where she was for perhaps a half hour. When she heard no more sounds in all that time, she wondered if it was safe to rise from her cramped position. Who had he been, that rider? Had he not seen her? Preposterous as it seemed, it must be so, for her hiding place was hardly cunning. Why hadn't he come back to find her?

She refused to believe he might have been a ghost.

But what kind of traveler was abroad on the open moors at night?

The desperate kind, came her answer, like me.

She didn't move for another quarter of an hour. The last echo of the rider's presence had long since died; the moors were completely silent in the light of the moon. There was no sign of anyone, but she walked faster now. Her way was lit by moonlight. The land rose and ascended endlessly through steep harsh country full of crags. She found another path and followed it, reasoning that it must lead somewhere. She was just beginning another ascent when, half turning, she saw movement among the half-dozen squat trees up at the top of the fell she'd just come down. She caught a glimpse, through the shabby remnants of those October trees, of a man mounted on a horse. He just sat there, giving her a look terrible and silent.

He was following her. He was keeping pace with her atop the black fells. Even as she strained to see him better, he disappeared, went behind the thicket . . . and didn't come out the other side.

She didn't wait to see if he ever would. She fled into the bracken herself, to hide again. She nearly fell over a broken bit of dry-stone wall. She didn't know what it was in the dark, until she made out in the bleak, uneasy moonlight, the shape of a three-barred gate rotting at one end. She crawled down beside the stones, between the wall and some gorse.

She listened hard, taut with strain, her body wound in a knot, trembling. After a while, she heard hoofbeats come near to where she lay flat beneath the thorns. The awful slow rhythm of those hoofbeats, which seemed to circle her all around, as if he knew exactly where she lay and was toying with her. She remembered everything she'd ever heard about highwaymen: the story Mr. Welby had told her about the one who had raped a milkmaid and plucked her eyes out; one her mother had told her in which the outlaw looked on travelers as a dependable source of venison.

Abruptly she heard his horse snort, shockingly near. She tried to knot herself tighter.

Eventually the horse wheeled about and off they went. The animal whinnied from some distance; the sound carried sharply through the stillness.

Jane was too afraid to move, however, and lay absolutely still. What if he came back? Clearly he knew she was in the area, even if he didn't know exactly where she was hidden.

Her fear-dazed mind skittered from thought to thought. *Did* he know? He'd come so close, almost near enough to step on her! But then why hadn't he routed her out?

He couldn't have known how. But he might be waiting for her to show herself again. And when she did . . .

She hadn't lived a sheltered life. She already knew the farthest reaches of cruelty to which a man could travel.

What should she do? If she rose up and ran, he and his horse would thunder down on her—and there was no one to help her.

She began to cry—for the first time—silently, painfully. Tears ran down her face in a film. She sobbed, though softly, softly, careful not to be heard where she lay, hidden and in fear for her life. She put her face in her arms and wept.

But not for long. She hadn't the strength to cry for long. Soon she was empty of tears, even empty of fear, worn out. Her body gradually loosened from its knot and she fell asleep again, like a boulder falling.

What was that?

Jane sat bolt upright, her heart hammering, for a sound had waked her—hadn't it?

She shivered slightly inside her cloak. She heard nothing now but the sighing of wind softly in the grass and the sound of water running somewhere close.

But something was wrong. The hair prickled on her arms. She felt a power in the atmosphere. What was it? Something more was about to befall her.

The light was subdued. Clouds were massed in the sky, pink in the east where the sun was rising, fading to white above, and dark and turbulent in the west. Was she alone? Was she safe? She looked about for evidence of last night's horseman, and though she saw nothing, she felt in no way relieved. Her heart went on hammering, her breath came short. What was she afraid of?

That he was still about somewhere, waiting. That he would return with the fall of dark.

She rubbed her forehead with the heel of her hand. I'm hungry, that's what my trouble is. I'm tired and hurt and hungry.

She found the source of the sound of running water and drank long and deep to fill her stomach. Then she started out once more, this time along the stream bank. Though the sky lowered over her, it was daylight and she could see where she was going. She might spot a herdsman or a hunter, a farmhouse, a hamlet. She must find someone, learn where she was, buy some food—

112

soup, bread, stew, porridge, anything at all. The very thought made her head spin.

And she must beg a safe place to rest for the night. In case the man on horseback returned to look for her.

Chapter Eight

> The villain still pursued her.
>
> Milton Nobles: *The Phoenix I*

The remains of the morning, the afternoon, the twilight flowed past. Jane was lost on the moors. She came across no village, no farm, no herdsman. Atop all her other troubles came a creeping fear that she might die out here, alone. Then, in the dusk, she suddenly found herself on a lighted crest where four rough snaking tracks met. Here stood a signpost resembling a gallows silhouetted against the sky. Burned into the splintered, weathered panels were words: WAKEFIELD, HUDDERS-FIELD, BARNSLEY, SHEFFIELD.

Wakefield. She'd heard of that. She gazed down the path that descended the moorland hillside. It seemed to lead more southerly than westward, and Liverpool, she believed, was pretty much directly west of York. But it was a town. There would be people. Carters, merchants, innkeepers, clothiers. Once there, she could take better stock. She would have to part with some of her precious money, but her notions of walking to Liverpool were thoroughly doused now. She would spend a guinea, two if need be. She was willing now.

She swayed. It came on like that sometimes; her

power was strained to the limit and beyond, turning her body traitor. Wakefield, she told herself. Everything will be fine as soon as I reach Wakefield.

She stared out again, and soon came upon the road she'd lost night before last. Suddenly her weariness of spirits was split by a kind of irrational joy. Yes, everything would be fine now.

Yet night fell and she still had not gained any sign of habitation. Soon, she kept telling herself, just another mile, around that turn ahead, over that crest. Meanwhile the overcast sky dropped, the wind came up stronger, and it started to rain. The road took her down a dip in a fellside. At the bottom was the still, black water of a small tarn. The dull surface was stippled by the rain and wrinkled by the wind. A lone traveler could fall into such a dark pool and never be found.

She must fight off such morbid thoughts. She clutched the hood of her cloak about her throat and passed by the water's edge. There was no moon this side of the clouds; the night darkened to its darkest. She could hardly see where she placed her feet. She must step slowly, carefully, so as not to fall and rip open her healing wounds. She could hardly see the long-drawn aisle ahead of her, yet she kept on, thanking this weather, this immense windy, clouded, rainy night, for certainly it was her savior. No one would be out on such a night, not even a brigand.

Beyond where the road was pinched between two huge boulders a path led off into the bracken. She considered taking that path, and finding some place to rest, a dry place under a rock if nothing else.

But what if she got lost again? Her head was spinning all the time now, even when she wasn't thinking of food. Her wet clothes stuck to her. She'd been walking for two nights and a day, plus this night, all the time hurt, famished, chased, frightened. She'd been on her feet this day alone for at least twelve hours. It must be ten o'clock—in those places where clocks still held sway.

As her clothes got wetter, her petticoats slapped and lashed against her knees as though to bind her. Mire from small puddles spattered over her ankles and shoes. Her thoughts began to take strange shapes, intruding like angles and pebbles in her trancelike urge to keep going. The stiff wind slanted the rain across the road before her. She thought she saw her father . . . there, just ahead. *Jane,* he whispered, thin as moonlight.

"Go away!" she cried aloud. Then bit the back of her hand to stop her voice. She halted—woke with a start actually, startled by the sound of her own voice. The vision faded.

Was it possible to sleep and to dream on your feet? She looked about, wiping the rain from her eyes. She saw the road she was on, and realized she'd been stumbling along as if blind. There was a copse of woods on either side. The autumn branches were pitching violently, the rain was blowing across the dark. There was no ghost, no one—

Suddenly a man rode out of the trees. Her mind screamed: *run!* Yet her reflexes were slow. She turned slowly, her feet moved so slowly that he cut her off before she could even leave the road. She turned back for the other side. There he was again, a man on a honey-colored horse. He seemed to spread around her like a flustering dream. Everywhere she turned, there he was. Dizzy, she stopped and stared at him, round-eyed. Seen against the wet sky, he looked monstrous.

"What's this?" he said with huge enjoyment, grinning, and she knew he was real by the sound of his voice. And because he was real, she realized her peril.

"Out for a walk, maid?"

116

He swung down from his saddle. She took advantage of that business and started to run again. He caught her cloak, then her arm. She towed against his hold and whimpered as she felt her back pull and sting.

"Now, now, where are ye going? Stay awhile and we'll dance us a bit o' a dance."

His horse was jittery; he couldn't let go of the reins, which meant he could only keep that one tenuous grip on her.

His hand slipped to her wrist, where the rope burn was healing. In the rainy dark—though her eyes were used to darkness now—she strove to make him out. He was hatless and had a round-as-a-ball head, and glistening, greasy-wet hair. Of his face, she saw only a short, wide nose. His neck and shoulders looked powerful, perfectly suited to the support of that enormous head. He wore a shabby gray coat with the pockets down low on the slightly flared hem. One of the large turned-back cuffs was gone. From his leather belt protruded the butt of a huge horse pistol.

Another horse burst out of the woods. Its rider drew rein. Two of them! Jane's legs nearly gave out; in fact, her knees bent, but at the last minute she forced them straight again, enough to keep that tension between her and the one who held her, enough so that he could not grab her more securely. She locked her knee joints.

The second man was doubly cloaked by darkness and the rain. She knew this one. It was him. "Let her go," he said without any particular urgency. "She's mine." Frost clung to the words. Jane recognized both the man and the strength of will underlying his solitary manner. In comparison with the man who held her, he looked almost elegant: black greatcoat covered tonight by a black tarpaulin cloak, black hat, shiny black jackboots that protected his legs to his thighs.

The man holding Jane's wrist grinned awfully at the newcomer aslant through the rain. "Who 't hell—?"

The horseman said, "The maid is mine." His black-as-midnight horse moved, started to circle the scene. "I've been following her for three nights."

He continued to ride in a calm circle about them. He held his reins in one gauntlet-encased hand; his left hand seemed to be hanging down his side beneath his cloak, as if injured. Jane's captor had to turn his head to glare at him. "And why didn't ye reel her in?"

"I had my reasons."

The man gripping her arm looked at Jane. He said, as if making a sniggering jest, "Sure ye have your reasons, sure ye do. And they're no different than my reasons. We're wise as wolves, the both of us." He looked back at the mounted man. "Ye're stepping on my toes here."

"Whose toes would that be, I wonder?"

"Name's Earl Nord."

"Ah, yes, *Grubneck* Nord." There was a small pause. "I've heard of you. A braggert and a bastard and a butcher, I've heard. And now it seems your toes are overlong, too. They're encroaching on space meant for other men's toes." He stopped his horse. "I suggest you curl those toes under a bit, Nord. Let go of her." He sat perfectly still on his horse. Jane watched him with edged fascination.

Grubneck Nord's fingers bit into her wrist. Jane spared him the merest glance. He still grinned. She saw the glitter in his eyes. He was like a man being quartered, with his nervous horse pulling one arm taut and Jane pulling the other—and he unwilling to let go of either. He yanked the horse closer and leaned into his arm to mop the streaming rain from his eyes. Jane sensed he was creating the business to hide the awkwardness of his situation.

"I would let go of her, aye, I would, but I suspect she's comely, and no matter how long ye've been following her, I'm the one who has a hold of her now. I reckon that makes her properly mine. And as soon as ye get the hell out o' here, me and her are going to dance a little cotillion."

He suddenly tugged hard on her wrist, as he had on his reins a moment before. Jane fell toward him. If he got his arm around her—! She caught herself at the last instant and managed to wince away again. She was not free, yet she was not fully captured either.

"Going to prance us a little prance."

She was hardly capable of connected thought. Life would never hold another moment as harrowing as this.

Grubneck laughed. "Comely, aye, and hot to have me muss her little curls for her."

"Comely? Yes, a man like you might use a word like that to describe her." His eyes slid toward Jane and just as quickly slid away again. "She's not for you, Nord. She's mine." What light there was glittered on his wet face beneath his hat brim.

The pistol butt in Grubneck's belt gleamed darkly. All he had to do was let go of his horse, or of Jane. He said, "Ye want killing, don't ye?"

Armed with nothing but a bland smile, the highwayman said, "Do you challenge me? I wouldn't. I'm one of those dangerous types, the kind who has nothing to lose. Absolutely nothing."

Thunder cracked suddenly, and lightning flared against the sky. Jane felt the electricity gathering in the night. Her scalp tingled. Her mind was like a mouse in a bucket. Her thoughts scratched and clawed and jumped and scraped. A quote from Genesis came to her all at once: " 'And he will be a wild man: his hand will be against every man, and every man's hand against him.' "

Grubneck laughed uncomfortably. "Ye seem damn

119

keen, a man wi' the habits o' a gentleman, so I tell ye what"—Jane felt his eyes on her—"why don't we share her?"

The frosted voice iced over completely. "I'm no gentleman." He now lifted his left hand to show he was holding a pistol. The world held its breath. Jane couldn't take her eyes away from that weapon. It had two barrels, and both of them were cocked. It came down, unhurried, steady, to a dead level. Jane noticed how practiced was the motion of his arm in this. The stone of a ring made a momentary flash from his little finger. "And I never share," he said.

The pistol spurted fire and smoke; instantly there was a deafening report. The blast shattered the air. Sparks fizzled in smoke, and there came to Jane an acrid smell of hot metal and tinder and burnt powder. For a fraction of a second she saw, in the white flash from his weapon, the highwayman's eyes.

She flinched—and nearly fell backward as the pull on her arm was released. At the same instant, Grubneck's smoked honey horse reared, turned, and broke into a panic-stricken gallop. The roll of the discharge reverberated around the fells. The highwayman remained erect in his saddle, grasping his own horse's reins firmly. The rain stopped abruptly, as if stunned by that shot. The thick, low-hanging sky suddenly thinned. A hazy rind of white moon showed itself briefly to light the scene.

Grubneck stood where he was with his legs apart, sagging but not yet fallen. His heavy round head was toppled back, his jaws unlocked, his breath loud. His eyes, in that opaline light, were those of a bull trapped inside a narrow stall, showing all the whites. He staggered back, tearing at the air. Finally he tumbled to his back on the ground, thick and solid, and with his arms spread out. Blood blossomed like a red rose from a hole in his shirt. .

The sky closed again. The heavy beat of the rain returned louder than ever. Thunder split the air overhead, and lightning followed in a brilliant flash. The highwayman slipped his pistol back into the case at his knee and swung down out of his saddle. Now Jane saw his face; a young man with dark hair. More thunder cracked and rumbled. She saw his eyes; dark—yet burning with light. She waited for nothing. She was into the woods in an instant, running madly despite her spinning head and her aching body. She heard Grubneck say, in a choked, sharp voice that traveled after her, "Yer prize is getting away."

"She's not going anywhere I can't find her."

The brief rift in the clouds closed completely. There were no stars or moon to take direction from—and no road, for Jane was in the trees. She couldn't keep a running pace for long, being three nights without a bed, and hurt, and sick with hunger.

An hour passed. She'd left the last tattered shadows of the copse behind and was back on the open moors. Pain and terror and exhaustion took their toll. A weariness grew, a heaviness, a yearning to quit, give up, lie down. She faltered to a stop and could get herself going once more only with a kind of plunge forward— and a little grunt of suffering. She walked with a jerky, driven gait. Her feet slithered in mud. She fell with a cry of pain, and toiled to rise again, to make herself continue on. She was cold, a chill not so much due to the weather but from within, radiating outward from the marrow of her bones.

Now her feet barely moved. If only she could sit down, lie down, stop, have a rest. It was so cruel, all of it, so cruel. She was near to tears again. And cramps gripped her empty belly. She was starving. The cramps, the pain in her back, the ache in her whole body under her rain-heavy clothes. Despair overpowered her.

She came to a stop once more and put her hands over her face. She listened to the rustle of the dropping rain. He was out there somewhere, with his horse and his pistols, following her, watching her. She knew it, she knew it. What did he want? To watch her die? She sobbed and rubbed her wet face.

The highwayman sat under his tarpaulin cloak in the rain. The wind soughed over his head. His horse stood patient beneath him. He watched the maid come on. She'd run exactly as he'd guessed, run until she met the beck and then followed it along its banks, followed it doggedly. Something in her seemed to say endlessly: keep going!

Why? What was she traveling toward, what illusion, what doomed hope?

He let her walk right past him. Sleepless and terrified, she didn't even see him, though nothing but a boulder half his horse's size concealed him.

Twenty paces beyond him, her heavy, jerky pace faltered. She halted. In the high grass, the wind tossed like the sound of the sea in a storm. She took a few more steps, stopped once more. She bent her neck as she once rubbed her face. The hood of her cloak had fallen back, and under the crowding sky her head was a white patch once more. She must be soaked through. Aye—he saw her shudder, saw a tremor race through her body. That was when he moved out from where he was waiting.

Jane fell a third time, and pulled herself onto a low stone and sat there looking at the ground before her shoe tips. The beck had seeped over its banks here, forming a little bog of something between earth and water. She gradually realized what she was seeing—a hoofprint. The warped indentation in the drenched ground, even as she looked, filled with moisture until it was level, and then began to overflow and the print began to dissolve.

She stood up as she heard the muffled sound of the horse. She turned, and yet still had to look around, for she was bewildered and could not get her mind to focus, let alone her eyes, which gleamed with unshed tears. She rubbed her wet forehead with the heel of her hand, and when she lowered it, she saw him at last. He did not materialize, or appear; he was just there. She felt . . . terror . . . and relief. It was over, at last it was over.

The wind caught his cloak and it billowed. He'd claimed to Grubneck Nord that he'd been following her since she'd left York. She knew he'd told the truth. From the first she'd felt him, that awful shadow of someone unobserved, just over her shoulder, just behind her, just out of sight. She'd seen his face, and it was a stranger's face, but the eyes . . . she almost felt she knew those eyes, dark yet burning with light.

He'd also claimed that there was nowhere she could go that he couldn't find her. Evidently that was true as well. What a sinister and crooked cunning he must possess. He seemed one with this shadowy cold, with this shadowy rain and wind, with the dark, with the night.

He'd just shot a man.

She took a step backward, and another, her gaze never leaving him. A whimper rose up in her; she battled it down.

He said with sudden lucid violence, "This has gone on long enough! You need a fire and food and a bed—

and I have all three. So let's stop this damnable game. Come with me now!''

His words struck her the way the east wind struck the grasses on the fells, so that they swayed and rustled with the shock. Go with him? To what end? He was a highwayman, a remorseless, treacherous (and no doubt lecherous), kindless rogue. She'd watched him shoot a man as casually as if he were tossing out an insult. Cunning? Perhaps. But a man of narrow nature, a hunter in the midnight, unfeeling and ferocious.

Yet even as she thought these reasonable and totally true thoughts, in her mind's eye she saw a bright small fire. He had a fire. And food.

Why not give in? It did no good to evade him. He pursued and pursued.

He wanted to roar at her, to release his passion in a sudden flood: *do as I say, maid!* He felt ice-white with fury. She had no place on this blade's edge she was walking. No right to make herself vulnerable to men like Grubneck Nord—men like himself! So that now he had to go against all his resolve and show her mercy.

But his was not a mercy without limits. He'd already made up his mind; if she didn't agree, he would simply leave her to her own fate. He would ride away without the least feeling of remorse. She was an impostor, no ''Rose of Midnight'' at all, nothing but a runaway scullery maid, whipped for whoring. For three nights he'd felt vicious with her, that she'd turned out to be so base, so utterly human. He'd followed her—not out of wanting to, but out of some need to take his disillusionment out on her. He hadn't hurt her, he had no bad conscience there; he'd only given her the sly little paw strokes the cat gives a mouse.

What was she doing out here! She had no business

trespassing into his world. The road! The road! What did she think she was going to find on that bloody road? She would never get out of these moors alive. She was going to die trying to follow his road.

Look at her, just look at her! Long strands of dark hair drizzling down her forehead. That look of pathetic misery. What keeps her on her feet? Stubbornness?

Desperation. You know very well that it's desperation. No one comes into this world of the night unless he—or she—has been driven to it, no one acts so rashly, so recklessly unless all hope for anything better has been ripped away. She's here because she's desperate.

He was furious, yes. And his anger was not against her so much as against her desperation.

At last, eyes glimmering, she nodded.

He hesitated a moment, surprised by her surrender despite himself. His thighs loosened, along with his stomach. Recovering, he barked, "All right then."

But then came the question: how to get her home? Would she get on his horse? If he suggested it, she would flinch, and he didn't think he could stand that. It would make him too savage. He was already too close to savagery. No, let her come to the idea herself. She could hardly stand, let alone walk much farther. Let her admit to herself that she needed help—his help. He would force nothing on her, nothing.

He urged Eclipse past her and started south. He did not look back, though he kept listening for the delicate sound of her following.

She did not hang back, and for a while did not falter. How did she do it? How did she manage to remain upright? By God's bright blood, he didn't know. And despite his fury, he had to grant her a distant and awful respect.

When her footsteps at last stumbled, and then halted,

125

he looked back. She was stopped, her head down. The rain was falling in thick, fat drops. He got off Eclipse and walked back to her. He didn't ask what was wrong. He knew. But he wanted her to say it.

She did, as if it were an effort even to speak. "I . . . can't go any farther." Those were the first words he'd heard her say, the first time he'd heard her voice. The calm, genteel accent took him by surprise. Was she a well-born lady or not? She was dressed like a servant, yet she was no round-faced, broad-beamed country girl. She was also no stately and perfumed goddess in white taffeta, her face pale and calm, her shining hair held back by a ribbon, her movements graceful and frozen in time.

He went back to Eclipse, took hold of the horse's bridle, and brought him around to her. "Get on," he said.

She looked at the stallion, at the saddle that came to the top of her head, at the stirrup which was nearly at the height of her waist. The last of her strength seemed to be running out of her now like water out of a broken bottle. She swayed slightly, as if any moment she might drop. He kept himself from putting so much as a hand out to stay her. She said, "I don't think I can." Her teeth chattered. She was drawn together, hunched up like an old woman, held up by nothing but will.

He couldn't help but measure her. She was at least a foot shorter than he was. Women were always smaller than him, but he'd never felt his size as something that put him in control of one like this. "I'll help you."

She backed away. Her face shone with rain. But it was *her* face, the skin as fair and as fine-grained as a child's. Again he felt that anger: what are you doing out here, your cap a sodden rag, your hair clinging to your face, your gown hanging limp and drenched around your body? He felt like grabbing her and thrusting her up onto the horse.

But he knew she would—somehow! weak as she was!—fight him, with panic if not with strength. He knew those awful wounds on her back would open up, and she would cry out, and her blood would flow.

Still wearing his riding gauntlets, he laced his fingers together and squatted down. Rain streamed off the back of his hat onto his cloak as he looked up at her. "Put your foot in my hands." There was a pause, filled with doubt on her part and a rigidly cold stare on his. He said it again: "Put your foot in my hands."

She weighed no more than a feather pillow even wet through. Once in the saddle, she stared at the pistol butts rearing from their cases at her thighs. For a moment he wondered if she would try to draw one and use it on him. He wondered this without much fear, confident that she couldn't manage it. But would she be so stupid as to try? He almost wanted her to. He gave her time. Pretending not to notice where her attention was, he pulled her petticoat and skirt down over her leg, walked around to the other side of Eclipse and covered the other leg.

Her hands never moved toward the weapons.

He patted Eclipse's neck, steadying him. "Slide back onto his rump."

He saw the questioning look she gave him.

"Did you think I was going to walk? I'd take the pillion seat myself, but I've seen your back." He poured these words out, heedless. "You wouldn't like me leaning forward against that."

Her expression changed—to surprise, and then to shame as she comprehended that he had spied on her whilst she was secret and half naked and suffering. She slid back onto the horse's rump and managed to find her seat, her back hunched, her face hidden.

127

The highwayman led the horse to a stone as tall as his own waist. He leapt up on it, then swung one leg over Eclipse's neck. He dropped into the saddle. Eclipse lifted his strong muzzle and stepped sideways.

Settling himself, the highwayman said grudgingly, "Rest against me if you want." He doubted she would, though. He touched his well-trained horse to a walk, soothing the beast with his hand. The maid was startled by the sudden motion. She grabbed at his rain-slick cloak. He said over his shoulder, "Lift that up—and my coat—and hook your fingers in my belt. Go on, do it! Or you'll fall off. Think how that'll feel."

She obeyed slowly. Besides her fear of him, he sensed her brain was muddled and weary. He felt her fingers work beneath his belt in the small of his back. Cold fingers, cold little knuckles. He clenched his jaw.

He touched Eclipse's flank with his spur; the horse moved into an easy cantor. They crossed the beck and entered some high bracken. Clouds hung over them like an immense, ragged, leaking black roof; the rain fell and fell.

He hadn't intended to rescue her, hadn't intended to take her to his hidey-hole. What else would he do this night that he'd never intended?

He needed all his self-control. As he rode, he girded himself to it and began to ready his will.

Chapter Nine

No Harm, No Harm

Jane looked at the back of the highwayman's head; she could see the serious stroke of his cheek and jawbone. He must be strong to handle such a horse. She couldn't imagine weakness in him under any circumstance. He seemed alien, unfazed by the fact that he'd recently shot a man in cold-blood. She'd assumed that bandits of his sort lived in squalor, but there was nothing squalid about him. His clothes were fine, his horse, his weapons, his speech. But he'd told Grubneck Nord he was no gentleman—and then proved the point beyond all doubt.

Though there was no path, he never hesitated as he stepped his horse across becks and traveled across unmarked open moorland. They moved through the soggy darkness, loud with rain. Jane's eyes fell closed. When she forced them open again, she was certain it was only a moment later, but their surroundings were very much different. The highwayman ducked some low branches, and she did, too, not an instant too soon. They moved through a mass of shrubbery, and around an enormous fallen oak, and finally he walked the horse right into a bramble thicket.

Jane thought the beast would certainly balk; then she saw a narrow opening into the thicket. They entered a bridle path so narrow it was almost unrecognizable as such: it was sunken into a deep cleft which could have been the bed of a gully but for the stones which walled its banks.

As they made their way down this narrow wynd, Jane's instincts rebelled. Where was he taking her?

They got closer all the time to the roar of a river in a rocky bed. She caught, once . . . once again, the muted scent of wood smoke, just the faintest whiff, as from a banked fire. The path sloped ever more steeply—toward that river? At the same time the brambles above curled up, entangled in one another, and made a hooped roof.

Just when Jane thought they must stop and somehow back the horse out of this dead end (impossible, they were trapped!) the path turned abruptly and emerged into an open space overhung with dark trees that made a roof over a cottage.

So this was his house, where he concealed himself by day, where he rested when he was not riding the highroad with his hat over his eyes and a mask over his mouth. This was where he would proceed with whatever dark intentions he had for her.

She looked back over her shoulder at the high hoops and tangles of briar. Already she couldn't see, in the dark rain, the place where the path had emerged.

She looked at the dark cottage. She had a fleeting vision of a bright little attic room in York, a sense of order and safety. But that memory was like a cork pulled out of a bottle. It had shrunk. It no longer fit.

She smelled the sawdust of a woodpile. Beyond the black shape of the cottage, she heard the river clearly now, a lot of water sweeping between man-tall boulders. On the opposite bank, the utter darkness hinted of cliffs ranging steeply upward, probably to a rolling treeless, empty height of moorland hidden beneath the clinging wet rags of cloud. The cottage was built on a bramble-protected shelf at the edge of a gorge, as secure a hiding place as a man of the midnight could want.

As he dismounted, his belt was ripped out of her hands. They were so numb with cold that she'd forgotten she was holding on to him. Now she had to accept his help in getting down. His hands were strong around her ribs, his thumbs under her breasts. He had hard arms and thighs. Briefly, she felt his warm breath on her cold face.

Her feet firmly on the ground, it was her turn to measure him—and be unnerved by his size. His lips parted in an abruptly cruel smile. A terrifying smile.

But she was not terrified. What might have terrified her last week, or even yesterday, or even this morning, had little power to terrify her now. She was sated on terror.

"What now?" Her voice came out small and husky.

He looked toward the cottage, and at the same time put his hand on her arm. Even in its gauntlet, she could tell it was a hard hand, hard as horn, and huge. She flinched from its contact. The hand dropped away. He moved alone toward the cottage door.

He left it open as he went inside. She lingered in the rain, watching his big, sturdy shadow find a candle and light it. She saw a longish room. It was a small cottage, simple in plan, but nicer than the one in which she'd grown up. Stones made a real floor, for instance. And it had two windows. One was shuttered, the other was not. He'd covered them with waxed muslin so that on sunny days the light would come through. She stepped up onto the stone porch, onto the lintel, but still didn't go inside.

He knelt at the fireplace in the far wall, where the fire had been banked during his absence. Soon he had a small blaze going. He swung a pot over the flames. He stood and came back to the door. She took in his silhouette in the frame of light, solid and rugged. He looked at her there, hesitating on the step. He gave her a long, slow examination, which took in her torn gown and her filthy cloak, her wan hands and face, her straggling hair. He held his chin high and gave her a glittering, disdainful look.

Yet what he said was neither glittering nor disdainful: "Upon my honor, no harm shall come to you under my roof."

It wasn't the first time she'd heard him use a gauged, quiet manner of speech. Where had he learned it, this man with such a deep voice and such big fists?

He stood aside, silently inviting her to enter. The fire glowed on its flat-stone hearth. The smoke rose straight up the chimney. She broke through the ache of her long, cross-country days and nights, through her fear and hesitation, and stepped inside.

He didn't come in behind her, but instead went out to close the shutter that was open to the rain. She was momentarily left alone to examine the place. It had a clean, well-cared-for look—not as clean as a woman would keep it, for there was dust, and things left lying about, a few tools and bits of harness, a rabbit trap, a wooden measure of some sort; the sort of things a woman would not have in her house—but it was clean for a man's keeping. No dirty platters and pots. No smell of past meals. No unlaundered, unmended clothes kicked into the corners.

There was a cooking pot, just as there would be in any household, and judging by the smell, it held the same kind of pottage everyone else ate—vegetables cooked with meat bones and herbs. Her mouth watered.

On the mantel were three books.

He came back inside carrying a pail of water. He took it to the fireside, then took off his hat and leather gauntlets and dropped them onto the table. He came back to close the door behind her. Again his hand touched her—her shoulder this time. She dodged away as though grazed by hot iron. "Don't ever put your hands on me!"

He stared at her with eyes gone to shadows. Without his hat, his dark, secret face was exposed to the light, to her stare. She stood shivering and dripping before him. And she knew it had been a silly thing to say. A silly, wild bit of bravado. She knew what he was and she understood what her being here signified. She was in the hands of, at the mercy of, this stranger. He would strike her down now, and rape her, and probably break her wounds open and cause her more in the doing. She saw clearly the violent emotions moving in him, heaving like dark clouds in a thunderous sky. Yes, he would hurt her now, and probably kill her.

But he only said, "Go over by the fire. I've got some stew there." He gestured to the blackened kettle. "You have to eat."

For a moment she didn't budge. Then she did as he said and moved to the fire. How could she not? Warmth and light and cooking smells, and the sound of his low-pitched voice still in her ears promising no harm, no harm. She stood dripping over the hearthstones. She found it hard to remain standing. There were two plain armchairs at the central table, both worn to the bone. He pulled one close to the flames. "Sit down." She wanted to weep. The resolve not to was ebbing from her.

She sat, stiffly upright, her hands clenched together in her lap.

"You can sleep there." He nodded toward the bed in the corner. "I shan't use it tonight."

It was a truckle bed, homemade of oak, with a patchwork cover. "There's water to wash with." He gave her another of those looks that made her feel dirty and bloody and ragged. He crossed to a chest and knelt down on one knee to unlock it. "Here's a shirt you can sleep in." He lay it on the lid as he relocked the chest. He looked her straight in the eye. "I won't be back till sunrise." His dark gaze reflected the fire and seemed to be filled with leaping light. There was silence, except for the muffled and constant sound of the river and the blustering beat of the rain. At last he turned.

His shadow was huge against the door; it got smaller as he crossed the room to join it. A draught of cold air wafted in as he opened the door—then he was gone.

He'd left her alone—and had done her no harm. She felt those two things as keenly as she felt her hunger. She realized it was going to be all right, at least for a while, and a weight rolled from her heart. Frowning into the fire, she found herself wondering how old he was. Very old, possibly thirty. Or maybe only twenty-five. He wasn't ugly; in fact, he had an austere male sort of beauty, a sort of sullen perfection.

Her stunned mind wavered, wandered. She saw her father's face flaring in the leaping fire. He stared at her, and repeated something in an urgent murmur, over and over, until at last she heard it: *Jane* . . . *Jane* . . . His cheek was snatched by flame, then his lips, his jowls.

She sat up straighter, alert to her whereabouts again.

The stew . . . she wanted it. God help her she could hardly think for wanting it. If he'd stayed . . . she wanted to believe that she'd inherited enough of her mother's proud and stubborn temperament to balk at eating in the company of a murderer. But he hadn't stayed, and alone, she couldn't even wait for it to warm all the way through before she picked up the wooden bowl left on the table and scooped it into the pot.

It was meaty and wonderful. When she had drunk all the juice and spooned out the vegetables and meat, she dipped herself another bowlful.

Now she tasted what she was eating. It seemed to be duck—shot presumably with the same precision with which her host had shot Grubneck Nord.

Her stomach packed to discomfort, she relaxed even more. The heat of the fire made her shiver in her drenched garments. She moved closer and closer to the flames—until she smelled her gown scorching against her knees. She stood and looked at the chest where he'd left out the shirt. (It was a wide, ironbound chest, locked. No doubt the highwayman's stolen treasures were arrayed within.) A man's white nightshirt, neatly folded on top of the heavy lid. She crossed to it, and brought it back to the fire. She shed her cloak, her shoes and stockings, her dress and petticoat.

She was almost surprised to find her hips were still wrapped by her makeshift moneybelt. She'd all but forgotten about it in the past few hours. It was of course as sodden as everything else. She untied it . . . and felt the first frost of worry. She was in the hands of a highwayman. She glanced at the locked chest, full of stolen coins and jewels. She didn't want her little hoard to get locked away in there. She must think.

Meanwhile, she reached to touch her back. It seemed a mass of softened crusts and scabs.

The bucket of water had been left by the fire to warm. A length of folded toweling lay on the mantel. He'd thought of everything, every essential. He'd known what she needed. He reminded her of a spider, lifting his long legs in pairs and weaving them with an awful grace, binding her while she was still stunned by his bite so that at his leisure he might suck the life out of her. He'd followed her, tormented her, played night-games with her . . . why? For the simple amusement of it? Yet as soon as she'd been accosted by Grubneck Nord . . . "She's mine," he'd said.

Where was he now? What was he doing? What did he mean to do with her?

She shook her head. He was too exotic. Her eyes could not see into such a man's heart, or gauge what he might do next or think to do. She slipped his night-shirt over her head. Its hem brushed the stone floor about her bare feet.

As she hung her clothes on some nails by the door where they might dry, she was aware of all the shadows leaping up the walls around her. She turned and considered her moneybelt again. Her eyes took in every little nook of the room. On a high shelf stood several pieces of dusty crockery. Toward the back was a chipped tankard with a broken handle.

She went to work at the knots of her belt. She fingered each coin with awe, discovered each anew. They were hers. Seeing them, counting them, some of her courage returned.

She moved her chair and stepped up on it, and put the coins into the chipped tankard, being careful not to disturb the dust on the shelf with so much as a finger-print. Now she pulled the chair back to the fire and sat forward, her arms wrapped around her breasts and resting on her knees. Her bare feet were almost in the flames as she soaked up the heat. Eventually she remembered to unpin her bonnet and cap; she unplaited her braids and let fall her damp hair.

The flames burned her face. The warmth seeped

136

through the nightshirt into her body. Her head nodded. She sat up with a start, looking around her—what . . . ? But it was nothing, only the rainwater that wrapped the house like a vine.

The fire had died down. She tended it.

The second time she nodded and startled herself awake, she looked over at the clumsily made bed. She slid the chair back from the fire and rose, painstakingly, for even a few moments of inaction caused her body to stiffen up. She blew out the candle on the table and took a step toward the bed, stopped, took another step . . .

She pulled the patchwork quilt open. She felt tense and daring, as if she were trespassing. Finally she lay down—in a strange brigand's bed, smelling the scent that must be singularly his.

She remembered suddenly how his mouth had twisted into that terrible smile. She made a tiny moaning sob of pure exhaustion, of complete surrender.

Though the idea was distasteful, using someone else's bed, a man's bed, the sensations were good, being able to stretch out at last. In less than a minute, she was still. Her heart continued to beat, but everything else was still.

The sun had been up for several hours, though it was hidden by the heavy clouds that rolled up the river gorge, bringing with them curtains of rain and twilight at midmorning. And still the maid slept on, unaware of the highwayman's presence, of his observation. The face was *her* face, his Rose of Midnight, the not-quite-real gentlewoman in the portrait, she who was secure from the travails of life. But the hand upon which her cheek rested (on his pillow) was very real—and work-roughened. The mark around the wrist was made by a hemp rope. Once she whimpered in her sleep, and once made a noise like a strangled scream. The sounds made him feel a new surge of fury—God's blood!—both at what had been done to her and at her recklessness in challenging the wild and lonely road.

He sat at the table, slumped in his chair, listening to the rain as it sizzled down the chimney. "Who are you?" he said softly, studying her moon-white face, her flower mouth soft with sleep, the shape of her body beneath his quilts. He felt a pang of desire. He wanted her, right here, right this minute.

He'd promised to do her no harm, and he would keep his word—as long as it didn't cost him a great deal. He lifted his elbows to the arms of his chair and steepled his hands and rested the tips of both index fingers against his mouth.

She slept on oblivious. She was a mystery. A man dripping with scientific degrees couldn't figure her out. She seemed as fragile as a hummingbird—and was in truth as uncompromising as a blade. The looks she'd given him! Those blue eyes like deep, quiet lakes . . . where corpses might be drifting along the bottom and no one would ever know.

She slept through the day and into the dusk.

Jane's eyes opened. It was either very early or very late, she couldn't tell which. She knew where she was, however. That awareness coursed through her. She was in the highwayman's cottage, in his bed, wearing his shirt.

Yet she was unmolested. And she was alive: her blood throbbed in her body, her breath moved evenly in and out, she was even dry and warm. She lay like a fetus in the womb of his feather bed—the bed of a strong, willful man.

She wiggled her toes. Could she really be safe here?

She turned her head—and saw something that caused her to rise up on her elbow, despite the painful complaint from her back. The cold she'd felt last night returned to her, permeating the hollows of her bones. For on the table in the middle of the room was her money, put into neat stacks: seventy guineas, six shillings, and four pence.

A soft wind was blowing when the highwayman pushed open the door and stooped under the lintel to come in. He saw that the maid was up and had helped herself to some more stew. Her money was still where he'd stacked it.

She sat by the fire now, still wearing his shirt, but with her cloak wrapped around her. Her feet were bare, and her long dark hair flooded over her shoulders and down her back. His mind overflowed with the possibilities, just seeing her there, in his house, his chair, before his fire, wearing his shirt, the seemingly infinite possibilities.

She sat forward in her chair, in a way that reminded him that she was hurt. He slung his greatcoat off and hung it on a peg. He stopped at the table and, with a slow blink at the glittering coins, said, "Never try to hide thievery from a thief."

He helped himself to the last bowl of the stew and drew the second chair from under the table. He sat sideways so that he could look at her.

She was shy of him now, couldn't quite look at him outright but only dared little glances out the sides of the moonlit meres that were her eyes. She said, as if it was an old story and all of its anguish was worn away, "That's my own money."

"Where'd you get it?"

A pause, then, "I didn't steal it. It's mine."

He saw he would have to ask many questions to find out just a few things. He said again, "Where'd you get it?"

"I worked for it."

In Hockness Hall, he'd been caught by her mystery. And again this morning, watching her asleep in his bed. And mystery she remained now, silent and enigmatic.

But then, unexpectedly, she emerged from her silence and volunteered, "I suppose you'll take it from me now."

So the money was that important to her—important enough to coax her into speech despite her shyness. He observed that her face was no longer a skull-face of terror and exhaustion; it was round, velvety—but its expression was not calm.

She'd worked for it? Then for certain she wasn't a lady, though she spoke like one. What kind of work? A lady's maid? Some of them learned to speak like their mistresses. Even so, most maidservants earned their bed and board and ten guineas a half-year and considered themselves lucky to be freed from the fear of starving. Where could she have come by such a hoard all at once?

"What kind of work?"

"I was a maidservant. And I posed for a picture, a painting. I saved everything I made for two years."

He could only stare at her. Who was she? What was behind her secretness?

"Why were you flogged?"

"For that." She said nothing more but there was an emotion in her eyes that was more arresting than the most articulate words: I have endured for that money, I have suffered, and I am willing to suffer more to keep it.

140

He rubbed one hand over his face, fingering the sore, stiff growth of whiskers on his jaw and lip. He hadn't shaved today, not wanting to disturb her rest. Silence closed around them until he could almost hear his own agitation tingling on the air. "You're going to have to let me have a look at your back."

"Why?" she said, startled.

He kept his face a dead blank. "It may need attention."

"No."

He checked the one or two ill-tempered comments that came to his tongue. Instead, he finished his stew and sat back and crossed his hands over his stomach for a while. She continued to look at him, steadily now, her small, obstinate face guarded and shut, her eyes showing only glints of emotion. He breathed in and out, oddly aware of how his chest moved. He pulled at his nose with his thumb and index finger; then, making up his mind all at once, he rose and stepped before her. Even before he could reach for her, however, she was out of her chair.

She went to her torn clothes hanging by the door and started plucking them down. "Where are my shoes?"

"What are you going to do? Run away again? Through the night? And the rain?"

"What have you done with my shoes?" It was daunting the way those eyes were different from the eyes in the portrait. Had journey and struggle done that? Had pain? It was almost as though she couldn't see with them now, as though she were blind. They stared at a point beyond him, and beyond the door behind him.

"In just three nights you've already crossed paths with two brigands. Have you not heard, Innocent, the roads are not safe." He couldn't restrain his sarcasm.

She paused, her clothes in her arms. She focused her eyes on him. A wary look clouded her eyes.

He let his gaze wander down her, as though idly. He tipped his head to one side. "You haven't got a chance in a million to get wherever it is you're heading. A woman traveling afoot—and hurt badly."

Her eyes narrowed. "Did you kill that man—Nord?"

He blinked slowly. "He'll live. But he won't uncurl his toes in my direction again." She was looking at him as if he were a cold-blooded murderer. He said, "A highwayman's reputation is his stock in trade. Nothing is so weak and insecure as a reputation for savagery not based on example. Think of the lightning, how it injures without warning. That's the reputation a man in my position must maintain, so that everyone will run indoors the minute they hear the thunder of my hooves.

"As for Grubneck Nord, I caught his horse for him, and put him on it. He was shot through the shoulder—not usually a fatal wound."

A moment passed. The wind sang around the corners of the cottage. She said, "Why did you follow me like that?"

"Because—"

Because I was furious to find you are mortal, that you can be as hurt and lost and lonely and desperate as the rest of us.

"Because I was curious. I recognized you, I know who you are."

Her mouth narrowed.

"Everyone knows about 'The Rose of Midnight.' "

"Even here, then." Her acceptance was as quiet as a thin blue spiral of smoke.

He wasn't going to let her turn him from the main

142

issue. He got back to his point. "Someone needs to look at your back."

"You said you already did." Her throat tightened around the words; they came out thin.

"Aye, and what I saw looked evil. Cuts like that can easily turn foul. You could find yourself very ill, possibly dead."

She lowered her gaze to a point in the middle of his chest. "You'll just look. You won't touch me."

"Unless you need touching."

She swallowed. He stepped closer. She stepped away.

"Yield, maid, because if you don't, I most certainly will resort to force."

Chapter Ten

They Began to Look Familiar to One Another

The frightened look returned to the maid's eyes. She shook her head, but then turned her back on the highwayman to hang her clothes on the nails again. Hesitantly, she removed her cloak and untied the neck of her nightshirt. She pushed it down her shoulders and lifted her hair, revealing the upper half of her back.

He wanted to rage. The least of the welts stood up bright and angry-looking. The worst of the cuts had healed and broken open and healed again. She would be scarred. But it didn't look as if any of the wounds were tainted. He needed to see the rest to be sure. "Lower," he said. She leaned forward, hiding her face and her breasts in the folds of her hanging gown as she let the shirt fall to her waist.

Pity coursed through him. All the pity he'd been tamping down and holding back for days. Without thinking, he lifted his hands to her bare shoulders and tried to turn her. His intention was to comfort—himself as much as her—but at the first touch of his hands she jerked away. "Don't," she said, turning and putting space between them. He caught a glimpse of her

144

breasts, lucent as moons, before she got the shirt up again and with both hands held the cotton closed tightly.

"Who did that to you?"

She caught the fullness of her bottom lip between her teeth, and shook her head vigorously. Her eyes flashed at him, wary and defiant.

He stepped nearer, wanting to shake the answers out of her: who are you? Who would do such a thing? Why? She backed away, looking around him at the door. She cried, "I shouldn't be here! Let me go!"

He brought himself up short.

He went to his chair, leaving her to stand lost and helpless in the middle of the room. He didn't dare look at her; he was distrustful of himself. His tone had a businesslike sound. "Let's try again. Let's start over. Shall we introduce ourselves? My name is Keith Cutler. And yours is . . . ?"

Her eyes foundered blankly. "I want my shoes. I want to go." After a moment, she added, "Please."

He looked back over his shoulder at her. "Why? What are you afraid of?"

She wouldn't say it.

"You're afraid of me. You think I'm going to drag you to the bed there and—" He stopped. "If that was my purpose, you wouldn't stand a chance, maid. You'd be taken already, in fact, and very sorry you ever ventured out alone on the road." He left a silence to give the words time to filter through to her.

She stared at him with eyes gone dark. He almost heard her mind working: *What am I doing in the house of a highwayman?* In the quiet between them, the dread she'd been too stunned to feel yesterday now ran through her body in an almost visible shockwave.

Yet she remained as impenetrable as ever.

He leaned back and folded his arms. "Sit down."

145

The fire burned bright and almost noiseless in the small fireplace. After a while she did as he bade her. And after another while her breath came evenly again. She raised her head and sat up. He knew she was calmer when her small pink feet slid nearer the fire. He felt pleased that he'd calmed her down, that he'd ridden down her hysteria.

"Now then, we are both comfortable and private, are we not? You can tell me everything, and I give you my pledge that I won't betray any of your secrets, for I'm not your enemy, maid."

She gave him an uncomprehending look, which was as good as a whole book of protest against his meaningless twaddle. "Why did you follow me?"

He checked for a fraction of a breath. No, he would not tell her the truth. He said, "As it happened, I was indulging in a late supper of some bread and cheese, thinking how quiet the night was, when, several minutes into my meal, something white-and-black entered the edge of my vision. I turned my head—and there you were.

"I thought, now who is this stupid wench walking right down the middle of the road in the broad moonlight?" He didn't know where this chatter was coming from, but it kept coming. "I thought you were probably a maid who needed a husband in a hurry, or maybe a servant who had stolen her master's cash. It was the possibility of the cash that stoked my first interest, I admit. But later you stopped, and you lifted your face to the moon, and I recognized you."

He watched the golden dance of the fire-flicker between his half closed lashes. " 'The Rose of Midnight.' In person. In my domain. There was more mystery about you than I could resist.

"When you left the road to find a place to rest, you took your cloak off—and I saw what had been done to

146

you." He moved in his chair. The wind had picked up outside.

He looked at her. He was determined to make her talk. "How did you keep up that endless walking?"

She drew her white hand back through her lush dark hair. Her voice was a whisper. "I kept telling myself that if I kept on it would come out all right."

"You see now that you were wrong?"

She gave him a look. "I didn't have any choice. I would do it again—I *will* go on again. I must."

"And the terror? And the hunger? And the predators, like Grubneck Nord . . . like myself? What about those?"

She shook her head distractedly, saying in effect, I can't think about that.

"You *are* innocent. I still don't know what your name is. 'The maid,' I call you when I think of you."

She gnawed her lips.

"I suppose I could call you Rose."

"No, not that—Jane, my name is Jane. Fitzpatrick."

It might be true, and it might not.

He pretended to stifle a yawn. "Well, Jane Fitzpatrick, you've certainly tired me out with your prattling conversation. You talk in a regular unbroken stream, don't you?"

She looked at him with pleading eyes.

"Why do you look at me like that? Have I hurt you? I promised that you would suffer no harm under my roof. I'm many things, but I'm not a liar. Not unless it serves me. Go back to bed; you can sleep every hour of this night without fear."

She looked at him with wariness. "If I take your bed, where will you sleep?"

"On the floor."

She said, looking at the fire, "Why are you being so kind to me?"

"Kind? I'm not kind." He laughed at the thought, a small outburst of breath. "No more than a wolf is."

She didn't flinch. "You promised not to harm me."

He smiled thinly. "If you trust me so much then why won't you tell me what happened to you? Those marks on your wrists and around your neck—you look like you've been half hung and whipped. What did you do? What happened? What did you do, Jane Fitzpatrick?"

"Nothing! My father . . . my father beat me."

He stared hard at her. Several notions ran through his head, ugly imaginings. "Why?"

She looked at the money on the table again. "I told you, for that."

Part of him was relieved. The man had just wanted money from her. He said, "But you still have it. How—"

"Oh, don't ask me any more questions!" She hid her face in her hands.

Her body shook with silent sobs. She was so pitiful, it took every ounce of his willpower to continue badgering her. "What happened?" She didn't answer. "If you want to keep your little stack of coins here, you'd better tell me."

That made her sit up. Her face was wet. The look she gave him was venomous, but at last she started talking. "He wanted my money. I'd been saving it to go to America—that's where I'm going. He came back from Africa and said he wanted it, just like that. He'd been gone for years and I never thought . . . just like that, all my working and saving. And Mr. Welby, my master, said I must give it to him and give up my position and go with him to help him restore our old farm—because he was my father." An edge of bitterness knifed into her tone. "But he didn't want to farm at all, he just wanted to get me off by myself. And Mr. Welby—

"Mr. Welby just wanted to get rid of me. He liked me too well, and saw the chance to rid himself of temptation."

She looked at Keith with eyes that were wet and dark. "As soon as we got out of the town and onto the moors, Father put a rope around my neck, a coffle, he called it. It's what they use on the African slaves to bring them out of their jungles. It was tight around my throat and around my wrists"—she demonstrated, putting her hands beneath her chin as though she were praying—"I couldn't do anything, I couldn't get away."

He saw her pathetically trying to defend herself; it was as clear in his imagination as the detail of a portrait.

She continued on in a low surge, "At our cottage, he tied the end of the rope up to the roof beam. It was rotten, that beam, and I was afraid it was going to come down—and all he said was that I shouldn't pull too hard on it! And he went out and came back with a whip, a cat-o-nine-tails."

Her eyes were huge, seeing things that weren't in the room with them. She shook her head. "But I wouldn't tell him where I had my money. I wouldn't . . ." She lowered her head and wept. "I might have told him," she admitted in a whisper, as if it were something to be ashamed of, "but after a while I couldn't. I couldn't even remember why he was beating me, not after a while."

It was a moment before she could go on. "He left me there, with that slivery beam creaking over me. I was out of my head for a while, I guess. When I woke up, I couldn't kneel down or rest. I had to stay on my

149

feet, you see, because I was afraid that all that moldy thatch would come down and smother me.''

She wiped her eyes on the back of her hand and took a deep breath. ''When he finally cut me loose, he said to start a fire. I was shaking so, it wouldn't start, and I was afraid. He kicked me aside and then—and then the beam broke! I got out the door just as it came down on his head, the beam, and then the whole roof.

''Smoke started rising through the thatch—from the fire we'd been working on—and I think I heard him— I think I heard him whisper my name! 'Jane.' He was trapped, he couldn't move, he was *trapped!*'' A shudder ripped through her body. ''And then, oh God, I smelled him.'' Her hands went to her mouth. ''I smelled him burning.''

''You only thought you heard him. The beam killed him. He was dead already.''

It was as if she couldn't hear him. Her face was as white as the shirt she was wearing. The pupils of her eyes were huge. He had to do something. He rose and pulled her up with him. ''He was already dead.'' He would have carried her to the bed, but he couldn't risk hurting her back, so he led her, and pulled the covers up to her chin.

She reached out to touch his hand, but cautiously, as if it were blazing and might burn her. He grasped her fingers. She looked up at him beseechingly. ''I couldn't go back to Mr. Welby. He wouldn't have wanted me to come back.'' She was trembling. Her voice shook. ''And I was too proud—I was still proud, even then.''

He squatted beside the bed. He could well believe this Welby had turned against her because ''he liked her too well.'' Keith Cutler had done the same thing when he'd found out she was real and human and not an ever-perfect image on an artist's canvas. In his guilt he had no comforting words to offer. Her eyes were still round and dark with fright. A rush of wind shook the cottage. He said, "Go to sleep. I'll make a pallet on the floor."

She looked at him; her vision seemed to recall itself from some place far away, and she looked at him as if she were seeing him for the first time, as if he were some shape that had just stepped out of the shadows and acquired human form. She looked at his hand grasping hers. She didn't pull away from the contact. She seemed to surrender, to place herself in his hands. She said again, "Why are you being so kind to me?"

He shrugged. "I don't know. I wouldn't trust it too far if I were you."

She moved under the bedclothes, the movement causing a clear look of pain to span her face. "You followed me because you thought I was her—'The Rose of Midnight.' But I'm not, you know. I'm someone else entirely."

And that might be the truth, and it might not be.

A pattern was established that night, of wind and rain and the muffled roar of the river without, and warmth within, and silence. The first day or two was hard for the maid, but after that some of the tautly wound springs inside her started to unwind, and then she was able to get respite for her body, her mind, her nerves. Sometimes the sky was like a scalded mackerel and the sun cast a fragile light; sometimes the clouds solidified and rained down upon the dusky moors. At night, Keith Cutler slept on a pallet opposite the hearth from his bed. The cottage and its silence surrounded them like a cocoon. In such close quarters, they began to look familiar to one another.

And Keith began to have shameless dreams.

151

He showed her where things were kept, and she mended her clothes. He hauled water so she could wash some of the stains out. She washed her hair as well, and left it loose to dry more quickly. Otherwise its waist length was plaited and pinned up for efficiency—and out of modesty. He'd once assumed a woman could not be truly beautiful unless she was a lady, ornamental and lovely, but watching Jane Fitzpatrick perform these homely tasks he knew he'd been wrong. Her beauty pierced him.

He returned her shoes to her and she went out. His place was located in a natural amphitheater beneath a two-hundred-forty-foot limestone cliff created by some ice age or other. A river fell from the precipice, and flowed south between channeling boulders. There was but one entrance and one exit, through the wall of brambles.

He never touched her money again. She put it back into the tankard on the shelf and it was never mentioned by either of them.

He attended to his winter wood cutting. His steel ax thudded into the logs he'd cut last spring with a blunt ringing sound which repeated off the cliffs. One Saturday he saddled his horse and rode to a market village in the direction of Mattock. He brought home food and she took it upon herself to cook it, as if she were his woman. As if he were her man. He sat at the table while she served him. He glanced at her, and bravely she held the look—until it proved too much for her and she blushed and turned aside.

She seemed to heal. His quick eyes almost saw her pain retract, withdraw its thorns. It struck again if she moved without thinking, but slowly, surely, it retreated. Then, except for seizures of itching, she seemed to do well enough. He could imagine the tender scars even though she never let him look at them again.

Once, when he was on his way in from his woodpile, he heard her humming as she put their supper on the table. A low, late light was pitched across the natural amphitheater and the river, throwing elongated shadows of sycamores and the thorn thickets before it, making objects far distant from each other seem bound together. The wings of the clouds were painted in watercolors of peach and gold. He stopped there in the midst of that sunset and listened to the woman of his dreams humming a song in his house, and for a moment his heart slugged up into his throat.

He'd known her a fortnight and she'd not let him so much as run his fingers though her hair. His imagination had woven stories about them, about the scared look she sometimes gave him whenever he happened to get too close, and how he overcame it; about the way she always managed to keep just beyond his reach, and how she one day forgot; about the breathless way she waited whenever he stood over her, as if she were afraid he might grab her suddenly and take her roughly, and how instead he eased her into his arms so gently that she was surprised and disarmed and willing.

She was small beside him, fine-boned, light, and strong as a blade. His nose knew the scent of her, faint, like rare roses. He knew her skin would be cream and silk.

Ordinarily he was a man who loved anticipation of any sort, loved to let it stretch until it was the finest, tightest strand, but finally he'd reached a point when he didn't know if he could wait much longer.

He turned, there in that sunset, and went to the stable instead of into the cottage.

"It's her spirit," he told his stallion, "her refusal to break." He stroked the muscled velvet of Eclipse's neck. Here was fire to meet his fire, grief to compare with his own, and a will as implacable as all heaven. "And yet, that's only part of it."

The stallion was mercifully removed from such foolishness. He lipped up the last of his sweet barley and cocked an ear. Would he be given more?

"Gluttony is a cardinal sin." Keith worked a tangle out of the dark mane. He could take her. But he wouldn't humble himself that way. He had no appetite for rape. Let her be.

"I'm a fool." He was as miserable as a highwayman with a reputation for cold-bloodedness might be with a beautiful maid in his grasp.

The stallion rubbed an itch out of his cheek and huffed through his nostrils. Keith stroked the warm satin neck, sighing a deep sigh.

He supposed she saw everything in his face. He knew for a fact that this very morning when he'd sat up in his pallet and looked her way she'd caught him giving her a stricken look. In return she'd got that pinched aspect he remembered from the first night. When he saw it, he wanted to say, I'm a man like any other, and you are provokingly fair. And provokingly near at hand.

Actually, she would have been amazed to know how close he was to innocence himself, how infrequently he had wanted a woman adequately to do what men did. He kindled slowly. But once he had begun . . .

He knew what he had to do. He must do it tonight.

After a fortnight of staying close to home and neglecting his regular business, the highwayman suddenly announced over supper that he would be gone until dawn.

The weather had lifted at last into gusty, drying days with the last of the cumulus drawn across the sky so that spears of sun broke through as if aimed over the land like search lamps. The lifting of the weather had heartened Jane so that she had baked some bread today. It was round and savory and still warm as she placed it on the table. Keith was wearing a plain woodsman's shirt and breeches and rough hose. The shirt wasn't laced. She refused to consider his bare throat.

"Will you be all right while I'm gone?" he asked.

"Of course." She was already beholden to him for so much, what else could she say? Even if the prospect of staying alone through the windy night terrified her. It was as though she'd used up all her courage in those three nights of desperation and had none left anymore. The one day he'd gone to the market village for food, she'd been so glad to hear his return that it had taken all her will not to run out and welcome him back with smiles and cheer and, yes, open arms.

She didn't ask him where he was going tonight, on what errand, toward what rough and revolting deeds. She had no need to: it was only obvious when he unlocked his ironbound chest and took out his black linen shirt and his side-arm sword and his pistols.

He was suddenly the highwayman again, the brigand who had ghosted her on the highroad, his cloak billowing, his hat pulled low. Only now he was something more, as well, for she knew that he was handsome and young, with great shadowy eyes and a completely unexpected vein of kindness.

Indeed, he was nothing of what she'd been led to expect. He did not shovel his dinner in with both hands. Or stink like a goat. In fact, he was fastidiously clean. And reasonable. And perceptive.

The highwaymen in legends, in tales to frighten children, came like spirits of the night, robbed, raped, killed, and vanished again into the moors. This one confused her. He didn't follow at all in the usual pattern. In his keeping she was let be, while he chopped wood and went—fishing! He kept an ash rod in the corner nearest the door and twice he had brought fish home from the river. He spoke of going char fishing.

"A char is something like a salmon, but you find it in fresh water only. Generally, only in deep water, in lakes. I've seen them ten inches, a foot long, up to three-quarters of a pound. You don't want them bigger—the bigger they are the older they are."

What kind of brigand enjoyed fishing? What would attract a highwayman to such an uncompensating sport? Here was no devil, no monster, no creature beyond a woman's ken.

Yet when he was dressed in his midnight finery, and had buttoned up his greatcoat and mounted Eclipse, he was, without a doubt, a highwayman. The fact checked Jane's impulse to wish him well. From his horse he looked down at her, a slow look. Then, giving her a little salute of his gauntleted hand, he rode off into the windy night.

His wraith continued to insinuate itself into her thoughts and interrupt her after-supper chores. In the middle of putting a plate away she found herself staring through space. Her fingers traced her mouth. She imagined her fingertips tracing his mouth, his high cheekbones, his hands, the hair caught back at the nape of his neck. She imagined her palms on the rounds of his broad shoulders, against the spread of his back. All these images obsessed her suddenly. As the evening wore on, she constantly pictured him again and again.

She was not introspective. She approved of who she was and of her own feeling without question, hence, although she was startled at the abruptness of this passion, she didn't try to analyze it. Instead she accepted it, and went over every look and gesture and word and event of the last fortnight with a potent blend of long-ing and apprehension which became combustible dur-ing those waiting hours.

She hardly slept at all. Awake, abed, with the fire banked, she asked herself why she was no longer afraid of him. Her tiredness when he had put her on his horse and brought her here was only a memory in her nerves and limbs; that sickening fear of rape and murder she'd felt when he'd stalked her was only a memory of her heart. Though she'd known all along the repayment he wanted for his shelter and protection, no awful gnaw-ing began in the pit of her belly anymore at the thought of it. There was no panic in her pulse now.

She'd kept most of herself hidden from him, and she knew that he, too, had kept more of himself hidden than he'd revealed, yet that comforted her, to know that he didn't care to thrust all of who he was at her. He'd shown patience, and restraint, and consideration. She owed him for all that, and perhaps for her very life.

He returned before he'd said he would, long before dawn, when it was still completely dark. She heard the soft clop of a horse's hooves in the muddy dooryard, and at first she was a little apprehensive, but then she heard his voice as he urged Eclipse toward the stable. She heard the saddle creak and the chink of bits as he dismounted. Then the horse's hooves, faint and un-hurried on the peat-based soil, until they were muffled by the straw on the stable floor.

He came in quietly, expecting her to be asleep. She didn't tell him she wasn't. He laid his pistols on the table, along with his riding gauntlets—and a weighted purse. He quietly brought the fire back to life, and took off his greatcoat. Before tossing it aside, he held it to the light. He was looking at a bullet hole in the cape, uncomfortably near the neck.

He put the coat aside and rubbed his eyes with his big hand, his left hand, which was the hand he ate with and held his cup with, the hand he favored. It was something else that was different about him.

Jane regarded him in a way she hadn't consciously done before: he was heavy, but favorably proportioned. And undeniably handsome. His hair was black as the midnight sky. His rough-hewn features were alive with willfulness and character. There was a smooth, brawny strength in his shoulders, and his thighs were sleek and powerful.

He moved a chair before the fire. He seemed tired. He pulled his sword from its scabbard and examined the blade. The glow from the flames glanced off the bright metal.

After a moment, he stood up and peeled off his black shirt. The method they had established was that he went out "to check on Eclipse" when she needed to dress or undress. And she turned her back when he got into his pallet or out of it. She had never seen him shirtless.

Now she did. Her eyes saw all too distinctly. He was well made, broad of shoulder, narrow of hip, muscles well defined by his labor with ax and saw—and pistols. He sat down again to pull off his boots. His legs were long, strongly molded by horsemanship. His bare feet were narrow. He stood again to take off his drawers, his breeches.

When he was done, Jane said quietly, "Keith."

Chapter Eleven

> One kiss, my bonny sweetheart,
> I'm after a prize tonight,
> But I shall be back with the yellow gold
> before the morning light . . .
>
> Alfred Noyes: *The Highwayman*

Keith turned to Jane, surprised. Some impulse of modesty made him grab his shirt and hold it to his groin. She almost smiled at the look on his face.

She lifted her hand toward him. His expression tightened. For a moment, as his eyes confronted hers, they seemed almost frightened. He padded toward her. She moved over, into the territory of coolness on the unoccupied side of the bed. For the first time she noticed that the wind had died. Nothing stirred. It was like a deafness. There was no sound.

At last he tossed the shirt onto the table and took possession of his own bed once more. He leaned up on his elbow, not touching her, yet just a little too near, barely crossing that invisible line where companionship ends, assessing it and testing its edges precisely, with some instinct of skin and hair tips. His eyes narrowed with lazy menace. She forced herself not to falter. And yet he *was* bigger, stronger, a man of mysteries and riddles and strange intensities, a highwayman who if anything appeared more formidable in his nakedness.

Who if anything burned the brighter unmasked.

"You told me never to touch you." His voice was thick.

"That was before." She stared up at him gravely.

She saw the softening of his mouth, the stillness of his eyes, and she was awed. His expression was intent, profoundly serious. She had seen such expressions on other men's faces, this same look, which she had thought made them all alike.

"Have a care," he warned.

She wasn't afraid, however. Awed, yes, but captivated as she studied him. She drew a breath, half glad, half shy, and plunged into the center of it: she reached up a tentative hand and touched his lips, and the hollow of his temple, wanting to know this appetite that enveloped him.

He cautiously took her into his arms, and held her loosely, until she put both her arms around his neck. His touch made her welts itch, but she ignored that as her fingers found the surprising softness of his hair. His hold tightened; he let himself settle slowly over her— and she felt herself go supple and quick as water beneath his weight. One hand was at her breasts, rolling the buds under her nightshirt and plucking them softly. The calluses on his fingers snagged the material of her shirt. "My hands are rough as old stones," he said. Then he asked, "Are you very sure, Jane?"

"Yes." She couldn't make her voice louder than a whisper. She felt such a sudden wondrous softening, his big hands were moving with utterly unexpected competence. With no experience to compare, she noted no clumsiness that might reveal a lack of familiarity

160

with what he was doing. His cold eyes had warmed almost to tenderness.

He pulled up her shirt and parted her knees with his leg and with his fingers opened her. With abrupt violence she pulled away.

Or would have, for his left arm was still under her back and held her to him. His eyes had gone dark, the color of rain at night, and his chin was set hard, and she knew that for now she was overcome by him. Would her strength endure? Could her body contain him?

She seemed to hear her mother speaking, a remembrance of words. "It's not a terrible thing. There is pain at the outset, and some blood, a little fright— nothing bad enough to warrant weeping over."

His lips touched her face, the barest touch, tracing the line of her jaw. His fingers between her legs delved. She gasped.

But a moment later she was losing her misgivings, warming and easing under his touch.

"Are you a maiden?"

"Yes."

"Then I'm sorry for not taking more time with you, but my business is of the kind that will not abide." He had a complete look of regret and contrition in his eyes, but the highwayman in him mounted her.

This was very far from what she expected. His patience in waiting for her to heal had prepared her for more patience. But it seemed he had none left.

He entered her. She was entered. "Stop! Stop!" But he did not stop. He appeared to be in a trance. He breathed in gasps. His weight and motion rocked the bed. The hurt . . .

There was hurt, but it passed quickly into a melting and a voluptuousness. And though she hadn't expected pleasure, there was pleasure. To be sure. So this was

161

what that ache in her had been about, that fire when she glanced at him or thought about him or was simply around him. She had no power to stop him—nor the wish to stop him now.

Within seconds he gushed his passion into her, and then they lay united, mixed and melded, pliant breasts beneath rigid chest, breath mingled. He kissed her, deeply, and within minutes he stood in her again and she fastened on him, and impulse drove them to mate again.

This time it was a sweetness long drawn out. There was a hint of hurt, faint enough to be ignored and soon overcome. She pressed tighter and tighter to him, her breasts crushed against his chest, her fingers spread out on his back, her knees pulling. Her upturned mouth instinctively found his—until she cried out, and heard him cry out.

When he released her, she took stock of her new body, which felt unlocked and handled and used—and knowing.

"Did I rob you, Jane? Is that how you're feeling now?"

She'd never in her dreams considered he might be unsure in this. He was a man accustomed to plunder. She said, setting it out in slow and cautious words, "It was the payment of a debt, not a robbery."

He fell back onto his pillow. "Ah, but I took something of yours, whereas I have lost nothing to you. You must not trust me too far. Villains can give you gentle looks and smile even as they cheat you raw."

She considered this. "You saved me from that man, Grubneck Nord, and you are giving me shelter. All I have to offer you in return is myself. When I go, I want to leave no debts behind."

Partly it was pride that made her speak so, pride that

hoped she wasn't really such a fool as she felt at the moment.

As if he knew exactly what she was thinking, he smiled a certain smile he had, a winsome, charming one. Was it a villain's smile? She found she didn't care anymore, much to her dismay.

Her nightshirt was bunched beneath her chin. Keith pulled it off her, and turned her onto her side away from him and gathered her hips into the cradle of his thighs. The lush curve of her fitted perfectly into his curvelessness. Her head came just to his chin. He arranged her hair, black and full and long, away from her plump breasts, leaving them naked and at his disposal. The tips knotted beneath his caressing fingers. He felt the wonder of how he and she were made, male and female, wrought flawlessly for one another. He felt the wonder of being alone with her in his own cottage, in his own bed. But what was it she'd just said?

"When you're gone? Where are you going, Jane?"

"To America, to Georgia Colony."

He smiled indulgently. "To America, where grapes grow on brambles and solid oaks drip honey."

"Yes," she said, half asleep, "and I'm going to live in a red-brick mansion."

He lay with his cheek against the top of her head. "My midnight rose."

"I'm not her, I'm not the person in that portrait."

"You are," he said.

She shook her head, dismissing the idea. "I'm me."

He felt an instant of panic as he realized she was still puzzlingly out of his grasp. Her body was solid in his hands, supple, his Rose of Midnight come to life—but so was all her elusiveness as well. "You're beautiful." He tried to describe her loveliness in caresses, but with-

163

out urgency, delicately, sleepily. He felt her fall asleep in his arms.

The fire burned lower and lower, becoming a hump of glowing embers. He found her hand, and set a kiss in the palm, and doubled her fingers over it. "Sleep well, Jane Fitzpatrick," the highwayman advised.

In the morning Keith was considerate, concerned that he might have injured her, disbelieving that she'd felt so little pain. She accepted his pampering with some surprise. Pampering gave way to fondling by noon, however, and by afternoon he carried her to the bed and loved her again.

His touch now had a new certainty. Now that he'd been allowed every intimacy she sensed a dash of the conqueror in him. She discovered that Keith Cutler, highwayman, was no more immune to the universal male pride of possession than any other mortal man.

She discovered several unexpected things about him in the next week; for instance, the completely unanticipated playful side of him and how useless it was to clench the coverlet and protest when he felt that way. And she couldn't help but feel a thrill, tinged with danger, when of an afternoon he suddenly came walking through the broad shaft of sunshine that fell across the doorway, his mouth smiling but his eyes intent and purposeful.

She was always aware of him. Days and nights elapsed, All Hallows' Eve, when the wind ran wild and an eerie glee passed over the earth, and All Saints' Day, and finally All Souls' Day, the time for mollifying the dead. For a week they made a world of their own, small but complete.

But that week ended and a new one began. Tonight, Keith stood at the washbasin shaving. Jane watched him scrape away at his lathered cheeks. He was humming. He was going out on the road tonight, for the first time since Jane had taken him for her lover. She felt an urgent need to think of some way to keep him from going. It was a completely foolish idea: he was a highwayman. She'd known that and had no right to try to change him. Yet she couldn't forget that bullet hole through the cape collar of his greatcoat. The thought hollowed her.

She moved behind him and put her arms around him. He made a sound. Whereas he was always surprising her with a kiss or an embrace, she seldom did such things. Once she had his attention, she said, "Since you'll be gone, I suppose I might as well go to bed early." Her hands reaching from around his back stroked up his bare chest, down his thighs. She nuzzled her cheek between his shoulder blades. The scent of him spun along her nerves.

He rinsed his razor. "Are you trying to seduce me, Jane Fitzpatrick?" He turned.

With a slight, neat turn of her back she deflected his reaching hand. "Of course not. You have somewhere to go."

"Um-hm." He leaned against the wall and folded his arms, at ease, half smiling.

She wandered toward the fire and began to pull at the laces of her bodice. He went back to his shaving, but she knew he watched her in his looking glass. Down to her chemise, she unplaited her hair. She combed it with her fingers so that it fell in a mass of waves. He seemed to have a special fondness for her hair. At last she pulled her chemise over her head, then pretended not to be able to find the shirt she slept in.

He was finished shaving by now (and had nicked himself, she noted from the corner of her eye). He rinsed his face and turned to watch her, dabbing at the

165

nick under his jaw with his towel. She found her night-shirt. He began to close the distance separating them. He did it with excruciating slowness, a hunter closing in on his prey. The cottage was not so large that it took him more than a few steps, but she had time to get the shirt over her head and to step back again from his reaching hands.

He saw the nature of her game, and smiled like a cat. His eyes glittered. "Come here, wench."

She knew what she was doing. She knew that he knew what she was doing. She barely blushed. "Why?" she asked, and blinked at him. "Won't you be late for your appointment? You'd best not tarry." He stepped toward her. She casually moved around the table, pretending to yawn. "I'm so tired."

He caught her from behind, and ran his hands under her arms to capture her breasts. He mumbled from deep in his chest, "I'll tuck you into bed."

His hands were kneading her deliciously. She leaned her head back against his shoulder. "I don't want to keep you. I can manage alone. Keith"—she got away from him—"I really think you'd better go. We can do this later, when you get back."

"You'll be sleepy and cross then. I'd rather have you now, when you're beautiful and fresh and will-ing." He caught her again and drew her against him so tightly that she could feel every detail of his cloth-ing—and his desire. She saw the stark hunger in his eyes. His hands were busy bunching up her nightshirt so that he could take if off her.

"No," she said, reaching to catch his wrists. "Keith, if you get started, you know how you like to go on and on."

"Mmm, yes, I know."

"Better not then." She tried to step out of his hold.

Impossible. He lifted her against him and turned toward the bed.

"Oh, Keith." She managed to sound disappointed.

He had the shirt off her soon enough, and had her on her back with her hands on his shoulders while he lay over her and talked—to her breasts!

"Now, look here, my choice pair, I have entertained thoughts of you through the long day—"

She laughed softly; he was a mad man.

"Excuse me," he said to her breasts. He looked up into her laughing face. "You're interrupting, you know. When you laugh, you make them bob like men in a boat. You really must be more considerate, Jane."

"Sometimes you talk just like my old master."

He raised his eyebrows. A shrewd look of calculation crossed his face. "Ah yes, the Honorable Mr. Welby, who took your welfare and your schooling so dearly to heart. A wonder you were still a maiden when I reined you in—but then didn't you say he was as old as God's voice in Eden?"

He returned to his conversation with her breasts. "She has glorious, great blue eyes, but she does interrupt—not to mention her penchant for tempting me into foolish things. Now, as I was saying, my thoughts over the long day—"

"Was it such a long day, Keith?" In fact, he'd wakened her to the sparkling morning with his lovemaking; and this afternoon when she'd gone to the river for water, he'd thrown down his ax and followed her and loved her there on a shorelike patch of bank, surrounded by fallen leaves and mushrooms and lovely late flowers. He'd likened her breasts to the dappled clouds, and their puckered tips to the fine-pleated undersides of the mushroom caps. He could wax exceedingly poetic. A pang shot through her as she remembered how, over his moving shoulders, she'd looked up with half-closed eyes at the curving shell of the sky.

The firelight played on his face now as he lowered his ear toward her left breast. "What was that you said? You'd like a kiss? Well . . ."

A week, and clearly his interest in her was undiminished. He was still avid to the feel of her breasts, her thighs, her hips.

Her seduction was not entirely successful. Though it was a long while later, nonetheless, as he lay there beside her naked, his eyes closed and his head turned aside, he recalled his night mission. "It's time I got to work."

With a sinking heart, she lifted and kissed his ringed hand on the pillow. She touched the long splendid line from his navel to his throat, and toyed with that peculiarly soft hair in the pit of his arm. She wanted to tell him that he was beautiful, but she was no good at saying such things.

She murmured, soft and cool, "I thought you'd already done your night's work."

Smiling, he said, "I know what you thought—that I'd love you and then be set upon by sleep and forget my rendezvous. But tonight's work promises to be too lucrative to let it pass."

"Do you need the money so badly? You seem to have quite enough in that treasure chest of yours."

He took her face between his hands. "It's no use trying to reform me, Jane. I am what I am—and damned good at it, too." He smiled with naked male conceit.

"No one is so good he doesn't get caught eventually. And besides, it's wrong."

"Give over." He swung his feet to the floor and stretched his shoulders. "In this world, the grand thief condemns the little pickpocket—but all men love to steal the belongings of others. It's a universal desire. Only the manner of each man's doing it varies."

"You're intelligent—you could live elsewise."

"How?" he asked with a placid smile. "Chopping wood?"

She hesitated, then said, "You could go to America, start over again."

He stiffened. "Yes, there's always Georgia Colony, isn't there? And who knows, I may end up there eventually. They ship convicts out on a regular schedule, you know. That's assuming they don't prefer to hang me and be done with it, of course."

"Knaves think they can do nothing without knavery."

"That's right, it's the outright narrative of my life. I won't be mocked or oppressed or wronged—not again—which is what happens to those who are less villainous than the rest of us. Look at yourself. It's high-time you learned what I already know—the virtue of necessity. Life is loaded against those of us who aren't fortunate enough to live in the comfortable world of the moralists."

A frosty silence hung in the air. Then she asked, "What happened to you, Keith? What turned you into such a criminal?"

He shook his head. "Open confession is not necessarily good for the soul. It's just as well if we don't delve into my history or rifle through my secrets. Besides, I have no time just now."

It was no use arguing with him. He rose and dressed. Seeing the beauty of his heavy, gleaming arms and throat, admiration filled her. She watched him put his black linen shirt on. He put on his belt, settled his sword on his hip, shrugged into his wide-sleeved coat. He brought out his pistols and took them from their cases. He set out his powder horn and shot flask, and picked up one of the double-barreled guns. He slipped the rammers from out of the chased stocks.

As he dropped into a chair, he drew back the twin

hammers and opened the primers. He rammed home the charges, wad, shot, and wad again, primed the pans and shut the primers, and finally slid the flints forward a little before screwing them into place.

He went through the same process with the second pistol, then slid the weapons back into their leather cases. At last he rose and reached for his greatcoat and tricorn.

Jane's heart spasmed. "Don't go, Keith." She rose up onto her knees, naked save for her hair. It rippled against her cheeks and arms. He turned back to her, his eyes hidden in the shadow beneath the brim of his hat.

God, she was beautiful, his own fair rose of the midnight. He'd robbed her again, taking the thing she'd offered knowing all along he was not going to give back what she wanted in return. He was apologetic. "I won't be long, a few hours."

"Don't go!" Fear was in her cry. Her eyes were rounded in fright.

"You said you weren't afraid to be left alone."

"I'm afraid for you!"

He didn't know what to say. "You needn't fret yourself over me. You wait here, and you'll see, I'll be back." He tried an open, frank smile. "I always come back."

"Oh yes, how dare I imply that you're not invulnerable! How dare I notice that new hole in the collar of your coat!"

He saw a glitter in her eyes. Tears? He thought, but didn't give voice to, a short, blistering obscenity having to do with fools and women's tears. Then he went to her, tossing his tricorn and pistols on the table. "Maid, you are not even modest. You know too well what you look like."

"I can hardly help it."

And he could hardly ignore it. At the side of her cheeks, the delicate down was like gold dust in the firelight. He smoothed the frown from her brow with a finger, and followed it with kisses, along the taut lines of her face, under her chin, to the sweep of her throat and shoulder, to the round fullness of her breasts.

Her heart beat light and fast beneath her warm, soft woman-flesh. He had come to know what it meant that she let him touch her like this. He knew her pride and her sense of privacy, and he was grateful. He lifted his head and kissed her mouth, hard, passionately. One hand moved to the round of her belly, to her navel which a better poet than he would fill with a jewel. Her hips flared wide and deep between his palms. Her buttocks filled his hands. He went to his knees as his mouth descended to her secrets, making himself dizzy with the scent of them. He urged her to part her thighs. His kisses made her moan.

Again he lifted his head, this time to kiss the tip of each breast lightly. "I'll finish this when I return. The waiting will make it sweeter."

"No—"

"There's gold to be had on the road tonight," he murmured, trying to make her understand. "And once it's mine, what better use could it be put to than to indulge my poppet?" He kissed her quickly and chastely on the forehead. "You'll have a new dress."

"Make it black, to wear to your hanging." She was obdurate and angry now. She was not mere soft skin and embering pleasure.

He let her go and took up his hat and weapons and went back to the door. He said nothing more, made no more promises, for it was easier to drop words than it was to pick them up again. Yet he looked at her with affection before he went out. She looked back with her eyes wide and blazing dry. Her hair was tumbled over her arms; one breast hid in the thick of it, the other peered coquettishly out: white, pink, beautiful, maddening. He went out the door.

In the stable he saddled his horse with practiced speed and led Eclipse into the yard. He was surprised to find Jane on the lintel with nothing but her scarlet cloak and the light from the open door thrown about her. She stood quietly by as he swung up into his saddle. He urged Eclipse close to the door and reached down from his saddle to finger a lock of her magnificent hair. He wanted her to smile, even if it was just the merest curving of her full mouth and no more than a polite exoneration. "Are you certain you want black? Blue would go better with your eyes."

She didn't respond. He saw the care beneath the anger in her face. He was surprised at the force of his reaction. If she took hold of his hand . . . could he leave?

To be safe, he pulled his hand out of her reach. "Think on it, maid, and I'll be back for your decision." He pulled Eclipse's head about and nudged the animal's underbelly with his spurs. The stallion snorted in anticipation. They swung away into the bramble thicket.

Once free of the path through the thorns, the powerful horse galloped easily, the long hair of its mane flying backward in the night, taking the highwayman toward his unrevealed destination.

Chapter Twelve

> He did not come in the dawning;
> He did not come at noon . . .
> Alfred Noyes: *The Highwayman*

Keith stopped to let Eclipse drink at a place where a beck widened into a mere beneath an ancient willow tree. The willow's great bole stood pewter in the night. His thoughts were all with Jane, her white skin as smooth and sumptuous as Devon cream, her dark hair, her delicate bamboo fingers moving like a lover's fingers on his body, warm, soft, the scent of her, like a musk rose, a scent that could make him feel as greedy as a fire.

Her smile—he'd supposed that smile was a painted invention, yet now he'd seen it with his own eyes. Hers was a beauty that cut like a sword. Oh, indeed, a sword, directly to the heart.

Sometimes he wondered how he'd won this good fortune, this prize. He took each coin of it out, a miser counting his treasure, and caressed it with his mind, examining each memory and basking in it. When he thought about her as she'd been when he'd first stalked her, mad with pain and dazed with fear, just keeping her feet on the thin edge of life, and vulnerable to every brigand on the road—when he thought of that, then it was as well that Rip Fitzpatrick was dead or Keith knew he would have to kill him.

And he could, too. He could do that.

The slow-moving water Eclipse drank from carried a carpet of pale serrated leaves. Keith looked up. The November moon was late rising. Though it was midnight, the lush field of the autumn sky was lit by naught but a million icy points of stars, each a crystallization of pure night.

Jane . . . thoughts of her kept coming back to him, along with a strange unformed longing. He smiled foolishly, he patted Eclipse's shoulder, he was like a man in his cups.

He understood perfectly that she was not so enthralled with him as he was with her. Not that he was in love with her or anything so dire as that. They said that everyone was doomed to fall in love at least once in his life; but Keith was just taking a good look into that abyss, he hadn't fallen over the edge. He felt that such a glance was good for him.

True love was like the noble ideas that Jane's master, the Honorable Mr. Welby, had filled her full of, foolish ideas—like that one about going to America. She didn't understand—a woman wouldn't—that the Crown only wanted the youngest of the thirteen colonies as a shield to protect the far more precious territories of North and South Carolina from the Spanish in Florida. Keith had heard something about a war, the War of Jenkin's Ear, all having to do with Georgia and the Spanish. There were pirates. And red Indians. And transported criminals, men like himself, or worse.

She thought she could sail off to a new land and, with Welby's notions about honesty and earnestness being their own reward, make a life shaped to her own will. Keith knew how a young mind could be influenced by such concepts. In his own youth, when he was supposed to be preparing for one of the gentlemanly professions, he'd been fed quite a lot of learning and philosophy—and too late found that a man must own a certain kind of life in order to use them.

Since then he'd learned a different set of rules. He could still hear old Georgie Moraga mumbling in the way he had of speaking, as if his mouth were full: "The biggest rule of all is that they what has the strength takes what they want." Keith had taken that as his motto, and he had forged a place for himself in this avaricious world.

What other choice did he have? Nothing else of any likelihood had ever suggested itself.

He swung himself easily onto Eclipse and gave the horse just a touch of his spurs. He needed to settle his mind on his business. He couldn't let anyone, not even Jane, distract him from the tight moments ahead. Jane was unhappy with him, but she would forgive him. He would find the door unlocked, the fire banked—and her tender heart lying in wait for him when he returned.

God's blood, it was time to stop swimming off on these thoughts of Jane Fitzpatrick.

It was time to let out the pent-up force of the true nature of Keith Cutler.

His nature was to practice the art, the sport, and the cunning pleasure of highway robbery. Why else would it feel so sweet, this tang of hazard, this bright edge of fright? He didn't think he could define, even to Jane, the excitement and the terror of his profession.

He rode toward that edge of hazard, and he was proud of his lack of fear.

* * *

In the dark November midnight, lit by naught but the faint glimmer of stars, the highwayman arrived at his destination. He was outside the city of Derby, in a place known thereabout as Kate's Thicket, a copse that stretched on either side of a beck spanned by an ancient, humped stone bridge. He was late in placing himself and had not more than a moment in which to roll down the tops of his jackboots so his knees could grip and firmly guide his horse without needing his hands. He lifted his neck scarf over the lower half of his face. Almost before he was ready, the magnificently appointed carriage and four of the Duke of Genthner came rocking along the road.

The vehicle's two lanterns swung fitfully, hopeful glimmers against the immensity of the dark night. The driver began to whip up the horses to take the humped stone bridge. That was why the highwayman had chosen this spot. There was the disadvantage of the driver speeding up, but he would have his attention on the bridge and would not be thinking of robbery. Such small details came into a road agent's calculations.

The lantern-lit carriage came on. Within a few heartbeats, the highwayman absorbed the sense of the great impending risk he was about to take, and he drew both a pistol and his side-arm sword. Fear tingled in his hands and thighs, his blood gleamed and fizzed in his head.

Perhaps the armed escort sitting high on the driver's box with the fat coachman was heavy with drink—or perhaps he was just a boy who had fallen asleep—but certainly neither he nor the horseman who followed the carriage seemed prepared to offer any resistance when out of the trees that lined the highroad cantered an iron-nerved horseman, masked and cloaked and with his weapons drawn.

The highwayman drove his horse to the very center

176

of the road, blocking access to the bridge. The coach-man threw all his considerable weight into applying the brake and dragging his team back from the run he'd just whipped them to—no easy task, since the duke kept four great ramping beasts with immense manes and tails for his carriage.

"Colonel! Whoa! Whoa, Peacock!"

Lurching and swaying, the vehicle slowed. The highwayman's stallion backed up to keep from being run down by the carriage team, but then the vehicle came to a stop. The highwayman's keen eyes detected the lowering of the passenger window by its leather strap. "What is it—what is it, Samuel!" called a querulous voice, clearly a product of the English upper classes. The highwayman glimpsed a man rubbing the sleep from his eyes. The driver, having applied the brake, said nothing. The mounted rearguard lifted his pistol. The highwayman turned his weapon on him in an instant; the gun produced a shower of sparks as one of the two barrels fired. The man ducked and his horse danced.

"Let no man move or speak if he loves life!"

The coach lanterns made an island of light in the darkness. The highwayman spurred his stallion onto the grass verge beside the carriage horses and with a single slash of his sword cut the traces. Sliding the blade back into its scabbard, he produced his second pistol. He bade the fat coachman, "Throw the reins over the backs of your steeds!" which the man accomplished without ado.

Seeing how matters were going, the mounted rearguard turned and fled. The highwayman was satisfied with this, but the passenger bellowed at him and started out of the carriage. The highwayman swung both pistols toward him. He quickly sat back in his seat, and banged his door closed. "My lord," said the highwayman.

As he nudged his horse toward the closed carriage door, the young guard on the driver's seat produced from beneath his cloak a heavy sword. He stood atop the carriage, the weapon swung back for a blow. He stopped in that attitude as the barrel of the highwayman's nearest pistol lifted toward him.

"Drop it," said the highwayman.

The lad held the weapon poised.

"Boy, are you mad? Think what you're risking. Surely your master can't be that exceedingly comfortable to live with that you're willing to die for him."

The boy hesitated.

In a quieter voice: "Lad, don't make me kill you, for I will, I swear it. I have no conscience to speak of."

With a dart of his eyes, the boy looked to the coachman. The portly fellow gave him a barely perceptible nod. The boy threw the sword into the roadway and settled down to watch what followed with a white face. The highwayman felt an immense potency descend on him, wrapping him like a coat of armor.

Now the passenger thrust out the open carriage window a rigid arm supporting a well-weighted purse. "Take it and be gone! And may you not long avoid the rope you've set your heart on!"

The highwayman took his road toll. "Your jewels, too—haste, my lord," he said crisply, laying the barrels of a pistol on the window's very ledge.

With a guttural groan, three rings, a diamond hat clasp, and a gold chain came out. "Things go ill indeed in this land when such as you can rob honest people. I'll cheer when you're at the gallows wearing your hemp collar."

As the highwayman thrust his booty away beneath his greatcoat, the robbed man, stirred by emotions deep

178

and angry, thrust his wig-framed face out the carriage—though it put his chest against the thief's pistol point. The carriage lanterns made his expression harsh. "You have what you want! Now away with you, you ill-bred scoundrel!"

The highwayman managed to hide his elation. He managed to seem indifferent as he considered the steaming splendor of the four horses and glittering carriage. "I believe I've heard enough of the coarse side of your tongue, my lord," he said, softly, softly, and all the more dangerous did he sound for his mildness. "Get out."

Up in indignation to his eyes, the duke nevertheless did as he was told. He wore a blue coat and waistcoat, and white short-bodied breeches, his wig was covered in white powder, showing him to be, indeed, a full citizen of the Age of Elegance. Yet his stateliness was beholden more to the tailor, the lace maker, the periwig maker, and the hatter than to nature. Beneath the opulence, he was a man with a fat round face and brisk little eyes like two flickering candle flames. He bared a gleam of teeth and looked up to curse his young guard for being such a cowardly fellow (of course believing himself a man of great pride and ferociousness). The highwayman bade the coachman, "Samuel, my friend, get down and retie your traces."

It took several minutes for the fat coachman to do as he was told. "Get on with it, man!" The highwayman's manner was meant to convey that he was becoming dangerously bored with this whole transaction. His horse mouthed its metal bit and stamped restlessly. Samuel's pace sharpened in a frenzy of obedience. He issued a stream of vile workmanlike cursing as he struggled at his task, but at last he was done.

He was so corpulent of build that the boy had to get

down and help hoist him back onto the box. The high-wayman said, "Get along on your way now."

"What, and leave him?" Samuel looked at his master.

"The walk should do him good," said the steely voice.

The two servants could barely suppress their smirks at the prospect of their master's humiliation. The coachman cracked his whip sharply over his team's backs and they were off, up and over the ancient bridge.

The duke and the highwayman remained alone in the road. The place seemed suddenly dark and desolate again.

The highwayman felt invulnerable. "It would seem, my lord, that for all your esteemed qualities"—a caustic measure crept in—"your servants don't much love you. Do you have a family? I wonder if even they feel much affection for you. Upon my short acquaintance with you, I perceive you to be a rattle and a scold."

"You filthy vermin, you think you're quite the dandy. We'll see how game you are when I set a reward of five hundred pounds on your head. I'll see you hang—and I'll dine out on the story many a time in the years to come."

The highwayman watched the nobleman's eyes—eyes flecked yellow like the predatory cats from Africa in London's menagerie. The sense of invincibility grew. Impulsively, he lowered his mask to grin, openly, warmly. "So you can recognize me when my hanging day comes."

Standing in his stirrups, he was satisfied to see the carriage and its lanterns disappear beyond the thicket. He looked up at the starry black sky. "The moon should be rising soon." He looked back at the duke. A crafty expression had come into the man's eyes. The highwayman wasn't certain what it meant. He said, "You'll find the road a pleasant place for a stroll. Be careful, though, I pray you; there are rogues about."

He backed his horse and sketched a bow. "Till we meet again." Laughing, he shook his reins and his stallion started off.

But as he entered the wood he discovered the reason for that crafty look in the Duke's flickering eyes. The mounted guard, hidden by the night, had doubled back through the gnarled and ancient trunks of the trees where, too late, the highwayman discovered the man was a crack shot. He heard the report of the gun behind him an instant before he felt the blow. It struck like a bolt of lightning into his back. "Unhh!" His spine arched and he saw the winking arrows of the sun in his eyes. But no, there was no sun, only the newly risen crescent moon, curved to cup the sky—all this in the instant before he fell forward again, nearly toppling over Eclipse's head.

The stallion started into a gallop, carrying its rider deeper into the blackness of the night.

Keith's head cleared. He was no longer in Kate's Thicket. Eclipse was galloping wildly up a grassy slope into one of those deserted hamlets with which England abounded. The horse's hooves pounded the coarse turf, throwing up fragments of dark soil behind them. It took every bit of strength Keith owned to get the horse under control. As far as he could hear, he was not being followed. He realized he was a long way from home. Eclipse's hooves slowed to move almost soundlessly between the crumbling, roofless buildings, gray as corpses.

Once people had lived here, had built these homes of the old mixture of clay and gravel and straw and horsehair, called cob; they'd rendered and white-washed them; they'd fashioned roofs of thatch. All that was left now were the walls, several feet thick. The place was gloomy and forbidding, with the look and feeling of what secretly haunted Keith Cutler: disavowal, renunciation, abandonment.

Using his teeth to pull his gauntlet off his right hand, he felt inside his greatcoat. His knuckles bumped against the lump of coins and jewels taken from the duke. Was it enough? The nagging fear was always present that when he reached the end of his forty guineas there would be no possible means to raise another penny.

No . . . that fear was out of the past. He must be delirious. He had money now, a chest full of money and jewels, all the money he needed. He laid his hand over his shirt. Blood welled between his fingers and dripped.

His mouth was dry. He could use a glass of pale derby right now. And he must get a blue dress for Jane, made of worsted stuff to keep her warm in the coming cold.

Poor Jane, without a protector in the world. Alone in the night. The urge to defend and take care of her suffused him like a flush. She thought she wanted to go to Georgia. He dismissed the notion out of hand. The climate was unhealthy. The attacks from the Spanish were unhealthy. Georgia was no place for her. Better for her to lie in his arms all the night long. Better by far for her to die of ecstasy than at the hands of red Indians.

His thoughts died away. He was barely conscious of being atop his horse, of moving through the night. What time was it? He looked about him. When had the sky clouded over? Why . . . it was raining. Eclipse had wandered up onto a moor top and Keith was actually riding through the rainclouds. He was totally enclosed by a barrier of mist that muffled all sound. He clung to his seat as the blood still flowed from his wound.

He became all but unaware; even the hole in him was forgotten. Eclipse stumbled on a rock. The horse recovered but Keith lost his seat. He fell hard and lay still, without the strength to rise. His eyes closed reluctantly.

For a moment he considered prayer, but he'd always been indifferent to religion. His mother had been attracted by the Methodists' enthusiasm, their vain belief in private revelation, but Keith had always known too well that God was nothing but what men made Him.

And to some God was a bullet, and to some He was a length of hemp.

The black stallion, freed of his burden, was nonetheless held by the weight of his saddle to his rider's wishes. As he grew cold, he nosed gently at the man lying on the wet heath. The man groaned. The horse raised his head and whickered softly.

Keith thought he heard a voice speaking so faintly he could just discern the words: *Keith, wake up now.*

His mother's voice? With quickening pulse, he thought he saw her chopping walnuts in her round wooden bowl, the one with the crescent-shaped blade. The ruched gauze trimming at the elbows of her sleeves danced with her labor.

Keith, life is too rich.

"What?" he answered drowsily from the furthest borders of slumber and the nearest borders of death. He opened his eyes, blurred more with confusion than pain now. Where was he? His fingers felt the drenched leaves of nettle, dock, thistle. "Eclipse . . ." He sensed the big horse standing over him. "Here . . . here, boy."

He had to fight to rise up onto his elbow. His left side hurt. He caught the horse's reins with his right hand and cautiously got to his feet. Standing, he swayed to and fro gently like seaweed in the surge of the tide. He drew the beast closer, feeling the muscles rise in his arms. He lay his cheek against the damp saddle for a moment before he lifted his boot into the stirrup.

Jane didn't fall asleep until near dawn. She woke with a start to discover it was late morning. The noise that had wakened her? Eclipse returning, walking more slowly and idly than usual. The sound of his hooves stopped in the dooryard, scuffled a bit, stopped again. And still no sound of Keith dismounting. She rose from the bed. The dull glow of the banked fire was lost in the light filtering through the covered windows. The cottage was cold. She stirred up the fire, expecting Keith to come in any moment. When he didn't a sudden fear weighted her. What if it hadn't been Eclipse she'd heard at all, but some other horse, bringing some other rider?

She padded barefoot to the door and opened it an inch. The fear fell off her. Clouds obscured the sky above the trees, but in the gray morning light she saw Eclipse reflected in the puddled yard—and that shape leaning forward in the saddle as if he were whispering to the horse, murmuring into its twitching ears, was Keith. He'd lost his hat; his hair was dark and gleaming with the night's rain. And he was drunk.

He slid out of the saddle and hung onto the horse in a way that said he was very drunk indeed. Jane considered all her sleepless hours. She felt like closing the door and turning her back on him. Let him take care of himself. And if he fell on the wet ground, so be it.

Let him spend the day there. If he chose to cleanse his spirit with this or that arrant behavior, let him suffer the consequences. He was a brigand. She couldn't deny what was true. She couldn't alter what he was.

He turned toward her, seemingly prepared to leave Eclipse saddled and standing in the open—which he'd never done before. He could walk, but he stumbled a lot. About halfway to the door, he said, "Jane." His eyes shone huge in the cloudy light. "It's my side," he said in a weak, small voice that made her heart give a mighty throb.

Hurt!

"Keith!" In an electric instant all her anxiety and anger dissolved into fear and passion and tenderness. Her brain was shot with a thousand wild embers, each a thought that flew to nowhere. Her mind held nothing that was not him. Barefoot, in naught but her nightshirt, she ran to him. She caught him just before he toppled. She got her shoulder under him, made a crutch of herself, and he leaned against her. He was heavy, deathly heavy, shambling and unseeing; his weight staggered her. She felt panicky. She willed herself erect and put her arms around his middle. Her hands went around his waist, under his greatcoat—and came out bloody.

He let her guide him into the cottage, moving where she led in a sliding, dragging way, without lifting his feet. All the front of his black shirt was slicked by blood. It had oozed down to stain his breeches and disappeared into the tops of his jackboots.

She sat him on the side of the bed. "I have to get your clothes off."

"Never mind . . . too tired." He started to fall sideways toward his pillow.

She pulled him upright again. "Keith, you have to help me."

185

"Thirsty," he said.

"I'll give you a drink if you promise not to lie down." It was the same tone she'd used to bargain over an oxtail for Mrs. Galbraith on market day, a calm, firm tone that belied the banging of her heart in her chest.

She gave him water. A swallow was all he could manage. She started to get his clothes off him. He couldn't help much. His dark eyes were almost uncomprehending. It was all he could do to remain conscious. His limbs, without life, were incredibly heavy. "Help me, Keith—oh my God." The blood, he was covered with blood.

He seemed not to hear her. ". . . stuck on a counting-house stool everyday for the rest of my life . . ."

If she prayed, she wasn't aware of it, there were no words in it. By persistence she got his greatcoat and coat and his long black boots and spurs and breeches off him. He cried out as she tried to work his bloodied shirt over his shoulders. In the end, she took a knife to the fine black linen.

His shoulders and arms were heavy, muscled, strong, the black hair on his chest glistened. But there was a chilling hole in the left side of his back, and another, even more hideous, where the ball had torn through in the front. She felt like someone staring at a place where something dear to her had stood after a cannonball had fallen on it. She must bind these wounds, and wipe away the blood.

She went at her task with the concentration of a surgeon. She cut a nightshirt into bandages, which she wrapped tightly about his middle.

"I'm cold." His voice was timid and empty, a boy's voice. His brows contracted in a hurt, puzzled way. "Cold to my bones."

The Keith she knew had a ruthless edge; this was

186

someone she didn't know, someone naive, unsure. As she worked frantically, he sat staring ahead with a resigned look, as if he were going to be hung as soon as she finished.

"Get under the bedclothes now. You'll feel warmer soon." She helped him lie down, felt his body give up, felt the tiredness of his muscles and sinews win over whatever will had kept him upright.

She covered him, and pulled a chair close, and fretfully stroked his hand. Presently he gripped her fingers. With the bedclothes hiding his bandages, he seemed sleepy-eyed and startlingly attractive, a handsome young giant. Somehow he even managed to produce a smile, that boyish and winsome smile that always transformed his face, the one that always dried the lining of her mouth. "Thank you, Jane," he said with timid gratitude. "It's not a mortal wound, I'm sure. I'll just rest awhile and it will heal. You'll see. Soon you'll be lying in my arms again." His voice died off.

"The ball went clean through," she said, reassuring herself as well as him.

He didn't answer.

"You just rest. Go to sleep."

He obeyed her. In a moment his face was slack. His breathing was shallow, a sort of panting; otherwise he lay motionless.

She couldn't just sit and watch him. She stood, full of purpose. She slipped on her shoes and cloak and went out where the light of the day had hardly strengthened. She tugged at the reins of his intimidating black stallion and put him to bed. The horse, like his master, was too weary to give her much trouble. She lifted down the saddle from his back, staggered under the load, and struggled to heave it onto the oaken peg where Keith kept it. She picked up a hank of straw and wiped the rain and mire and watery blood from the leather.

When she came back inside, she brought Keith's pistols.

Next she washed out the remains of his black shirt, which would come in handy for more bandages. He didn't wake when she gently cleaned the bloodstains and mud from his face and throat.

Eventually came a time when she'd done all she could. He lay still, his eyes closed, breathing shallowly. His breath was perhaps a trifle slower and quieter now. There was nothing left to do but sit with her hand on his.

He had never looked so mortal, her highwayman. Once or twice she stroked his soft, springy hair back from his forehead. She kept watch beside him all through the remainder of the day, only stirring when the fire needed rekindling. The hours crawled by like years. Stark with fear for him, she kept touching him, to be assured that he lived. Only once did she weep aloud: "I don't know what to do! What should I do?"

Chapter Thirteen

> He repents in thorns,
> that sleeps in beds of roses.
>
> Frances Quarles: *Emblems*

If only Keith's side didn't hurt. His arms and legs weighted by fatigue—he could bear that; if only the sword wouldn't drive into his side, a bit deeper now . . . and again . . . and again, he might be able to console Jane. He heard her weeping for him, and he didn't have the strength to hold her, to comfort her.

You. You are my completion. You, the rose of my midnight, beyond all expectation, you make me want to live. He hadn't cared much about living for a long time, but now he knew that he would feel a great regret at never seeing her again. He said, or meant to say, *You are warmth.* He meant to tell her many things, but the sword drove into him deeper again. *You are sunlight.* Why had he left it to so late to say these things to her? She couldn't hear him now; he couldn't speak aloud because of the sword beneath his ribs. He couldn't move. The pain was so intense he sometimes had to clench.

He knew she was there, though. He lost track of the

time. The world became narrowed to her hand on his, and he was consoled when she stroked his hair.

The wind sat north. Keith slept. Slept without moving—without breathing, it seemed. Jane reached over in the dark cottage yet again to feel for the warmth of his breath on her palm.

Yes, he still breathed. And the bleeding had not begun again. He was sleeping, and with rest and good fortune, he would live.

It was perhaps four in the morning when he half awoke. His side hurt. His tongue was dry and swollen behind his teeth. It seemed he'd been thirsty for hours. But he was not awake enough to give voice to this need. Someone at hand to help him. His mother? No; a small round eye opened and closed in his memory, disclosing a scene, with terrific clarity, all reconstructed in a flash, complete with even the kind of shadows on the fallen leaves and the kind of weather in the air. It was the day of his mother's burial outside London when he was nineteen years old.

He didn't want to remember that. He struggled against it and the immediate flare of feeling it brought. He wished he could open his tired eyelids and see the woman who was beside him. Like his mother, she was a woman who didn't smile a lot, but she could make him forget.

Keith Cutler, born Keith Solomon, was the son of Laurel Solomon, a dark-haired, smooth-cheeked, very mannerly yeoman's daughter briefly desired by an officer of the Royal Navy, Lieutenant Thomas Grayson. The tall, rugged, fair-haired lieutenant seduced her. For her favors, he presented her with an opal set in a silver ring, which she mistakenly took for an engagement token. Sixteen, she had no understanding that gentlemen of his sort regarded women of her sort as legitimate prey. She had the usual girlish visions of love overcoming the social barriers.

As could have been foreseen, the handsome officer quickly got over her and was annoyed when she tenderly announced to him that most common of all commonplaces: that she was expecting their child. The only thing he could do, of course, was disclaim any connection with her. He did this with such ease that she was stunned. Indeed, it was several months before she realized how completely he had abandoned her.

The lieutenant's older brother, Francis, secretly took pity on the ruined girl. The two Grayson brothers had little in common, no mutual pursuits or affections. Francis was the heir-apparent of the Grayson estate, located between Malvern and Worcester, in Derbyshire. He was a staunch Whig, which is to say he was Protestant, enterprising, for Parliament and against royal privilege, in favor of the new Hanoverian dynasty, and passionately opposed to all Papists. He owned a pleasing informality of manner, and thought his younger sibling rather dull-minded, perfectly suited for the military life he'd chosen.

"Fudge"—Francis still referred to Thomas by his baby nickname when speaking to his friends—"will steadily tug at his oar all his life without ever realizing how little advance he's making."

When Francis learned that Laurel was refusing to follow her family's wishes and give her baby to a child-taker, who would place the infant in a foster home, he admired her courage. Hence, he didn't bother to inform his younger brother when he settled enough money on the girl to allow her to go away to bear her child and rear it in a quiet, secluded place.

Shortly after jilting Laurel, Lieutenant Grayson became Captain Grayson. And only months after that, to his great shock, his military career was necessarily ended. Francis died of the smallpox and the Grayson estate fell to the young captain's care. Suddenly Captain Thomas Grayson—Fudge—was a wealthy squire, a landowner, a man with multiple responsibilities. As he shed his naval uniform, he realized suddenly that now he would need heirs, he would need a wife. Shortly after Keith's first birthday, when the rose garden of Grayson House was sweet and musky with summer flowers, Captain Thomas Grayson married.

Except that she was redheaded, his wife was nondescript, plain in looks and personality, small and gentle and rather mawkish, seemingly content to be her husband's wife and wanting very little more. She performed her marital duty admirably by bearing a daughter and then a son. Thomas was not in love with her, in fact he found her very easy to ignore. Nature never intended him to be much good as a husband, especially to a quiet wife. He thought that as long as a woman was silent, nothing ailed her, and she wanted nothing. Since Mistress Grayson did not complain of loneliness, loneliness must please her. Since she expressed no bias for this or dislike of that, she must have no biases or dislikes.

After her second lying-in, however, she faded. Thomas hardly knew why. He made no pretense of understanding women, they were different, an inferior order of existence; a woman could not be a friend, much less a confidant. When his wife one day, abruptly—for he had scarcely noticed her decline—took her leave of him and of life together, she left hardly even a memory of her face or being in his mind.

His daughter Stella, so much like her mother, he naturally did not educate beyond the talents of the governess she shared with the daughter of the local vicar. Otherwise, he had masters to Grayson House to teach her dancing and French, writing and music. He believed wholeheartedly in Jean Jacques Rousseau's philosophy: "The education of women should always be relative to that of men. To please, to be useful to us, to make us love and esteem them, to educate us when young, to take care of us when grown up; to advise, to console us, to render our lives easy and agreeable. These are the duties of women at all times, and what they should be taught in their infancy."

His son Burne, however, had all the advantages for learning that could be imagined. First there was a tutor (a descendant of the French refugees of the 1680's), then, in the course of time, the boy was enrolled in Hillsburrow Grammar School, which had been attended by Grayson boys for three generations. There young gentlemen of his class were boarded and taught Latin and Greek and the other subjects needed to prepare them to be sent on, at the age of twelve, to the great schools of Winchester and Eton.

At Hillsburrow, Burne discovered and began to idolize an engaging fellow of very promising qualities: Keith Solomon, three years his senior.

Laurel had been careful with the money settled on her. If she was very thrifty, she'd reasoned, her son could attend a good school. He could pursue a career. She lived poorly in order to provide the background of a gentleman for him. It was not so much selflessness as it was a way of fighting against the sense of rejection which enveloped her. Spurned by everyone who had loved her, cast out, her spirit was broken in every respect but this one.

The child she had borne grew comely, keen, and strong. She saw his father in him at every turn—except that he had inherited her dark hair, of course. Her ambition for him grew when she learned of Thomas's ascension to master of Grayson House. Keith must become so eminent that one day his father would realize he'd made a mistake.

The mother Keith knew presented a still surface, like glass; she was capable of little more than reflection. Yet in the formative gristle of his youth she somehow fostered in him a hope of one day being reconciled and accepted by his father. He would live in Grayson House then, and for that he needed to be "ready." To this end he studied harder than any boy of his acquaintance; he made extraordinary efforts to succeed in everything he did.

At Hillsburrow, he never needed a whipping for wandering attention. He did everything well—sports, academics—and he was popular, too. He found learning easy, and seemed able to disentangle any skein of thought. He outdistanced other boys with so little trouble that he was marked out by his teachers as a boy of amazing intelligence. The world and his future looked bright and strong, like a full moon rising on a fair summer night.

When eight-year-old Burne Grayson began to follow him about, Keith managed to appear half irritated. In fact, he was very pleased. He took the younger boy under his wing, helped him with his assignments, helped him better his game on the cricket field. It wasn't long before it was noticed that though Keith was dark and Burne was fair (and possessed two natural dimples which, according to Thomas, were nothing but a weakness in the muscular structure of his face inherited from his mother), both were unusually tall, husky, handsome youths. They looked so much alike in fact that they began to be teased for being long-lost brothers. With the brash honesty of an adoring schoolboy, Burne told Keith, "I wish it were true!"

That was the day Keith told him that it was.

Once Burne digested the situation, he started planning. When Christmas arrived, he arranged with his father to bring home a "friend." "I'm sure the minute he sees you, and sees how much alike we are—how like him, actually—he will repent his treatment of you."

Keith, reared on the illusions of his mother, was sure of it, too.

Grayson House was all he had dreamed. It stood on a southeast slope, sheltered by a grove of old oaks. It was high enough to enjoy the graceful prospect of a river-watered valley below.

The minute he saw Keith, Captain Grayson seemed suspicious. But the boys had wisely schemed to say nothing at that first moment. Burne had even thought up a fictitious surname for his brother: Cutler. Keith took off his hat and disposed it under his arm. His bow to his father displayed as much grace as the action would allow. He wanted to make the impression that he had been brought up as mannerly and cultured as if he'd been to dancing school.

Stella was let in on the secret. At nine, she was a pleasant, plain girl with her mother's carroty hair and jutting teeth and rather long, narrow cheeks. She also owned a heart of the tenderest sort. As soon as she heard Keith's story, she took him into her arms and with tears in her eyes, said, "Welcome home, dearest Brother."

Though a big lad of eleven, Keith wept. To be raised from the mud to this.

The two Grayson children eagerly gave him a tour of the home they were prepared to share with him. Keith was awed. Nothing his mother had told him could compare with the reality of the fine bindings in the library, the shadows on the snow in the formal garden, the painting in the gallery of a water jug, a dish, two lemons, and a pear. Here were so many superior things, things of the heart and spirit, things Keith felt were his by natural right. At last he was to have what he'd wanted since he was old enough to comprehend his mother's stories. She'd told him that no one could ever be melancholy here, or plagued with the little cares of the world. And he believed her.

That night, Christmas Eve, the children were allowed to join their elders at dinner. Burne was almost bursting with suppressed anticipation. Captain Grayson had guests: a jowly-faced neighbor, Mr. Bernard, and his falcon-eyed wife; the local vicar and his pink, foolish-faced dame; and an old military friend of the captain's on a visit from Chatham. The table talk was predictable: "Hunting fox is the best sport in the world," the clergyman said to the old soldier. Mr. Bernard wanted to talk about the tax for newspapers, the Government Stamp, they called it.

Keith's eyes were on his father, whom he thought a most extraordinarily handsome being. He watched the captain's hands, which were the same shape, and would one day be the same length, finger by finger, with his own.

Burne waited until the claret was poured, then he made his announcement.

It was met by silence all down the satinwood table. His father went white. Keith felt an uneasy fear. "I'll be damned," the jowly Mr. Bernard said aloud, with a wheezy laugh. The vicar adjusted his neck-band and straightened the periwig on his head. The expression of the military man did not alter, unless it grew more stern. The ladies stopped eating. Mrs. Bernard's falcon eyes glinted. Time slowed, and slowed, and then it seemed to stop.

The captain stood, and after a moment he laughed, looking at his guests. "It has been many an honorable man's fate to pass for the author of children he never wrote." The tension cracked like overheated glass; relief descended down the table. Turning to Keith, the captain very politely asked him to get out of his house. Keith was more aghast at this courtesy than he would have been at a curse.

While the vicar remained at the table, mumbling from the litany—" '. . . the deceits of the world, the flesh, and the devil . . .' "—Stella cried and followed her new brother to the door. Burne turned on his father. Outraged, the captain had the boy carried to an attic room often used for punishment when the Grayson children misbehaved. Stella, though distraught, managed to speak well for Keith, with moving candor. There was a goodness in her that Keith recognized, even in those ugly moments.

The situation asked too much of Captain Grayson, however; it strained his small spirit too far. He saw only the boy's mockery of his credulity, his gullibility, his stupidity, all engineered with unbelievable impudence by the bastard son of a peasant girl. When Stella put her arms around the boy, Captain Grayson pulled her away, saying with the severity of his character, "Let him go! He's nothing but a low brute, not fit for you to touch." Keith felt the man's fiercely strong and hurtful fingers viselike on his arm as his father put him out the door.

It was December. There was snow on the fine lawn that sloped downward from Grayson House. The oaks were as bare as hands under the thin, pale, delicate shine of the moon. Where was a boy to go? How was he to get home to his mother? These were the questions that faced Keith the moment the door to Grayson House was shut behind him. He had no food with him, no shelter but his coat. He was eleven years old, but he grew up in that moment. And a small part of him grew old. He had tried to invade the realm—and had at once and humiliatingly been thrown out. He felt the sharp edges of his father's last statement. Nothing but a low brute, unfit to be touched. It did something to him.

The visiting neighbor's wife came to the rescue. While talk at the table limped along around the subjects of the awful winter and the vicar's recent conversation with a Methodist, Mistress Bernard surreptitiously saw to it that a stableman was sent out to pick up the outcast along the road, take him to the nearest public conveyance, and see to his transportation home to his mother.

No one, however, came to Keith's aid when Captain Grayson engineered his expulsion from Hillsburrow School immediately following the holidays, nor was anyone there when Laurel became ill with a coughing sickness soon after. Her health was not helped by the way she fretted over how her medical care depleted the trust settled on her. Keith, naturally enough, felt like a dog that had been kicked out of the way, and he yearned to curl up where no one could see him—but it was obviously time for him to make himself useful. His schooldays were at an end. Chin up, face resolute, he took an ill-paid job in a counting house.

Sometimes the two Solomons subsisted on stale bread and buttermilk for dinner, a glass of ale and a crust for breakfast. A fine, strong lad, Keith could have made more income as a laborer, but his mother would not let him stoop so far down. He himself had a thorough aversion to going into service, that is, to be a servant.

His own drive to gentility would not let him be content in the counting house either. He had a fine hand and a fine mind; these were facts. He began to build his hopes again, this time of gaining a position under a magistrate. There he could at least read for the legal profession.

The Bar, of course, closed its eyes to anyone without affluence and nobility, but there was room for such as him in the lower ranks of the attorneys. These were commonly regarded with disdain as batteners upon the misfortunes of others, a society of men bred from youth in ways to prove that white is black, and black is white, according to who paid them. Their drink was hogwash and belch.

Keith dreamed of becoming something unheard of, however: a good attorney, someone who helped those who came to him. Though no magistrate appeared to offer him a position, the dream assuaged the numbing hours on his stool in the counting house. His mind had been shaped into an urge to be a gentleman, or at least to rise up the social scale beyond what he was now.

So boyhood passed into adolescence. His mother was increasingly tormented by ill-health. She'd had a dozen incisions cut in her arms to drain the noxious humors. She bathed weekly in a time when nobody dreamed of taking even a monthly bath unless following the precepts of Sir John Floger, an advanced physician who held that a bath was actually beneficial.

By Keith's eighteenth year, Laurel was deteriorated to the point where he felt she required a better surgeon than the one who had been attending her. Maybe an apothecary, such as the London middle classes were doctored by, would be able to cure her.

There was no one to help with the expense, but she was all Keith had, and it was not in him to let her go without a struggle. He pawned all their belongings, garnered forty guineas for them, quit his job, shut up their humble cottage, and took her to London. From Lichfield it was a three-day coach journey.

In the long, late light of the year, they crossed the Thames, glittering under the blue English sky. From London Bridge they saw the rising current roaring and rushing beneath the arches. Below the bridge foreign merchant vessels anchored in rows all but concealed the river.

London was everywhere full of excitement and color and piping times. They passed St. Paul's, brand new and deemed one of the three most beautiful churches on earth. It was said the view from the top, smoke permitting, was magnificent.

Keith settled his mother into lodgings in Little Britain, the favorite street with the book trade—and also noted for its whores. There was one woman of a lewd and loose nature who every time Keith stepped out the inn door stroked his cheeks and neck and teased him with promises of ecstasy. But he had more important matters on his mind.

London was full of things, people, enthusiasm. Determined though he was to cling to his pride, Keith was hard put not to gawp like a yokel. For a price there were theaters, cotillions, assemblies, waxworks, taverns, gardens, grog shops, and bawdy houses. The city catered to every taste and purse. The shops were fascinating, stocked with eery imaginable and unimaginable thing from the four corners of the world, save when several corners were warring with each other—not uncommon.

Exquisitely painted shop signs swung over the streets like triumphal banners. Those of medical men claimed cures for gouts, catarrhs, rheums, cachexias, bradypepsias, bad eyes, stones, collicks, crudities, oppilations, vertigos, winds, consumptions, and innumerable other diseases. Though an apothecary was considered better than either a surgeon or a barber, a physician was regarded superior to them all. Naturally Keith chose the best for his mother. As for the expense, it was easy for him to give the impression that he was a gentleman of means and good credit. He'd spent his youth cultivating the ability to give that impression.

It was madness. To gamble—there is no other word for it—to gamble everything. At night he lay awake, feeling in his very body the dwindling and then the absence of his forty guineas. And then feeling the mounting of his debts like a weight on his chest. And the pity of it was that Laurel died anyway. Died so swiftly one day that Keith was left dazed.

He saw her buried. The afternoon was windy, raw, with sunshine and dark alternating over the hills and meadows outside London. As they shoveled dirt over her coffin, he didn't have to fight to keep his face empty of emotion. The suddenness of her going held him in a kind of astonishment, a doubt of the very truth of it. The chaos of the funeral created a fog inside which he chose to let linger.

How could he dare wake up and feel anything? Feelings all led him to the undeniable sense of relief that he no longer needed to think of his mother being ill anymore.

And to the inescapable horror that her burden of being utterly alone in the world had now passed to him. He had no parents anymore, or any kin to take refuge in, no friends, no advisors, no one.

He looked away from the dirt falling on his mother's coffin; he looked up at the great gray sweeps of cloud that furnished the day with silence, with an awareness of the tears and sorrow and hopelessness that he dared not feel.

The room he'd shared with Laurel seemed unnaturally large and silent. He stayed on there, not even realizing how swift and hard the tide was rising against him. The physician who had treated Laurel was a solid young man with a faint and permanent frown, very full of his own dignity. He waited until after the funeral to present his bill. And waited another month hence. But at last he wanted his fee.

So did the innkeeper, a little puffy-cheeked old man. And the gloomy mortician. When the three discovered that Keith was not what he'd said, and that he had no money, they didn't rant. No, they were all three as even-tempered as dead fish. Instead, they simply had the youth seized for debt by the sheriff's bailiffs. Keith realized at last that his crime was not simply going to be forgiven. He had half believed it would be, being young and unhardened.

Taken to the Old Baily, the criminal court adjoining Newgate Prison, he didn't have the half crown necessary to be put in the bail-dock. He went instead into the hold. He was on his own, alien and isolated, among criminals resembling so many sheep penned up in Smithfield for a market day. The space was scarce so much as he might swing a cat in.

Here such as were committed for housebreaking swore stoutly they couldn't be cast for burglary because the incident was done in the daytime; those committed for stealing a coachman's cloak vowed they couldn't be cast for felony or robbery because the coach was standing still. The legal terminology which distinguished a felony from a misdemeanor was ambiguous, and whether the accused went out of the world "by the steps and the string" or were allowed to live on often depended on the interpretation of the statutes. Hence, everyone was eager to reason that his conviction would be adjudged a lesser offense and therefore not punishably by hanging.

Hanging was very much on everyone's mind. There were nearly two hundred hanging offenses in Britain.

To ease their minds, alcoholic drinks were allowed

for prisoners able to pay for them. For amusement, the eldest made shift to get the youngest drunk before they went up to the bar for arraignment or trial. Keith was marked as their especial target. "Look-it how he struts, as noble as a beadle!" He was intimidated and frightened; they didn't have to hold him down and pour the liquor down his throat. The drink they had somehow procured was a dark, full-bodied sack, potent, especially for a boy unused to spiritus liquors. It went down his throat like a lance of fire and hit his belly like a burning coal.

Chapter Fourteen

'Tis the most certain sign the world's accurst
That the best things corrupted are the worst.
Sir John Denham: *The Progress of Learning*

Keith woke up from his drunken stupor to find himself not in the rough hands of the criminals of the hold, but in a courtroom among attorneys such as he had once hoped to become. His mind whirled with the drink forced on him as he sat through the murk of legal rituals and the cases called before his own.

This was a time when criminal biographies enjoyed unusual popularity. Pamphlets, songs, and broadsides describing the crimes and the dying utterances of thieves and murderers were common reading. Keith had read "Hell on Earth," a pamphlet by John Hall, a famous housebreaker imprisoned in Newgate, and he was afraid as he sat, half inebriated, in that courtroom.

One man was just being transported, banished to the tobacco and cotton estates in America, where he would endure nine years of servitude in alternative to hanging.

For stealing five pewter tankards, a woman, obese

as a pudding, was committed to three years in Gate-house Prison in Westminster.

Two soldiers, one grave and embarrassed, the other with his face set like iron, were bound to Newgate for four years, for clubbing a watchman who'd found them breaking into an inn.

A young woman was sentenced for breaking into a chamber and filching some goods from her mistress—a silk dress and a pair of silver buckles. The mistress was present, glaring at the justice, silently demanding a hard sentence. The maidservant was given ten years. As she turned from the dock, her eyes stumbled onto Keith's, and locked in fury. She was upward of twenty years of age, barely pitted with pock marks, with a high forehead, fresh coloring, light eyes and brows and hair, about five feet tall and nearly five feet around. What would she look like in ten years? What would she be?

Keith heard one of the attorneys grumble that the prisons were quite full. "Where are we going to put these villains we see every day, especially with this late increase of thieves?"

"The more we hang the better," said another with a dour flourish. "Justice Covell is too soft."

The justice was being easy. It was common for quite small thefts to be punished by death: a boy of ten was recently executed at Norwich for stealing a penknife. And yet perhaps the justice was not being so merciful as he thought, for everyone knew the prisons were schools of corruption and breeding grounds of plague. There were no separate cells, and as Keith already knew, the small offender was herded together with the most depraved. The dirt bred a lethal and highly in-fectious disease called gaol-fever.

Keith straightened when he was called to the dock. The somberness of the proceedings had sobered him. Justice Covell was no more than ceremoniously interested in the recitation of his crimes. Soon enough the man was intoning, ". . . I do commit you, Keith Solomon, for offenses against your God, your king, and your fellow subjects, to Bridewell Prison, located in Tothill-fields, Bridewell, for a period of two and one-half years."

A very light sentence. Yet Keith realized, with total clarity, and no sensation at all, that now he was a prisoner of the state.

There are young men, lean, well-built and clean-faced, with luminous eyes and thick hair, and an open, cheerful look, who invite good sentiments and make things pleasant where they are by the pure morning glow that is on them. Despite the disappointments of his youth, Keith Solomon was still one of these—up until the day he arrived at Bridewell Prison under the warrant of his commitment.

The turnkey opened the door into that so-called house of correction, using a key the size of the weathercock on St. Peter's Church in Cornhill. And Keith stepped over the threshold into one of the most concentrated spectrums of criminal consciousness in existence. To the right and left of him, before and behind him, his eyes met nothing but poverty and low reputation and desperation and distress.

Bridewell housed chiefly prostitutes and women debauched from their childhood, vagrants, debtors, and disorderly persons, but there were prisoners of all sorts and all crimes, prisoners of all ages and both sexes, including children, all driven together indiscriminately into this din of horror and darkness.

At the grate, the door locked behind him, he was immediately delivered up to the wolves who lurked there for prey. Out jumped three truncheon officers demanding that he "distill a little Oil of Argentum," by which they meant that he grease their palms with silver. "I am here for indebtedness, I have no money," he told them truthfully.

Truth wasn't worth much here. They took him to their apartments where two held him while the other one culled his pockets, claiming his last six shillings.

When they turned him out, he found other criminals hovering about him asking for their garnish—eight pence—apparently an old custom, "for coming into the Society." Since Keith had not so much as a farthing now, he was stripped down to his shirt and breeches, and they would have taken those as well, except that one of the women took pity on "the poor wretch," and so they only beat him a little with their fists and thrust him into that cold country which lies beyond fear.

He was without friends, without shoes or coat, without help or a helper in the world.

His loss of clothing was the least of his worries. To be out at the elbows was the fashion there, and it was a great indecorum not to look threadbare. Within twenty-four hours he became all too intimate with this fact and with the ploys of these convicts, with their fever-breeding filth and their relish for brutality. Within forty-eight hours he knew every square foot of Bridewell Prison—the dungeons, the cells, the iron gates, the fasting rooms. (These last had an especially good reputation for calming anger and rebellion among his fellow inmates.)

Bridewell contained an unbelievable gathering of human affliction. The faces of not only thieves and cutthroats, but of fools and madmen surrounded Keith day and night. His first occupation was to fight off the thugs addicted to sodomy. He was lucky to be still healthy and able. Though several of the vicious sodomites might attack him together, he was able to break free, and even to land a few blows that earned him respect.

His robust health was not to last, however, for he must depend on what meager fare the prison afforded those poor prisoners who, for lack of friends, had nothing to subsist on but bread and water. He watched with hollow eyes as the gray-pease woman strolled through at seven or eight o'clock each night crying, "Hot gray-pease, hot, hot!"

The nastiest place in the gaol was assigned to its most pathetic inhabitants, the debtors, of which Keith was one. When he walked, lice crackled under his feet, as noisily as if he were strolling on shells strewn over a garden walk. The destruction of his spirit and body was swift. He came down with a headache in his second week, then found red spots all over his body. He lapsed into a fever and might have died but for the interest of a shadowy figure who said her name was Madge.

She was the mistress of one Georgie Moraga, a mumbling, malevolent man who looked fifty and was "a solid Tory if ever there was one!" Georgie was unconcerned about Madge nursing the younger, handsomer Keith through his bout of gaol-fever. There wasn't much need for jealousy. The woman was eight months pregnant and due for the gallows as soon as she gave birth.

Madge had at an early age huddled up her life as a thing of no use. She'd worn it out quickly, the faster the better. She'd been burnt on the forehead for theft when she was eleven, and whipped at the cart's tail for petty larceny when she was thirteen. Now nineteen, she'd been convicted of putting herself in a grand dress, taking an empty bandbox and going to a lady's house where she knocked and asked the servant, "Is yer mistress stirring yet? I brought the suit of knots she ordered."

As the maid went upstairs to acquaint Madame of the message, Madge stepped inside and filled her band-box with the silver left out on the sideboard to be polished.

As Keith drifted in semiconsciousness, he was aware that Madge and Georgie were often beside him. He dozed fitfully. His eyes kept opening, and what he saw was his caretaker lying upon ragged blankets on the prison floor beside him, coupling openly with the aging felon.

Keith got well about the time Madge's baby was born. Once it was taken away, she was promptly carted off to Tyburn, never to return.

Georgie, without female distraction, quickly grew surly. He nearly strangled a dwarf who stood no taller than Keith's waist and whose head was so outsized it looked as if it might topple from his shoulders. Georgie claimed the freak had tried to steal his two ragged blankets, yet he was taken away to be punished anyway, in the pressroom. There his hands and feet were stretched out to iron rings fixed to the floor, and a great heavy press, made like a hog trough full of weights, was lowered on him. In this torment he lay for three days, having nothing to eat or drink but water. When he was returned to the general society, it was Keith who nursed him.

A bond of sorts formed between the two. The aging felon took this talented youngster (so reserved and polite in his demeanor) under his instruction and began to share with Keith his own peculiar talents.

Keith hence became a student of iniquity. In the school of Bridewell the students, instead of holding debates in philosophy or mathematics, argued about the law. It was a school that taught ample wisdom, but it was better to be ignorant than to go there to master it.

Georgie being the offspring of generations of de-

209

bauchery and corruption, was quite willing to give an account of all his vicious practices. His ways were "as dark as the inside of the devil's arse." He was currently in gaol for beating a constable, but his true occupation was highway robbery. (He had also raped and killed a young woman with a garrote, but he didn't feel this really counted, as he'd never been caught for it.) His code of honor insisted that he could sooner accept the gibbet than a mean trade.

For Keith, who had always been facile and quick to learn, the next two and a half years were exceedingly fruitful. By the age of twenty-two he had learned every essential of his future trade, and had consciously rooted from his mind every humane and gentle virtue.

Georgie shook his hand the day of Keith's release, and gave him this final counsel, mumbling as always as if his mouth were full: " 'Tis a cold, condemning world, my boy. No place for people with dangerous impulses to 'rise' or to get in with 'nice people.' Such tendencies I have wrung from me own constitution with great success, I'm glad to say."

Though they exchanged promises to "crack a bottle or two, and get drunk and mad" when Georgie was released, Keith knew he would never make an effort to see the old man again. He turned. He stepped away from his mentor without saying goodbye. He stepped through the grate of Bridewell Prison and faced the bright sun of the world as an outlaw with a darkened mind.

As he lay in his outlaw's bed now, half awake at four A.M., he was hardened in his sin, unrepentant of his villainy upon the road, a criminal inured to wearing a mask, to wearing always a guise, an identity not his own until, at last, after years of deception, he had lost track of his earliest shape and aspect altogether. That former Keith had stopped having any significance for

210

him. As he moved in his bed, he remembered that he had slept on straw, and filthy straw at that, in Bridewell Prison.

Yet he also "remembered" the architecture of the clubs he had hoped to join, the good homes where the time of day cascaded through the windows onto all the insignia of luxury and repose, the fine emporiums with wide-board floors upon which he had never set foot and never would. It is simple, at four A.M., to feel exiled. And he was exiled, forever and ever, from those hopes of his youth. He now considered the moors his home. He had made a life of sorts. And yet he remained a man who remembered.

Keith lived through that night, and through the next and the next. He was alive, his blood pulsed in his head and throat and chest. But he didn't feel much like living. He was weak, and he hurt, and that made him irritable. He slept a lot, and every time he dozed, he fell into restless dreams: thunder cracked in his ears. The night yellowed under a flash of lightning. He saw by its glare a young woman with a face like a rose. She wore white silk; her skirt swung in the wind like a bell. He wanted her, and he wanted to say so. He wanted to take her into his arms, but he was covered with blood.

The dream swirled around him as he opened his eyes. And there was Jane, her hair tidy, her face lit by the yellow light of the fire as she leaned into the kettle over the crackling flames. Nothing was a dream. Except that she was not wearing fine silk; no, she had nothing but that mended purple Sunday gown of a maidservant. He hadn't got her a new dress after all. But he wasn't covered with blood; all the blood was washed away.

211

He was so glad to see her there. Yet glad as he felt, he couldn't seem to say any of the things he wanted to say.

Seeing he was awake, she came to help him sit up a little, propping a pillow behind his back. But as soon as she turned away he dozed off again. He couldn't have been asleep more than a minute. He dreamed about his mother this time. She was stitching a piece of rough fabric by the light of a guttering candle stub. She lifted her face and said, *Keith.* Her voice seemed to trail long threads that his fingers could almost catch hold of.

"Keith."

Jane's voice, not his mother's. Thank God. He dreaded when those years spilled over into his sleep. It was Jane waking him again; she was sitting beside him with a bowl of gruel and a spoon.

Jane, not his mother. Jane, but not in a white silk dress. And there was no lightning. And all the blood was washed away.

So much dreaming in such little winks of time.

He took a spoonful of gruel. Swallowing, he said, "You ought to go now. Take that purse I took off the good duke and get yourself a coach seat—go anywhere but here."

"I have my own money," she said primly.

"Then take it and go!" he said, his exasperation with his own helplessness bursting out. She winced. So did he; such an eruption was not achieved without pain. "It's dangerous for you here. There could be soldiers combing the area this very minute. I don't need you anymore. In fact, you're a hindrance. Alone, I'd be able to act unfettered."

Her jaw set, her blue eyes were severe. "That's the purest nonsense, Keith. What could you do better alone, except get yourself shot again, or hung?"

He hadn't the will to argue like this. His muscles ached; he felt ill and vexed. He looked at the calm, soft, yet somehow relentless face of this woman he had saved against her will and who was now returning the favor. She placed a spoon of gruel before his lips. He hunched up miserably. "Not hungry."

"Keith—"

"Not now."

She put the bowl on the table and took up a cup. "Drink something, anyhow." Her eyes were enormous, like the eyes of a saint in a mosaic. This was how it had been for three days. She tended him, and was forbearing, submissive, soothing, and untiring. She slept at his bedside—in the chair, like a passenger in a coach! While he, brooding and childish, grumbled and fussed and was an abomination and a beast. He'd never been confined indoors so long since his time in Bridewell. His locked, airless mind reeked.

He took the water she wanted him to drink. For a long moment she was so close he could smell the distinct womanly scent of her round breasts and her fragrant hair. Night-colored hair, kept in two heavy dark braids that coiled around her head like serpents. Her chin was soft when he took it in his right hand. He said, "Jane . . ."

But nothing more would come out.

For three days Jane had stayed inside the cottage with him. By the second day he'd opened his eyes more often. And begun to take broth in slow careful sips, and seemed to breathe more easily. Now his dark hair stood out from his head; the stubble of his beard was thick; he looked grave and haggard. Jane felt sorry for him—yet now that she knew he was going to live she accepted that only time could knit him completely. At

213

the moment she was more anxious about their food supplies than his irritable complaints.

She said, "If you would eat something—you ought to eat, Keith."

He took an interminable time to answer, but at last he nodded. "All right."

When she had spooned the bowl of gruel down him, she checked the pot. There was one more bowlful for his dinner at noon. For herself, she attacked the last piece of hard, dry bread.

"We're out of food, aren't we?" he said, his eyes closed. She'd thought he was asleep.

"There's enough for your dinner."

"What about yours?"

She didn't answer.

He took a deep breath, storing up strength to talk. "There's an inn about five miles from here, The King William. The innkeeper is Alan White, a man of habitual melancholy, probably because he's wed to a Gypsy of grotesque appearance. Her name is Sal; she's recognizable by her mustache."

Evidently the gruel had fortified him. He went on; "Alan sometimes acts in collusion with a certain road inspector who makes the lanes here about a terror." He opened one eye to look at Jane. A little smile now, it curled the corners of his mouth. "The innkeeper shelters the brigand when he needs sheltering, and he also supplies much valuable knowledge from the conversations he overhears in his establishment. When there is profit, the twain share the spoils."

The eye was shut again, the smile was gone. "If you go there, he'll supply us with food—and he'll know what's afoot in the neighborhood, as well."

The idea frightened her. She mopped her palms against her skirt. "When would be the best time to go?"

214

"Leave here at sundown. The Whites will put you up for the night, then you can come back at dawn. That way you won't have to be out in the dark too much. Take Eclipse—"

"Oh, I don't think—"

"—and leave off that damned white coif of yours; it shines out like a star in the dark."

He would know, he'd had experience in stalking her.

"Maybe I could dress altogether like a man."

The smile came back to the corners of his mouth. But his voice was thinner now; he was tiring. "Not a chance. First of all, I don't have anything that wouldn't wrap around you twice . . ." He didn't give a second reason.

"How will I find this inn?" She was forgetting to be afraid.

He gave her the directions: over a beck that ran into a tarn, Gwilt's Tarn, then to a place called Dannel Common. "There's a butcher and cattle dealer who owns a farm there. You can't miss the stench. Go around it, keeping to the woods to the north—to your right." He suffered a twinge of pain and turned his fiercely contained face away from her. "I assume you know your left from your right."

As the sun set, she put on her scarlet cloak and went out to saddle Eclipse. She looked up at the sky, surprised to realize the weather had cleared. In taking care of Keith for the past three days, she'd been living in the climate he created, which had been gloomy to say the least. It was chilly out; November was facing toward December.

She entered the small stable, skirted a pile of straw, and came upon the gleaming rump of the stallion. He was more used to her now that he'd been dependent on her for his mash. And she was more used to him after three days of edging past his flank to hold the pot

215

to his muzzle and listen as his strong teeth chew between bouts of snorting.

She lifted down the saddle she'd somehow hung on a peg the day Keith had come home so near death. She struggled with it back to where the stallion was standing at the mouth of the stall. In the dim light, she reached up and with aching arms threw it over the horse's back. Or tried to. When she slumped down, the saddle was still in her arms.

She made another effort, and this time successfully heaved it up. She managed to buckle the two straps of the girth. At last she took the horse by the bridle and backed him out of the stable.

All this took her longer than Keith thought it should, and he began to worry. If she did it wrong, she could fall off and be hurt. He fretted until at last he forced himself to slide back the covers, angle his bare legs over the edge of the bed and, with desperate ferocity, lift himself into a sitting position. Then he got to his feet, head spinning, and tottered to the door.

She was just bringing the horse around. He loved the way she bound her head around with the plaits of her hair. He loved—

"Keith!"

"Walk"—his voice stuck in his throat; he tried again—"walk him around in a circle so I can see if you've got everything buckled right." He stood in the door wearing nothing but his bandages and his drawers, holding firmly to the jamb to keep himself from collapsing. He felt himself go hot, then cold.

"I did it exactly as you said." Offended, she walked the horse in a circle anyway. "Now get back to bed."

"What, no kiss for luck?" Propped reasonably securely, he held his right arm out to her.

The look she gave him! Yet she came and went up on her tiptoes. The lights from the fire behind him

216

gleamed in her eyes. But her lips were cool. It had been three days since he'd had his mouth on hers. Did she miss his kisses, his hands? He put his right arm around her. Her whole body softened, like wax under the candleflame; she seemed to melt.

Now. Tell her now.

But he didn't. He couldn't. The words, just waiting to leap out of his mouth, wouldn't come. He glowered at nothing, at everything, at her.

The twilight lay heavy. She should go now if she was going to go at all. She said, "I'm not leaving until you get back into bed."

That witchy reserve, that calm. There was a part of her that never laughed, but always stood apart and watched. He shouldn't be sending her out like this; but there was no choice, there was no time. He said, trying to sound fierce, "Let me see you get up on him."

Once he'd cupped his hands for her shoe and lifted her easily up to the saddle. Now she must stand on a round of log and hitch her skirts up high and reach her foot up to the stirrup and, by gripping the stallion's mane and the horn of the saddle, somehow haul herself onto his back. She slipped her toe into the far stirrup and took up the reins. Eclipse stood through it all, his round eyes on his master.

"Hold the reins between your thumbs and fingers." Keith remained standing; he held his leg muscles stiff so they wouldn't quiver. "Hold him firmly, then he will know you're his mistress."

"I will."

The silence fell again, charged with doubt. Keith moved a drift of hair off his forehead. He felt weak, and at the same time stiff, sore, glum. Night was drawing its cloak. The silence and the shadows hovered around the horse and its rider. He doubted her ability to remain in charge of the great brute. She needed gloves, but his leather gauntlets were too big for her hands. She needed her stirrups adjusted. He doubted this whole scheme. But there was nothing he could do. Nothing he could do. He saluted them both and, summoning what strength he had left, turned for his bed, closing the door behind him.

The cottage seemed empty. Doubt, like a voice, plucked at his shoulder. If he were going himself, he would not scruple to take his pistols, both ends of which were pretty useful. But she wouldn't know how to use them. Anyway, without a horse he was helpless here. Keeping the pistols might at least give him a chance, should anyone come.

He felt so sleepy. You'd think he'd soaked up enough sleep to go without for a month. He'd come to think of sleep like a wild beast that turned its victim over slowly, seeking the soft spots, the tender places where its teeth could sink deep. As he closed his eyes, he heard Eclipse take her out of the dooryard and into the brambles. He heard the horse's hooves crunch and splash along the damp narrow pathway.

You are the center that has suddenly given my world a shape again. You are the voice of a new spring in my heart. I love you, Jane Fitzpatrick, I love you!

Chapter Fifteen

The King William Inn

Beyond the close bramble path, Eclipse shied and backed. Jane felt exhilarated, and at the same time frightened by the height from which she found herself looking down at the ground, and by the power of the beast beneath her. Her insistence that she could handle the horse was all based on a moment's courage, summoned up from God knows where.

She pulled on the rein. As the horse felt the bit in his teeth, he backed again. He would respond to the merest touch, she discovered, and she was on her guard.

The stallion tolerated her inexperienced fumblings reasonably well. She followed Keith's directions with no sense of haste. She felt a strange, easy timelessness.

She found Gwilt's Tarn. From there she found Dannel Common by the bawling of the cattle and the charnel house stench from the November slaughter. She turned toward the wood to her right.

In the full dark, the country here seemed a network of cart tracks and sheep paths. She feared several times that she was hopelessly lost. The tracks all met, finally, at a hostelry, the King William Inn, beside which a very wide and straight highroad ran due east and west. It had all gone better than she'd expected. She leaned forward and patted the black neck of the stallion in relief and gratitude. She suspected he'd brought her here despite her attempts to direct him elsewhere.

She studied the peak-gabled, bow-windowed, galleonlike bulk of the inn. Its roof was dark against the evening stars. A low wall enclosed the cobblestoned courtyard, in the middle of which stood a well. A coach and four great black horses stood before the door, along with several carts and dray horses, and quite a few saddle horses. The opaque horn windows of the ground-floor taproom dripped with steam. Behind them moved the shapes of men with tankards in their hands. The King William seemed busy for such an out-of-the-way place.

She circled it at a distance, and then jumped off the horse and left him in the woods while she picked her way on foot to the back door. Before she reached it, a dog rose up and strained against his rope and filled the air with savage barking. Jane stepped back. The large black dog went on barking. A pregnant scullion poked her head out from the kitchen. "Who's there!" she shouted above the din.

Jane instinctively made her voice low. "Someone who wishes to speak to Mr. White."

The scullion scratched her bulging belly. "What dost thou want?" she shouted, then added, "You, Dorado, shut up!" The fierce-looking dog obediently backed off and sat on his haunches. "What dost thou want wi' the master?"

"That's between me and him."

"Oh aye?"

She stared at Jane, then turned and disappeared inside. The dog snarled and growled, warning Jane not to come a step closer. Instead, she took a step back, under an overhanging tree.

The rear yard was narrower than the main innyard, and ill-kept. The low barn opposite Jane had a broken door. To her right lay a vegetable garden, overgrown and rank with decaying cabbage stumps and full of muck and litter.

A second woman, this one with an empty wooden platter, came to the door. She peered out, saying, "Who wants to see my husband?"

Jane hesitated, then stepped forward into the light. The dog rose again immediately. The woman kicked at it. "Sit, Dorado!"

Dame White was not attractive, and she did have a mustache. Also she was frog-eyed and corpulent and definitely unpleasant, in both looks and manner. Giving Jane a narrow-eyed look, she said, "You're the one they're looking for out of York, 'The Rose of Midnight.' "

Jane shivered with surprise. "Who is looking for me?"

"No need to run off; I know how to mind my tongue."

"Who is looking for me?"

"The soldiers, of course. For murder." Dame White's eyes narrowed. "You didn't know? Or leastwise you didn't expect it."

Jane couldn't take this in. It was too preposterous. A trick was being played. "Who . . . who do they think I murdered?"

"Your father."

Her lips fell open, but no sound came out. Dame White left the doorway and came toward her. "Pretty as they say, ain't you? Now, what do you want, girl?"

Jane's urge was to back away, to turn and run. Murder? She shook herself like a sleeper waking from a dream into deathly reality. She whispered, "I didn't murder him."

The woman shrugged. "That's what they all say, I expect. But you don't have to convince me. It's matterless to me what you did or didn't do. What do you want?"

She had to search her mind: what did she want? "I was told to come here—"

"Told by who?"

"By Keith Cutler."

The woman considered her, then suddenly laughed. It came as a jarring sound to Jane, who had thought the woman incapable of mirth. (And she was still paralyzed by the news that the law wanted her for a murderess.) "The hypocritical rogue! He kept the smock with him—and now she runs his errands! Grubneck said Keith took a girl away from him. He didn't see you clearly, but the soldiers, they put one and one together and figured it had to be you, fleeing from what you did at York." She laughed again. "Leave it to Keith Cutler to get the prettiest runaway on the road— and the only one that's wanted for murder! He never does nothing by halves!"

Jane kept trying to digest all of this: wanted for murder . . . Grubneck . . . soldiers knew she was with Keith . . .

Dame White looked at her closely, then laughed again, an ugly Gypsy's cackle. Then, as quickly as she'd fallen into mirth, she sobered. Her humors were sudden to come and sudden to go. "I take it he's hurt. The duke's man is bragging all over the district that he shot Keith Cutler."

"He's hurt, but not dead. I think he's on the mend."

Mr. White finally put in an appearance. He came out wearing a soiled apron and holding up a lamp. He was a nondescript, blunt-featured man. "So what's this?"

"It's her," his wife said, " 'The Rose of Midnight.' "

The man leaned to look closer with his lantern at Jane. "So I see."

Jane wanted to cringe back from that examining look. Dame White said, "They say your old cottage was nothing but a mound of rubbish. 'Twas a terrible blaze. And your father naught but a skeleton, the flesh all burned away."

Jane felt ill. "It was an accident."

The woman shrugged. "Them who knows say he was mean enough to deserve what he got, however it come about."

"Why . . . why do they think I *murdered* him?"

"Your old master says he heard you threaten him."

"Mr. Welby?"

The woman shrugged again. "Says you had some bit of money you vowed to keep if it meant seeing him dead."

Jane couldn't respond.

Dame White said to her husband, "She's come here because of Keith Cutler."

Jane mumbled, "He's hurt. He said you would give us supplies—food."

The man took this in slowly, and exchanged looks with his wife. "There are soldiers inside, you know. His fine grace, the Duke of Genthner, sent them out. They're bound to find Keith or the duke will know why not. I don't suppose they'd mind taking you in to York as well. It'd make a fine spectacle, the two of you hanging from the same gibbet. Their sergeant is talking to Grubneck Nord this minute. You couldn't have come at a worse time, lass."

Jane flinched back under the overhanging tree. A leaf dropped down and stroked her cheek damply. She shivered at its touch.

Man and wife exchanged glances again. Mr. White shifted the lantern from one hand to the other, wiping first one bony palm and then the other on his dirty apron. With an awkward twitch of his shoulders, he screwed up his blunt features. "The duke got bills printed with a full description of Keith. Seems Keith bared his face and told the duke to have a good look. The rogue—what makes him do such foolish things? His grace is offering two hundred pounds for him. They're distributing the bills among all the coach guards and carriers up and down the road. And anyone who sees you will know who you are."

Jane glanced behind her, where she'd hidden Eclipse in the woods. They wanted her to go; they were saying it was too dangerous for them to help her and Keith. But without food, Keith would die. She looked back. "You have given him information about travelers. If he's caught, you will want him to recall that you've been generous toward him. And if he's not caught, you won't want him to feel angry with you. I saw him get angry with Grubneck Nord."

The two stood regarding her, their thoughts busy, until Dame White made up her mind. "Alan will get some supplies together for you."

"And you must hide me for the night. I can't ride back in the dark."

The Gypsy woman didn't like being threatened. "Come with me!" She gestured for Jane to follow her. "We got a room you can stay in, where we put Keith when he comes about."

"Inside? What about the soldiers?"

"We'll get you by them."

"If you turn me over to them, Keith will know."

Mr. White looked at his wife. She said nothing, only went into the inn, saying in effect, Trust us or not, the choice is yours.

Jane hesitated only an instant more, then started after her. Mr. White stopped her with a hand on her shoulder. "I always liked Keith Cutler. He's not a man to take note of warnings, but you tell him Alan White says he'd best stay low." He pondered his own words. "No, now that'll scarce suffice. How can he stay low, when as we breathe and speak Grubneck Nord is telling Jamesy Amos just whither his cottage is? No," he thought hard, "you tell him he'd best disappear from these parts whilst he can."

"And how can he do that?" said the wife, who had paused when she saw her husband had stopped Jane. "How can he disappear whilst he's so laid up he has to send a chit of a girl out to fetch and carry for him?"

Mr. White scratched his chin. At last he said, "Keith'll think of something."

Impatient, his wife said, "Find Eclipse and put him in the stable and have a boy brush him down and feed him." She didn't wait to hear his answer. She took Jane's arm and hurried her through the kitchen. They passed the pantry, where hams dangled from the low ceiling beams and bags of flour and huge barrels reeking with ale stood on the floor. Evidently they must also pass by the taproom door. "Pull that hood over your face."

Jane paused to draw her scarlet cloak about her. Her stomach crawled with the new knowledge that she was suspected of murder. She'd never considered the idea that people would find her father and think she'd killed him. And the men who were looking for her were right here, just on the other side of this wall, through that open door. And Grubneck Nord was there, too, telling where Keith was, where she'd been staying with him.

And Keith so helpless! If not for him, she would escape this minute, and take her chances alone on the road. But Keith . . . they would hang him.

She'd thought to hold her head down and pass by the door quickly. But she couldn't. She glimpsed the light of a blazing fire, the red curtained windows, and the pewter-hung walls; and though Dame White urged her along, some fascination caused Jane to stop, and to peer from beneath the folds of her hood into the large room.

It was crowded and full of clamor, heavy with the smell of ale, with lamplight clouded by thick, pungent blue tobacco smoke and cheap tallow candles offering more smoke than light. Her eyes watered. Along with the smoke wafted the undeniable and inimitable stink of a cramped crowd of freely sweating men. Two very young girls dressed in ragged woolen gowns and beer-soaked aprons carried wooden trays laden with leathern jacks and jugs between four or five tables set close together on a flagged floor. A yeoman stood before the hearth, his breeches unbuttoned and his shirt raised. He was urinating into the fire, the jet streaming between two great logs and hissing in the glow of the ashes underneath. At the side of the hearth slept a cat, a velvet semicircle of contentment amidst that disorderly scene.

The soldiers were unmistakable in their red uniforms. Light slid down a sword sheath as it moved on the hip of a young corporal. Jane also recognized Grubneck Nord. He had one arm in a tattered sling. He sat with one of the soldiers at a table near the fire, a dice box between them. The sergeant was drinking down a cup of ale as if he had a terrible thirst. Jane felt held where she stood, as tight as if in knotted ropes. She saw his rabbity little eyes above the rim of his tankard. When he finished, he belched. And belched again. He took up the dice box, shook it, and upended it so the dice rattled out.

Dame White murmured, with some derision, "That's Jamesy Amos. It's not been so long since he got promoted to sergeant. This is the peak dignity of his life. He's got five men with him, all of them armed, of course."

Grubneck grimaced as he saw the result of the sergeant's throw of the dice. " 'Od's blood!" Many of the others looked over at his exclamation. There fell an instant of silence in which Jane heard the whispering snicker of the fire. A purplish flush touched the sergeant's cheeks. He emitted another long belch and let all his teeth show in a big grin. Conversations started up again, but the yeoman who had been at his private business at the hearth turned and looked Jane's way.

Dame White pulled her away from the door, turning her firmly toward a set of stairs. "It's not safe." She led the way upstairs with a brisk rustle of skirts.

Feet had kept those steep stairs dusted in a narrow track up the middle. Jane looked up into the shadows above her. She held small hope of any comfort. She'd never stayed in an inn before, but they were well-known to be deplorable. Beds shared with strangers were common. And bugs were rumored to be active in the mattresses.

Hence she felt no surprise at the sort of room she was shown. Located at the very top of the building, it was small and stale and dirty.

"I'll send you up a fried mutton chop," Dame White said. "Then you can rest. I'll wake you early enough to be off before the soldiers stir."

Jane felt she would not be able to rest a wink. Could this be a trap? Had the Whites reasoned that the two hundred pounds reward for Keith was a lot of money? The very air of the cell-like chamber seemed charged with uncertainty and fear, with an untellable dread. She could not like the Whites, especially the frog-eyed, corpulent, disagreeable dame. Nor could she trust them, knowing that they made part of their living off the scandalous and unlawful trade of highway robbery. If she had any sense in her head she would run downstairs and gallop back to the cottage right now.

But what about the darkness? She would never find Keith's secret hiding place again if she weren't very careful to retrace her steps exactly.

She must trust the Whites. She had no choice. And she must be content with leaving very early in the morning—if she wasn't arrested herself by then. Meanwhile, maybe she could think of something, form some plan to get Keith out of the cottage and away.

She sat in the one chair, at a small table that held a single candle, and stared at the rough plastered walls until her mutton chop and a cup of refreshment arrived by way of one of the girls from the taproom. The child's hair fell loose over her shoulders. She giggled as she set down the cup and the sizzling platter of meat. "Are ye a Quaker?"

"What?"

"Are ye a Quaker? Can he sleep wi' ye—the highwayman?"

"I don't know what you're talking about." Quakers? Weren't they that odd sect which went so far as to pronounce war unChristian?

"Oh we all know about him, how he's a Quaker and can only sleep wi' other Quakers. It don't matter to us, we wouldn't none o' us gi' him away to the Pope—or even to Parson Gupton who says Quakers is all tainted with Catholicism and damned to hell—but he's strict like is Keith Cutler. Won't sleep wi' none o' us."

From the moment she'd arrived here, Jane had been beset with a feeling of unreality. She couldn't even think of a civil response to this mad child and her prattling.

The girl hardly noticed. She sighed, then blathered on, "Even so, he allus remembers us wi' a little coin or two—shillings, not farthings. Why, I could go to Liverpool and paint snuffboxes for a farthing each I tell them as'd gi' me so little value! Anyway, he gi's us a little something when he comes round—though I'd say no need for that if only he'd just gi' me an hour alone wi' him.'' She grinned. "Aye, I'd do it wi' him for free! I just love all that black, tousled hair spilling about. And them tall, shiny jackboots. Ye've slept wi' him, ain't ye? Ye must be a Quaker like him.''

Jane hid in the cool manner she'd learned from Mr. Welby. "You're impertinent, girl.'' She picked up the cup before her and drank deeply. She'd expected water; she'd seldom tasted wine, and judging by this had missed nothing. Yet her long ride had left her thirsty.

The girl giggled; clearly she didn't understand the meaning of the big word Jane had used. She leaned across the small table and her presence filled the chamber—or was it just her smell? She was close enough for Jane to smell her hair, her skin—both of which gave off a fetor that threatened to make Jane ill. She wore no smock. The neckline of her dirty woolen gown exposed her pale, mud-hued shoulders and her breasts right to the pink edges of her nipples. She said in a tone of confidentiality, "Last time he come, I was going to slip into his bed like. I never found one who wouldn't roll over if he felt ye naked—but wouldn't ye know it, my woman's tokens come, so I couldn't.''

"How unfortunate for you.'' Jane took another drink of the sour wine. She felt the spirits coursing through her.

"Oh I'm allus glad to see my tokens,'' the girl winked cheerfully as she backed toward the door.

"They get in the way now and again, but better to have 'em than to miss 'em—if ye know what I mean."

Jane ate. The muttonchop tasted surprisingly good. Then she lay down atop the disreputable-looking bed. She would not go so far as to crawl beneath those dank and fusty bedclothes, however. Stiffness from her ride on the big stallion over the rough paths and tracks crept through her limbs. She felt drowsy. A peculiar drowsiness. She wished she hadn't drunk that cup of wine. She should have asked the girl to bring her some water. She couldn't afford to fall asleep. She had to think:

Soldiers were here; Keith couldn't leave the district, couldn't even stand without support; what if she missed her "women's tokens?" Keith had always been generous to that silly young slut . . . even a fourteen-year-old girl's face could be full of autobiography. She must not sleep, must not sleep . . . must not sleep too soundly, for soon she must rise . . . wake up . . . long before dawn . . . must get back to Keith.

The sweet, heavy, yeasty odors of beer and ale rose up the stairs from the taproom, along with men's voices. Both poured into her ears like a drug, spreading through her and drawing her down into will-less action.

The King William Inn gradually grew silent. And dark. Out in the night was no sound but that of branches clicking together, moved by a vast, far skein of wind out of the night dark sky.

Jane eased the stallion through the brambles. It could have been a cavern for the amount of light she had to see by. She came into the clearing just as the sun shafted its first light through the tops of the trees.

Ever since Dame White had awakened her, she'd been in a panic, almost an hysteria of urgency. Though she'd left the King William before the soldiers, Sergeant Jamesy Amos surprised the Whites by waking much earlier than expected. As Jane slipped out the back door, she'd heard the sounds of iron-rimmed wheels on the front cobbles as the coach pulled out, the sound of horses' hooves, of the roosters. The black dog rose up and started immediately to bark at her. Alan White himself brought Eclipse. "Be off with you!" he yelled at his dog. "Back away!" He helped Jane onto the horse's back. It had not yet struck six, yet she felt she was late, late, very late.

Mr. White said, "At least Grubneck won't be leading them today." He grinned. "I gave him a special drink last night. He won't be rising from his bed today, and maybe not tomorrow either."

By the silver light of the near-dawn, the farm at Dannel Common looked neat. The paths, enclosures, and yards were all clean. The cattle in the pens appeared well-fed and in good condition. Only the stench remained.

Beyond Gwilt's Tarn, she urged the stallion to a canter. He broke into a full gallop along the narrow track of beaten gorse. Bracken and huge outcrops of boulder spun away on both sides of Jane, and the air was so edged with cold it hurt to inhale it.

All along the route back, she'd felt she was being followed, that she was about to be overtaken by men much surer of their mounts and of their way than she was.

It was too much to bear alone, this fear. She needed to tell Keith. He would know what to do. He would save them both.

Her breath made white puffs in the frosty air. *Home,* she thought, reining Eclipse before the cottage. Tears of relief burned her eyes. No time for that, now. She'd come many miles, but the most dangerous distance lay ahead.

Keith opened the door, just a crack at first, then fully as he saw it was her. A pistol dangled from his hand. A grin curled his pale lips. He looked white and weak, despite his sturdy arms and shoulders and the fullness of his figure. His unshaven beard sculpted his unmasked face.

Keith, she wanted to say, we're in danger! What shall we do? But one look at him told her she must save them; he couldn't. If there had been any chance of his being able to travel—but he couldn't stand any sort of a journey, she saw that clearly.

She said, kicking her feet out of the stirrups and slipping from Eclipse's saddle, "Get back into bed."

His welcoming smile disappeared. "What's wrong?"

"Nothing," she snapped. Was she angry—on top of everything else she felt? Evidently so. "I have some work to do. I know you're hungry—get back into bed, Keith."

The fire had sunk down and the cottage felt cold. He hadn't even found the strength to tend it in her absence. The weight of her responsibility for both of their lives almost crushed her.

Ignoring the soreness of the insides of her thighs from her long ride, she quickly stirred up a blaze. She'd plunked the sack of food Mr. White had given her on the table. "Here's a cheese and some bread." She cut a thick slice of each for Keith. His face, looking up from his pillow, was full of questions, but she didn't have time to answer them, let alone risk getting into an argument over her answers. If she told him that Jamesy Amos and five armed soldiers were coming for him—who knew what he might try to do?

His weakness compelled her to be strong. She

brought him a cup of water to wash down his dry meal. "Now you're to stay put."

He didn't like any of this. He was suspicious. "Jane, what's wrong?" When she would have turned away, he gripped her wrist. Helpless as he was, he held her there, for to pull away would cause him hurt.

She gave him a look. "I have trusted you with my life, Keith Cutler. Now you must trust me with yours."

Chapter Sixteen

Dugs Like a Cow

Keith regarded Jane unblinkingly. Though she stood still by his bedside, her head throbbed with the knowledge that danger was near, very near. She sensed it like a noose closing around her neck.

After an eternity he let go of her wrist. She felt the release through her whole body, felt herself spin back into the need for action. So sudden and so strong was the sensation that black motes reeled before her eyes. She must think now. "Do you own a spade?"

He told her where to find one; she heard him as through the narrow end of a funnel. She went out.

First she took Eclipse into the woods near the river and tethered him in a thicket where enough grass grew for him to graze. She took his saddle off and patted his nose. She realized she'd lost all fear of the great beast. There were so many other things to fear more.

Nearer the cottage, she found a spot where the ground looked tolerably soft. She marked out a rectangle. She fetched Keith's spade from a little shed and began to dig. Her years on the farm aided her now. She worked efficiently though she felt light-headed and kept feeling an impulse in her mind to just give up. She recalled something her mother had told her: "We often come off best when we're most afraid." She hoped it was true. If what she planned didn't work, she and Keith would both likely hang.

The intensity of her fear became too great. Her concentration focused on driving the spade into the stony ground, lifting the earth. Her thinking mind went blank.

Sometime later she came back to herself. (Where had she been?) She breathed deeply of the frosty air. At her feet lay a small hole three feet deep, two feet wide, and about three feet long. She went back into the cottage where Keith lay dozing. He woke when she started to drag his ironbound chest across the floor. "What—?" He started to rise up.

She straightened. Anger burst through to the surface of her again. "I'm doing what I can to keep you from the gallows! You must trust me."

Perhaps the fierce look on her face quelled him. He nodded, and lay back on his bed, but not without doubts.

She dragged the chest out and got it in the hole. The sun was well up now. She prayed that Alan White had given the sergeant all he could drink last night. If so, maybe he would linger at the King William long enough. But if not . . .

She buried the chest, working as fast as she could. She piled the earth high over it so it made a mound. She felt the passage of each minute. Hurry! her heart warned, Hurry! She found two small pieces of wood among Keith's pile. The sense of urgency in her prompted her to take them inside. She handed them to him, along with a strip of cloth. Her hysteria mounted; to hide it she controlled her voice tightly. "Can you make a cross with these?"

"A cross?"

"Can you?"

"Of course I can, I'm not helpless." Yet she saw how it pained him to move his left arm.

Among the food the Whites had sent was an onion. Just as she cut it in half, she heard the first muffled sounds of horsemen looking for the opening that would bring them through the brambles. The cross Keith made was clumsy, but that didn't matter. She grabbed it from him, along with half the onion, and she ran out to where she'd buried the chest. She thrust the cross into one end of the mound of dirt and knelt beside it. She tore at the onion, then recklessly rubbed the juice into her eyes.

The stinging! In an instant, she was crying. She thrust the torn onion into the loose soil, and at the same time gathered up some of the dirt and smeared her wet face. Her eyes hurt so badly she could hardly bear to take her hands away, which was all to the good. If they got a clear look, if she was recognized . . The Rose of Midnight . . . murderess . . .

Six scarlet-coated horsemen cantered one at a time into the clearing. They found a woman kneeling beside a small "grave," sobbing so hard she seemed hardly to take note of all their clamor.

A man dismounted. "What's your name?"

"C-Cathleen!" She forced her eyes to open a slit. She recognized that rabbity stare—Jamesy Amos. He looked tolerably sober, but not especially clearheaded.

"Is this where Keith Cutler lives?"

"C-Cutler? He sold this place to-to Lester last month."

"Who is Lester?"

"My husband—h-he's awful sick! This here grave belongs to my . . . my poor baby Andrew. He took a troublesome cough and broke out wi' t' pox just day

236

afore yesterday—barely five years old and now he's d-dead!''

The sergeant stepped back, no longer such a racy, rough character. "The pox?"

"And my baby Kate—just nine months—she couldn't even suckle, though ever'body says I got good, full breasts—a pair of dugs like a cow, my Lester used to say. She couldn't even c-*cry!* I buried them together . . . and now poor Lester—oh, he don't look so good!'' She tried to open her swollen eyes enough to see through her fingers. "It's the pox, I'm sure. They's ugly, ugly sores. Have ye ever seen it? I just don't know what to do! Won't you come in and look at him and see—''

Jamesy Amos was looking at his men, who were looking back at him in horror. Common soldiers in the King's Army were drawn largely from men incompetent for any other job, or from the gaols, and they naturally preferred their own safety to taking any sort of risk.

"Please! Ye got to help us!'' Jane bellered. She climbed to her feet.

Jamesy stepped back, maintaining his distance.

"Help us!'' She reached out with both hands, daring to bare her face.

Before she could touch him, he swung up into his saddle. She ran toward him and clutched his leg. He kicked her off so hard she fell, and there she lay, sobbing, rubbing her eyes.

He seemed to feel repentant, for he tossed down a few coins. "Here now! I wish you luck, good dame, but there's nothing I can do for you. We're out on the matter of the arrest of a dastard by the name of Keith Cutler. Pick up that money, now, and buy your man a fever powder. Maybe that'll do him some good.''

Before she could respond, he and all his men turned

tail to ride away. There was some jostling for position to get into the narrow lane through the brambles. Horses reared and whinnied in panic. There was cursing, words that soon burst like soap bubbles, leaving nothing but the memory of their bright sound. Then the clearing was empty. Silent. Full of daylight now, but a misty light that seemed no warmer than at midnight.

Jane couldn't stop crying. Her eyes hurt something awful. She stumbled to the door of the cottage—and there was Keith. He'd somehow got into his breeches and a shirt when he heard the horses and the men outside. He led her to the water bucket and helped her rinse her stinging eyes.

"I should wring your neck!" he muttered between curses. "You never said a word!" He handed her a towel. But then, even while she was still sobbing, he made his wending way to the bed and sat on the side of it and started to laugh—cautiously, holding himself protectively around the middle.

"My God, what a woman you are! Dugs like a cow?" He couldn't hold back a wicked grin. "You're a natural."

"A natural?" she said from behind the towel.

"Outlaw."

In an instant she was raging. "I'm not!" She even took a step toward him.

He held out his hands to ward her off. "All right, all right." He eased himself back onto the rumpled bed. But he was still grinning. "Dugs like a cow."

Her eyes burned. She rinsed them again. After a while she heard him say, "But didn't it feel good, Jane?"

She lowered the towel and looked at him. He winked hugely at her. The fear she'd suffered rose up in her belly. She gave no sign of the sour taste that came up in her throat with it. She swallowed it back down. She gripped the towel as if to tear it in two. "I'm not an outlaw. You think I'm like you, but I'm not."

As he regarded her, all signs of humor left his face. "I think you are a woman of spirit. And courage."

She wanted to fall on her knees and lean into him and hide her face and cry some more. I was so afraid! she wanted to say. But she mistrusted her own responses. And she realized that the anger his teasing had brought out was only the tip of some anger that had sunk down deep in her. He'd fallen in love with a portrait, and it just so happened that she'd been the model for that false image, so he had used her for his pleasure.

She wiped her sour mouth with the back of her hand. She must look a sight, with her eyes swollen to slits. She smoothed her tatter of a dress, touched her hair. She felt like something wilted to the ground after a terrific frost. She turned away from him. "I'd better get Eclipse."

He ran his fingers through his untidy hair. "Yes." He lay back and let his helplessness fall over him once more.

Ten days passed after Jamesy Amos and his men ran away from Jane. Keith was confident that they wouldn't return, not as long as there was any possibility of small pox.

He was improved. Rested if not entirely hardy. At his insistence, Jane had been sharing the bed with him again. Something had changed about her. She wasn't eating well. She'd begun to have the transparent look of a china doll. She'd withdrawn into herself, retreated into that remoteness and secrecy which had kept him from touching her when he'd first brought her in from the moors. He thought it had to do with that escapade with the soldiers. She'd been so magnificent!—but she wasn't proud of it, and wasn't able to laugh about it.

He watched her undress tonight. It was a rich pleasure just to watch the way she tossed her head back, slinging her hair out of the way so she could take off her garters and roll down her stockings. "Ooh—" she said, lifting one bare foot off the flagged floor and then the other, "—it's cold."

"Come here," he said from the bed, putting all his desire into his voice, trying to enchant her.

For a moment she looked at him, her mane of hair hanging dark as rain down her back. Then the enchantment worked. She came to him and lay down in his arms. He loved the dreamy, almost stunned look she got whenever she knew he was going to make love to her. He murmured, "Shall I get you warm?" He turned her so he could get behind her and hold both her soft breasts in his hands at once. He nuzzled her hair aside and kissed the back of her neck. She was ticklish there; his kisses made her shiver.

She murmured something.

"What was that?"

"I said, I'm not a Quaker."

It took him a moment to understand. "Was it Christine or Salome? Which one?"

"I didn't ask her name. She was dirty. And young."

"They're all dirty, girls like that. And all young."

"And all heartbroken that your religious beliefs won't let you sleep with them."

He chuckled. "Well, it's hard to be a good Quaker."

"You aren't one really, are you?"

"I knew one once. A woman who visited . . ." He'd almost said Bridewell Prison. He'd done that once or twice before—unconsciously told her things about himself. "She saw herself as a missionary to the lost." Something seemed to tear in his chest. He wanted to

240

drop the joke now. "Me, I'm no more Quaker than I am Wesleyan, or Deist—or a Jew."

He ran his mouth down her naked shoulder. She shivered again.

"Well, I was brought up Church of England, and if you only sleep with Quakers . . ."

He bent his head to kiss her jaw, laughing soft and deep. "I make an exception where you're concerned."

"So do I, Keith," she answered quite soberly. "Ordinarily I never sleep with highwaymen."

What was that soberness? What had happened to her that he didn't understand?

His concentration slid elsewhere. He felt a strong, swimming longing in his loins. He turned her and kissed her mouth, light and swift. His lips trailed down to her breasts. His kisses circled them. Then down, down.

He felt that guardedness in her relent. She melted on his tongue. She flowed. She opened. She swelled and blossomed and sang. His mind traced the path within her, where his tongue could not reach. It was familiar yet mysterious, perfect and womanly. He heard her breath catch: a sob. As for himself, he could not breathe. Could hardly see. Joy. This was joy.

He must go deeper into her, discover once more that dark, secret center of her. He rose up over her and took her and made her cry out. He loved the look of hungry appeal in her face. "Jane," he murmured against her lips. He felt his blood bubbling. "Jane." He couldn't hold back any longer. The pulsing spasm of his pleasure began. White mad joy.

After the storm, the peace. He lay utterly still. She was as beautiful as she had ever been, lying beside him, naked, warm, and richly pleasured. He must tell her what he felt for her. The words hung on his lips. But the dolt in him, which was a large part of himself, disavowed it, called it all delusion.

She moved against him. His passion rose again. He bid it be silent. He was not as strong as he would like to be yet. It irked him but it was true. Soon he would spend the whole night kissing and caressing the landscape that was her. But not this night.

Long after he'd fallen asleep, Jane's body tingled. He lay with his arms around her. She felt safe, surrounded by his powerful legs and his massive chest. Safe from soldiers, from magistrates, from hangmen. Yet she also felt captured, captivated, completely entranced. When he tightened his grip on her possessively in his sleep, it caused a little torrent of lust within her. The comfort they gave one another was great—but it was the only comfort they had.

She drew away from his embrace. He protested, muttering something before relapsing back into his dreams. She couldn't help but feel that she did herself some wrong every time she joined with him. With this rogue. She could almost hear Mr. Welby admonishing her: "Consider, child . . ."

And yet, except that he was a professional thief, Keith Cutler seemed entirely admirable to her. He'd saved her from certain rape. He hadn't stolen her money. Or her virtue. He seemed educated, mannerly, intelligent. She could love him. Latterly, she had felt herself falling in love with him.

Yet she couldn't make herself be blind. How long would it be before he went out into the night again? How long before she waited for him to return—and he didn't. How long before she heard he'd been caught, arrested, that they were going to hang him?

If they didn't catch her first and hang her, that was. No, don't think that way.

She knew so little about him. He'd let it slip that

he'd been in a house of correction once. Likely he'd been a miscreant all his life. She knew just how ruthless he could be; she'd felt his malignity those nights he'd stalked her; she'd seen him shoot a man. He was a man of the midnight, who, when exposed to the bright cruel sun, was immoral, evil, corrupt.

She looked at the ceiling of the cottage. She'd come to think of this place, nestled as it was between thorn and precipice, as home. But what kind of a home was it? A place in which they lived like lepers, driven out of society, hunted for wicked and reprobate persons. What kind of a home was it that you had to crawl into as varmints into a hole?

What are you doing here, Jane Fitzpatrick?

She was no criminal. No matter what people believed, she'd done nothing wrong. She'd always tried to be a good, honest, plain girl, and never vain and never wanton. She'd lived innocent of any outlaw design. And she did not want to end like this, with every gate shut against her. She didn't want a future in which the dread of someone coming up behind her suffocated her days and haunted her sleep.

She looked at Keith, at his sleeping mouth. His lips were soft from the kisses he'd given her. She loved that mouth—and heartily despised herself for loving it. He was a highwayman, he robbed people, and he did it with relish. She turned her head away, stiffened by some pride that nothing could snap. Sooner or later it was inevitable that someone would bring him to justice.

There was only one answer for her: to leave him and continue her journey. It was time she went on with the plan she'd begun in so much desperation. And so much hope. She'd never meant to stay with Keith. Now it was time to go. Already it was mid-November; another fortnight and the roads would be impassable with snow.

Another fortnight and she might be caught and hung for a murder she never committed.

Another fortnight and she might be with child.

She took a deep breath, moved her hand over her abdomen. Keith's child.

She felt safe here, but she wasn't. In America, in Georgia Colony, no one would know her, no one would seek to find her. America was a world away.

Keith moved in his sleep, searching for her. He took her in his arms again, gathered her up, as if in his dream he heard her thinking and believed that his strength alone might will them to go on as he would have it.

Keith reached for Jane several times in his sleep. He kept both remembering and dreaming of the damp softness of her inner thighs and the feel of her mouth under his.

When his arms found her side of the bed empty and cool, it woke him. He turned to look at the faintly lit room. She wasn't there. He waited a few minutes, thinking she might have gone out to the privy. The night was extremely still. Five minutes passed, then ten. He sat up. He was stiff and sore. He rubbed his side. It was still tender. There was no medicine for that but time.

The cottage was cold and had an empty feel. Her clothes were gone. A chair was standing beneath the shelf of crockery. He rose and checked the chipped tankard, knowing what he would find in it—nothing. He spoke her name in the night's hush. "Jane."

Nothing of her remained, not even the trace of her scent, that floral delicacy. It was as if she'd never been here, as if he'd dreamed her from the beginning.

Gone without a sound. Without a word.

* * *

The moon slid under a single thick cloud. The night was chill with the icy breath of November. Everything seemed so strangely quiet, as in a lull between storms. Jane followed the small bridle path that had taken her and Eclipse to the King William. She would sleep in the woods beside Dannel Common until daylight, lest she lose her way among the many paths there in the dark. Tomorrow she'd find the inn, and she would take up the road west.

This time at least she had some food with her, and was rested and well. She wondered how far she'd have to walk before she could feel safe enough to hire a farmer and his cart. A coach seat was out of the question, considering her infamous face. A cart would cost less, anyway.

She had her money wrapped around her waist again, with the three shillings the sergeant had thrown at her added to the total. She wasn't wearing her coif, not since Keith had warned her about how it shone out to eyes used to the dark.

Good-bye, Keith. You'll be angry to find me gone. I can't help that. I owe you nothing, though I love you well.

A moody silence prevailed. She crossed the beck that ran into Gwilt's Tarn, passed Dannel Common, and went into the woods. That was when she heard hoofbeats behind her, coming fast and hard, echoing and ringing through the eaves of the forest. Though she looked neither behind her nor to the left or right, her heart beat up. She felt an urge to run, to hide. She hadn't expected him to discover her absence so soon. She'd hoped she might be able to just disappear.

Suddenly the full moon broke free of the cloud overhead. It stood high and remote and sent its damning light down on her. She forced herself to keep her pace, going no faster, no slower. The horse came nearer, and then there it was, riding around her, wheeling, stopping in her path, a great black horse that reared up and neighed, for Keith was taking his anger out on the reins.

He glared down at her for several breaths. He was dressed in his full night regalia, complete with pistols and heavy leather sword scabbard. He was back in his frozen-faced role, the highwayman. He said coldly, "I take it you think you're leaving."

Their eyes met. His whole being seemed to quiver, as from surprise, or a blow. She looked away. They were silent until at last he said, "You might have said goodbye."

She was filled with a sense of inexplicable shame. She drew the hood of her cloak off her head. "I was afraid you wouldn't let me go."

"Think I'd coffle you?"

She couldn't see his expression beneath the shadow of his tricorn. She was a good deal more afraid of him than she'd expected to be. She surmised his face was as flat and cruel as the moon's. She wondered at the unself-consciousness of him when he took on this role, the authority, the completeness that was like a wild animal's. As a highwayman, he was a great strange creature.

"Maybe beat you a little?" he added. "Keep you in my bed with the aid of a stout stick?" He spoke quietly, yet she was aware of a ringing in his voice, muted, but telling. He was in a black wrath.

She answered, "I don't know."

"I realize that my manners are not the finest, but have I ever done anything to you that you didn't want me to do? That you should hasten from me like this? As from a cold-hearted murderer? Is that why your eyes look so dark and frightened just now, because you think I'll harm you?"

She felt more ashamed. "No." Yet she was uneasy.

He sat above her, vengeful, raging. She felt the great will it cost him to put aside these feelings and say, "I admit I don't want you to go."

She couldn't look at him.

"We're good together."

She took in a shallow breath and let it out quickly. "We're good at hiding together. I can't do that forever. Do you expect me to stand by your side right up to the gallows-foot?"

He remained stiff for a long moment, then he seemed to slump a little. He fingered his left side with a gingerly touch, and commented with a sort of bewilderment, "I'm sore as hell."

Her own anger rose up in an instant. "That's what happens when you get yourself shot! When you go out at night and rob people! When you live as if your life doesn't mean a thing, not to you or anybody else!"

"You've developed a nasty tongue, Jane Fitzpatrick."

"Yes, and that's another reason I must go—to recollect myself."

She started around him. Eclipse moved, always at his master's subtlest command. They blocked her way. For a moment she glared up at Keith. "I don't need any more of this! I don't need any part of you. I have enough problems of my own without getting involved with a highwayman."

"If you didn't want to get involved with a highwayman," he informed her with a fierce smile, "you shouldn't have come out on the road to play games with one."

Chapter Seventeen

Jenny Somebody or Other—the Whore

Keith swung off his horse. As he did, Jane took the opportunity to duck under Eclipse's head. The horse snaked and sidled; Keith caught her hand. Despite herself, she was afraid of him.

"I don't like how you live, Keith Cutler," she said in a smaller voice than she'd used before. "You took off your mask. You *dared* the Duke of Genthner to hang you."

"You're not responsible for how I live."

"And you're not responsible for keeping me from going where I want to go! I've paid my debt to you, I gave you what you wanted. I owe you nothing more. I'm on my way to Liverpool, and from there to America."

"Ah, yes, America—Georgia Colony! Where you're going to live in a red brick mansion. But did it ever occur to you that your brave New World might have its own evils and problems? You know what kind of people have found asylum in Georgia? Human wrecks, hundreds of them. The gaols and the almshouses have provided the quota for those wilds."

"They're giving away land to people who want to better themselves."

"To paupers and convicted criminals. To such as are idle and useless and cannot be transformed overnight into successful farmers. The scum of English cities. Coarse, evil-smelling, and brutal. And into their midst suddenly arrives a young and beautiful woman, all alone, without protection. Consider it."

"I can take care of myself."

"You think so? Have you, by chance, peeked into a looking glass in the last decade? Or have you heard of the current prevalence of lawlessness in the world? Do you know the kind of men who people this earth? The kind of men between here and Liverpool, the kind of sailors there, the kind who make pirates on the high seas? And the kind of women? There are bawdy-house keepers, Jane, here and I would lay odds, in your precious Georgia, too, who would make a fortune from having you tied down to one of the their flea-infested beds. Think of that, the men, fine colonists all, lined up outside the door, the bulge in their breeches quivering with excitement."

She'd seldom talked about her plan with him, sensing how skeptical he was of it. Now the depth of his scorn was blatantly apparent.

"Do you have any notion how far away America is?" He laughed humorlessly. "Do you even know how far away Liverpool is?" Another contemptuous laugh. "Do you even know where you are right this minute?"

She felt undermined. She knew she was *here,* and that somewhere ahead was a road that would take her *there,* but otherwise . . .

"And you think you can find your way to *Georgia?*"

He said it, as if it were a curse word.

Humiliation warred with desperation. She wished she'd never told him where she was going. Speaking of it brought it out into the light too much, and suddenly it looked impossible, a worthless and silly dream, doomed never to come true. He was stealing her hope from her just as surely as he stole jewels from the rich. She'd never come so close to hating him as she did in that moment.

"I'm going, Keith. I have to. I don't want to stay. I can't." He still had hold of her hand. She was suffocatingly aware of him. "I *can't*, don't you understand? I'm . . . they're . . . I can't stay in England!"

"Why not?"

He was too tall, too big, too strong in every way. She felt smothered by his nearness. Without struggling, she said, "You must let me go."

He didn't. He wouldn't. She knew it then. She'd thought she could slip away from him, but she'd only wakened his ruthlessness. He was, after all, when it came down to it, a highwayman. She should have waited until he was better, until he'd gone out into the night to take up his trade once more; then she would have had time. She'd been mad to venture it now. She'd been worse than mad, she'd been stupid.

He was watching her. "Why not, Jane? Something's been on your mind—what?"

She didn't want to tell him, didn't want to give voice to it. But he would never let her go elsewise. "They found my father. And they think I did him harm. I don't know—that I hit him over the head or something, and set the cottage afire around him. They think . . . they think I murdered him."

It was a long moment before he reacted. "I see. The Whites told you."

She nodded.

"But you didn't tell me. You faced those soldiers . . ."

"I have to leave England," she whispered again. "Please . . . do you understand?"

250

Silence. Then: "With me," he said suddenly. "You'll go with me. To Bristol, not Liverpool. You said yourself your father saw your portrait there. At least we have no *proof* that 'The Rose of Midnight' has made it to Bristol, which is, in any case, farther from York than Liverpool is. I'll see you there, and see you on a ship—if you still insist on your foolishness by then."

She stared at him, utterly taken by surprise. Her free hand went to her throat, to keep her emotion down. "You'll help me?"

He gave one nod, sharp and swift and resolute. His face was dark, set.

An astounded bliss grew in her. Not alone! And who could say, once they were on the highroad to America, he might even get a sense of where it could take him.

"Are you not afraid?" the highwayman in him said. The moonlight fell pale and thin on his black hat and greatcoat. "You were a moment ago. Consider: I could well devise a journey for you that ends in nothing."

She shook her head.

"Are you certain? Are you really so certain of me? I wonder. You were too unsure to tell me of your danger. Too afraid to say goodbye, to even give me a parting kiss."

He pulled her closer, reined her in, drew her against him and lowered his mouth to take hers. She felt his anger in that kiss, and his hurt, and his passion. The kiss lasted, there among the moonlight, till she knew he wanted her. Wanted her exceedingly. He'd never used so much strength to hold her, never kissed her quite so savagely. She stood enfolded, suspended on the balance of his will. He was no one she knew anymore. He was that masked horseman who had hunted her, who no matter what she did would not grow weary of his search and pursue some other prey.

251

With one powerful arm surrounding her, holding her, he shrugged off his coat, his hat, his sword belt. He pulled her down to the ground.

"Keith—"

"You're not under my roof now. My promise of mercy held only under my roof. There I obliged the woman who would keep to herself, who would not be handled—though my hands itched to handle her. Now you've ventured back into my other world. Give way, for you're about to be ravished by a highwayman."

He pulled her skirts up and sought her out with his hands and made her ready for him. It was indecent. He panted, " 'Tis very unsafe to go out unaccompanied after dark. There are men—"

He took her quickly, and hard. She made a sound.

"—men who rob . . . beat up . . . gouge out the eyes of . . . of their hapless victims . . . who rape . . ."

She was left gasping when he was done.

"Now you know what Grubneck Nord would have done to you. What will happen if you're ambushed by thugs."

She lay unmoving beneath him, limp with the violence he'd done her.

He gave her a sullen look. "When I saddled Eclipse, I counseled myself, I will not treat her badly."

"Then why did you?"

He shook his head imperceptibly. His expression changed. He seemed regretful as he laid his big calloused hand on her cheek. "I don't know. Which of us is really lost, Jane? Sometimes I think I need a navigator more than you do."

His voice was low. This was the Keith she knew. Who was that other man? The one who wore a mask and did things, dangerous things, terrible things? Her arms tightened about him. She felt a wild need to weep. "I don't know you." Her voice was a mix of her pain

252

and her confusion. "I want to be loved again, Keith. Not by a highwayman, by *you*."

He gave her a brief smile. He murmured, "Well, we can neither of us get lost if we don't go anywhere." His head bent down. His eyes were all her world. A moment more and she would drown in them. Her hands gripped his neck and pulled his mouth hard onto hers. Her body shuddered.

They went back to the cottage so that he could pack for the journey. They opened the "grave" containing his treasure. He took the money, but left the jewels—except for the opal ring that glinted on his small finger. They reburied the chest. Keith felt it was as safe where it was as anywhere. No one would dare open the grave of the two young pox victims.

He told Jane it was too dangerous for them to follow the highroad hence. So come morning they set out along the bridleways that wound between gnarled and rough hawthorns and connected hamlet to hamlet. No one coming upon them would guess that the bundle strapped to Eclipse's rump contained a small fortune.

They were in Staffordshire, Keith said. They bypassed Uttoxeter—a market town, Jane recalled from her geography lessons. It had held a prosperous Wednesday cattle market since the town's first charter in the thirteenth century.

She caught no more than a glimpse of Burton-upon-Trent, wherein she spied a few of the typical Staffordshire half-timbered houses. Mr. Welby's voice played in her mind: "Burton-upon-Trent has been known since the Middle Ages as a brewing center." She fancied she smelled hops and malt in the air.

She sensed that Keith was in constant argument with himself about what he was helping her to do. She knew he hadn't been clear as to his intent in promising to help her. He'd no doubt thought the impulse over since then, and regretted it.

The first night they camped in a copse. His love-making was like a rough wind. Jane's zenith was a dark point, breaking into bits, raining motionless stars over her.

Afterward, she recognized that she had given herself to him not to repay her debt. Such debts were no longer owing. The two of them had simply come to a point where they shared whatever they had that merited sharing.

Despite his protection, she spent an uneasy night filled with dreams and wakenings. The weather turned very cold before dawn. Frost glazed the earth with brittle glints and plated the branches with rime. The rising sun, small and cold in a bright sky, sent shadows westward from every break and hummock on the landscape. The air was raw. They rose eager to get on the move and warm themselves.

They traveled beyond Cannock Chase. They passed only two signs of habitation. One was an old cruck cottage built of cotswold stone. Whoever lived there was not at home this day. The other was a great white colonnaded estate set in beautiful grounds, with acres of lush farmland.

The sun shone through the morning without heat. Just before noon, the day darkened and a few drops of rain spattered Jane's face. She looked up to see massing gray clouds overhead. Thunder rolled, and lightning made a hundred breaks in the murderous sky. She'd heard tales of men stunned in exposed fields by lightning, and of milk curdling in cows' udders. But beyond a few sprinkles, the storm held off. They crested some gritstone uplands and came up onto the rim of new country, intensely green and pleated. Knolls wrapped around the slate-hung cottages of a village, like an eiderdown. Everywhere on the slopes sheep made their reedy demands.

Hence they came into the best of Derbyshire. These fertile farmlands bordered Birmingham. As they went on, the panorama included a slow-flowing river, and hills that rose sharply and were just short of being mountains. Jane spied another great country home in a horseshoe of hills and woodland, probably owned by one of the nobility. She saw several smaller manor houses. Orchards paraded their tidy military rows of leafless fruit trees.

Though nature's mantle had fallen gently on this district, the beauty of the view didn't seem to please Keith. A frown tightened between his eyebrows. His mood seemed as dark as the day.

Jane grew tired. She began to ache after two days in the saddle. She felt unwell. For the last hour or so a shivering had come on her now and again. It worried her, so that when Keith inquired if she was ill, she was unwontedly sharp in her denial.

He wasn't fooled. He examined her with a hard clear stare, his eyes taking in every weary inch of her, and in the end he said they would go down into the very next village and find a place to stay for the night.

"Is it safe?"

"Nothing is safe. But sometimes you must go counter to the wheel's turn."

He meant to find an inn. She was to keep her head down, her face hidden, while he arranged for a room. She was afraid. After all, she was wanted for murder. And what about him? Handbills with his description had been distributed to travelers and coachmen. Someone might have brought one here.

But she was too tired to protest his ready bravery—or rather the perversity in him that made him ready, even eager, to stake his lifeblood on the next cruel test. She was not like him, not at all. She was wanted for murder and it disturbed her profoundly; and she couldn't take it for granted.

A shiver shook her. Would life ever slow down to let her think through the awful events that had dropped like cannonballs all around her for the past month and more?

The next village was built mostly of gray limestone. Jane was surprised to realize it was Saturday, market day. She'd been in the wilds for so long she'd forgotten what day of the week it was. Though it must be three o'clock, the place was still full of stalls, animal pens, and carts, and packed with country people. The cobbled street was littered with straw. The air was thick with the noise of cattle and the rough shouting of men. Keith helped her down from Eclipse. She was to walk along beside the horse with her hood pulled up and forward to hide her face. Why wasn't fear, or at least wariness, filling all the interstices of her mind? Not because she'd learned to accept these moments of uncertainty with a quiet heart. No, rather it was because she felt only a flat exhaustion, and no will for anything except what Keith told her to do. She was glad, for once, to be venturing under a highwayman's wing. She felt his nearness like a hand on her skin. Wherever he led, she would go.

Her mind was on one thing, a bed. She looked forward to stretching out on a real mattress—though she hoped it would have no bugs. But even if it did, she thought she might lay down on it anyway. In fact, she didn't strictly require a bed. She would settle for a cattle stall or a hayloft. She was aching that badly, she wanted that badly to fall asleep with the pleasant sense of a sheltering roof over her head.

The shivering came and went again. Maybe there would be a cheerful blaze?

As they wove their way into the heart of the market, through the heavy, jostling crowds, she didn't dare look up at the tattered canopies of the stalls, or the overhanging gables of the timber-fronted houses. A horde of grimy children populated the street before a puppeter's stall. Leading Eclipse, Keith's spurs clinked on the stones. He paused here and there to ask about the possibility of a room for the night. Some of the stalls were beginning to be dismantled; a few carts were being loaded for going home. The throng seemed to be thinning out.

At a bookstall, Keith was told of an inn at the end of the street. To get there they must first push through a crowd packed shoulder to shoulder. Jane felt trapped in the center of all this humanity. Too late, she discovered what these last hangers-on were assembled to see.

Near the village church, next to the Hadaway Inn, were a pillory, the village stocks, and the whipping posts, all set into the cobbles. Whipping was often carried out in public. Between the posts ran a horizontal rail a foot or so above head-high. A village girl stood under this rail, her arms bound above her head with thongs. Her hair had been drawn up roughly under a coarse wool cap. Without regard to the chill weather, her bodice and chemise had been torn from her, so that her body was naked to her waist. Her white skin was drawn into gooseflesh. The whiteness of her small breasts, with their clenched nipples, made her look twice as vulnerable as any man in the same position.

She was young, shapely, though a trifle gaunt, as with long acquaintance with hunger. Her feet were bare. Evidently she'd been kept there for quite a while, for all the market visitors to witness her shame. She was drooping, hanging by the thongs about her wrists.

257

The constable guarding her lounged at his leisure with his wooden club.

Keith was still moving forward, trying to find a way through the crowd to get to the inn. The door of the Hadaway opened, and Jane glimpsed animal skins, wolf and deer, affixed to the walls with wooden pegs. A man came out with a long whip coiled in his hand. Jane stopped. Keith went on without her, unwitting.

The man with the whip was a swarthy, rough-looking fellow. He walked straight to his trussed victim. He ripped her skirt of cotton stuff a bit more, just to hear the crowd's reaction, it seemed. The waist of the girl's skirt fell to the swelling tops of her hips. Her body was naked now to the divide of her buttocks. She stood straighter and whimpered against her bonds. The people bunched closer with horrid eagerness. A dame shouted in a voice that reached into Jane's very backbone, "Whipping's not good enough for her!" Jane looked to her right and saw an older woman, the sturdy, laboring sort, with strong, robust shoulders, and heavy, drooping breasts. "She'll only be improved by hanging, that one!"

Her husband gave her a jerk. "Hush thee, Esther Raithcock! The lass will be dealt with as warranted." He glared at her, though she didn't have the grace to seem abashed.

Standing in a cart off to one side was a black-coated figure brandishing a black-bound book. His eyes shone with scalding, gospel vehemence. "Aye, she'll get as she's warranted, here and in hell!"

The man with the whip turned to his audience. A smile flickered then went out. He said formally, "Jenny Cliffwood, twenty lashes, for fornicating with various men." This was met by a stolid, humorless silence. The only noise came from the beasts in the market. He let the wicked-looking knotted end of the whip fall. A young couple near Jane held up their children to see.

When the first blow fell, Jane flinched. Suddenly she felt gauntleted fingers around her wrist. Keith. Something in her winced as if he had touched an injury. She felt the pressure of his hand pulling her away—but she was rooted to the spot. As the whip sliced through the air again, every noise in the square merged into a single sound that was like silence to her ears. She fisted her mind against the blow, yet she felt the second smoldering welt rise on the girl's white skin.

Keith put his arm around her and forced her through the crowd. There were complaints. Eclipse was blocking a farmer's view. " 'Ere now, get out o' t' way!" Jane looked back. It was as if she couldn't prevent herself from watching. She tripped, and looked down to see a homemade box full of russet apples. "Clumsy hussy!" scolded a woman who was all severity, coiffed as relentlessly as a nun. Jane felt Keith's hands on her waist. He lifted her abruptly. She saw Eclipse's saddle and involuntarily grabbed for it. She looked back. She could see better now. The girl, alone, so obviously alone, and so vulnerable. There were three welts on her white back, the newest rapidly becoming a red oozy trail.

Jane felt the movement of the stallion beneath her. Keith was leading her through the edge of the crowd, making people give way or be trampled. He had to stop for a cart. Jane heard the whir and snap of number four. She swayed heavily against the pommel and clung there for an interminable moment, dizzy and sick.

Eclipse's hooves clattered on the cobblestones as they started up a dark alley, away from the marketplace. Jane heard the fifth snap of the whip, and now a spasmodic, gasping cry. Jane cried out herself.

"Something wrong with your lady?"

Jane looked down to find two men in scarlet livery, two exotic cock pheasants, both haughty with their uniforms and their authority. She quickly hid her face in her hood.

Keith said, "She was upset by the whipping."

"Ah, yes, Jenny somebody or other—the whore," the nearest soldier muttered, continuing to study Jane. He had his hat under his arm and his hair was so importantly waved and burnished and combed that the face under it gave the effect of zero. Rigidity was Jane's one protection against his eyes. His companion was just as busy looking at Keith.

Keith nodded and started to move along. The second soldier barred his way. His eyes looked drunk. Keith waited in a patience that bade fair to break, and soon. His composure awed Jane. It was moments like these when his distinctly alien nature was bared. She needed no magic to know what he was thinking: if only I had my pistols! These two cock pheasants would be easy prey.

Too easy, Jane thought.

The soldier stood with his legs braced and his arms folded across his chest, a challenging stance. "Do I know you, sir?"

"I think not," Keith said. Jane felt the edge of violence in his tone. "Though I've been to this market several times lately and perhaps you've seen me about."

"Perhaps." His narrowed eyes seemed less drunk now. They were the color of bright brown wood.

Keith glared back with fine fierceness. "If you'll excuse us, I'd like to get my wife home."

"Where is home?"

"I beg your pardon, sir? Am I being hampered and questioned for any good reason?"

The soldier with fancy hair came to the rescue. "Here, Ingram, let the man pass. Can't you see his lady is ill?"

She felt movement under her. Eclipse. With strange reluctance, as if she had been asleep and didn't want to wake, Jane acknowledged that Keith had led her away from the soldiers, down an alley and into the wynds, the narrower lanes and alleys of the village. Here the clamor of the marketplace seemed curiously distant. She was relieved that he should have assumed so much responsibility for her, for she could not have taken herself away.

Yet even here she couldn't get it out of her mind, the whip, the snap, that cry. It had a hold on her memory as vivid as paint.

But between then and now . . . what had happened to her? Where had her mind gone? It frightened her to realize that several times lately she'd lost her consciousness and her vision for long minutes, and when she "woke" again, she had no memory of what she'd done or where she'd been.

Oh God, what had happened to her life—the orderliness, the serenity, the routine? Since the day she'd found her father in her chamber in Mr. Welby's house it was as if she were on a runaway horse: everything occurred so quickly there was no chance to react to events. The only thing she could do was hold on tightly and try to stay lucid.

Chapter Eighteen

She Seemed About to Slip From His Grasp

Keith rode pillion behind Jane. Twilight fell early.
Dark gray clouds in heaps tumbled overhead. The
thunder returned, and the lightning, and it started to
rain hard. Jane could not forget what she had seen in
the market village. Or the way those soldiers had looked
at Keith. She was tired and ill, and she felt despairing.
They passed a cottage where they might have begged
shelter in a barn, but Keith wouldn't stop. Jane sensed
he had been more startled by the soldiers than he
wanted her to know.

She saw a road marker that pointed one way to
Worchester and the other to Malvern. Both were close
by, but Keith would go into neither place. He said he'd
rather press forward to Ledbury. Jane surmised that
this might take them into the night. She dared not
complain, not when that drunk-eyed soldier might have
already sobered and realized that the man he'd thought
seemed familiar today was the one described on the
Duke of Genthner's handbills.

Keith got down to give Eclipse a rest from their double weight. He squared his hat and led the horse for-

ward under a fell with outcrops of toppled stone. He did not share his thoughts. She wished she knew what was going on inside his clever head. But how could she, when she didn't even know what was going on inside her own? What was this despair, this weary sadness, this relentless urge to weep? She gripped the pommel of the saddle, unaware of the grand and horrid scenery all about her. Tears leaked down her rain-damp cheeks. Keith looked anxiously at her over his shoulder. She was ashamed of herself.

Even if he'd wanted to stop here, there was no place, no shelter from the storm and the night. She was compelled to journey with him through this arched and steep landscape of darkness and stone.

The faint outline of their track now followed a river that talked to itself where it hid in black bushes and a few stark, lonely trees. As the rain continued, the waterway grew swollen by the innumerable becks which poured down from the steep fellsides. It made a ceaseless gurgle as it pummeled the banks of its course. These water sounds gradually grew into a fountainous roar. Keith shouted, "A miller's pond."

Jane drew herself up with effort. What had he said? A millpond? She now recognized the sound of a rain-flooded dam of the sort used to direct the water onto a waterwheel. When a heavy sprout of lightning branched overhead, she saw the rush of the plunging waterfall, the fume at the bottom, the churning beyond.

The path they were on led to a wooden footbridge. It swayed and shook with the force of the water dashing beneath it. Jane turned her head to shout, "It's too dangerous." The rain pelted her cold face like small wet gravel.

"It will hold," Keith insisted. He took the horse by the bridle. The moonless dark made a shadow of him; he was carved out of the substance of the midnight.

Not a man to vacillate, he led Eclipse onto the bridge. The river was coming to flood. The bridge shook so badly that even Eclipse balked. Keith breathed a bitter, blasphemous expletive. It was all Jane could do to keep her terror quiet. Keith had to take the animal's bridle in both hands and lead him by walking backward before him. Alone in the saddle, Jane clenched herself so tight she was rigid.

They reached the middle, however, and she began to think they might make it.

But the bridge suddenly gave way. Eclipse tried to keep some foothold. Keith swore as the animal's bridle was wrenched out of his hands. Jane's last glimpse of him showed a white visage of fear. Then Eclipse went down, taking her with him, down to where the water ran black.

The millstream was cold! Cold! As cold as it ought to be in November with the coming of winter. She hardly had time to gasp as she plunged into that harsh iciness. So cold it was hot. Like falling into an icy inferno. Ripples of cold flame licked her body, sizzled her flesh.

She lost her hold on Eclipse, though she felt the big horse struggling. One of his great hooves struck the back of her head. So instantly numbing was the cold, she didn't feel the blow in terms of pain. There was no sharp dizzying hurt, only a slam that knocked her head forward and down, and an abrupt zigzag light.

The powerful current caught her heavy cloak and skirts and she was suddenly ripped away from the wrestling horse. She was carried to the surface, but tumbled and tumbled. Her wheel of fortune was spinning in a fury. The noise of the flooding river pressed against her eardrums. Then the malevolent current took a better grip on her; she was pulled under again.

The river closed over her. All was silent; her ears

heard nothing but the echo of the frenzy above. The water set fast about her, tighter and tighter, trussing her in cold iron. She stopped tumbling. The coins wrapped around her waist weighted her. She was pushed into an embrace of roots. A submerged tree. Her whole body writhed in resistance, but every move tangled her further. Her hair was caught, her cloak and skirts, one foot. The current shoved her deeper into that tentacled clutch. The water stopped her nose and her mouth. It pressed her eyelids open. Her breath swelled in her chest. She had to let it out. She had to breathe.

At first she thought of nothing except a yearning to be saved. Then, like a rabbit doubling before a fox, her mind suddenly ran back through her life. She felt again Keith's first fierce entrance into her body, followed by the surging pleasure. Back, her mind ran. She bolted over the black moors rife with brigands. Memory upon memory slammed through her mind, all reaching backward. *Jane,* her father whispered. There was fire, ashes to ashes, heat beyond endurance. She saw the ceiling beam come down, *thunk,* as it struck Rip's skull. She heard with perfect clarity the spine-chilling whistle of the whip behind her, her own voice rising in a thin scream. Backward, it was all reversed, her remembrance was racing the wrong way. She heard her dress being rent from her back, the look on Rip's wrinkled, winter-apple face. The old cottage, decayed to its heart, its roof about to fall in. Hockness Hall, the great lawns, the baron with his paintbrushes. She lifted the heavy skirts of the white, sack-backed gown. Mr. Welby's house, a meat pie on the table in the kitchen, the sun falling through the windows in the dining room, the order, the peace. Her mother's grave, the neglected graveyard, the untidy rose at the gate. The farm, the cottage again, the spring shearing, the pitiful harvest, the wind catching the chaff as she and her mother threw up the flailed grain. She saw their lives, the years of poverty and struggle. She saw her father with her mother, young they were, and she saw herself, very young, a child, an infant in a basket staring at fire-shadows on the ceiling.

She traveled back to where it had all begun. And by this review, she recognized that now it was over. Something in her gave up. Her mind, drawn taut in resistance for so long, announced, *No more.*

Keith's side of the bridge held just long enough for him to leap to the bank. He started along the worn path at the far edge, trying to keep Jane in sight. She was swept along faster than he could follow. What was that old saying about a straw in a millrace?

Lightning bolted from the cracked and fluent heaven. Something large and dark rose up against the night: Eclipse clambered onto solid ground, blowing like a whale, eyes popping in panic. Keith gave the stallion little heed, for at that same moment Jane disappeared.

He ran on along the track that followed the river, among gnarled trees and dark, mossy boulders. His boots sank in the mud. He ran under the lurid sky calling, "Jane! Jane!" Fear chased along his spine. Would it finish as abruptly as it had started? Fear made his heart pound. And worse than the fear was the anguish, and the desperate denial.

In the next flash of lightning, he caught sight of a shape snared in a sidewise tangle just beneath the surface of the tumbling flood: Jane's neat, modest figure snared in a mass of tree roots. He threw off his greatcoat, his hat, his sword and scabbard. He was swift for her sake, yet he seemed slow. He stepped off the bank.

The water swirled over his boot tops, immediately

sloshed around his crotch. He gasped as though prodded by a blade. As he pushed further into it, the cold rose to his belt, the current beat at his legs. Another step and the water would be over his head.

He'd never learned to swim. Why hadn't he? Why had he never foreseen this critical need?

In books, men said they would die for such and such a woman. Keith had long thought this a sentiment that made pretty poetry but didn't mean anything. He understood it now, however, as meaning exactly what it said. He'd been blind and Jane had appeared to him, and seeing her, he'd seen the world again. Days and nights had meaning again, for she had touched him and that touch had retaught him the language of humanity. Nothing was changed, but sometimes it made sense. And sometimes there was beauty. He'd been afraid to see all that beauty, the beauty of the world. He'd been afraid.

He plunged into the roiling river. The cold made him want to scream. It was as if he were cut, burned. Things hurt. Everything. The highwayman had been numb. The narcotic was worn off. Keith Soloman lived again, he felt pain. And inside the pain was hope, hope beyond calculation. The name of that hope was Jane.

The cold locked around him and turned each movement into an agony of sluggish motion. The current wanted him. He fought it. He came to the surface for a breath. The black water was speckled in a billion places with rain. He dove under again. He felt the boiling waters close over his head. He kicked. He reached. He felt her face. Her throat in his hands was a wonderful thing, as delicate as a flower's stem.

He found her shoulder, fumbled, caught her around the waist. She didn't help him. Her eyes were open but he couldn't tell whether she was dead or unconscious. He kicked with his legs and surfaced. She lay heavy in his arms, her face white, waxy. She was whiter than he'd ever seen her, as white as death. The current still clutched him, but he would not give himself to it, nor would he give it Jane.

Lightning continued to electrify the air. He got close enough to the edge of the torrent that his feet touched bottom. He lifted Jane over his shoulder and struggled for the bank. He carried her to higher ground, into an orchard where the naked boughs were like roots striking into the sky. Her face was more blue than white now. Her lips were blue. Her hair, most of it pulled loose from her heavy wet braids, trailed in streams over her open eyes. She wasn't breathing. He knelt beside her and labored to make her breathe. As the seconds passed, he willed her to move, to blink. Angry tears clouded his eyes. "You always fought, Jane! You always fought!"

At last, at the end of two or three infinitely long minutes, he felt her ribs move slightly beneath his pressing, squeezing hands. He felt a sense of terrified elation. He wanted to laugh and groan together. She coughed, gasped. Her mouth filled with swallowed water; he turned her so she could spew it out. More coughing. Keith's breath snagged on something— laughter, a sob. He fought the urge to sit on the ground and weep. He bit his lip. His mouth twisted into a grimace. He inhaled in quivering gasps.

Though she was still limp, he helped her sit up. He stood, slowly, like an old man with rheumatism. It was the release from fear; he was stunned. "I'll go get my coat—and Eclipse."

He returned with his sword and his hat and his greatcoat. Eclipse was still saddled, even the pack containing Keith's money and pistols was intact. "Can you stand, Jane?" She was looking at the river, at that black cold muscle of water. Her eyes were open but still unseeing. He gathered her in his arms and lifted her to her feet. For a moment he held her to him without speaking. Then he lifted her toward the horse. She managed to shove her foot into the stirrup and put herself in the saddle. "Put this around you," he said. "Wrap it well."

She looked at the greatcoat but didn't take it. Her mind seemed sluggish. It's the cold, he thought, even her brain must be frozen.

"Take the coat, Jane."

Eventually she did. She managed to pull it around her, over her own cloak, which was sodden.

He swung up behind her and put his arms around her to take up the horse's reins. She was shivering.

"You need a fire and a bed."

A fire and a bed. But where was he to find them? He couldn't risk going to an inn after that close brush with the King's Army today. Clearly the duke's handbills had found their way even this far south, for they'd almost recognized him. But Jane needed care, a bed, maybe even medical attention. And someone to hide her at the same time. But the Rose of Midnight was wanted for murder. She must be hidden while she recovered. Where? Where?

She put a hand to the back of her head, then looked at it. He saw what she did, the blood on her fingers. He examined her head with one hand, felt the lump. The cut didn't seem serious, but it would explain her sluggishness. He suddenly knew where he must take her. It was the only place where she could get the care she needed.

His arms were around her. She leaned against him and closed her eyes and seemed to drift into a doze. Her body went quite slack; her head leaned sideways.

She didn't rouse until he stopped Eclipse outside the imposing entrance to a manor estate. Keith hesitated.

The shape of the big house loomed against the blackness of the wooded fellside. It stared at him from behind its black metal railings as though sensible of its superiority. What had made him think he could bring Jane here? The owner was not one of those charitable persons who are ready to bestow meat and lodging.

He spurred Eclipse through the wrought-iron gates. He felt a fierce, raging determination. The last time he'd come to this place, he'd believed he was about to make a mighty leap upward in life, a great rise in the world, but he'd been wrong. He recalled the night, a Christmas Eve he'd never forget. A feeling of unease undermined his rage.

Jane dozed along the drive. The gravel crunched loudly under Eclipse's hooves. Keith realized he was wearing a berzerker's smile. He swung down before the house. Jane looked at him dully. In her eyes was a kind of lost and sad look. Her face was still ghastly white. He held his arms up to her. "Jane?"

She gave him a glazed stare and no reply. Finally she slid sideways, a dead weight for him to catch. He tried to set her on her feet, but her legs wouldn't hold her. She seemed about to slip from his grasp. She watched some point vaguely over his shoulder. He was frightened, and more frightened by what she murmured as he lifted her into his arms to carry her to the door:

"Why . . . why do you call me that?" Her eyes barely brushed his.

"Call you what?" he said very gently.

Her groggy mind seemed to be trying to put things together. "Jane."

His stomach churned with vague apprehension. He didn't like this. He struggled to keep the tremor out of his voice. "Because that's your name."

The monstrous dark clouds overhead flickered with internal lightning. The air felt heavy with water. She frowned, seemed to think very hard, then said, "Is it?"

His lips parted; he felt a chill. Suddenly the trusses of reality had moved backward about ten yards. He still clung to a shred of groundless faith. "You know who I am—don't you?"

She studied him, then moved her head: no. A spasm shook her; her teeth chattered. He smiled at her uncertainly. "You're freezing." He carried her up the steps.

He was not a fool to think it would be so easy as simply knocking. This house had been forbidden him. He was without a face here. He wasn't seen, wasn't heard, wasn't received. There was no place by the hearth for him, no food for him to eat, no chamber for him to rest in. He was a fatherless nobody here, a low brute, a bastard.

He sat Jane on the steps, pausing only to arrange his greatcoat around her, then he went to look through the downstairs windows. Two were lit in the salon. Though it was probably near midnight, in the circle of a warming fire sat a lone woman with hair the color of a new copper pot. Keith recognized that face despite the years, despite the fact that it was reddened and cratered by firelight and shadow. Stella. She was wearing a countrywoman's workaday dress, turquoise blue, with a tight, boned bodice and full skirt over petticoats. He watched her without feeling. The shock and fright of almost losing Jane had burned away all feeling save a dull, cold sense of purpose.

He went back to Jane, who was just as he'd left her, huddled and listless, with that glazed look on her face. He got her on her feet, keeping her curiously limp body braced against him. He muttered, "This is a damned dangerous thing." Dangerous for her even more than for him. "If I had any idea what else I *could* do . . ."

She seemed not to hear. "I want to go home," she

said in a small voice, her teeth chattering a little. "I just want to go home."

Keith had never seen her like this. His free hand, with absent gentleness, stroked her hair back from her face. He laid a palm over the ebb and return of the pulse in her cool throat. Then he lifted the ram's-head knocker and let it fall lightly against the oaken door.

No one was awake in the interior of the big house but Stella Grayson. She'd made it a habit to stay up late, alone, so that no one would think it unusual. She sat by the fire in the salon doing some sewing, or rather, staring blindly at the needlework which she'd taken into her lap to give the appearance that she'd been sewing. Her square-toed shoes were damp. She hoped her heavy petticoat was not crusted with mud. She must remember to clean them both before she went to bed— which she would like to do now, but she wanted her father to see her here when he came in.

She smiled, remembering the hour she'd spent earlier. She recreated the scene, treasuring every detail: she was in his lap, and he was laughing in delight. She was grinning herself, even though she wanted to hit him for teasing her.

Why couldn't she be with him all the time?

No. She must not consider that. Think only of him, of the light in his face and the warmth of his body, the strength of his hands, the joy when she could be with him, when she could escape for an hour, live free for an hour.

The quiet knock at the door shocked her rigid. She hadn't heard the carriage—anyway, Father always used his key at such a late hour. All manner of things ran through her mind at the sound of that knocker falling against the door so lightly: whoever was there didn't want to wake the house. Was it someone who knew she was still up? Something dark and haunted in the back of her eyes woke up. Was it . . . ? But no, of course not, it couldn't be. He would never follow her back here, never.

She rose from her tall-backed chair, dropping her handiwork in the basket from which she'd taken it. She almost called for Daniel, Father's manservant, to come and answer the summons with her, but then she chided herself for being a coward.

Still, as she came into the polished black marble entrance hall her heart beat harder than normal. Reason warned her that any visit coming so late must be momentous in some way. Maybe something had befallen Father coming home in this nasty weather from his regular game of whist.

She fumbled with the lock and opened the door a crack, expecting some unpleasant discovery. A face, masculine, not Father's—though it looked like Father's, only younger. And not Burne's either. Keith.

She opened the door fully as she saw Keith Solomon for the first time in fifteen years. Yes, it was Keith, there was no mistaking him. Her eyes met his, direct and mute. She felt herself go white with excitement— and with sudden, piercing terror, for Father could return at any time.

Her lips formed his name, but before she could give voice to it, he pulled a greatcoat off an ill-looking young woman and thrust her forward, dripping with water and blue with cold. Stella had no choice but to take the girl into her arms. Still rocked by the sight of Keith, she registered nothing of the girl but an impression of white, wild beauty, and hair that could only be a fantasy, rivers of it.

Keith said, "You once showed a willingness to be my sister. If that feeling was true, I ask you to show it

273

to this girl now. She's nearly drowned, and has a lump on her head, and doesn't seem to recall who she is at the moment. Her name is Jane. She's in danger, Stella, so if you take her, you must promise to protect her. Keep her hidden until she's well again and I can take her away again. Can you do that? Will you?''

Stella nodded, hardly knowing what she was promising. She continued to stare at him. Willing her mind into focus, she found her voice. Something in his attitude told her she must be quick. "Keith, I think of you, I always do, wherever you are.''

She thought she saw a little twitch of the corner of his mouth. "Thank you,'' he said.

Keith! How are you? How do you live? Are you happy? All this she wanted to say, but before she could make her voice work, he was backing away. She had both arms around the girl, this Jane person, who seemed unable to stand without support. Stella felt the girl's cold, wet body slip; she stiffened, becoming a brace. She could not follow Keith, though she longed to with all her heart. Already he was down the drive where his horse waited for him. He swung up into his saddle and wheeled his mount, and giving her one last piercing stare, he galloped off, disappearing into the dense blackness of the rain.

From behind Stella came a voice—Burne's: "Who is that?''

Stella was practiced at stealth, but it seemed to take her a fearful amount of time to remember what she'd promised Keith: help the girl, protect her, hide her. What did it mean? Until she knew, she decided that not even Burne must know this secret. She pushed the heavy door shut with her foot, closing out the sluicing ice-water air, and she turned to her brother with a look of innocent surprise.

Chapter Nineteen

Tied About the Girl's Hips
Was a Curious Moneybelt

Burne came down the stairs wearing a robe and bedroom slippers. His eyes were all for the girl in Stella's arms.

"I found her on the doorstep."

Burne's mind seemed blurred, full of sleep. She felt a great relief: he hadn't seen Keith; he would believe her. "Help me carry her up to a bed."

Scowling, Burne took hold of the limp, listless Jane. "What's wrong with her? Why—she's soaked!"

"She looks half drowned."

It was odd looking at Burne just minutes after looking at Keith. Though one was so dark and the other so fair—and Burne had his dimples, of course—they would be marked as brothers by anyone. Burne was as tall as Keith, and his body was nearly as thick with muscle, kept strong at the hunt. He had no trouble lifting the girl, who was no bigger than Stella, which was not particularly big. He swung her easily up into his arms. For once he seemed surprised enough to forget to punctuate his every move with his usual fire of wit, perhaps because the girl was so ill. Or perhaps because she stared up at him with such round, lovely, lost blue eyes.

"Where'd she come from?" he grumbled in his deep voice. "How'd she get so wet?"

"I don't know. She was leaning against the door and simply fell into my arms when I opened it." From outside came the sound of gentle thunder, sonorous and moving away, like gods in the storm.

"She's shivering. Let's get her upstairs."

Stella hurried ahead. Which room? The Empire Room was the nicest, but the White Room was farthest away from her father's suite. She led the way to the White Room.

Burne seemed completely mesmerized by the girl in his arms. His face was a complete blank. With all the gentleness in the world, he laid her on the White Room's high bed. Stella had to ask him twice to go downstairs and rouse Catherine, their woman servant.

As soon as he left, Stella hurried to undress the girl. She'd never performed such an intimate service, yet she did not hesitate. Keith had asked something of her, and she would do what she promised. To accomplish that, she would have to employ a vast amount of cunning. For Father would think nothing of putting the girl out—unless Stella could somehow make her acceptable to him.

Tied about the girl's hips was a curious sort of knotted money belt. She instinctively hid this in a cupboard. She dried the girl—and caught her breath to see the scars on her back. What mystery was this? Was the person who had done this the "danger" Keith had mentioned?

The girl was in no condition to say. She was groggy, as if under the influence of a drug. Stella felt the lump on the back of her head. It had stopped bleeding, and didn't seem serious. To protect the pillowslip, she put a towel beneath Jane's head.

Stella next flew on tiptoes to her own room for a smock, and was struggling to get Jane's limp body into it—to cover those scars. She must do that, she knew intuitively. She was nearly finished when Catherine came.

"Here, madam! Ye should've waited for me to help ye." Catherine was worrying her uncovered black hair with her fingers. She had ears that stuck out, and a space between her front teeth, and was otherwise thoroughly ugly, though Stella had long ago accepted her looks as one accepts a piece of furniture that's been around most of one's life. The woman was surprisingly agreeable at having her sleep disturbed. In the constricted atmosphere of Grayson House, such a novelty as this must seem delicious.

Stella said, "She was so cold, I had to get her out of her wet things. Just pull that hem down over her legs."

Once Jane was under the bedclothes, they spread out her hair so that it would dry. She might have been dead, she lay so still—and yet her eyes were often open. They did no more than stare into nothingness, however.

"Light the fire, Catherine; it's miserably chilly in here; then go get me something hot to give her—tea or broth, it makes no difference as long as it's steaming. I wish I had just a small vial of sal volatile."

While Catherine was gone, Stella furtively rolled Jane's sodden clothes into a bundle and hid them in the cupboard with the money belt. Her father mustn't know that she'd come dressed in such poor things, for a plan was already forming in Stella's mind.

She was surprised and more than a little proud of herself. She was thinking far faster than she'd believed herself able to do. Still, this thing she was planning, if

Father—his heart was a cold clenched thing, a knot of ice beneath his breastbone—if he should find out the girl had been brought by Keith—no, he wouldn't find that out.

She touched the girl's forehead. My, but she was beautiful. No wonder Burne had been bewitched. Beauty like that could pierce a heart as tough as a cannonball. (Pray that it can pierce Father's!) Such long thick hair. What was it like to be so beautiful? What would it be like not to have people's glances slide over you like rain down a windowpane, but instead stop and try to penetrate? She felt a pang of jealousy. She stifled it.

Who is she, Keith. What does she mean to you? What danger is she in? What happened to her?

She must save this girl and protect her for Keith. She remembered all too well the one and only time she'd ever met her half brother, that terrible Christmas Eve. She remembered Keith's eyes just before her father had shut the door on him, eyes blazing with hopeless courage.

Catherine brought back a steaming bowl of barley broth simmered with some herbs. Burne came with her. He had a flask of brandy. "Might revive her a little." He went to the bedside and gently lifted Jane's head.

"Watch that lump. She's been hit by something."

Burne examined it briefly, then forced the liquid into her mouth.

It came out again. Catherine was ready with a towel. But the spirits made Jane's eyes open wide.

"Can you speak?" Burne asked her.

She only stared at him.

Stella said, "Best leave her to us."

"Yes, if you think so."

When he went out, Catherine lifted the bowl of broth. Stella took it from her. "I'll do that, Catherine. You may go back to bed."

The servant's homely face closed like a fist below the black tangle of her hair. Clearly she didn't like being excluded from this excitement. Nonetheless, she left.

Stella spooned the broth into Jane a drop at a time. The girl wouldn't take much, and it was as if she did not know that she swallowed what little she did. Through it all, her eyes seemed mere objects, registering nothing, revealing nothing.

"Jane," Stella murmured.

There was no response. The blue eyes simply stared.

"Jane? Do you hear me?" She leaned close to the silent girl. Carefully, she moved her hand before the half-open eyes. Not even a flutter. Puzzled, she pulled a chair near the bed and sat back. The girl was alive. And yet—

She stood and tried a third time. "Jane?"

The eyes moved, looked at her, but that was all. She wasn't blind, she just was . . . unseeing.

"What happened to you, Jane?"

No answer.

She could do nothing more for the girl, but must leave nature to fight it out. Eventually Jane's eyes closed and she seemed to sleep. Stella heard the carriage bring her father home. She heard him come into the upper gallery. She half expected to hear Burne's voice, telling him about the girl in the White Room. But Burne evidently had gone back to sleep. Good. Father didn't need to know until morning. By then Stella would be ready.

The chamber was warm now. Stella sat on alone by the bedside. She covered her mouth and yawned till her jaw cracked. Her eyes felt scratched and swollen. When she was sure her father must be abed, she went to the cupboard and took out that odd moneybelt. She picked out the knots that held the coins in the long strip of cloth. When she had them all free, she counted seventy guineas, nine shillings, and four pence. Not a large sum to someone like Father, yet as much as three years' wages for someone like Catherine.

What would it be to someone like Stella Grayson?

What was it to this girl?

Other questions rose, one upon the other. If the girl had so much money, why was she dressed as a pauper and a vagrant? Why was her back scarred? How had she come to be nearly drowned? What was she to Keith? Who was she?

Stella burned every fragment of Jane's identity. She first used the shabby rag that had been the moneybelt to clean the mud off her own shoes, however. She mustn't forget that. There must never be any evidence that she'd been out earlier tonight herself.

As she worked, she thought about Keith. He'd grown so tall, become so much more handsome, even drenched. It was a mixed blessing to have the past return this way, but finally she could do something for her lost brother. Though she was not clear about what it was she was doing.

She sat back by the bedside and once again looked at Jane's money stacked on the table there. Seventy guineas, nine shillings, and four pence. Father would insist on keeping that for her. He hated a woman having any money of her own.

Stella's imagination suddenly ignited. She felt her emotions rise. Eyes bright with defiance, with a kind of fury, she rose and went to the chamber door. She opened it cautiously. The gallery was dark. She tiptoed to her own chamber. With only a candle to see by, she passed her great curtained bed. In her wardrobe she found a little purse for which she'd had no use but once, many years ago, when she'd hung it on her arm to complete an outfit during a brief visit to "that sink of wretchedness"—her father's term for London. He wouldn't remember the purse. She took it back to Jane's chamber.

He would keep Jane's money if he knew about it. But what if she must leave quickly—and secretly—with Keith? Although a purse with a little money in it would help Stella convince Father to let Jane stay, Stella needn't account for all of it. She put ten guineas and all the shillings and pence in the purse. That would satisfy Father. The rest . . .

Stella would keep the rest.

For Jane.

Captain Thomas Grayson, a large man of late middle age, walked with a slight bend of his head, as though always anticipating trouble from behind. His long oval face usually wore an expression of gloom. His eyes were slate gray, his nose straight and even—he was pure English. He was an amateur musician, a keen sportsman, and in his younger years a full-hearted naval man. He was a model of personal fastidiousness, with a passion for clean linen.

Even before his breakfast today, he was informed that a young lady had been found on the doorstep in the night and taken in by his children. Burne wasn't up yet. It was Stella (still in her dressing gown and slippers) who came to his library at this early hour to inform him of the visitor occupying the bed in the White Room. His pipe was suspended halfway to his mouth when Stella said, "Her clothes were in such poor condition, I had them burned. But she had this." She handed him a lady's purse.

The captain set aside his pipe on his desk, opened the purse and counted the coins inside. Not a great sum. He examined the purse. It was not something a common poor wench would have—unless she'd stolen it. Smoke continued to waft from his untouched pipe.

Stella stressed, "She seems of good quality."

But of course the captain must visit the White Room to see for himself.

He let Stella go and waited until he was sure she was at her toilet before he went up himself. He wanted to look over the girl and make his decision without his daughter's hand-wringing presence. He stayed just long enough to ascertain that the creature was not foul or diseased. She was not; indeed, she seemed particularly attractive—for someone who was not conscious. With her hair lying loose over her graceful arms and slender neck, she looked as peaceful and sweet as a sleeping cat. And her face—well, she had a face that was quite amazing.

Stella, usually so compliant, became difficult when later that morning he insisted on sending for Bradley Barceloux. He felt it necessary to obtain a professional opinion, however. Hence a mounted messenger was sent for the physician.

Captain Grayson disliked Barceloux, who had been a youthful friend of the captain's older brother, Francis. The two had been Whigs together, which meant they were no great respecters of either persons or traditions. They craved a new world, with new liberties and new "advances." They vehemently discussed Whig policies and read Whig newspapers and met with others of their kind in boisterous Whig coffeehouses. The captain hadn't had much truck with Barceloux since Francis' death. Something glinted in the fellow's eye that Thomas Grayson found insolent.

The doctor, a tall, lantern-faced man, came wearing an elegant redingote, with his cupping case under his arm. He took out a spirit bottle and the lamp to heat the cupping glass. With a scarifactor, he made an incision in the skin of the girl's shoulder. She whimpered as he placed the hot glass over the incision. She would have moved if he hadn't seen beforehand that her arms were bound in Stella's tight hold. The idea was for the cooling cup to create a semivacuum and consequently a sucking action.

Captain Grayson felt some satisfaction in seeing that very little of the girl's blood would flow. For two hours the man tried all the secrets of his art, and when he could accomplish no more (nothing, in fact), he supplied Stella with a bottle of tincture of laudanum—in case the girl needed it for the blisters left by his treatment—and enough camomile for purge. And a jar of leeches with instructions to apply them every day. As dusk began to settle, the captain saw him down to the hall. Barceloux draped his redingote around his shoulders, took his cupping case, and left.

Only a trace of light remained, faintly edging the bare oak trees before Grayson House, firing the only cloud that remained from the recent storm. Looking out the front doors, the captain's satisfaction in seeing Barceloux discomfited gave way to the realization that the strange girl was about to spend a second night in his house.

Daniel, his manservant, reported within a half hour that Stella had ordered him to throw Barceloux's leeches in the cesspit. He suspected Stella had similarly disposed of the good doctor's camomile purge. On the one hand, it angered him to pay for medical advice that was then ignored; on the other, it gratified him that someone else thought as little of Barceloux's competence as he did.

The next day, while Stella dealt with the circular blister left on the girl's shoulder, Captain Grayson sent Burne out about the district to see if he could discover any reports of an accident on the roads. Though the

283

rain had turned to sleet, Burne left cheerfully enough. He considered himself a notable horseman—and perhaps he was. The captain thought that maybe a carriage had been found overturned somewhere, or a gig. But no, nothing, Burne could find no search afoot for a missing woman. How had she gotten here? Had she walked? The girl seemed to have stepped out of the night into Grayson House without a background, without a name, without even a personality.

As the days passed and she continued in her listless state, not conscious yet not dead, she became a presence with which the captain was seldom bothered. Occasionally he saw his daughter coming out of the White Room with a tray or a basin. He didn't wonder at Stella's concern for this complete stranger. She'd always been one to bring home injured birds and field animals. She'd even named the girl: Jane. The captain thought that was a fitting appellation for a person who was essentially no one.

As for who the girl really was and from whence she heralded, he had to be content with hoping that it would all come to light sooner or later. It was not unusual to hear of people who had met with misadventures on England's horrific roads. Someone would eventually come looking for her; or she would rouse herself and tell them who she was—or she might simply slip into death. Women tended to do that. Mostly she seemed dead already. A beautiful corpse.

Meanwhile, the captain had things to occupy him: he'd lately found the Methodists in the local village more infuriating than usual. And he'd been approached to accept the post of justice of the peace, which had fallen empty. The post bestowed power to grant licenses, keep up the roads and bridges, oversee the workhouse, and administrate justice. He didn't like to say no to the honor of it, in fact, he felt he really *should* accept it, which made it hard to do what he wanted, which was to turn it down. On top of that, there were the coming holidays to concern him. By tradition, Grayson House was the scene of a large party every New Year's Eve. The captain didn't like to entertain, and he always began to worry about it long beforehand, to dread it even, but, well, it was a Grayson tradition.

Thus he often forgot for long periods the girl who lay in the upper reaches of his home. The days became weeks, and true winter arrived with the first snows. Advent began, and brought Christmas Day, and then the New Year loomed on the horizon.

Though she had no perception of time passing, she was not totally lost to sensation. On occasion she became aware of people handling her, lifting her up, for instance, and supporting her in a sitting posture. Food was spooned into her, and water. Sometimes she was aware that she rested against something soft, a cushion or a mattress, and that she felt easy and comfortable. The first thing of which she became fully conscious was the light.

She'd been dreaming. In her dream, it had been night, and she'd been in the grasp of a forceful man. His eyes were dark, brooding, and mocking. His body huge, sinewy, muscular. He caressed her, and finally possessed her. She was caught in a whirlpool of passion . . . then, somehow he was separated from her. He was astride a black horse that reared back and neighed loudly.

She'd wakened with the sound of that horse. She was awake, and it was daytime, she was sure of it. Her eyes were closed, but she knew that it was a bright day.

She opened her eyes. She was lying in a bed and

looking at a ceiling. It was quite high, that ceiling, and clean, absolutely unspotted. She blinked once, let her eyelids come down over her eyes and raise. She didn't think she'd ever seen that ceiling before. How did she happen to be lying beneath it? She felt the pillow beneath her head, fresh and cool, and the weight of the bedclothes over her. She lifted herself up a little. Her limbs were painfully stiff. She was struck at once by what she saw all about her: order. Cleanliness. Sunlight coming through a window. Peace and charm.

A dormer window was hung with simple white curtains, pulled back so that she could see out onto a field of white snow. The bed was white, too: white counterpane, white bedclothes. She looked at the fine weaving of the linen sheets. At the sleeve of the white smock she was wearing.

How quiet it was. She felt like she were still in a dream—but she was awake. In the dream she'd *felt* more awake, however. There was some familiarity underlying the dream; here . . . nothing seemed familiar. It was a giddy sensation. There must be some reasonable basis for her presence in this bed. She must discover what it was; she must consider it.

But not right now. It was too much to consider right now. And really, there seemed no reason for any immediate alarm. Everything was so fine: flaxen sheets and pillow cases; on the table beside her bed a decorative chinaware dish and plate. Nothing alarming, nothing to fear.

The door opened. Someone came in. "Good morning, Jane." The speaker was a woman, perhaps twenty-four years old, with carroty hair and slightly protruding front teeth—not pretty, yet somehow restful-looking. She wore a light blue dress, well tailored but functional, covered with a white bib apron. She had a tray in her hands. "Are you hungry? I

286

brought some toast and tea—a most temperate beverage tea, not like Father's coffee.''

Jane thought she recognized that voice. Someone had stood over her, the face a blur, without feature. Connections vaguely floated, like strands of spiderwebs floating in a breeze, connections and considerations. ''Who . . . ?'' It was something of a surprise that her voice wouldn't work. She could only mouth, ''Who are you?''

The woman paused, startled out of her humdrum performance. Her smile broadened. ''You're awake!'' She put down her tray and leaned into the bed and kissed Jane's cheek, light and swift. ''Bless you, dear, I'm Stella Grayson. I've been taking care of you.''

Jane managed a whisper: ''What's wrong with me?''

Soothingly, Stella took her hand. ''You nearly drowned. It made you ill.''

She pondered this. ''I don't remember.''

Stella frowned, yet her eyes remained sympathetic. ''Do you remember anything at all, dear?''

She looked backward with her mind . . . and found only darkness. For a moment she tasted this new ignorance, shifted it on her tongue. It was as if Stella's question had opened a door, a frightening door beyond the threshold of which she was blind. ''No, nothing. I don't . . . I don't know who I am.'' She grew more frightened. She felt an odd whir, like wings, in her head. What was she to do? Whatever would become of her? What would this soothing stranger think of her?

Stella didn't seem amazed at all. She remained moon-calm. Very kindly she said, ''I know your name. It's Jane.''

Was it? How could she be sure?

The girl had wakened at last, and Bradley Barceloux was called back. The tall, lantern-faced physician told

Captain Grayson that "Jane" was suffering from something called hysterical amnesia.

"What does that mean?" the captain asked. He'd invited Barceloux into his library for a glass of port and a smoke. Barceloux accepted the drink, not the pipe.

"It means she doesn't know who she is or where she's from or anything else about herself. Amnesia is the severe loss of memory. Stella says there was a small lump on the back of her head when she came. It could have something to do with that. Or perhaps some shock. Do you mind?" Barceloux rose from his chair to inspect the library's shelves. He and Francis had graduated from Pembroke College, Oxford, and he considered himself a clever fellow. "I wish I had the funds for a more extensive library of my own. As it is, I must condescend to the circulating library. They offer very little above the quality of cheap novels and plays."

Captain Grayson gestured in irritation with the bowl of his pipe. "Please, feel free to borrow anything you like." He had little sense of possessiveness about the wealth of works on divinity, travel, philosophy, and science at his elbows. They were all just books to him, valuable only in that they had been assembled by the masters of Grayson House before him.

"She can't remember anything at all?" he said. He felt his unsought accountability for this girl expanding into the future indefinitely. The idea irritated him. Wasn't Grayson House enough of a responsibility for any man? He'd wanted to be a naval officer. He'd never asked for any of this squire-of-the-manor business. He wasn't any good at it. He'd let the post of justice of the peace go to Ernest Adams, who was struggling to live as gentry on a few hundred pounds a year and hardly capable of the job. Captain Grayson's father would have taken the position. Francis would have

288

taken it. The captain felt a keen shame in letting it go to a lesser man.

Barceloux's solid personality remained detached. "It's hard to tell yet whether the amnesia is partial or total. She hasn't lost the ability to count, for instance. And she knows that German George is sitting on the throne at the moment." He briefly gave his host a wide, ripping smile.

When the captain did not respond, he went back to pulling out this book and then that one, making a random exploration of history and classical literature. Opening one of the beautifully printed and illustrated travel volumes for which Francis had satisfied an insatiable appetite, he chuckled, "I remember when Francis and I . . ." He didn't finish.

"I find this hard to believe."

"What? Oh, the girl's amnesia?" He put the book back in its place. "It's a well-established medical phenomenon, Thomas."

"Oh well then, that's a relief." Captain Grayson showed a gleam of teeth that would have to pass for a smile. "Come now, Barceloux, you medical fellows often don't know your humors from your horse fleas. Surely I can be pardoned for a modicum of suspicion."

"You can believe me or not; it won't change the fact that the girl doesn't know how old she is, or where her parents live, or indeed, if she was raised by human beings or by African apes."

"How long is it likely to last?"

"That is also hard to tell. Her memory may come back in a flash, or in bits and pieces, or it may never come back at all. These things are largely in the realm of God."

The captain made a dismissive gesture with the hand not supporting his pipe. Physicians! Whenever any of their sort didn't know something, they started talking about God. "What is to be done with her meanwhile?"

Barceloux kept a bland expression as he folded his long legs and arms into his chair once more. He adjusted his ruffles. "She's physically healthy, rational. Alert. Collected. As undismayed over these odd goings-on as anyone could be. A remarkably calm and practical young woman, that's my impression. Feed her well, see she gets out for a walk now and then—but not too often. She isn't 'sick' in the sense of needing to remain bedridden, but she should get plenty of rest. Indeed, rest is probably the only thing that will do her any good. Otherwise there is nothing special I can recommend. We must simply wait and see."

"Which means I'll have to keep her here longer."

Barceloux shrugged, "Stella seems pleased to have something to occupy her."

"Stella loves nothing more than to have some injured creature in her plump little lap. She should have children of her own, a husband."

"Every female must have companionship, married or not."

"My wife didn't."

Barceloux didn't comment. He took his glass of port, which he hadn't yet touched, to the tray on which several decanters stood. "May I?" The captain waved to him to do whatever he liked. Barceloux opened the decanter of *cappilaire,* syrup flavored with orange-flower water, and added a generous measure to his wine. He took a sip, and then another. "Would it be such an inconvenience, Fudge, to keep the girl awhile longer?"

Fudge! God's blood, he hadn't been called that since he was a boy. Not since Francis had died!

"From what I can ascertain, she seems intelligent and polite. A little confused and frightened, of course, but—"

"Did you question her closely? Are you absolutely sure—"

"I don't recommend too much questioning."

The captain threw up his hands. "And just how are we to jog her memory then?"

"My dear Thomas, if it was a shock that led to this state then we must be very careful—unless you wish to risk pushing her over the edge into real madness."

"Are you telling me I have a female in the house who may be on the brink of madness?"

"Well, you know women." Barceloux's tone became jocular, one man to another. "Not a one of them is all that stable. It's all those strange compounds of ardencies and illusions that swirl inside them. They can get frantic over the most foolish things." He smiled hard. "This girl is probably just a bit more sensitive than most of her sex."

"I thought you said she seemed calm and practical."

Barceloux shrugged again, a most irritating habit. "Before the bump, she may have been jilted by her beau. Or suffered the dire humiliation of being a wallflower at an important ball—though with her looks, I doubt that." His eyes suddenly veered toward the captain's. "And then again, she might have been out traveling and become the victim of a 'road inspector,' as they call themselves. Rape . . . such a young girl . . . perhaps even attempted murder. Stella says she seemed nearly drowned. A highwayman would think nothing of silencing his victim by whatever means. And who knows what effects might follow upon such doings? What young woman would want to remember something like that? Much easier to forget, much easier on the mind."

"Hmm . . . that's an interesting theory—a highwayman you think? Heaven knows they're as ubiquitous as flies. Which means she might have been taken from a coach or a carriage at some distance from here—abducted.'' He puffed on his pipe. ''That would account for Burne's not being able to find anyone searching for her in the vicinity. When you looked her over did you find any signs of violence—besides that lump on her head? Is she not a maiden?''

The doctor stiffened as if insulted. ''Thomas, mine is a gentleman's profession. I do not 'look over' young women. Your daughter was with us the whole time and can attest that I did not stoop to any improprieties.''

''Yes, yes, I'm sure you're a very good, very sound and moral sort of physician,'' the captain grumbled through the haze of his pipesmoke. ''Still, you could have sent Stella out for a moment on some excuse. I don't see how you can tell what's wrong with the girl if you don't examine her.''

Rigid, Barceloux said, ''Whether the girl is a maiden or not bears very little significance in how her amnesia must be treated. I would simply humor her, Thomas— and wait.''

''Easy for you to say. You come, drain off a little of her blood, then you leave. You're not the one who might be murdered in his sleep by—''

''There's no danger of that. I've told you—''

''You've told me a lot of things, Bradley—and exactly nothing at all.''

Chapter Twenty

Do You Dream of Me?

"Yes, Father?"

Captain Grayson looked up from his desk at his daughter. Burne was off to one of his shooting parties. He was always hunting or angling or hawking, no matter the season. "Barceloux has left."

"What did he say?"

"Nothing he hadn't already told you, I'm sure." Fudge! He'd called him Fudge! "The man is hardly worth the money he charges."

"What . . . ?"

"What do I intend to do with the girl?"

"Let her stay, Father!" Stella leaned over the desk in a beseeching manner that his wounded dignity found very pleasing at the moment.

"We don't know a thing about her, Stella."

"But she's very nice. And lovely to look at. I think she might be of the nobility."

"Now don't start spinning fairy tales. As I said, we don't know a thing about her. And I'm not altogether convinced she wouldn't be better off in, well, an asylum."

"No!"

He raised a silencing hand. "Listen to me. She can stay." He let that sink in. It gratified him to see her relief and know she had him to thank for it. "But not as a houseguest," he added. "Barceloux says she can get up when she feels strong enough, that she can do things, take walks and so forth, as long as she gets plenty of rest. But I will not have you adopting her, Stella, do you hear me? She's not a houseguest, to be diverted and amused. She's staying as, well, as a charity case—until we know more about her, anyway."

"Yes, I understand, Father. But if she does prove to be of the nobility, we won't want it to be said we treated her shabbily."

"Of course we won't treat her shabbily. Still, you're not to include her when we have callers. Certainly not when we entertain. Even if she turns out to be nobly born, her family might not thank us for parading her current infirmity of mind before the district." Particularly if the girl had been molested. "She's to stay out of sight, do you understand?"

"I do, and I agree completely."

Well! This was a nice change. Stella was being very agreeable indeed. He'd expected much more argument, at the very least that she would want to take the girl to church services. He sighed. Barceloux was right about one thing—if nothing else!—that women are a strange compound of ardencies and illusions and not a man alive can predict what they might do next.

Jane experienced strange sensations those first days of consciousness. She lay in the unfamiliar chamber, deep in the soft, goosefeather bed, her head propped on pillows, properly attired in bedgown and cap, alternately dozing or blinking sleepily in the winter sunshine that came through the dormer window. Her mind floated, but never far. She felt moored to this bed, the terrain of which stretched out before her, completely white, completely blank. She was content to be here for now, to be waited upon and spoken to soothingly. She was content at this point to be treated as a child. She accepted the servants, the help, the luxury. Every essential was furnished and she was content to be ruled by these kind strangers.

She was weak. Stella said she had lost weight. It seemed Stella knew more about her than she knew herself.

A knock at the door roused her. Her voice had come back with talking to Stella and Dr. Barceloux. She called, "Come in."

A man came through the door, tall, handsome, smiling, young, gorgeously well dressed and recently barbered. His blond hair had been cropped for wearing a wig. He was smiling as if he knew her—and he had such a winsome smile.

"So, our mermaiden is awake."

She didn't know who he was, yet something about him felt right, familiar. As he came closer, without thinking, she lifted her hand. He took it and bowed over it, his smile becoming concerned at her expression. "What is it?" She couldn't say. She felt odd, examining his face. Then . . . a quick glimpse of a man wheeling a horse and galloping off into the dark. She gasped audibly. Her whole heart rose, her soul sat up and leaned toward him, yearning, beseeching, seeking more than this slender spectral wisp, seeking remembrance.

But nothing more came, and he offered no help. She tried to keep her face calm—but her hands were shaking. She didn't want him to feel that shaking. She removed her hand from his and fell back against her pillows. His touch had left her skin electrified. "You must forgive me. I thought for a moment that I knew you."

"But you do." His smile was teasing now. "I'm the one who carried you up here the night you came. And I gave you some of my best brandy."

Could it be that she remembered those events? Those hands, the hands of a strong but privileged man lifting her? In her dream the hands seemed hard, forceful.

"All drenched, you were, you soaked my robe." A small ruffle of laughter. He had a dimple at each corner of his mouth. They disappeared with the smile. "We think you must have fallen in the river somehow and then wandered here."

"Yes, that's what Stella says." It was easy enough to believe, for dozing this afternoon she'd come awake once with a sense of panic, of struggling to the surface of her sleep, as if to breathe.

"You were very beautiful, mermaiden, even fresh from your mere. You were a rather vivid blue with cold—but a beautiful blue." The smile flickered, deepening his dimples—astonishing! All she could do was stare at him, lost in the warmth of his voice and the look on his face.

"I must have looked a fright. Stella says she had to have my clothes burned . . ." Was it proper to be talking to him about her clothes? She was aware of strong undercurrents, of implications, of connotations.

He remained smiling. "My name is Burne. I'm Stella's little brother."

She smiled faintly at the word "little," which she sensed was a joke of that old and comfortable sort which exists among people who feel affection for one another. Stella might be a year or two older than this man, but she was considerably smaller. Burne had probably been

296

calling himself her "little" brother since the day he'd topped her height and had means at last of teasing her.

"I regret that we meet under such a shadow," he said in a soft voice that made her think of silk over steel, "but I think I would like to meet you under any circumstances."

Jane's eyes fixed on him as if she would devour him. As he talked on, about this and that, she kept returning to that feeling of familiarity. Was he that sudden dark silhouette who embraced her in her dreams? The man in those dark, moonlight visions? Those caresses, that final possession . . . she felt herself blush scarlet.

He noticed. He smiled, and his dimples deepened again. "What is it?" he asked in that deep satiny voice. "Did I say something?"

"No, nothing." She couldn't look at him at all now.

When he left, he left behind a dozen confused impressions.

Luxuriously unrestricted by time or obligation, she slept again. The last of another dream slid past: firelight, the snatch of a voice. "Beautiful," it said. Keen, eagle features, love that touched the edge of joy. *I am his*. Then it all changed. A whir, like wings. A great cry swelled inside her, filling her, till certainly she must burst. Terror rose up and drowned her. She started awake. But confused by sleep and urgency, she still heard that wailing cry, and that other noise, wings, or wind through an empty place. There had been terrible, heart-withering pain, pain like madness, sweeping her into darkness.

But there was no terror here. It was quiet in her chamber. And light, as always. The darkness lay inside her. Her memory swam in and out of it. She must concentrate.

Before the pain there had been that other dream of faint, indefinable sweetness. That glitter of firelight,

297

that face, that man who would not be denied, who made love persistently and potently to all her senses, until she was left amazed and grateful and full of love. Who was he?

She'd learned that she'd been in this room for six weeks. Since the end of November. All of December had passed without her knowing. Christmas had been celebrated all over the country, undoubtedly with the usual cheer and presents and dinners and evening parties. What had happened to her six weeks ago?

She didn't know. She leaned back with resignation on her heaped pillows.

The Graysons themselves were to give a party tonight. It was New Year's Eve. Stella came in to wish her a good evening before she went down to the salon wearing a thin yellow muslin frock with scarlet ribbons, with her hair in elaborate ringlets. She was in a rush, being late for her own party. She said, "I'll leave your door ajar, so you can at least hear the fun."

Hence Jane heard the sound of a harpsichord played below, and the bustle of servants, the jingle of glass and china as refreshments were passed, the hum of voices. She dozed a little, and woke again. Long did the hours seem while she waited for the departure of the company and the sound of Stella's step on the stairs again.

Stella sat on the end of her bed and told her everything that happened, what they'd eaten, how the captain had grumbled at the pounds he'd had to spend on candles to make the house blaze. Stella seemed to Jane to be the finest, the kindest being on Earth.

A dark horse and rider stood stone-still outside the gates of Grayson House. Every window downstairs burned with light. Through the steamy glaze the col-

298

orful shapes of gentlemen and ladies, all the best of the district's gentry, moved and drank and ate and laughed. There was music. Was that Captain Grayson himself playing the harpsichord? Or perhaps Burne, the heir apparent of all this gaiety?

The highwayman's eyes traveled to the upper reaches of the manor house. All was dark. He spurred his mount and began to circle the property. He found one window that had a pale light, as of a candle left for a person abed.

He stared hard at that window. *Do you dream of me? I remember everything about you, your beauty, the sound of your voice, the scent of you.*

Later, the blazing candles were snuffed, and then the windows in the upstairs chambers grew amber with light. One by one, they all grew dark again, including *her* window. The highwayman lingered, unwilling to go. He sat slumped in his saddle. A tardy autumn leaf, frozen brittle, fell somewhere in the night. His horse stirred impatiently.

A noise harkened him. He straightened, and saw a form coming out of a small, almost hidden door at the side of the house. A cloaked woman stood for a moment, as if listening. He felt a freshet of hope. Jane? Suddenly the woman darted across the snow-mounded rose garden, heading for the orchard. A maidservant out to meet her lover? But the Graysons' maid was middle-aged and stout, of medium height, while this form was small and quick. The hood of her cloak fell back a little, showing hair that even in the dark was carroty. Stella!

The highwayman's great fist of a heart loosened and was freed again to beat. He spurred his mount. This bore looking into.

* * *

299

Though Jane had not the least wish to go into company, she soon tired of idleness. Ungoverned thoughts took over any vacant hour, thoughts that scurried and circled and got her nowhere. Her mind wearied of looking back on itself, peering into that darkness that was her memory. It terrified her to think she might never know anything about herself, that this state might drag on until she was balding and aged. She simply couldn't lie still when that possibility occurred to her. Stella, who was as good to her as any sister, encouraged her efforts at regaining her strength, and when she discovered Jane trying slowly and awkwardly to get out of bed, she didn't scold; instead, she helped her.

Within two days, Jane was able to walk about her chamber. Then, dressed in a borrowed robe of white quilted satin, and slippers to match, she ventured out for a jaunt along the dimly lit length of the polished upstairs gallery. Her bed-weakened limbs made painful, slow work of it. She was gasping for breath when she arrived back at her chamber door. But she felt triumphant, too.

In the three days since his visit to her chamber, she had not seen Burne. He had been elsewhere, riding out. She'd been abed or moving sluggishly about, taking her meals alone. (Yet she had felt full of Burne Grayson, and worthless at thinking about anything else but how familiar he seemed.) Her escape from bed did not go unnoticed by the other male in the household, however. The day after Epiphany, Captain Grayson requested her presence at dinner.

She'd heard her host's voice often, but had only glimpsed him once, out her window, when she'd seen him riding a chestnut stallion up the side of the snow-covered field. He was a tall, formidable, barrel of a man with yellow hair, dusted with powder on that occasion, and was clearly a person of importance, a man

300

accustomed to taking control. Though he was called Captain, he was a squire, with a country estate that was large and richly remunerative. (This she'd learned from Catherine.)

Jane had felt sheltered and befriended by Stella, and by Burne, too, but now the master of the house wished to meet her. She wasn't sure she was ready. She willed the command away. She didn't want Captain Thomas Grayson to see her as she must look now: pallid, lank-haired, indistinct.

A spell of gray, cold, snowy weather descended that afternoon. As the early dusk fell, Stella took Jane into her own chamber and bid her choose a gown from among the many in her wardrobe.

"Oh, I couldn't."

"But you must. You have nothing of your own to wear."

The logic was inescapable. Jane might have lost her memory but she still had an uncompromising intelligence. She chose what seemed the oldest gown among the dozen or so hanging there. Stella shook her head. "No—here, this one." She reached for a confection of rich royal blue.

She dressed Jane herself. A corset. A plain quilted petticoat for warmth. A chemise with ruffled sleeves. Panniers. A quilted, pale blue satin petticoat. The royal blue overskirt was bound with tapes that Stella tied at the back of her waist. It opened in front to display the paler quilted petticoat beneath. The boned bodice fastened in front with hooks and eyes. The ruffles of the chemise showed below the sleeves. Dressed thus, Jane felt uncomfortable. She believed she'd worn such a gown before—but when? And if she had, why did it feel so awkward? The panniers that held the skirt out at the hips seemed strange in the extreme. She didn't

301

know what to do with her hands. She blurted, "How will I ever sit down?"

Stella seemed startled at the question. She recovered and went to a yellow wooden chair and sat herself, saying, "Like this. You sort of perch."

Jane tried. It wasn't difficult. Yet the gown seemed to require a different sort of movement from what felt natural to her, a more sedate step. She felt certain she was a person who walked quickly, with more purpose than such a wide-skirted gown allowed.

"Stella, is it possible that I'm not of your sort?"

Stella went to the window and looked out. It was a long moment before she turned back. "I'll tell you the truth. You didn't come here dressed as a lady. I'm the only one who saw what you were wearing when you arrived—well, Burne saw you, too, but he didn't notice your clothes. I burned your things because if my father had any shred of evidence that you aren't a lady, he would, well, I'm afraid he might—I don't know, put you in the workhouse or something. He can be cruel. So you must never give him any reason to think you aren't a gentlewoman, Jane. Promise me you won't. In fact, if you can, be careful of what you say to him. He will no doubt ask you what you remember. Tell him only what will serve—if you understand what I mean."

Jane's heart throbbed.

Stella went on, "Despite what you were wearing, I still think you must be a lady. You have an erect posture, you walk with a natural grace—in fact, you are as graceful as any lady of my acquaintance." As she talked, she moved about the room, unnecessarily touching this and that. "And your hands—Burne mentioned just yesterday how slender and tapered they are, and how you move them in such easy, graceful gestures, all of which bespeaks a gentle breeding."

302

Jane felt flustered. She should have realized that she had been a topic of conversation in the house. So Burne had noticed her hands, and in such close detail. "But if I were a gentlewoman, why would I come here dressed in—what *did* I have on?"

"Rags, a maidservant's dress, ripped and then mended." She crossed the room and took Jane's hands. "I have a theory. I think you might be a lady who disguised herself to run away with her lover, someone your parents couldn't approve of—though probably quite wonderful. You took your maidservant's poorest gown and put it on as a disguise."

Jane's lips had fallen open. It was so confusing.

"It all makes sense when you think about it. You have so many qualities of the gentry. You can even read. How many people of the lower classes can read?"

"I don't know. Quite a few. There are dame schools and grammar schools—"

"But not many can afford them, or care to attend. Most of those children never learn to read or write or understand numbers. You can do all those things."

Jane absorbed that not only had she been discussed, she'd been tested. For instance, Stella had brought a book into her chamber one day and casually left it on the bedside table. Jane picked it up quite spontaneously and began to read. She understood now that it was part of a careful investigation.

There were other incidents, too, now that she looked back, in which she showed that she could write and do simple figuring. She recalled innocent-seeming occasions as when she performed such simple tests as telling the time. It heckled her to think how planned it had all been, how she'd been manipulated without her knowing. She'd been content to let them rule her—and so they had. Probably they'd even talked of her in the servants' quarters. It gave her a queer, depriving feeling, being assessed like that, like an object.

Stella drew her to the full-length pier glass. "Look at yourself, Jane. Is that a maidservant you see?"

Jane looked. She saw a woman like a wax figure, composed, transfixed, standing in a frame of some sort. That it took her so long to identify the woman as her own reflection was telling commentary that she didn't know herself. But it was Jane she saw. Once she realized, she lost all power to look away. Was that what she looked like, that girl whose eyes glowed like the blue silk she was wearing, whose cheeks were pink, whose lips glistened? Why, she *was* beautiful.

She gave up trying to identify that beauty as herself in the surging wave of the next moment. The bodice of her gown had a low décolleté. Her fingers touched the faint, fading mark left by Dr. Barceloux's cupping glass. Stella said quickly. "Here, let's cover that with a kerchief. It's too chilly to go downstairs bare-shouldered anyway. And really," she laughed nervously, "we should make some alterations to that bodice before you wear it again. You're better endowed than I am."

As Jane turned to let her put the lace-edged kerchief around her shoulders, she caught a glimpse of her upper back. "Wait—what is that mark?" She twisted her neck, trying to see her back in the looking glass. "It's a scar. What is it?" She began to unfasten the bodice. She wanted to have a look.

"Jane, no." Stella stopped her. "You were . . . I think you were whipped."

Jane went very still. She looked at herself again. The mirror was still dizzy with her presence and, astonished, gave back a too-immediate image.

"The marks are fading, most of them."

"Why would . . . ?" A sound: that whirring of

304

wings, but not wings, a whip. A series of almost invisible shudders took her. Her nerves and muscles tensed, as if to resist a cutting scourge.

She stood like a dressmaker's form while Stella refastened her bodice and covered her bosom with the kerchief. "Thieves and harlots are whipped," she said, not knowing where that knowledge came from. "Whipped through the streets for vulgar crimes." Stella moved away and she looked at herself again in the dimly gleaming pier glass.

Stella appeared at her side again, and gently urged her away. "We'll have to talk about it later. We're late already, and Father will be restless."

A heavy mood weighted Jane as she let herself be led along the gallery. Their gowns rustled. She tried to fit together Stella's insistence that she was a runaway daughter of gentlefolk with the scars on her back. You've been whipped, a voice whispered; someone's flogged you.

An aroma of baked beef floated on the air. She stopped on the top of the stairs. She suddenly didn't want to go down there. She felt a totally unreasonable fear of being looked at, by anyone. Her mind scrambled for some way to get out of it. "Stella! I don't think I know how to eat in polite society."

"Don't worry," Stella said, though Jane could see she was nervous, too. "Do exactly as I do. It's not difficult."

Before they got halfway down the stairs, they heard the sound of men arguing. The elder voice said, "I'm disappointed in you, Burne."

"Yes *sir*," Burne said, coming down on the second word with force, like a lame man stepping. Jane didn't hear Captain Grayson's answer, for Stella whispered, "My father can be rather difficult at times. He has what I choose to think of as a fundamental frailty. It

prevents him from being a totally considerate man—
or a totally thoughtless one. Whatever inner shakiness
you feel, Jane, you must try to keep up a bold front
before him.''

Chapter Twenty-one

They Were Not a Contented Family

The storm outside continued. A bitter wind whipped across the dale, and low clouds frowned and snowed. Anyone with the bad luck to be out tonight would be cut to the bone by that icy wind.

Inside Grayson house, all was warmth and comfort. Wallpaper imported from the Orient graced the dining room. The narrow satinwood table was set with Oriental porcelain. A heavy wooden chandelier hung from the ceiling beam, from whence six candles gave light.

Captain Grayson greeted Jane coolly. Burne bowed over her hand with more feeling. He wore a long, full-skirted ruff coat of blue, with enormous cuffs of brocade that matched his inner waistcoat. Both men wore wigs. The captain's was powdered a shade of blond near his natural coloring; Burne's was done in blue.

Once they were all seated, the servants came in with the first course, consisting of an enormous pike, fried sole, and trout. These were accompanied by German white wine. Jane had already surmised from her meal trays that the captain kept a grand table. Even so, she was impressed by the array of food set before her. True to her word, Stella proved a perfect example of the protocol of a gentlewoman at table.

The captain was obviously uncomfortable; he didn't know how to treat Jane, hence he barely acknowledged her. Instead, he launched, with an awkward self-consciousness, right back into the middle of the conversation in which he and Burne had been embroiled before:

"Politics are the highroad to fortune in all walks of life, and the knowing father gets his son into the House of Commons as soon as he comes of age."

"And you are a knowing father," Burne answered, cutting into a fresh loaf of rye bread. The hint of sarcasm in his tone wasn't particularly hidden. "It's just your misfortune that you are cursed with a son who doesn't want to go into politics. Let it be said that you did your best, but you could not breed me to a profession I disliked."

Jane was a little tardy in taking the meaning of this. She was busy comparing Burne with his father. Captain Grayson was an older, stouter, sterner model of his son, with the same long limbs and the same straight nose and fair coloring. The solemnity that Burne only played at was the captain's natural state. If there was any lightness about the older man at all, he didn't display it to strangers.

"What *do* you want to do, Burne, besides sit well on a horse? You don't want to marry Mrs. Bennet—"

"That I don't. Arlene Bennet is a thirty-two-year-old child. A child-widow. The very idea of marrying a woman that much older than I, who nonetheless behaves as though she needs a nursemaid, doesn't interest me."

"Her inheritance ought to interest you."

"But it doesn't."

Now and again the door to the pantry swung open,

and a cold draft sliced through the warmth as the two house servants, Catherine and Daniel, came in and out from the kitchen. The Graysons didn't seem even to see the people who waited hand and foot upon them. They carried on as if they were totally private.

"It would interest your children," the captain said.

Burne laughed, that soft, confident ruffle of amusement Jane had heard before. "My children, if I sire any, will have to be happy with what they get. I will never satisfy my pocket in marrying and not satisfy my fancy." Despite his fair coloring, his rich, dark voice gave Jane the chills. "I don't have your dynastic attitude, Father."

"You think of yourself as a gallant, a lover. No doubt you have some private friendship with one female or other. Be careful, however, for you may find yourself called a fop, a man of small understanding and much ostentation, a man with very little weight in him. It is my sincere opinion that you and Mrs. Bennet would get on splendidly. You're both equally childish." His slate gray eyes snapped. Reaching for his wine, he said, "Get yourself a rich widow. There are enough of them about, I dare say." He drank. "That's my best advice."

"And it's perfectly reasonable advice; I'm just not sure I want to take it." Burne flicked a bread crumb from his mustard yellow silk neck scarf. When he looked up, he showed that his blue eyes could snap as sharply as his father's gray ones. "Perhaps you should marry Mrs. Bennet yourself, Father, since you see marriage to an heiress as a regular means of advancing the family fortunes. It worked out quite well for you with Mother."

"That's enough."

"No, really, you're not too old to take another bride. Some easily led creature whom you can bully."

"I never intend to take a second wife."

Jane shivered in the cool draft from the pantry. Catherine came in with a bowl that was giving off steam.

"It is enough, I agree," Burne said, all the light sarcasm gone from his tone, "and I would appreciate it if you would not bring up the Widow Bennet to me again."

Something in his attitude must have penetrated Captain Grayson's sensibilities, for he let the matter drop—after muttering, "You have a name to uphold, remember that."

The cold dispelled as soon as the pantry door closed again. This was Jane's first look at the relationship between father and son. Apparently Captain Grayson kept an iron grip over the household, but there were points beyond which he did not push Burne.

Stella, on the other hand, he pushed as far as he liked. While Jane was still looking from one man to the other with blank, dazed eyes, amazed at the exchange she had just witnessed, the captain turned toward his daughter.

"I can't seem to convince either of you of the wisdom of marrying well, though common sense would tell you that I have only your interests at heart. You," he said to Stella, "seem to prefer spinsterhood to decent matrimony. Marriage is the only reasonable option for a young woman. I've worked hard on Grayson House—the gardens, the park—all for the enjoyment of my grandchildren, which I begin to despair of ever being conceived. Are you, like your brother, going to spend your life asleep to the opportunities I put before you? You do nothing to make yourself charming. It's been near two months since you've even had a caller."

Stella said nothing.

"Ah! Now she's going to sulk."

Jane tried to take a deep breath, but the tight lacing of the stays beneath her gown wouldn't quite let her. She picked up her knife and fork and tried to eat what the servants had just put on her plate.

Burne said, "If you'd let Stella spend just one Season in Town-"

"Town?" His sharpness and bitterness increased. "I know what the young rakes do when they go to London for the Season." He was like a man running down a steep hill path, unable to stop himself once he got started. "They get up at nine, languish till twelve in their nightshirts, steal down to Whites and spend four hours at the tables, sleep through their suppers, and finally make two wretches carry them in a chair—along with the three pints of wine in each of them—five miles or more to some ball given for a girl whom they treat as if she had the morals of a strumpet. Is that the kind of suitors you want for your sister? I might as well take her to a statute hall and sell her to the highest bidder. No sir, she will not spend a Season in Town, not when she's turned down good men right here."

"Good men? You mean Ralph Fetter and Cyril Todd? If I were Stella I wouldn't ever marry, not for the world and a woodcock, if those were my only choices. Ralph Fetter gets as drunk as a lord every night of his life. He has the manners of a dancing master and a head so hard he could break a door with it—and a reputation with the ladies as respectable as the bottom of a ditch."

"It's all right, Burne," Stella said to him, her eyes pleading for peace.

"And your fine Mr. Todd thinks of nothing but fox hunting. I doubt you'd get many grandchildren out of him, not unless Stella visited him in his stables with his hunters, which is where I believe he does most of his—''

''Burne!'' Stella was pale. ''Please!'' She signaled with her eyes toward Jane. ''Can't we just make pleasant conversation for once?''

Jane wasn't sure either of the men could put aside their ire. But she was wrong. Burne looked at her and suddenly grinned in boyish embarrassment. ''Forgive us, Jane. Father and I have been going at each other for so long that it's become a habit. You mustn't notice it. We hardly do anymore, I assure you. In fact, we actually enjoy it, don't we, Father? Though I don't suppose it's so much fun for a listener as it is for us.''

How Jane liked his voice!

The captain offered no apology. In fact, he hadn't quite given up his topic. He said, to no one in particular, ''I suppose she wants to pick her own husband— ha! If daughters were allowed to wed whom they please, we'd all be ruled by strolling minstrels and dark-eyed outlaws.''

Evidently browbeating his children gave him courage, for he turned to Jane at last. She braced herself.

''So, mistress, you are feeling better?''

The manservant, Daniel, poured his master more wine.

''Much better, thank you. You are so kind to let me stay here.''

He waved away her gratitude. ''Barceloux tells me you can't remember anything of your past.'' He made no attempt to hide his displeasure.

She looked at her plate, afraid to make any answer lest that displeasure boil over.

''You had some money on you.''

She looked up quickly. Her glance went from him to Stella and back again. ''I didn't know.'' Instinct

312

told her he was considering carefully everything she said.

"Well, it wasn't much."

"I'm sorry, Jane," Stella said. She'd turned a bright red. "I guess I forgot to mention it."

"A few guineas and shillings," the captain said dismissively. "I've put it in a safe place for you."

Jane felt an odd urgency. She looked at Stella for direction, but Stella only smiled weakly—and continued to blush, visibly uncomfortable under Jane's gaze. To the captain she said, "May I have it back, sir . . . please?"

"Do you think I'm not to be trusted?"

"No, of course not, I didn't mean . . ." She lowered her head again. "I must owe you quite a lot for your hospitality anyway."

"My dear girl, I don't run an inn. This is Grayson House, not the White Swan or the Blue Goose."

Stella gave Jane a warning look.

"I don't mean to be offensive, Captain Grayson. I'm still a little confused."

He seemed mollified. "I understand. As for your little purse of money, it will be waiting for you when whoever you belong to comes to claim you."

Whoever she belonged to? She felt shooting tingles in her hands and legs. She tried to eat, but the food was tasteless now. She felt marooned on an island of anxiety. She'd arrived here with some money. At last she said, "Captain, I really would like to have my purse returned if you would be so kind. It would make me feel better."

He lifted his head to give her a look of sheerest indignation. "It's improper for young ladies to have money. I give Stella what she needs when she goes shopping for her fripperies and so forth, but I don't like to think of her having cash in her chamber or about

313

her person. It's not safe. There are so many brigands about these days"—here he seemed to give Jane a particularly keen look—"and they're not above breaking into country houses to get what they want. Or stopping people on the roads." That look, what did it mean? "As long as you're under my roof, I'm afraid you'll just have to abide by my policies."

Burne seemed absorbed in one of the buttons of his ruff coat. And Stella wouldn't look at Jane at all. She knew that she'd done the very thing Stella hadn't wanted her to do: she'd made a bad first impression. She wondered if any woman in Grayson House had ever contradicted the captain. The man was nothing but a petty tyrant.

The meal went on in heavy silence. She knew she should give up, apologize, humble herself, and hence make peace with him, but there was an implacable knot of anxiety in her that refused. She stared for long seconds at her host's stern face, and finally said, "It is mine, is it not?"

"My dear young lady!" he exploded, "I have nothing but your welfare at heart, pray believe me! If you dislike anything of my hospitality, you know you are at liberty to leave it."

She stared distractedly at the windows behind Stella. The night beyond was a whitish gray void; there was nothing for the eye to catch on. It was crazy to prolong this dispute. Yet she plowed on. "I'm only asking for—"

"Ah!" Burne said, "here comes the roast beef!"

"Father," Stella said brightly, "did I show you the embroidery Jane started?"

"Jane, won't you have some of this beef?" There were sharp teeth in Burne's question. "You hardly ate any of your fish. A woman who doesn't mind her belly will scarcely mind anything else." The warning was clear.

The expression on Captain Grayson's face was sufficient to make her wilt. She accepted the beef and let the discussion move briefly on to needlework.

The captain also accepted the distractions thrown out by his son and daughter. Rancor remained in his heart, however, and of course he must have the last word. Taking some beef, he muttered, "The woman wants discipline."

Jane's anxiety could scarcely be contained.

In candlelit solitude, in the King's Head, in Ledbury, Keith lay on the rack that was his bed. He'd seen Jane at dinner at his father's table. He'd been excited to see her up and about. But then, though he couldn't risk getting close enough to hear their conversation, he'd seen the way her eyes, through the glass, reached like the hands of a drowning person beseechingly out of the water.

Jane was soon about the house more and really starting to grow well. The weather continued silent and snowy. At night, snow fell in the woods of the park, drifted deep, creating a pristine world. During the day, north winds brought such heavy falls that there was not much chance for anyone to get out. Jane continued to have her meals in the dining room with the family. They were draining, exhausting, those meals. She had to be so blithe, so careful, so carefree and false, assuming a hope and a certainty that were wholly without foundation.

She didn't quite understand her position in the household. She was a sort of lower member, not ser-

315

vant, but not guest. The ambiguity of her status didn't trouble her as much as the ambiguity of her own mind. She wasn't offended not to be allowed to meet any of the Graysons' infrequent callers. She was completely disinclined to meet anyone. In fact, at the first sound of someone at the door she moved rapidly from wherever she was back to her chamber. There she sat, her hands trembling and gathered tightly in her lap. Why? What was this fear of being seen?

Though they'd learned nothing about her, she'd learned much about her adopted family. By standards that prevailed, Grayson House was neither very large nor uncommonly impressive, but it achieved a flourishing, dignified, consequential air. Its grounds took up fifteen acres of the whole property. The residence stood on a knoll behind three acres of lawns set with lofty old oak trees, all bordered in the summer by flower beds.

An iron fence crossed the front. In the back was a rose garden separated from a fruit orchard by a dense high hedge. Beyond the orchard, a small park had been carefully conceived to include shrubbery and wandering lines of trees, a picturesque miniature summer house, and a spring-fed pond.

Stella and Burne believed such surroundings were normal. Jane felt increasingly convinced that she didn't.

Today, as a gray, cloudy morning led into a gray, dark, late afternoon, she sat alone in the salon, alternately watching out the mullioned windows and reading. She came downstairs rarely, always feeling clumsy and out of place when she did. Except for the rustle of the fire in the huge hearth, the silence was perfect. She had a copy of *The Essence of Style*, by Georges-Louis Le Clerc de Buffon—not a riveting work, but she'd learned to fear the hours of stagnant idleness forced on her.

She must fill them somehow, and she couldn't expect Stella to spend every moment with her. Hence she was drawn irresistibly to the captain's books.

Stella was upstairs, napping through one of her unhappy moods. As Jane had got to know her better, she'd discovered a deep melancholy in the woman, a private despair, of which everyone in the house seemed fully aware yet no one ever spoke. Once in a while a gloom seemed to fall over her and she would simply retire from life. She became distant, almost physically transparent.

Jane wondered why in this prosperous and accomplished household, in which everyone seemed to practice Chopin preludes on the harpsichord, every occupant should seem so disappointed with his lot. They were not a contented family, the Graysons.

She finished her book and rose to return it, but again was drawn to looking out the windows. The mullioned glass of this room, the dormer window of her chamber, even the little window on the stairs drew her continually. She stared beyond the snow-covered drive, beyond the smothered rose garden, beyond the fields of snow surrounding the house. And she waited. It wasn't a resting, easy wait. Those days in which she'd lain in her feather bed content to float were over. They'd ended the night she'd discovered the scars on her back—and that the captain had a purse of her money. Now her whole body was screwed tight with tension.

She recalled herself. Book in hand, she turned for the library. As she started across the polished black marble floor of the hall, she saw the library door was open. She sniffed the unmistakable scent of the cook's fine tea pastries. She stopped when she heard the captain's voice:

"It's the most reasonable theory anyone has come up with so far."

"But . . ." That was Burne's dark voice.

"You don't want to believe it." The captain's answer was dry and sneering. "You've become increasingly close to the girl, and unseemly attentive, Burne. I wouldn't, if I were you."

"She's a remarkably pretty and fresh young woman. You must acknowledge that she is very handsome."

"That's not the question. She's attractive enough. But we don't know but what she hasn't two pennies to rub together."

"She has a few pennies. That purse—"

"I'm talking about a dowry."

"Beauty is a dowry, and good temper."

"She may have been ravished. You'd not be the first."

"She's an innocent. You can tell by looking at her, by watching her; she's an innocent."

"You can't know that. You want to believe it and so you refuse to see the points of my theory."

"It's so lurid! No, I don't want to see the points of it. Abducted by a highwayman, raped, and thrown into the river to drown? No, I don't want to even consider it."

There came a long hush, broken only by the sound of pouring tea, the clink of china and spoon. Jane stood riveted to the cold marble floor of the hall.

At last Burne said, "I carried her upstairs myself the night she came, and I didn't see any signs of rape."

"What signs would you see, unless you'd undressed her?"

"Stella undressed her; she didn't mention anything."

"Would Stella know what to look for? Would she know how to interpret what she saw? And Barceloux" the captain made a snorting sort of noise—"that pompous ass felt himself above taking a real look at her." After a pause, he went on, "I don't like the cut of her jib. And I don't like you paying so much attention to her. There are too many questions about her. If she's well born why has no one come looking for her?"

"I think she was simply traveling and met with some accident, and whoever was with her drowned. Maybe she was an only child, and her parents—"

"No bodies were discovered, no coach found, no stray team. An accident? More likely a robbery, and murder—admit the possibility, at least—and the bodies of her escort hidden, or buried, and her equipage sold for profit."

"You've worked it all out rather elaborately, Father. I had no idea you had so much imagination."

"Laugh if you will, but the girl has mystery hanging around her as black as a widow's veil." A moment passed; then he added, "And meanwhile you're falling in love with her. Don't try to deny it. I can see what's happening. I'm not blind."

Jane could almost see his angry, slate gray eyes, his unyielding back, and she heard the edge in his voice.

"Barceloux says we must wait—but I don't wait well, I tell you. I'm going to start making inquiries—in London, to begin with. That seems the most likely place. I'll put a squib about her in the London papers and if nothing comes of that, well, I'll advertise in the north counties. She has a hint of northerness in her speech, don't you think?"

Burne's answer was not audible. Jane's emotions were an indigestible ball in her stomach.

"Someone must know her," the captain went on. "A girl so remarkable does not spring into womanhood without someone noticing her; she just doesn't flit out of the shadows like a gray moth."

Jane forgot what she had come into the hall to do. She quietly crept back to the salon.

Chapter Twenty-two

Booted Footsteps

Jane was looking out the windows when Burne came into the salon a little later. She knew his step now without having to turn to look at him. She heard him close the doors of the room and cross to her. Before he said anything, she confessed:

"I heard you and your father talking. I didn't mean to eavesdrop—but I heard."

There was a long silence in which she could almost hear him trying to think of something to say. "Father has a more vivid imagination than I ever expected. I'm sorry you heard him going on like that. He has no proof, of course, not a shred of evidence to back him up."

"But it could have happened just as he says. It would account for . . . I certainly wouldn't want to remember something like that. If he's right, I don't think I ever want to remember it."

"Jane," his voice was close behind her, "you mustn't let him upset you. He has no proof. It's all theory."

It was a far cry from Stella's theory that she was a

lady running away to meet her lover. But Burne was right; there was no point in agonizing over the unknown. She tried to direct her mind onto a more positive path. She said, "He's going to advertise for people who might know me."

"Does that disturb you?"

"It frightens me a little. What if someone comes, someone I don't even recognize, who expects me to . . ."

"To what?"

"I don't know. To love him—or her—and I won't be able to because I won't know who he is."

Burne was quiet for a moment, then he stepped even nearer and put his hands on her waist. He murmured close to her ear, "Did you also overhear Father say that I was falling in love with you?"

She didn't answer.

"You and my sister have grown to be close friends. Do you think you could ever feel close to me?"

She put her hands over his, lifted them from her waist, and turned to face him. The snowlight from the windows was on his hair, making the deep, rich blond gleam with silver highlights. He was the most vital figure in the small, eccentric company of this household. The most picturesque and powerful element. She said, "I don't think I should answer that."

His lips curved, the dimples flickered at the corners of his mouth. "In my experience, that's a feminine way of saying yes." His hands clasped her waist again. He closed in. She rested her hands on his upper arms to prevent any additional familiarity.

"Burne, what if I'm bound to someone else?"

"That's a risk I'll have to take." His mouth lowered.

She pushed away and stepped around him. Though it took him an instant to recover it, he had his sense of humor in place again when he turned to follow her with

322

his eyes. "Poor Jane, you look so bewildered. I can almost see that muddled little brain riffling through the possible responses: 'Should I weep? Or laugh? Or run away from him?—Or just wet my drawers?' "

"Burne!" Her hands went to her mouth—yet she couldn't help but laugh.

"There, I think you've made the right choice."

"You're outrageous!"

"I know." He was content that he'd amused her. "Think what fun it would be to smile in the dark beside me."

She tried *not* to smile at that. But the truth was, she believed she could lie comfortably next to him in the dark. She almost felt as if she had already, at one time or another. But that was silly.

He was closing in on her again. "Let me kiss you, Jane. I've wanted to for so long."

Her back was to the fire. She could see in his eyes the reflections of the flame tongues lashing upward in the huge grate.

"I've had such an urge to touch you, to just brush my hand over your cheek. But I've held back. Don't make me hold back anymore. Just one kiss."

That low voice, gentle, caressing, wrapping her, holding her as in an embrace, sapping her will to resist. She let his arms go around her. She shivered. Her hands pressed flat against his chest inside his unbuttoned coat. She could feel the warmth of him through his shirt; his heart was beating hard against her palms. As his head lowered, she reached one hand up to stop him.

But when she touched his mouth, and felt his cool lips beneath her fingertips, she was lost to curiosity. Her hands smoothed around his neck and she lifted her face in acceptance of the inevitable.

323

His kiss was comfortable. *He* was comfortable. She liked him.

His lips left her mouth and trailed down her throat. She tried gently to push out of his hold. "Don't go." He pressed little kisses to her eyelids, her cheeks, her lips. His hands were light around her back, but she could no more have escaped them than if they'd been steel.

"Your father might come in." Her face was turned up as his kisses continued down her neck again.

"I don't care. I should have kissed you that first night, when you were limp in my arms."

She ought to stop him. The situation was getting out of control. "Burne, where would I go if the captain asked me to leave?"

"I'd take care of you. I want to kiss you again. I want to hear you laugh. Do you know that's the only time I've ever heard you laugh? It was like water bubbling up—"

"Don't, Burne."

"—like a spring bursting forth in the desert."

"Someone will hear you."

"Like—"

She covered his mouth with her fingers.

He smiled behind her hand and flicked his tongue out at her fingers. She pulled it away. And took advantage of his distraction to leave his embrace. As she did, his hands slipped from her waist and trailed under her breasts.

"You're incorrigible."

"I know." There was a chuckle in his voice. She felt the delicious danger of being alone with a pleasure-loving and full-blooded man. "And I'm stubborn, as well."

He was both, in truth, and when he tried to catch

her in his arms again, she had no choice but to flee upstairs to her chamber.

He was falling in love with her. What was going to come of it? How would he go about trying to foster a like feeling in her? Already he'd convinced her to let him hold her and kiss her. And she'd enjoyed being that close to him, she'd liked the feel of his arms around her. How would she respond to his next advance—she knew there would be a next one. She should avoid him, and say no when she couldn't avoid him, but—there was no doubt he was perilously attractive. It would be so much easier if he were ugly, with a big bent nose and a squint.

She remembered his hands moving on her back, unknowing of the scars hidden beneath her gown. As she went to the dormer window and looked out at the winter afternoon, she unlaced her gown a little, and felt, as best she could reach, the three raised ridges, the seven pink diagonals, and the dozen silvery lines that were branded there. Where had she got them? They didn't quite fit with Captain Grayson's theory. Nor with Stella's. There was even more mystery hanging about her than any one of them imagined. Mystery in the lap of beauty.

Would Burne still think he loved her if he knew about those scars? Would he think her so beautiful, so desirable?

She comforted herself with the hope that he didn't really love her, that he was merely infatuated, that he was amusing himself as best he could until spring came again and released them all from this winter prison.

A flight of blackbirds rose abruptly from the snowfield beyond her window. They'd been disturbed by a man riding a black horse along the near edge of the field. So clear was her view she could see his breath smoking, though his hat was pulled too low for her to see his face. He seemed to be looking up at the house, though, right at her window. She couldn't help feeling startled. She backed way and laced her gown.

She had her own small looking glass now, so that she could dress her hair. She went to it. For an instant, her face astonished her. It always did, hence she usually avoided looking too closely. She concentrated instead on tightening the combs in her heavy braids. But then she stopped. Boldly, she viewed precisely each feature of her face. She closed her eyes and contemplated the image.

A different image intruded: *think what fun it would be to smile in the dark beside me.* Burne's mouth coming down on hers with sudden shattering hunger. In a moment she was being fiercely kissed.

Mentally she flung herself away from him. Her eyes flew open. He hadn't kissed her like that!

But someone had. In her dreams . . . it seemed to be Burne and yet her mind slipped away from that idea; it refused to accept such an intimacy with him. If not him, then who?

The glass gave back her reflection, that youthful, exquisite face, softly marred now by her own derision. "You don't even know who you are," she murmured. Then she added, "That's not true—you *do* know! Tell me!"

Sometimes she thought she almost knew. Sometimes she thought she almost had a grasp on a thread of a clue. And if she could only catch hold of that thread, she felt sure she could pull the whole cloth into view. Sometimes after an explicit dream she could almost recount the shadowy events in which she'd been so actively involved. Often there was a sharp and arousing tone, or a taste . . . but she could never pin it down.

She felt like a phantom. It was as if she didn't cast

a shadow where she walked as other people did. If she could remember just one thing, just one, then she was sure she could remember it all: her past. The closeness of it and her inability to find the door into it was enough to drive her to tears.

Meanwhile, she felt more heavily each day a sense of time passing. If the captain was weary of waiting, then she was growing frantic with it. Was she a lady who had been violated and left for dead? Had she been running away to be with her lover? Perhaps both theories were right.

Or was she merely a maidservant on the road looking for a new position?

Or simply a madwoman escaped from some asylum?

Or a harlot, a thief, a criminal? Those marks on her back—who? why?

She wished Stella weren't so distant today. She wished, at that moment, that she might bring herself to trust Burne enough to express all her unease to him. There was nobody else to whom she could talk. She was alone.

An image leapt up in her mind: she was carrying a candle, climbing steep stairs to an attic room, she reached for the door . . .

Then it was gone. She almost cried out in frustration. She felt close to the painful edge of some truth. It was there, just *there* . . . why couldn't she grasp it! She looked about at her chamber, the whiteness, the blankness. This room, this house, suddenly they seemed too close for her. She felt as if she couldn't breathe. She rushed to her cupboard and found among the clothing Stella had lent her a heavy purple cloak.

The cocksure boy, Keith Solomon, had held fantasies of his father being a man impossibly distinguished.

Then had come a time of complete disillusionment. Now the highwayman, Keith Cutler, was learning about the real Thomas Grayson. Mostly this education came from conversations in taverns and coffee houses about the district. But Keith had also learned many things firsthand. With cunning, he'd charted the habits and pathways of "the captain."

Thomas Grayson had a deep regard for books—for their bindings, at least. It was not known whether he ever read any of the volumes in the large library left to him.

He was also considered something of an accomplished gourmet. His table was laden with the best English food. His notions of a good dinner were delicate—a leg of pork boiled till it dropped off the bone, veal pie with raisins and sugar, an outside cut of buttock of beef; these were his favorites, though he also loved soups and sauced puddings with plenty of melted butter.

Above and beyond all this, as far as Keith could ascertain, his father had one driving, obsessive, uncontrollable fervor: Grayson House. For this he would sacrifice anything and anyone.

Keith understood, for he, too, loved Grayson House. He'd thought that those feelings had vanished forever in Bridewell Prison—and they had! The amazing thing about this revived emotion was its power to reconstruct all the pain of his youth. It made him bold; it made him impatient with stealth. Today, openly riding the perimeter of the grounds, he relived the whole set of emotions, every one that he had felt as a rejected youth—for once again he was outside while everything he wanted was inside.

He wanted Jane. He wanted her more than he wanted his next breath.

She was a topic in the taverns, naturally, the woman

328

slipping around Grayson House like a shadow. No one had seen her, and engravings of the portrait of her had not made it this far south of Yorkshire. Yet, simply because she was such a mystery, there were many stories about her. There was one about her being an heiress run away from her husband. And another that she was a nurse hired secretly to take care of Stella, who was gradually going insane. Some had it on good account that she was the captain's mistress. Or Burne's. So it went. Keith found it intensely annoying to listen to these reports, or the ones that said knowingly that she had a wooden leg, or leprosy. But there was no end to this sort of legendry.

The Graysons' coachman spent his free time in Marydale, in a tavern run by one Dame Diana, two hundred pounds of female all in one package. The man, whose name was Jones, had a long, bony face, a protruding jaw, and lank black hair. He was the sort who felt most comfortable with a tankard of ale in his hand, and he'd earned many a free drink lately from a certain stranger, on the basis of his regular reports about the girl who had wandered to Grayson House the night of the big storm last November.

She was beautiful, the coachman said, "So lovely she be both pleasure and pain to look at." But she seemed unhappy, even when she smiled. "O' course, the maid's a little soft in the head." She had something the doctor called "historical amnesia." No one was supposed to question her, because if she were forced to recall too suddenlike what fright or shock had knocked her memory out of her, it might send her right into madness.

That chilled the back of Keith's neck. Jane, who had been so full of the future, a future he'd never been able to envision, but a future, nonetheless. Calm, practical, stubborn Jane. Could she really go mad? He'd seen women, and men, too, go mad in prison. A person you knew became different. Sweet, tender souls became coiled, silent, brooding figures, lost to the shadows. They even started to smell bad, as if they were rotting from the inside. You began to avoid them, even those you used to admire. And the more you admired them, the more you eventually grew to hate them.

''The doctor says she might remember everything in a flash—or she might never remember naught at all.''

The words struck home, sharp, steel-shafted. Keith could only hope that as long as she didn't recall herself, she was safe where she was. As long as the captain believed she was a lady come upon misfortune he wouldn't toss her out the front door, out into the snowy night.

On the other hand, if he did toss her out, then at least Keith could collect her. As it was, he couldn't get near her.

Meanwhile, here he was, despite the risk of being identified—at more risk than her, as it happened. The duke's handbills had come farther south than the engraving of ''The Rose of Midnight.'' Most of the handbills had been used for pipe-lighters by now, but some people, soldiers in particular, had long memories. He lingered, however, because he must. He kept moving every few days. He'd moved from Ledbury to take a room in the Druid Inn, located on the highroad, a very small plain spot sunk deep in rural lassitude. He was using a false name. He was keeping his eye on Grayson House, on Jane.

He'd watched her last night. One of his father's proud lavishnesses was candles, making it easy for someone lurking outside the house to see in. Snow had fallen around Keith again, holding him in its hushed, insistent patter as he watched Jane with Stella through the windows in the salon.

Her body seemed to move lightly, gracefully again, and her skin had regained most of its fresh vitality. He'd watched her speak. She sounded so natural. So familiar. And then Burne had come in.

He entered the room like a long sharp knife, and cut the ladies' boredom to shreds. Keith saw that Burne was falling in love with Jane. No great surprise. But could she love him back? He was a pretty fellow. Washed, combed, shaved, powdered, he appeared to be of a different race of men from Keith Cutler. Keith had done a lot of silent, sulphurous cursing over his handsome brother since then.

It took no great wit to realize he was jealous. Not only was he wild with anxiety for Jane's safety, he was jealous. He'd been jealous now for seven weeks. Not just of Burne, but of the captain and Stella, too, because they had Jane and he didn't. But mostly he was upset by his bitter envy of Burne. He knew this was an absurd feeling, but he had it anyway, vicious and strong.

As for Stella, he'd discovered she was a shy, miserable woman. The locals said her tendency to melancholy was inherited from her mother, but Keith's opinion was that much of it came from being stunted by her father. Keith knew for a fact that she had hidden qualities. And that she led a hidden life.

There was a steadily building tragedy there. Keith was grateful to this lonely, unhappy sister for taking Jane in and making her presence palatable to her father. Hence, if there was anything he could do to avert the tragedy he foresaw, he most certainly would do it.

As he rode around Grayson House today, the gray clouds of the afternoon began to filter toward the charcoal of twilight. Jane's chamber window was unlit, but he thought he glimpsed her form.

In a place where he couldn't be seen from the house,

he tied Eclipse. He found the small break in the hedge that protected the orchard, a narrow gap he'd used before, and he pushed through.

He was at the gate of the rose garden, looking toward the back of the house, when he saw a door open. A woman stepped out. Members of the family so rarely left the house since the snow had fallen that Keith was amazed to hear, "No, I won't be long; I just need some fresh air." The one voice on earth that was Jane's hung above the evening snowgarden like a ghost. His heart hammered up. She'd seen him from her window and now she was coming out to him. She remembered! He felt released, triumphant, as if a great victory had been accomplished.

But wait—what if she just wanted a breath of air, as she'd said? He mustn't startle her. He must be careful.

Since the last time a path through the ghostly garden had been shoveled, another eight inches had fallen, making Jane's walk awkward. Hers were the first footprints to deface the unblemished surface. She went toward the gate into the orchard, paused, then decided that since her shoes were already soaked she might as well go on.

There were footprints in the snow on the other side of the gate. They led to the left. She looked that way but saw no one. Perhaps a gardener had been here today? The going through the orchard was much harder than through the rose garden. Here there had been no shoveling done since winter began. She sank up to her knees more than once.

At the far end of the orchard, another gate in the hedge led into the park. It was Jane's first time here. She trudged on, though her feet were numb with cold. She discovered the sturdy miniature summer house, its roof pitched as steep as praying hands, icicle-fringed, and nearby, the little mere, gray with ice.

The complete solitude of this half hour allowed a relaxation of her natural guard, so that more images flickered and vanished in her mind. Still, nothing came completely clear.

She thought about Burne. He was a good man, attractive, strong. But she didn't think she could ever bring herself to love him. She didn't want to love him.

At last, aware of the fading light, she turned back toward the house. Following the narrow trail of her own footprints, she soon came across a larger set. She felt a tang of fear. They hadn't been there before. She looked about nervously. Who had come behind her? The deep prints mingled with her own for several hundred yards, then turned aside. Someone had followed her, then veered away as she'd doubled back.

She made it to the thorny hedgerow outside the orchard. As she reached for the gate latch, she heard a rustle. A dark form suddenly stepped out of the hedge and bolted toward her. She blinked like an owl and backed away. A man. He was before her in an instant, his great-coat billowing, his hat pulled low over his head. The sight of him gave her an immeasurably queer feeling.

Belatedly, she thought she ought to run—but she'd backed away from the gate and now he was between it and her. He had her cut off from the house. Her hands twitched up in an incomplete gesture.

He caught her easily. "Jane," he said gruffly.

She struggled in that grip, but it was too strong to break. He knew the name Stella had given her. She scraped together her courage and looked into his face, overwrought with anxiety and fear. The little she saw of his hair was the color of midnight. His features . . . his expression . . . "Who are you? What do you want?"

"You don't know me?" His voice was deadly gentle. His eyes were alert and dangerous, like the eyes of a cat that smelled a nest of baby rodents. He put his left hand on her cold cheek. "But Jane, I know you."

"You don't!" Her voice threatened to rise beyond her control. She twisted her arms, trying to escape his hands.

"Look at me." His voice was deeper even than Burne's. Curiously, it made her think of water falling.

She did look at him; she was suddenly dizzy.

"I know you. You know I'm telling you the truth. I've never lied to you."

She'd stopped struggling, she was so dizzy. His hold on her relented. She broke away and almost fell backward, trying to put some space between them. She set her teeth; the dizziness passed. Her mind began to stir, but it was barbed and rejecting, insisting that this stranger go away. He was staring at her, waiting. His gaze was very strange. His eyes were full of dizzying lights. For a moment she was trapped by the truth in them: he was the man in her troubled and violent dreams. Him, not Burne. Her throat tightened and her tongue dried and she felt baited, as though a game were being played, with her as the victim.

Those eyes went on regarding her carefully, counting every second, waiting to see what she would do. There was something about him, something secretive and voluptuous and treacherous. She was attracted to him—and that attraction frightened her. Had he flogged her? Had he tried to drown her? Had he raped her? In her dreams, his possession was an ecstasy; but how far could she trust dreams when she couldn't even trust her waking mind? She stood where she was, fixed in ambivalence.

He moved toward her again. "There is something you have to know. You're in danger." At the same time he said this, his greatcoat opened. She saw a sword! And a pistol thrust into his wide belt! She recalled Captain Grayson's theory—a highwayman, a brigand who prowled for prey and perhaps had vandalized her life with malice and murder.

"You're in danger, Jane."

He was inching toward her, watching her from under lowered lids. She heard again, unaccountably, water falling, water going over a mill dam. The sound—the memory of the sound—horrified her. Somehow this agile and powerful stranger was related to the horror of that dream in which she struggled in the embrace of something, or someone, that held her beneath the surface of a torrent, that dream from which she woke gasping for breath, for life.

She started to the left, miraculously got around him, and fled for the gate.

"Jane!" There was a ring of despair in his voice that frightened her as much as anything. She let the gate slam behind her and didn't pause.

The lighted house stood too distant to hear her should she waste her breath trying to call. Through the deep snow in the orchard she ran, slithering and falling. She was not yet as strong as she might be. Her legs ached, her lungs ached, her breathing was loud and ragged.

Beyond the gate, in the rose garden, the going was easier, and because it was easier she was that much more afraid of being overtaken. Her nerves pricked at the least noise. She could shout for help now—but something stopped her, some intuition, or premonition, or instinct.

It was nearing full dark. The house was lit like a lantern. She went in through the back door, took the back stairs up to her chamber. She forced a smile when she met Catherine coming down. "Mistress! Did ye fall in the snow?"

"Yes . . . yes, I did. Clumsy. I'm going up to change."

"I'll bring ye a hot drink."

"No, that's all right, Catherine. I'll be down soon for supper."

At last she closed the door of the White Room and stood with her back to it, as if she believed the stranger might follow her even here.

Quiet.

So quiet there in the darkness. The quiet, unstudied elegance of Grayson House stood all about her. She held her breath and listened for the sound of booted footsteps, for another's breathing beyond the door. But there was nothing.

Of course he wouldn't come right into the house. Of course not.

How could she know that? How could she know what was in him? He'd come right into the orchard, hadn't he?

At last she took one step, then another, as if walking a thin line, as thin as a blade's edge, toward her window. Would he still be down there? She was afraid to look.

I know you.

A bolt of blue fire arced through her. Who was he? Intuition whispered, Look . . . look, Jane, and you will see who he is—*look, Jane!*

She flung herself to the window, but it was a night-mirror and she could see nothing beyond it. She saw nothing but her own face—that face that she didn't even recognize!

Something huge in her swelled, choking her. It burst its bonds and she broke into a fit of weeping. Tears as large as beads dropped to the floor.

Chapter Twenty-three

A Man of Tenderness

Keith stood behind the orchard hedge with Eclipse.
His fury made him feel like weeping. He had cast himself too far forward. He must pull back, recover the equilibrium he'd started with.

But she didn't know him! Why not? Was there some change in his face? She'd looked at him as if she'd never seen him before. Worse, as if he had no human reality at all. Deprived of her acknowledgement, he felt robbed of life itself.

The effort to restrain his hurt left him rough-minded. He uttered a brief obscenity. Hurt became anger. He wanted her back, and he wanted her *now!*

He rubbed his hands over his eyes, regretting that he could remember everything so easily when she could remember nothing. He should never have let her run from him. Why hadn't he simply reached out, caught her, pulled her into his arms and held her tight? He could have forced her through the hedge, rode off with her. She was well enough in body now.

But her mind. He couldn't take chances with her mind.

Eclipse bent his neck and blew out his nostrils. He should be stabled, rubbed down, fed.

Keith's helplessness was intolerable. He'd been the one to set this coach rolling, and now he could not command it. He slinked along the roads hereabout with his hat dragged forward, all to catch a glimpse of her, and now . . . he was *tired* of this useless sneaking life!

A yearning fell on his heart like a warm hand. He wanted her back. He ached with wanting her face, her strong warm presence, her stillness which no storm could disturb.

But he couldn't risk driving her mad. He loved her too much for that.

He tossed his head and cursed both tears and self-pity.

The next two days and nights the clouds bared neither sun nor stars. Then the clouds broke up into fleecy puffs and drifted one after another out over the fells. Three days of bright, warm, clear skies ensued.

The stranger in the orchard had not returned. At least, Jane didn't think he had. She daren't go out again, so she couldn't be absolutely sure.

She hadn't told a soul about him. It was too frightening. And what good would it do? Even if he were apprehended, she didn't know him, didn't know if he'd done her harm; she couldn't act as a competent witness against him. A man like that, armed and treacherous— she wanted to believe that he was just someone who had heard of her amnesia and had come to take advantage of it somehow. But more likely was Captain Grayson's theory, that he was someone who had abused her and tried to kill her and now was chagrined that she was still alive and possibly able to recognize him. It frightened her to think he'd come to finish what he'd started.

Yet he'd had every opportunity to do just that in the orchard. He could have strangled her with those big gauntleted hands. Or struck her down with the butt of that huge pistol. Or carried her off to do whatever he wished with her elsewhere.

This morning, as the maidservant came in to light her chamber fire, Jane lay in a half-sleep. She heard the woman bustling about her work, but she didn't open her eyes or stir. She listened as Catherine spread her smock and stockings to warm before the fire. When she left, Jane finally slipped out of bed and with her white satin wrap pulled about her, went and crouched in front of the grate. Her mind was fully awake to the usual grind and gnash of what-if? who? and why? All her questions centered around that stranger in black.

He was somewhere outside, waiting. For what? She didn't know for certain. But he was there. She could comprehend his presence, even without the sun casting a shadow, even without the noise of a footstep. He was near, and he would accost her again if she went out alone.

She dressed in a sleeveless bodice of green glazed cotton, with a wide neck that showed off her white lawn chemise. She puffed the white sleeves. The skirt was striped in brick red and pale yellow; it was wide and circular to her ankles. She took her hair back from her face and pinned it up in a fairly high chignon at the back, with some curls hanging from it.

When she went down to breakfast, she found Captain Grayson alone at the table. He was reading a newspaper. He put it down politely and said, "Will you have some coffee?" He even discomposed his features so far as to show a gleam of teeth which Jane understood must be his smile. It was clearly something very unusual for him. Jane, helping herself to some fresh white bread, understood his awkwardness. No doubt he hardly knew what to do with her company, any more than she knew what to do with his.

What had he asked her? Oh, yes—coffee. For breakfast? He had it every morning. Neither Stella nor Burne drank it, both preferring tea. The captain had not offered it to Jane before. "Thank you," she said and accepted a cup from him. She tried it, and found it terrible, bitter stuff, ground from bark or something. She took another sip and smiled at him. She was growing so tired of being polite.

He looked out the windows and narrowed his eyes against the morning sun. A spell of bright, warm thaw weather had set in overnight. "Stella must be sleeping off her cold."

"Yes." Jane felt inane.

Yesterday, after returning from Sunday services at the little church in the hamlet of Marydale, Stella's mood was suddenly lifted, after a week of melancholy. All afternoon she'd seemed cheerful and so pleased with everything. Then, at dinner, she'd coughed and said she felt a cold coming on. She excused herself even before the dessert, saying, "I think I'll retire." Jane hadn't seen her since.

The captain noisily sucked at his coffee cup. "And Burne is gone."

"Oh?"

"Yes, he'll be gone for three weeks. We decided late last night. He's off to London to do some business for me."

You sent him to check for answers to the advertisements about me in the papers, Jane thought. The captain must be anxious indeed to get rid of her to expose Burne to the dissipation and licentiousness of Town during the Season.

340

Was she going to miss Burne? She didn't allow that thought to take definite shape.

Several minutes of uncomfortable silence followed. Finally the captain said, with a bit too much heartiness, "What have you in mind for the day?"

She felt put on the spot. Could she say, "Nothing?" She didn't like to. Looking out the mullioned windows, she thought quickly and answered, "I thought I might take a walk in the park.'

Where had that stupid idea come from?

"In the snow?"

She nodded.

"If you're really in earnest," his tone indicated he thought she was mad, "I'll accompany you. I should take a look at the roof of the summer house, to see that it's shedding the snow properly. This little thaw isn't likely to last."

Captain Grayson had decided to question the girl. He was beyond all patience with Barceloux's advice. And he was restless because of another matter. Perhaps a walk would clear his head.

The other matter was Stella. She was getting to be eccentric, what with her moods, ecstatic one day, morose the next. Taking to her bed on the excuse of a petty little cough. He'd been too lenient with her. He should have forced her into marriage years ago. She would have settled to it, and would be the mother of several children by now. His sentimentality, his sensitive, susceptible, generous nature made him act the fool. He'd let her make him feel guilty about that time years ago when she'd set her affections on that boy who was so totally unsuitable.

When she was but eighteen she'd opened her heart to the nephew of a neighbor. She just couldn't under-

341

stand that he wouldn't do. Although the fellow was a good enough horseman, and supposedly handsome, he had not the entreé to any worthwhile social circle, for he was known to have no wealth and no expectations.

Henry Hanson. That was his name. The captain suspected all along that the boy wasn't so much drawn to Stella as he was thoughtful of the main chance. The dowry left for her by her mother was not considerable, but it was more than Hanson had at his own disposal.

The captain sent her off to various places of resort until the young rascal engaged himself to some other poor wretch of a girl. Stella stopped talking to him for months. She just couldn't believe that he might be able to see farther into the thing than she. That was the way it was with children; they couldn't believe their parents might have felt the passions that so plague the young.

He vaguely remembered the embarrassment of his own infatuation with a pretty cottage girl, a farmer's daughter. For a spring and a summer he'd met her in a secret copse at the edge of Marydale. What was her name? Ah yes, Laurel Solomon. A lovely girl. She'd worn her dark hair back from her forehead with a center parting and put up in a knot at the top of her head. She hadn't powdered it, or worn a wig, of course, being of the working class.

It was not love, just an infatuation, and he'd reasoned that an attractive woman, even a peasant, was better than taking chances with harlots. He'd had a hard time at first just convincing her to give him a few kisses, but after that, well, girls like that were a lustier lot than women of his own class. You couldn't really blame them for their failings; it was simply a weakness in their natures.

After he'd possessed her the first time, her mind became oppressed, something distressed her. To get her to let him have her again, he'd had to give her an opal ring, quite an expensive trinket to pay for a peasant girl's favors, but at the time he'd thought her worth it. He himself had been young and hot-blooded, and she was such a pretty, dark thing.

Then she'd had the bad grace to get pregnant. Well, what did she expect when she had given him the freedom to use her as a harlot? It was her own fault. God knew, and so should Woman by now, that sometimes a young man couldn't contain his appetites. When a youth got that ache in his groin, that craving like no other craving, it was the woman's responsibility to say no.

He'd never regretted how he'd handled it. Best to cut such mistakes back coldly, prune them, lop them off.

Even so, it had come back to haunt him. One doesn't play dice with God. He sees that you're reminded of your sins. The girl's bastard child, a boy, had come right to Grayson House once, pretending to be Burne's friend. Shameless! He'd been attending Hillsburrow School, though heaven only knew where Laurel had got the money to send him there. No doubt she'd sunk into dark circumstances. After all, she was a woman who'd lost her reputation.

That had all been long ago, yes, long ago, yet it proved that though some might think him unfeeling, in truth he'd plumbed the very glittering iris of human passions.

"Daniel! Where are my heavy boots?" Where was that false, shuffling, prevaricating scoundrel?

The girl wanted to go for a walk in the snow. He sighed hugely. For the millionth time, he wished Francis hadn't died. He'd never wanted to be the squire of Grayson House. In all fairness, he'd come to the position unprepared.

Francis was a dazzling older brother, an even-handed, noble-hearted boy. He laughed a lot—called it "the wise man's substitute for lamentation." Both their mother and father had fixed their hopes on him to carry on the Grayson heritage, as had Thomas. And when their mother died, followed soon after by their grief-stricken father, Francis stepped into place as head of the family as gracefully as could be imagined. And then came the small pox. Thomas remembered him in his coffin, his face leaden gray. Only Thomas remained then, alone in a world he didn't understand, facing responsibilities for which he had not been prepared by either nurturing or training.

Still, on good days he believed he made a kindly overlord, taking interest in his tenants and workers, mixing with his sheep shearers and overseers—as well as one can mix from atop a chestnut stallion. On occasion he even ventured down into the village where he performed with creditable elegance.

On the infrequent not-so-good-day, however, he knew that he was arrogant and exacting, lashing out against the smallest offense. He'd struck one fat little woman with his riding whip during threshing season last autumn, for letting her child get dangerously in the way of his horse's hooves. She was the wife of the local wheelwright, he believed. He'd done her no lasting damage—and damnit! she should have been watching the child. Of course the story was repeated, drawn in the worst colors possible. For weeks thereafter he'd felt the eyes of his people following him, and not with the respect or affection he craved.

His mouth foolishly twitched, remembering those looks.

Francis had never gone about creating such a pocket of gloom around himself. His life had always had a bloom to it. He should have been the squire and Thomas should have been the successful naval man

344

who came home to visit during his shore leave wearing a fine uniform with a bright blue coat and broad lapels. Why, he'd made captain of his own ship by the age of twenty-three! Captain Thomas Grayson of *The Crusader*. He'd loved that ship as he'd never loved a woman. The sea was his proper arena. The navy way was the only way he really understood, and he tried to run Grayson House like a ship. But it didn't always work out right.

Wearing his redingote, he met Jane at the door leading to the rose garden. She moved with the light grace of a carefully bred person. She'd covered her colorful dress with a purple cloak, all cast-offs from Stella's wardrobe, though on her they looked new and fresh. They went out.

His mind caught again on the problem of Stella. She'd read too many novels. He tried to keep them from her, but somehow she always got her hands on them. They put in her head a lot of fanciful notions about marriage, such as that it should be accompanied by love. What nonsense!

The girl at his side, Jane, slipped in the snow, which was melting and slushy. He gallantly offered his arm. He was never quite sure—did an early thaw like this mean the winter was going to be short—or longer than usual? Francis would have known. Short, the captain hoped. The shorter the better. Then he could enjoy the first fresh meat of spring.

The girl's hands grasped his arm to steady herself again. Small hands. The crescent moons of the nails were pearly. *Pearly*, a nice word, a tender word. He prided himself on being a man of tenderness. "Careful," he said, feeling expansive and strong and masculine next to her smallness and weakness and pitiable female frailness.

He cleared his throat. She had a problem and as her

protector it was his duty to go to the core of it. "It seems the doctor was able to do you very little service, Jane; you mend slowly."

"I'm getting stronger, sir. I feel fine."

"But you aren't completely well, are you?"

She gave him one of those looks of hers, seemingly modest, though he couldn't help but suspect a degree of cleverness. What went on in her mind? Women with beauty learned early to use it. And she was decidedly beautiful. Who was she, this girl who had dropped into his life as from out of a cloud?

He said, not looking at her, "I understand that we are not to plague you with questions; however, it seems that just waiting for your memory to return is doing no good." He directed his voice to something a little before and above him. It was technique he'd learned from his senior officers. A man never looked so profound and in-charge as when he stood at the rail looking out at the sea. "It's my opinion that a few questions might be in order, might even be a help."

"Truly, I remember nothing of any value, Captain." Her voice was like soft, slithering satin.

He looked down at her, severe and disapproving. "I find that hard to believe. I'm not accusing you of withholding information; it's just that I can't imagine anything so odd as not remembering, well, one's own name, for instance."

She sighed. "It is odd, Captain. Odd beyond belief."

"Well then, I urge you to examine your memory for some correct answers."

"I'm certainly trying, sir, every minute of every day. But it's hard to remember anything by the exercise of will. More often things come to me when I'm not trying at all."

He pounced on that. "What things?"

346

She paused before she said, "I get glimpses now and then, little things that come bobbing to the surface like corks—but then they're dragged below again before I can get a clear view of them."

He felt certain she was hiding something. He pressed on, his voice more demanding. "Please try to be more explicit. What do you glimpse?"

The snow-humped rose bushes glittered and dripped in the bright sunlight. Here and there a bare stick of a branch thrust through.

"I've heard the sound of a great rushing of water, a mill damn, I think. But I suppose that comes from when I nearly drowned, so it can hardly help to identify me."

"But you see, you're wrong! The nearest mill dam is not on the highway—and all along we've assumed you were traveling on the northern road that night. This may put the location of your accident at Hobart's Mill—though I can't imagine what you were doing there on such a night!"

They passed into the orchard. As he closed the gate behind them, he looked at her for a moment, at her hair neatly put up under her white cap. Then he restored his glowering address to the unseen ocean. "What else?"

"I've seen myself standing beside some rough field-stones stacked into a wall."

That didn't seem of much help. "Go on."

She put her free hand to her temple, as if his question were crackling inside her head. "Fells," she said, "bare fells, very green, with sheep."

"Yes," he rapped out, "England is full of fells, green and covered with sheep. Is there anything more?"

She shook her head, looking fraught now. "Nothing that makes any sense."

"I only hope Burne finds out more in London."

"I hope so, too. I worry about it constantly. I can't see that being faced with the truth can be any more shocking than to be faced with this . . . nothing."

They walked on for a moment, then she added, "I do hope you know how grateful I am, Captain, for your patience and your hospitality. I realize that you can't be expected to accommodate me much longer and I'm trying to remember, truly I am, all the time. I feel a very real anxiety whenever I consider what I am to do with myself—should I never recall anything, that is."

He frowned at the air. "Yes, well, a woman with your physical, er, beauty shouldn't be terribly hard to trace."

Neither of them said anything more as they trudged on through the orchard. This softened snow was a real trial, and the captain would have turned back the instant she suggested it, but his core of vanity wouldn't allow him to be the first to mention that he was as cold as the wind in each particle of his being.

They reached the gate into the park. The captain was proud of this addition to Grayson House which he himself had added. The best of the nobility were all adding parks to their country estates these days. Captain Grayson always dreamed of seeing his son a great man like those. Burne had the ability—he had the funds and all the charm—to make a marriage into the nobility. Of course, he'd never get a title himself, but his children, the captain's grandchildren, might inherit one.

The girl seemed to know the way to the summer house. He hadn't looked the building over since before Christmas and he supposed it was as well that he take this opportunity to examine it.

He was looking down at the placement of his feet as they plodded around a big, lichened, gray rock which had been strategically placed to separate the summer house from view until one came upon it suddenly, when Jane abruptly came to a halt. He lifted his head, and in an instant he saw what she'd seen.

On the porch of the building was Stella—not back in her bed at all! But looking as if she'd just risen, with her carroty hair loose, her gown not quite laced—and her feet bare! Worse, she was in the arms of a man who was holding her intimately and kissing her deeply. Roughly. But she wasn't struggling; her arms were locked about his neck.

The captain's heart went suddenly and hideously still. Then he started forward as if he'd been shoved from behind.

Jane caught at his arm. "Captain!" He threw her off.

Her outcry alerted the two at the summer house. Stella broke free of her lover's kiss and gasped. She stepped out of his arms—flinched away. The man dropped his hands and stood with a blank expression on his face. Beneath his open coat he wore a sleeveless leather jerkin over a broad-cut shirt and breeches, the clothes of an ordinary village laborer. Captain Grayson recognized him now, Hart Baywood, born near the village of East Fox. His father was a farmer. The family attended the same church as the Graysons.

Farmer Baywood was by no means a dimwit. In spite of his humble birth, there was a dignity about him that had always pleased Captain Grayson. He was progressive; he used new systems, such as Townshend's four-course rotation of crops. But the man was hardly a local worthy. His wife Sarah was of slightly better breeding—as the world reckoned such affairs in a village like East Fox. Her own father was of yeoman status or perhaps a little more, a small-scale landowner and a man of some cultivation. There were connections there, by marriage, with the gentry and with the professions.

The family lived in an unremarkable yellow and pebbledash house. They farmed a freeholding of fifty acres. Their fortune varied according to the price levels, which depended upon harvests, tariff policies, natural catastrophes, and foreign wars.

Hart was in his middle thirties, of common height, very dark, very angular, with a long aquiline nose and an obstinate mouth. Captain Grayson went right up to him and lifted his hand and struck the man. The fellow's head and upper body swiveled with the strength of the blow. When he stood straight again, his eyes glistened with hot anger. The captain said with studied civility, "That, sir, was a challenge. I presume you know the exercise of a gentleman's weapon, since—"

"No, Father!" Stella's voice came out brittle and high-pitched. She had her hands in her hair like a maddened thing.

"—since you seem to know the exercise of a gentleman's daughter!" He gave Stella the look he would bestow on a slut. "Put yourself together, hussy! Put your shoes on!"

She turned quickly and mindlessly to the open door of the summer house. Beyond her the captain saw the fire they'd made. Its glow edged the wood and china and pewter pieces that ornamented the interior. The house had been built for small tea parties. On the table was a jar covered in wicker-work, of pottery, used to hold water, and beside it, the remains of a quarter loaf of bread. There was only the one room, no bedchamber. They had made a mattress of quilts and coverlets on the floor before the hearth. Romantic indeed.

He turned back to Hart—nothing but a hob-nailed farmer's son! My God!

The younger man's face was inflamed. He said. "If there be any dishonor here, 'tis mine alone, sir."

The captain said, "What do you know about honor? But you will bear your responsibility in this, never fear. You will meet me tomorrow morning at Jose-on-Tees, at dawn. Do you own a pistol?"

Baywood shook his head.

"Of course you don't. Never mind, I have a matched pair."

"Father!" Stella was back, frantically worrying her hair again. Maybe she was a little demented. There were rumors—he'd heard them; he heard every spider on the wall. Maybe he would have to have her put away.

"He can't go against you. You know he can't. It's madness! It's an excuse for murder!"

"And what do you call this?" He gestured to the tumbled bedding beyond the open door. "What is this an excuse for?"

His rage was increasing with every minute that passed. The moment clanged; rage and terror cavorted. He turned and shouted at Hart, "Get off my property, you varmint! Before I go back to the house and get my fowling piece!" He wanted to kill the man, he really did, it was his soul's wish, his heart's dream, his blood's will.

As the younger man stepped off the porch, he gave Stella a look devoid of all emotion. Her own eyes were full of tears. "Hart," she said in a watery voice, "don't meet him. Don't." She smiled through her tears at him, almost gently. "I'll understand."

The captain ground out, "If he doesn't, I'll see that everyone for fifty miles around knows what a coward he is. And how little he cares for you, by the way." He gripped her arm and pulled her off the porch.

"No!" She struggled. "Hart!"

"Show some dignity, trollop!"

The walk back took much less time and was much less stately than the leisurely stroll out. Whilst he pushed Stella through the door into the warmth, she said in a blurred voice, "I love him. He won't meet you. He'll go away, and then I'll find some way to escape you to be with him. You can't stop me this time."

He exploded in a fury, smacking her insolent face twice. Jane cried out, "Captain Grayson! Stop!"

Stella nearly fell from his blows, recovered herself, and looked him straight in the eye, long and deep. And with an unbearable smile said, "You can't stop me this time."

He had to admit she was a fine, fierce sight, with her uncovered hair all disheveled, standing up to him like a warrior woman out of the far past. Either she was mad indeed, or she was someone he had never suspected.

"Can't I?" he said. "We shall see about that."

Hence he had his wayward daughter locked inside the small room at the very top of the house, from which any escape was impossible. For now, at least, she was secure. Whether she would ever be allowed out again was a matter he would consider later.

Chapter Twenty-four

An Expert Shot

The day was long, but gradually the first stars appeared and grew fixed and bright and glittering—much like the sharp glitter of conviction in Captain Grayson's face. He and Jane sat alone at the satinwood supper table. His mantle of authority was clearly in place. She kept hearing those two rapidly delivered, stunning slaps, one to each side of Stella's face. The echo of those blows resounded through the still house.

The night was longer than the day had been. The wind still had the sting of winter in it. It blew up the valley while Jane struggled in her warm bed with a nightmare: there was pain, and a voice, *Jane*. There was a dreadful fire. It had some awful and ominous import, that fire. She woke gasping. She could almost . . . *almost* remember. Her eyes wide and staring, she looked inward, strained to see . . .

But her brain seemed to move ineptly, and the sensation of being so close, so close, faded away. A veil descended, cutting her off from . . . what?

She'd left a night light burning by her bed. She rose and, taking it with her, padded to her looking glass.

Who are you? It was no use. The candle glimmered on the glass. She saw only that same woman she'd been seeing for nearly a month now, since she'd awakened in this strange room, a stranger to herself, beautiful but incomplete and ridiculous, part of her mind stupidly misplaced.

She went to the dormer window. She thought she saw a figure below in the rose garden, dark, straight, motionless in the wind, outlined by star glimmer. But then it seemed to blur into the swaying hedgerow and there was nothing but the diffuse dust of starlight over the surface of the snow.

She did not go back to bed, but spent the rest of the night sitting wrapped in a shawl by her banked fire.

Before the first wash of dawn, Captain Grayson left for Jose-on-Tees, wherever that might be. No sooner did she hear him ride down the graveled drive than she dressed and went to the servant, Catherine. She demanded the key to the attic. The woman was still sleepy and easily intimidated.

Though Jane knew she was stepping perilously close to the edge of prudence, she unlocked the attic. The tiny cell had no window; with the door closed it must be blind dark. It was hardly larger than a closet, used to store old ledgers and accounts, bare of any comfort, full of dust and cobwebs and cold. Stella was on the floor, awake, yet lying curled like a grieving child. Her face and body seemed shrunken. It wasn't until Jane had her in her room, in her warmed bed, that Stella began to cry again, as she must have done for most of the night.

The suffused early sky-bloom came through the windows. Stella wouldn't let go of Jane's hand. She wouldn't eat the bowl of thick porridge and chunk of bread that Catherine brought. She sobbed, "He'll kill him."

"No," Jane murmured, sitting by her in the yellow wooden chair.

"He will, he's an expert shot, while Hart doesn't even own a pistol and has never fired one that I know of—and I know him better than anyone." Her voice was thin and soft with weeping, like fabric all but worn through. Outside her door, Catherine was going about her morning chores. Jane heard her sweeping away down the gallery.

"Father will let him choose one of his own pretty pistols, and then he'll kill him, and no one will be able to do anything about it because it will all seem *honorable.*" Her breath trembled. "How else should a father deal with the man his daughter has deported herself with, a man not her husband?"

She looked away. "I dare say you must think none of this bears any honor, Jane, and me as dishonorable as any."

"Oh, Stella." Jane thought it best to distract her. "Tell me about Hart. How long have you known him?"

"All my life, but when his mother got a fever four years ago, I went to their cottage every few days to help her. The Baywoods are a large family, all sons. Hart was always so kind. At first it was as innocent as that. We contrived to meet when I was out riding, or when I visited the tenants. But it got so that wasn't enough. Talking and holding hands wasn't enough. We decided to meet in the summer house on the fourth Monday of every month, when Father goes to his whist games. We've been lovers for the past year."

Her eyes were enormous in their dark sockets, all deception charred away. "It wasn't always possible. Sometimes he would wait in vain for me. If Father didn't go to his game, or even if he did and Burne

355

decided to spend the evening at home . . . I couldn't risk giving them the least suspicion, not the least.''

Her moods came clear now. The despair, followed by lightheartedness and animation.

''Why did you go Sunday night then, Stella? Your father was here, and Burne, too.''

''Because I was so lonely,'' she whispered. ''I saw him at church, and . . . we have signals. I *needed* to see him, Jane. Can you understand? Sometimes it's so painful, the loneliness, I can't bear it anymore.''

''But why didn't you come back before morning?''

''I wanted to be with him all night, just once, all night. I wanted to talk until there was no more to say. I wanted to fall asleep with him, in his arms, to pretend . . .'' Her eyes, like a rabbit's, intercepted Jane's for some sort of assurance. ''I can talk to him. I can talk about my inmost feelings. He listens. I can open my heart to him. He loves me. He makes me feel . . . pretty. When he looks at me I'm everything I crave to be.''

Jane tried to reconcile this image of tenderness with the older man she'd seen kissing Stella so roughly yesterday. Had Stella's instinct led her to someone rugged, someone older, who might just have the courage to rip her away from the spiderweb her father had spun around her? She'd loved the thrill of forbidden wine with him, and his coarse caresses. It was a pity. She wanted so badly to live.

Her hair was tumbled loosely, orange-red on the white pillow. Jane suddenly felt a wave of love for her. ''Stella, it's my fault the captain found you. I led him there. I wanted to go for a walk. I had no idea—''

''You couldn't have known. You mustn't blame yourself.''

''If only I hadn't—''

''There is no reason to blame yourself, Jane. I al-

356

ways knew he would find out. I think I wanted him to. Yes. And so Hart's death will be my fault. All my fault.''

Her eyes watched something Jane couldn't see. "Hart has nothing. There is no possibility of him taking me into his father's house; the Baywoods couldn't afford that, for Father would ruin them all. I have a bride's portion coming, but Father would never give it to me unless I married exactly who he wanted me to. He's mean, I've always known he was mean. He never lets me have any money out of which I might save something. I tried to save what I could from my little shopping excursions, but even after four years there's hardly enough to buy a single coach ticket.

"But I love Hart so! I don't know if I want to live without him." Her eyes had a look Jane had seen before; now she understood that profundity of sadness, that despair.

"Sometimes I get so lonely for him, seeing him at church and knowing I dare not look at him for too long, and never touch him or smile at him. It hurts so, Jane, it hurts so.''

Jane stroked her white cheek. *"Shhh,* try to rest now.''

Stella rolled her head helplessly on her pillow. "I can't rest when he's about to be killed. How can I rest?''

She did grow still, however, and Jane watched her eyelids fall. Her plump, amicable face seemed to have shrunk; she'd become older sometime in the night.

An hour passed. The sun came up. It seemed to mean business. There would be bare patches of ground showing through the snow by the end of this day. The light came in through the window onto Stella's face. Her closed eyes flickered. Jane gently pulled her hand away and rose to close the shutters.

She paused to blink at the raw light first, and savor the warmth of the sun on her face. She looked across the melting fields, wondering about that figure she'd seen in the dark last night. Had it been her imagination? Directly below, she saw Catherine come out a side door of the house carrying the night-soil buckets up the path to the pits by the woods. The woman plodded along, her neck stretched out like she was being towed. Jane suddenly knew that she'd felt the weight of such buckets in her hands before. A gust of familiarity, almost like homesickness, shook her.

She stood there for a moment like a stopped clock: nothing seemed to be happening within her at all.

She shook herself. Homesick for carrying night-soil buckets? She supposed that was of a piece with the rest of this accursed day. Grayson House, they called this place. A madhouse it was. A most genteel madhouse.

A whisper of sound brought her about. Stella's water blue eyes were open. "Jane," she said, her face set with some resolve, "we shall always have an affection for each other, won't we—no matter what?" Her voice was raw.

"Yes, Stella, always, no matter what."

"And you will forgive me?"

Jane's eyes squeezed shut. Tears seeped from beneath her lids. "Forgive you for what, Stella?"

The snow-covered land was still, still, everything quieter than the very earth, stiller than stone. Hart Baywood walked through that cold, still morning twilight toward his death. His brother Richard, a gawky young man of bad coloring, was with him, to serve as his second. Richard looked heavy-eyed and rather creased. He'd put on his mittens but forgotten his cap, and now his ears were bright red with the morning chill. He concentrated on his chew of tobacco and said nothing; nor did Hart speak. They walked quickly, intent on covering ground, as people who owned no saddle horses were used to doing.

About a mile from Jose-on-Tees, as they slithered down into a steep and very narrow ghyll that crossed their way, a masked horseman spurred his black mount out of the thin line of trees along the bottom of the ghyll and stopped them. With his left hand, he brought out a pistol. He gestured with his weapon and bade Hart's brother leave them. The youth nearly choked on his chew of tobacco. He spat it out as he bolted back up the snowy slope and disappeared over the top.

Hart stood alone, held by the highwayman and his gun. The brigand lowered his mask to reveal an appalling smile. Hart wiped his mouth with his hand. There were words exchanged, a dry, stumbling conversation. What it amounted to, no one but the twain involved would ever know. The highwayman did most of the speaking; Hart answered only now and then with a grim and desperate taciturnity.

Suddenly the highwayman lifted his gun and aimed it at the farmer. His eye was keen and his arm steady. He might have been sighting a deer instead of a man. Hart's face drew up with shock and dismay, yet he stood his ground.

The gun cracked. The explosion shattered the air again and again as it echoed back and forth across the narrow ghyll. Hart staggered, dropped to his knees, fell to his side. A red stain soaked into the porous white snow. The highwayman sat stolidly upon his mount. Here was cold-bloodedness worthy of the ancient Mongol conquerors.

In another moment, he rode off. His horse broke into a cantor, throwing snow up behind its hooves as it climbed out of the ghyll.

Hart's brother peeped his head cautiously over the top of the opposite slope. His face was white, his forehead crawling with wrinkles. When he saw Hart lying on the ground, wounded, perhaps dead, he covered his mouth with his mittened hand. He made very sure the highwayman was gone, however, before he ran down to his brother's prone body.

Captain Grayson waited at the appointed place, a level spot near a stone bridge over the River Tees, called Jose-on-Tees. The cold air numbed his cheeks and neck. The sky lightened, a few rooks began to prattle and caw. The sun rose, surprisingly warm. Part of his mind thought, If this weather holds, the snow will be gone by next week.

His second, a neighboring landowner by the name of Harold Dayton, paced beneath the towering oaks that shaded the place. Dayton was a pudgy man with a pink, pock-marked face and a small soft mouth like a child's. He wore a soiled ragged wig over his black hair. His coat had a heavy skirt and cuffs. He urged, "Give it up, Captain. The scoundrel isn't coming."

Captain Grayson wrapped his redingote tighter about him and stared straight ahead. He felt peevish and sulky. "It would be like his sort to say he arrived a bit late and found me already gone." Pride, like a shrill of trumpets, sounded in him. "It's not necessary for you to stay, Dayton, but I'll wait until there is not the least possibility of his attendance."

"Probably he's already on his way to London, or even to Bristol, to leave the country, hey?" Dayton was not affected by any extreme of refinement. In fact, he had a reputation for being coarse and outspoken. The women in his family were as rough as men. Much too rough and overbearing. Dayton was generally liked, but he did not always please. Once he got excited and had drunk a bottle of sack, he invariably went too far.

The captain said, "I hope you're right, for if he thinks he can stay in this district without my wrath finding him out, he's going to be sorely surprised. He can't treat my daughter like a woman of his own sort and get away with it."

The minutes continued to mount, they became an hour. The night's freeze gave way to the sun; the air filled with the seethe of water beneath the porous snow. Creaking cartwheels with a whip-crack announced the passing of a peddler over the bridge. Soon the place would be public.

When even the captain was ready to give up and go home, two men came into view, one helping the other who was walking very unsteadily. Captain Grayson watched them approach. He recognized the man who was staggering: it was Baywood. The oaf had risen too early to shave: with his farmer's hat pushed back from his forehead the captain could see the midnight stubble on his face, made darker against the unusual pallor of his complexion. Had he spent the night drinking? No doubt that was why he was stumbling so.

The Honorable Mr. Dayton strode out to meet them. The younger man helping Hart crooked his fingers against his forehead. He and Dayton spoke. Captain Grayson heard their voices indistinctly and muffled, as through a cloth. Overhead were the excited sounds of the rooks.

Harold Dayton came back to report. His thumbs somehow found room to hook between his thickened waist and his strained belt. "Sir, I am afraid you must call it off."

"Is the man playing ill?"

"Not playing; he's already been shot once this morning, by a highwayman they claim. I saw the wound myself, clear through his upper right arm, it is.''

''Then let him take his chances with his left arm.''

Dayton's childlike lips tightened with vexation. ''Captain, do you want people about to say you killed an already wounded man? It wouldn't look good, hey?'' He scratched his pockmarked forehead beneath his ragged wig. ''An incident of that sort could let loose a swarm of tales. It would ruin your reputation. Come now, it's not wise to be anything but realistic, hey?''

Captain Grayson saw all this, yet he was bitterly disappointed. ''This is a curious sort of justice, when an honest man can't avenge himself for fear of incurring disgrace. You tell the varmint I'll have my satisfaction sooner or later.''

He pushed Harold Dayton aside to deliver the message himself. ''I know where you live, Baywood! That little squeezed, miserable place. As soon as you're fit, we'll meet again—either that or I'll find a brush and tar you!''

He returned to Grayson House with his head down, his shoulders hunched, his skin gray with outrage. He never said a word to anyone, but went straight into his library and sent the door crashing shut behind him.

Jane had no idea what had happened beneath the oaks and beeches at Jose-on-Tees, and she was afraid to ask. She felt some hope however, for the captain's manner said clearly that things had not gone exactly as he wished.

Catherine brought the two women a dinner tray at noon and whispered, ''Master's in a real sour mood.''

Stella roused a little. ''Perhaps Hart didn't go.'' Her freckles darted as sharp as needle pricks from her shocked face. Her surging blood bleached her skin.

In the long bright evening, Catherine again came as the bearer of tidings. Handing in a supper tray, she

362

whispered, "Coachman says Hart Baywood was shot down by a highwayman afore he ever reached Jose-on-Tees."

"Shot down!" Jane exclaimed. She looked quickly back at Stella, who had risen up onto her elbows.

"Only shot through the arm, he was," Catherine reassured them quickly. "He's alive, and well enough, considering. But the master couldn't shoot him again, you see." For the first time ever, Jane saw a little smile on the ugly woman's face.

Jane was nearer to weeping than Stella, who took the news with a single sob. She looked at Jane as if she didn't dare believe it. Slowly she said, "A highwayman."

Jane too slowly gathered the import of those words. They permeated every fiber of her being. Not him. It couldn't be the armed man who had accosted her in the orchard.

I know you, Jane.

A chill trickled down her spine.

The news affected Stella like a revelation. "Thank you," she whispered—not to anyone in the chamber.

Her momentary rapture soon succumbed to a bitter, bone-deep trembling. Jane put aside her own confusion and took Stella's hand. "It's all right now. He's safe."

A long minute passed. Stella gradually stopped trembling. She lay still, rigid almost. She said with suddenly ferocity, "I want to *hurt* Father!" Her vehemence took Jane by surprise. "I want to show him he shall *not* have everything his own way."

It snowed again, then cleared again. The dawns following the incidents at Jose-on-Tees brought lovely mornings, light and snow-glistened. Though the sun shone all day, the weather remained cold enough to

363

keep the new snow solid. Today Captain Grayson stood at the windows in his library filling his pipe and tamping the tobacco with consideration. He lit up and drew in the smoke.

Stella. He folded his arms tightly across his chest, as if to keep himself from hitting someone. Stella was of course glowingly ecstatic these days. She'd learned somehow that her lover had wormed his way out of facing up to his crimes. Captain Grayson wanted to shake her, he wanted to shout at her, Don't be so smug, young lady! You're walking against the wind here! He felt quite outside all the world's beauty and happiness. For three weeks he'd seen nothing that wasn't tinged with red. He was convinced that with Burne gone there was no loyalty whatever to him in the house. Therefore all his gentle treatment was at an end.

He had laid down several new decrees: Stella was not to go anywhere without two chaperons. "You have been foolish and corrupt," he'd told her. "You will begin to entertain suitable gentlemen for dinner every Sunday noon with the idea of finding one who will marry you, sullied as you are. And you'd better not be late! You're always late—for meals, for church, for bed—but not anymore. I won't stand for it."

Her response was to widen her plump little expression into a parody of alarm. It was all part of her new contempt for him. There was something different about her now. Oh, she looked no more clever than she ever did; a round, cozy, faintly silly woman, the kind people went to when they wanted sympathy or comfort or unquestioning approval. But now, something forbidding stiffened her, something tightened her face—and it was not attractive, no more than her foolish contempt of him was. Well, he'd see how contemptuous she felt when she sat down to dinner next to Cyril Todd this Sunday.

Burne had returned from London just last night. He wouldn't like it when he learned of the invitation to Todd—but Burne was not master of Grayson House, not yet.

And as for Jane . . .

The captain took his pipe from his mouth. He'd been ready to throw the girl out when he'd discovered she'd taken it upon herself to let Stella out of the attic. Daily his feeling had grown more frosty toward her, until now he could hardly bear to see her going about as if she were a regular resident of his home. The atmosphere between them had grown cold enough for snow to fall inside the house.

He didn't quite know what he was going to do with her yet, but he must do something. Perhaps Burne would report some news this morning that would facilitate his eagerness to be rid of the girl.

Burne came in just as the captain was thinking about him. Captain Grayson turned and gave him a look.

"What is it?"

The captain realized he was giving his son a cold stare. He blamed Burne for not being home during these past trying weeks. He'd been the one to send Burne to London, but that didn't matter at the moment. At the moment he only felt that Burne's absence when he was needed, and worse, his affection for Jane, was a willful betrayal.

"What is it?" Burne asked again, coming further into the room.

The captain told him. All of it. The whole dreadful story. They hadn't had a chance to talk last night. Burne had arrived home so late, after one o'clock, that it seemed best to let it wait until now. As the story unfolded, the captain expected his son to look surprised, shocked—he would have felt satisfaction seeing those reactions. But he was not prepared for the haggard expression on Burne's face.

"Hart is at home?"

"Yes, but by God he'd better flee the district, the wretched coward, for the minute I hear he's well—"

Burne made a gesture that said he didn't want to hear the end of that sentence. He took a seat. His voice was soft and husky, but completely steady. "Father, have you ever wondered why a man should be cursed to be most inept where he loves the most?"

The captain didn't quite know who, or what he meant, not at first. Then he did. And he was stunned. Inept? His son had called him inept. He opened his mouth to deliver some withering retort—and could think of nothing to say, nothing at all. He turned away, speechless, and went to the fireplace. He put his hand on the chimney piece, which was of the finest marble. He looked at the festooned vases of blue-john and ormolu, and at the urn of Josiah Wedgewood. He knew they were valuable; Francis had thought them valuable, and so he prized them, too, without quite knowing what it was about them that made them worthy of Grayson House.

In time, Burne moved in his chair. "Here." He reached into his inner coat pocket and drew out a many-folded sheet. He shook it open and handed it to his father. Captain Grayson paused for an unsteady breath, then took the sheet.

It was an engraving, a young gentlewoman whose beauty touched the edge of pain. " 'The Rose of Midnight,' " he read aloud. A measure of relief washed over him. "It's her."

Burne's eyes were serious and remote. "Yes. I found it quite by accident, hanging in the salon of one Honorable Mistress Meadows. Seems she traveled through Yorkshire last summer and came home with that. She

366

says the engravings were all the rage up there, one hanging in every inn.''

"The girl's from Yorkshire then. Of course. That northerness in her speech. Didn't I tell you so? What's her name?''

Burne shook his head. "I don't know. Mistress Meadows didn't know either, and I couldn't discover anything else. The 'rages' of Yorkshire don't amount to much with the mistresses and milords of London. As for your advertisement, it drew nothing but the most ridiculous responses. Ridiculous stories that didn't bear investigation.''

The captain started for the door. "I'll have her come down.''

"I don't think you should show her that.''

"Why not?'' He looked back at his son, who was sitting with his head thrown back against the chair. The captain shut the library door. He tried to understand what weighted Burne's mind. "You don't want her to remember. You're afraid.''

Burne lifted his head and rose and turned toward the windows. He stood slumped, staring at a bruise-colored thunderhead that had come up out of nowhere and was already blotting out the sun. "I'm afraid of shocking her. Remember what Dr. Barceloux warned. She's been ill. We still don't know what happened to her. Your own theory of abduction and rape and attempted murder—I just think we should be very careful, whatever we do.''

The captain saw he was anxious from the way he rubbed his fingertips together. "All right,'' he said. Personally, he thought all this caution unnecessary; he couldn't really share Burne's concern. He saw nothing but what his mind was set on. "I am going to send to York for information about her, though. We've dallied too long without doing anything at all.''

367

Burne straightened with a grunt of agreement. He looked at the captain and nodded his head.

"I'll start with this engraver."

"I suppose that would be wise. But we agree that Jane isn't to know about this?" Burne gestured to the engraving still in his father's hands.

"For the time being." The captain went to his desk and took up his pen.

Chapter Twenty-five

Besieged on All Sides

The sky blackened. A thin snow was hardened by a freeze. The weather vane on the roof of Grayson House stood unmoving, stopped between north and east; but Jane couldn't get over an indisputable impression that winds of change were blowing.

Stella was changed, certainly. She was so openly scornful of her father that the friction in the household was almost unbearable. Even Burne couldn't smother all the sparks that flew whenever father and daughter were in the same room.

"Your conduct is disgraceful!"

"You're a tyrant, a mean, petty, little tyrant!"

So it went. Amazingly, her rebellion seemed to give Stella a growing sense of gladness and power. She'd never looked so pretty or carried herself with such confidence. Her delicate skin blossomed—while the captain seemed to age under her visible and palpable rejection.

The maidservant Catherine, between bustling about, lowering the wooden chandeliers and wiping the glass holders with her apron, sweeping down the backs of the chimneys, and serving the meals, brought regular reports about Hart, which she got through Jones, the coachman. First they heard Hart was up and about after his ordeal, his arm in a new white sling. Then Catherine reported that he'd fled the country.

Stella retreated to her chamber, seemingly in a melancholy that was beyond the power of tears to assuage. Jane overheard a conversation between her and Burne. "Father has taken everything from me. Hart and I were so happy with our plans and our schemes—oh yes, I see them for what they were, impossible schemes—but father crushed him, Burne! It was the wickedest piece of business he's ever done."

Something about Stella's curiously dry-eyed tone struck Jane as false.

On Sunday the household prepared to attend church. Jane was excused from going, as usual. She helped Stella get dressed. The captain and Burne were waiting downstairs, and Stella was late.

As she scurried about in her chamber, Jane went behind her picking up this, putting that away. Stella couldn't dress without strewing things about. Her wardrobe doors hung open, powder was spattered on the floor. She was as heedless about order as she was carefully elegant about her person. Jane was setting straight her bottles of rosewater, lavender water, and potpourris when Stella said, "Jane, you shouldn't do the maidservant's work."

Jane felt more and more certain that a maidservant's work was exactly what she should be doing. "Your father is waiting," she said.

Stella made a little moue of her mouth. "Let him wait." She seemed oddly buoyant today. "If Catherine had got my green gown ready—"

"You look just as lovely in that one."

"You think so?"

"Indeed I do. Stella, you know how Burne hates the way the parson stares when you arrive after he's started."

"Yes, yes, all right, where's my prayer book?" She took from Jane the leatherbound book which contained the responses and collects she would mouth with the others of the congregation. "You see? I'm ready."

Jane went down to see them off. Burne looked especially nice today. He'd taken advantage of his time in London to order a new suit of clothes, a long black coat faced with jade, ornamented with white lace; a jade waistcoat and breeches, white gaiters, white neckcloth, and a buff belt. His wig was clubbed—plaited, bound up, and tied with a ribbon. He looked every inch the gentleman of means that he was.

Jane felt almost dowdy as she watched the family disappear toward the village. She looked down at the dark blue gown she had on—which was not her own. She had nothing of her own. Except the money which Captain Grayson would not let her have.

She tried not to think about that money, because it always made her feel so anxious. Lately, however, she'd begun to wonder if maybe she shouldn't leave Grayson House. Why should she stay? She was only an unwanted burden on the captain. She was no business of his. But she had a niggling instinct that he might not let her go, that he would try to keep her by withholding her purse. And without money she could not so much as buy a loaf of bread from a baker's cart.

She wandered through the house aimlessly while they were gone. These walls were beginning to close in like cell walls. She'd now been cloistered behind the fastness of Grayson House for two and half months. She felt daily more certain that it was time for her to leave. But where to go? How to earn a living? She failed completely to solve that question. She believed she had been a maid at one time; but without a reference, without a family name or any information about her background, it was unlikely she would find employment.

When the family returned, Mr. Cyril Todd was with them, which meant Jane was excluded from joining them. Nonetheless, she heard some of their conversation. The talk was easy, of country subjects. Stella came upstairs briefly, looking very vexed. "That man!" she said, coming into Jane's chamber. "All he can talk about is horses. Dinner is like a fence I'm going to have to ride at, my heart in my mouth, till it's over and I've cleared. And I must smile, Father says." She put her fingers on the corners of her mouth and pulled it into a big revolted grin.

Jane would like to have a look at this notorious suitor, but Stella had something else to say, and she was in a hurry. "Jane, I left my prayer book behind at church." She glanced at Jane's door to make sure it was closed. "I'm afraid if Father finds out, he'll send me with Cyril to go get it after dinner. The oaf will try to hold my hand or something equally odious the minute we're alone, I know it. Would you go and get it for me? Now, while Father and Burne are busy and won't know that you've gone out? It was my mother's book and I wouldn't like to see it lost."

Jane had been reluctant to walk alone even in the orchard since that awful evening when she'd been accosted by the stranger, but she owed Stella so much, and something in her friend's look made her say, "Of course."

"Use the door Catherine uses out the side of the house. Once you're past the cesspits, you only need to push through a thin spot in the hedges and you'll find the path easily enough. No one will even know you're gone. Thank you, Jane."

Jane went dressed in her indoor clothes with only a

rose pink shawl thrown about her arms and shoulders. She'd never used the side door before. It was used only by Catherine, as far as she knew. Its one advantage, she discovered right away, was that one could leave the house in reasonable secrecy. Jane suspected it was how Stella had left when she'd gone to her midnight rendezvous with Hart.

Once Jane passed the cesspits and pushed through the hedge, she found herself in an intervening weald that seemed full of secret places, becks winding under dense rhododendron, and deer trails that threaded through bracken. Patches of hard-frozen snow still lay beneath the densest growth. She found the path to Marydale easily enough, however; she couldn't mistake the worn way the masters of Grayson House had used for generations to lead their families and servants through the woods, all afoot, to Sunday morning worship.

As she walked along, she glimpsed now and again the spire of the little church and she had no fear of getting lost. The afternoon was quiet; it was the dinner hour; she felt reasonably safe from meeting any of the locals.

The only thing she had to worry about was meeting *him*.

She scolded herself: she would hurry to the church and hurry back, and not give in to senseless anxiety.

Placing her attention elsewhere, she tried to put her finger on the changes she felt at Grayson House. At first she'd attributed it to the captain's disapproval of Stella. And Stella's own dramatic change of personality. But it went beyond that. Even Burne was changed. He hadn't sought Jane out since his return, hadn't pressed her with half-joking words of love. She'd always believed his affection was built more on her availability than on anything else, yet she felt oddly bereft.

She still had dreams of him—she thought it was him; erotic, disturbing dreams of lovemaking that woke her to a yearning and a need to weep.

Before she knew it, she was at the lych gate of the small stone church. She'd met with no one, and was encouraged.

The church was located on the edge of the village of Marydale. She paused to take in the modest gray cottages grouped around the green. One or two were prosperous-looking with lattice-windows. But there were also one or two mud hovels. Most of them were the middling sort of houses seen in every English village. The peat smoke rising from the chimneys seemed to stand as straight as columns.

She heard a woman scolding in a crow-harsh tone, then a girl came out a door. She was wearing a faded, much-mended, somber gray gown and a ragged but clean apron. Her light brown hair fell thin and straight from her frayed cap to her shoulders. She was not a pretty girl; she had a large mouth like a cat's without whiskers. She spotted Jane and stopped to stare at her. Jane turned away quickly and walked up the moss-covered footpath to the church. She lifted the iron ring and opened the door.

She went into the cold gloom. Though the noon light outside was not enough to dazzle the eyes, she felt nearly blinded by the dark interior. She stood beside one of the unadorned, rough-stone pillars and looked up the nave to the sanctuary, letting her eyes adjust. Gradually she made out the familiar altar furnishings: a plain polished brass cross, a lectuary and Book of Common Prayer resting on mats. She walked slowly around the last pews, under the low floor of the musician's gallery, and up the central aisle.

The stout, square box-pews contained wooden benches. Heat was provided by an open fireplace, probably tended by a village man wielding a big brass poker.

She found the Graysons' pew at the front of the nave, right against the chancel step, facing the raised pulpit. Jane could almost hear the drone of some odious little sexton peering down into the pews from his high pulpit.

Where had she heard such a drone? Why did she feel she was an unconvinced Christian?

Her thoughts were interrupted by one of those queer lightning-storm moments she had when she saw something of who she was. The environment of the church had an effect on her. She saw herself kneeling down with her hands together palm to palm. Who had taught her to do that? Who had been her mother when she was a child?

She opened the small door of the pew and stepped inside. An iron stove stood in the corner, with logs and shavings ready so that the family and their servants might worship in comfort, all but out of sight of the congregation of laborers, herdsmen, and their families. Jane found Stella's leather-bound prayer book. As she picked it up she noticed that one of the pages had been dog-eared.

She opened it and found printed in the heavy-black of a lead pencil, "Exodus 10:12," followed by the verse, which was about Moses and locusts. Perhaps it had some personal meaning for Stella. She left the page corner crimped as she'd found it, though it seemed odd that Stella had defaced the book so wantonly. She claimed she revered this little memento of her mother.

Jane left the church and went out into the cold sunlight. She went through the lych gate feeling faintly apprehensive. She sensed she was being watched. Just outside the village, she looked back. The churchyard and track behind her were empty. No one was following her. Still, the feeling remained.

She started back to Grayson House, hardly aware of her surroundings. The path came out of the weald and paralleled the orchard hedge. She looked for the place where she should push through, found it—and it was there that she met the highwayman again.

For an instant her face went blank. He seemed to be there so suddenly, standing before her out of nowhere—though clearly he had been waiting for some time, watching her coming along—and his horse! she hadn't even seen that great beast! She spared the animal a glance, and saw its black nostrils flare, its lean ears quiver.

"Jane." The man's black clothes made him both handsome and menacing.

"I don't know you." She felt something like anger. "Leave me alone ."

"I can't, Jane. There's danger in your staying here any longer. Don't you recognize me?" He stepped closer and pushed his tricorn back a little. He was remarkably large, larger than Burne—or was it just that he seemed larger because he seemed a hundred times more threatening?

She clenched Stella's prayer book tightly against her chest with both hands. "I don't recognize you because I don't know you."

A sudden glare come into his eyes. He hesitated, then reached for her. She shrank away as if he were leprous; it did no good. He got her by the shoulders and shook her once. "Don't do this, Jane!" His face was close. "Don't you turn me out, too."

"I don't know what you're talking about. If you don't let go of me, I'll scream."

He didn't let go; instead, he dragged her closer. She felt breathless held so hard against him.

"Listen to me. Your name is Jane Fitzpatrick." His voice seemed to come at her like the clang of a great bell. "I'm the one who brought you here—don't you remember even that much?"

Stella said she'd found her on the doorstep. Jane didn't remember anything about him . . . except for that vision of a man on a fine black horse that reared and then galloped away into the dark.

His eyes raked her expression. "We were traveling together. You were riding Eclipse, and the bridge over the river broke apart in the flood. I fished you out and brought you here. Try to remember, Jane!" He was holding her so hard he was hurting her.

"I don't know you. I don't *want* to know you." She tore herself away from him. But she didn't run. She pressed the heel of one hand to her forehead. That sound of flooding waters . . . she felt a cold breath of fear down the back of her neck. "If I know you at all, it's because you tried to kill me."

He stepped near again. "Where do you get that idea?"

She stepped out of his reach.

"I've never harmed you. You have to *remember*, Jane. I can't leave you here any longer. Someone is going to recognize you—and then they'll send for the soldiers."

Soldiers? What had she to do with the soldiers?

"Burne found out something about you in London. They've sent a letter by way of messenger to York. Whoever they wrote to, he's sure to denounce you."

A whimper escaped her. That sound of water . . . she was quaking. His hand reached out and smoothed down her arm. She yanked away. "Go away! If you touch me again, I'll scream, I swear I will. You'd best get on your horse and get away from here!"

Her threats didn't stop him for a minute. Did he guess how much it was costing her to fight down the

377

urge to run screaming for Burne, for the captain, for any help at all? Evidently so, for just as she took her first step he lunged forward and caught her wrist. She barely felt it, though all her strength did nothing to break her loose. He pulled her into his powerful arms again, with effortless ease, so tightly that there was no possibility of escape. She struggled; he merely wound his arms around her tighter, until she was held motionless.

"Jane," he said right into her ear, "don't be afraid." He dropped his cheek to the top of her head. "Don't be afraid of me. Listen, this is what I want you to do. Tell Stella that you met me, that I said you're in danger."

"Stella!" She struggled a little more. He was solid against her.

"Stella knows I brought you here. She knows who I am. Are you listening, Jane? I want you to talk to her—today! And then I want you to meet me tonight at the summer house in the park. Ten o'clock. Stella will tell you it's all right to come to me. You'll do what she says, won't you? You trust her. You *must* trust her." He loosened his hold fractionally. "I'm going now. We'll talk again tonight." True to his word, he released her. "You needn't be afraid of me, Jane." He swung up onto his horse, paused to lift his hat to her, then wheeled and galloped away.

The familiarity of that action struck her. Who was he? What was he to her? She couldn't remember. God help her, she couldn't *remember!*

He was gone. She must try to pick up the shards of the day. She pushed through the hedge and saw Grayson House. It stood there as her only sanctuary.

She met Captain Grayson in the gallery. She'd expected the family to still be downstairs entertaining their guests. He stopped abruptly and stood looking at

378

her with a slightly vacant look in his face. He took in her shawl. "You've been out?" His disapproval crystallized at once.

She held up the prayerbook. "Stella asked me to go get this. She left it at the church."

What was it she felt radiating from him? Suspicion?

"She didn't want it to be lost, and since you had company . . ." She left this thought dangling; she was too distracted to consider at the moment why the house was so quiet. "Well . . ." She felt besieged on all sides and never more insecure in her peculiar situation. "I was very quick going and coming."

"I daresay you were, but I thought we'd agreed that you wouldn't leave the grounds." He stood nervously thwacking a thick copy of *The Gentleman's Magazine* against his thigh.

"It was just this once." She must find Stella. She indicated the book in her hands again. "If you'll excuse me, I'll take this to Stella's chamber."

Stella was there, pacing. The light falling through her windows drenched the room and made her hair glow red-gold. Jane briefly wondered what had happened to Cyril Todd. Stella turned. "Oh, you got it! Oh, Jane!" She took the prayerbook immediately and turned so that Jane couldn't see; but Jane thought she opened the book—at the marked page?

Stella sighed heavily and lifted her face to the ceiling, as if to God. What did Moses and locusts say to her to bring her to such a stance of reverence?

She turned wearing an almost beatific smile. "Dear Jane." She sighed again, softly. Then suddenly her expression changed. She giggled. "You missed the excitement. I told Cyril Todd what Burne said about him—you know, about his affection for his hunters? He left in a flaming rage. Oh, it was wonderful. Of course, Father is furious. I think he would have locked

379

me in the attic again, except that Burne stopped him. He says I'm confined to my chamber for a week. Imagine, he still thinks he can order me around.''

"*Stella,*" Jane said anxiously, "a man stopped me. This is the second time now. I didn't say anything before because he frightened me so." She was very near to shattering. "He says he knows me. He says to tell you I met him, and that I'm in danger."

It took Stella a moment to take this in. Gradually her face sobered. "He's spoken to you? When? How?"

"Once in the orchard last month. He came through the hedge and caught me alone." She experienced that silent burst of terror in her soul again. "He had a gun in his belt. And a sword. I ran away from him. And just now along the path to Marydale. Who is he, Stella? He's so dangerous-looking. I think . . . ," she ended in a whisper, "he might have tried to drown me."

"Oh, no, Jane! He didn't." Her tone implied it was the most remote possibility in the world.

Jane wanted to weep. "Please, whatever you know, you mustn't hide it from me anymore, even out of kindness."

"I can see that. Come and sit with me on the bed."

Stella was so different, so definite and certain. So happy! How could she be so happy with her lover gone, crushed, as she had told Burne?

Jane sat and Stella put her arm around her. "It's all right. His name is Keith—and Jane," she seemed ready to break out into laughter, "he's my brother. Yes, mine and Burne's—our half brother. Oh, it's such a sad story. Father sired him before he married our mother. He would never acknowledge poor Keith. They say the girl, Keith's mother, loved Father entirely beyond reason. What she saw in him I'll never know. But it was a great scandal in the village when he refused to marry her. It broke her heart."

Stella clearly thought this a marvelous tale, despite its tragedy. Jane couldn't look at her; she stared at the white lawn fichu tucked into the front of Stella's bodice.

"Her name was Laurel, and they say she was beautiful. Keith gets his dark hair and eyes from her, but otherwise he looks so much like Burne—and like Father when he was young—why, there's no possibility he could be anything but our brother."

She had a glow in her eyes. "Anyway, somehow Laurel managed to send Keith to school—and that's how he met Burne. At Hillsburrow Grammar School." She seemed to think this very clever. Jane, however, didn't understand.

"Burne admired Keith so much that he was sure that if Father only knew him he would love him as he should. So he brought Keith home, thinking to effect a reconciliation.

"That's when I met him. Oh, you shouldn't be frightened of him, Jane." She laughed low in her throat. "I remember how he kissed my hand so charmingly, though we were both just children. He made me laugh with his flattery. But then—oh, it was awful, Jane. Burne disclosed his identity and—just like that! Father threw him out. Keith was only eleven years old. It was so cruel." Her expression hardened. "Father has always been cruel. And he can hold a grudge, but soon he will find that I can hold one, too."

She brought herself back to the moment. "We never heard of Keith again, until the night he brought you here."

Jane stared at her wide-eyed. "Someone did bring me? And you're sure it's him, your brother? He said so, but . . . I don't remember." She shook her head miserably. This was like having a strange man looking through the window at her. "Your father and Burne

381

think I was abducted by a highwayman, and—'' she searched for words—''and used . . . to satisfy his lusts; and when he was tired of me he tossed me in the river to drown.''

''Dear Jane! Now don't cry. Father and Burne— why, they don't know anything about it! Keith asked me to protect you. He brought you to the door that night and said you were in some sort of danger. I was to keep you out of sight. Of course I knew I shouldn't tell anyone you'd come with him. Not even Burne. I know how to keep a secret.''

Jane calmed herself. ''What is he to me?''

''I don't know. There wasn't time for us to talk. You were very wet and cold and ill-looking, and at any moment Father might have come home and seen Keith at the door. There was just no time. But as I told you from the first, I think you might be a lady who loves him and who had to run away from her family to be with him. There is no reason to be afraid of him. He won't hurt you.''

Jane saw exactly how Stella had settled on this conclusion. A lady running away from a cruel parent to be with a lover considered beneath her. Stella had projected all her own fantasies onto Jane.

But there were so many holes in her arguments. ''I don't think I'm a lady, Stella. None of this life seems natural to me. Not the clothes, not the idleness, not even the meals and the conversation. And what about those scars on my back?'' There was a silence, then she added, ''I don't know who I am, but I'm not a lady.''

Stella kissed her cheek tenderly. ''These are questions only Keith knows the answers to.''

Jane must try to think. She felt as if Stella had just gone at her with a broadax. If the man wasn't her enemy, then . . . was he her friend? Could he truly be trying to protect her from something? What? The soldiers, he'd said. Why? Was she an inveterate criminal? She already had the scars of flogging. And now it seemed she was in league with a highwayman.

"He says I'm in danger."

"Yes, that's what he told me. But Keith won't let anything happen to you. You must trust him."

"But I don't *know* him. I was so afraid when he stepped out in front of me." She put her head down into her hands. "I'm so afraid of him!"

"You just don't remember him, Jane."

Was there a difference between not knowing and not remembering? It didn't *feel* any different. "He wants me to meet him, tonight, at the summer house."

Stella was silent for a moment, then she said, "Then you must go."

"I don't want to."

"But Jane, he's Keith, my brother. You're not afraid of Burne, are you?"

"This man isn't like Burne."

"They're so much alike they could be twins, except that Keith is dark and doesn't have dimples. I'm surprised you didn't see it immediately. Keith looks just like Burne."

"Not quite," Jane said. "This man carries weapons—he looks for all the world like a highwayman, Stella."

This brought a totally inappropriate grin to Stella's face. "Yes, he does, doesn't he? The night he brought you here, he was dressed all in black. Riding a big black horse." She was looking at Jane meaningfully, waiting, it seemed, for Jane to make some sort of connection. "And Hart was shot by a highwayman—do you see?"

"Oh, Stella, I was afraid it was him. I'm so sorry."

"Sorry?" Stella's face was blissful. "No, don't you

383

see? He did it to *save* Hart.'' She seemed almost stupid with happiness. ''Father would never had aimed for Hart's arm—he would have killed him. Keith wounded him so that Father couldn't kill him.''

Jane's tears dried. ''Is that what you really think?''

Stella gave her a squeeze. ''It's what I *know*. Why would a highwayman want to hold up a man like Hart? He obviously has nothing worth stealing.'' She seemed ecstatic over Hart's poverty. ''Oh, Keith! Dear, dear Keith!''

While Stella danced on the crests of her private ecstasy, Jane sank into a dazed dread. Who was this man, this highwayman? Why couldn't she remember him? What was she to him?

Chapter Twenty-Six

And therefore, since I cannot prove a lover,
      I am determined to prove a villain.
Shakespeare: *Hamlet*

In the end, it was Jane's need to know that convinced her to meet the highwayman.

Stella was a better conniver than she was, having longer practice at it. She planned exactly how Jane would pretend to retire early whilst Stella asked to speak to her father. She would give Jane a half hour to get out of the house unseen. Later, when Stella went upstairs, back to her confinement in her chamber, she would murmur, "I'll just look in on Jane."

She would look in all right, and perhaps even speak a few words through the door—but Jane would not be there.

Perhaps all this subterfuge was inescapable; but before any of it could take place, Stella insisted Jane must get ready. After supper she must order a bath. She must come back to Stella's chamber to have her hair dressed and put on a special gown—as if she were going to meet a lover.

The afternoon crawled by. Supper with the Grayson

men, without Stella, was onerous. But the bath afterward was heaven. Stella loaned Jane a cake of soap scented with roses. Daniel brought up the heavy, wooden-slatted leather tub, and Catherine filled it with steaming water. Jane stepped into it and sank down. She lay observing the steam rise, almost invisible, off her body and the water surface. Relaxed, her mind opened to the memory of those dreams she had of a man caressing her. The dim images sharpened. He was kissing her—he was tall, his head was bent to the kiss. And she kissed him back, with an abandon that would have shamed a whore.

A face coalesced: dark brows, dark hair, dark eyes, a chiseled mouth. It was him. She sat up so quickly that she splashed water on the floor. She'd let him make love to her, at least in her dreams.

She went to Stella's chamber to have her hair dressed. Stella seemed to still feel that same odd, wheeling jubilation she'd shown earlier. She fashioned Jane's hair into an artful but rather insecure coiffure. Then she forced on Jane a beautiful dress, lavender with silver trimmings. She insisted Jane borrow her lapis necklace as well, and of course the eardrops that went with it. She continued luminous and immeasurably happy. "These were my grandmother's jewels. I only get to wear them until Burne marries, then they must go to his wife."

Jane felt as hung with jewels as a sultana. Stella was treating this as if she were going out on a high adventure.

All went according to plan, at least up to the point when Jane drew her purple cloak tight about her and went down to the side door. The house was carefully locked up each night. She must draw back the heavy iron bolt, taking care to be quiet, raise the latch, and go out into a surprisingly cold, windy darkness.

The weather had suddenly become blustery with nightfall. Jane pulled the door shut behind her. There was no moon; she really needed a lantern to see where she was going. As she hurried through the snow-crusted rose garden, the wind swept into her cloak, flapping it about so that she must hold it firmly. Her cap was almost whipped from her head, and the curls Stella had pinned up loosely underneath promptly fell down about her face and arms. As she entered the orchard through the hedge gate, her streaming hair caught on a branch and she lost a few strands.

She had little fear that the captain would find out about her absence. She feared more that what she was doing was simply unwise. Stella's blind optimism did not comfort her out here in the dark. Outlaws were desperate, and there was no telling what might happen to her before this night was over. She picked her way slowly through the slippery, thin-crusted snow of the orchard, not at all certain she wanted to go any further. Danger was ahead in one form or another, and she could not count on herself to act rationally. She had to pause often, partly to remember where she was—the moonless dark made it all different—and partly to recharge her small store of courage.

The wind caught her cloak and lifted it out of her grasp, high above her waist. At the same time it reached beneath her wide skirts and billowed them above her knees. As she struggled to keep her skirts down, while also reaching upward to grab her cloak, she came to a halt beneath an apple tree. A few shards of ice pelted her, cracked off the dancing black branches over her head.

With her cloak wrapped firmly around her again, she found the stump of another tree by stumbling over it.

This was lunacy! She should go back to the house.

What was she doing meeting a highwayman? He couldn't be innocent of blood. She *knew* he wasn't—he'd shot Hart Baywood. And how many others? How many people had he murdered outright?

As she hesitated, the minutes ticked away to ten o'clock and just past ten o'clock. She remembered the man, his largeness, his arms around her, so strong she couldn't escape. She also remembered his words, so at odds with his size and his strength: "Don't be afraid of me."

He hadn't forced her to go with him when she didn't want to. He could have. She should be able to find some assurance in that. And he was Stella's brother. Stella and Burne's. He was a Grayson of sorts.

More important, he said he knew her. He'd brought her to Grayson House. He could help her remember.

She started forward again. The trees before her presented a dense curtain of pitch black. She soon slipped on a patch of icy snow covering a pothole and stepped into the mire beneath. She lost her balance and fell back onto her bottom. For a moment she sat on the cold ground, trusting like an idiot that time would go frantically backward and undo what had just been done to her shoes and stockings. Of course, it didn't, and she must scramble to her feet again.

She searched for the gate that led into the park; she knew it was there, somewhere, hidden in the hedge. She pictured it in her mind, small, weathered, to her left? To her right? At last she found it. She unlatched it and went through. As she turned to relatch it, a hand came around her from behind, covering her mouth. An arm circled her waist and pulled her back against a large, hard body.

"I was about to come get you," he murmured in her ear. "Ten minutes more and I would have broken into the house and seized you right out from under the captain's nose.''

She knew that voice. Dark, deep. She'd been refusing to know it. She didn't struggle; she steeled herself to be passive. His hand over her mouth loosened tentatively, then dropped. She turned in his hold. He kept her tight against him, his head was down, bent as if to kiss her—as in her dreams. His mouth was almost on hers.

''I came,'' she said, at the same time pushing at his chest. He let her step back, though not quite out of his arms. ''Stella says you know me.''

He let out a little puff of a laugh, a sound that was lost in the wind. He held her by her upper arms. His words were carried to her by the next blast. ''We can talk at the summer house.''

He hurried her along, keeping one great arm about her; the other held her cloak closed around her.

The little house was dark. She knew the captain had ordered it to be locked. Locked and the windows boarded up. Did this man have a key? No lock on the door stopped him from ushering her inside. Abruptly, all was quiet. The dark shape of the highwayman moved to the hearth and crouched down. He struck flint to steel until a spark came to life. Soon he had flame going, then the beginnings of a blaze. By its light, Jane saw that the lock on the door behind her had been broken. The wood was splintered in such a way that she guessed he'd probably kicked it in. Everything about him shouted that he was a man of violence.

She clutched her cloak about her to conceal the shabby state of her dress. Stella had gone to so much trouble, yet the wind and the mire had undone it all. Jane could hear the wind outside yet, wild, coming out of the south.

He was feeding the fire, preparing it to last. She had

time to study him. He did look like Burne, only dark where Burne was fair. Dark as midnight eyes where Burne's were a pure, piercing, Esfahan blue. Why hadn't she seen it from the first? The two were about the same height, but the highwayman had wider shoulders, a more powerful build. She'd been attracted to Burne from the first. Had that feeling been only a mirrored reflection of something she'd once felt for this man? A feeling her mind wanted to reject, as it had rejected her memory?

"Now," he said, rising and turning his full attention on her, "we've got a night's toil ahead of us."

She glanced into his eyes and away, unable to stand it. Her temples were pounding with her pulse. A slow, inescapable awareness, begun only seconds before, grew clearer and clearer. Some strange bond did attach her and this man, where no bond (she'd known it instinctively all the time) attached her to Burne. She couldn't believe that this attachment was other than evil, however.

She suddenly felt how isolated they were. She wouldn't be heard if she cried out. Whatever he chose to do to her, no one would know.

"Don't try to run out on me," he said ominously, taking a step toward her. The muscles of his jaw made knots along the sides of his face. "My temper is uncertain at its best." His expression was frightening in its intensity. Her eyes once again slid off his. Her heart beat in quick, solid thumps. This was like galloping headlong down some mountainside, and God alone knew what was at the bottom.

The man took off his black greatcoat and laid his weapons on the tea table. She felt marginally less afraid of him with that done. She blurted suddenly, "Are you the one who whipped me?"

He turned his head to look at her like an eagle—one

eyed. He regarded her steadily but didn't answer. Instead, he sat down in one of the fragile-looking chairs and crossed his booted ankles, for all the world making himself at home.

"Come and sit down, Jane."

She watched him steadily.

"I said, come and sit down."

When she didn't, he stood. She turned for the door. Before she could get through it, his arms were around her. There was no escaping them. He was too quick and too strong. He pulled her back into the room, pinned her between him and the wall, and began to unlace her cloak.

"I knew you were a villain," she hissed.

"I am a villain, make no mistake about it. And no doubt I'll end my days on a gallows, but if you think I'm going to rape you tonight—I told you once that I have no taste for rape. But I suppose you've forgotten that, too, along with everything else."

Roughly, without any sign of pleasure, he took her cloak off and dragged her to the center of the room and forced her down into a chair.

He sat down himself, near enough to touch her. He watched her for a long minute, to see if she was going to try to run for the door again. Then he sat back, crossing one booted foot over the opposite knee.

Her chest heaved up and down. Seeing her fear, his own expression relented a little. "Don't be afraid," he said.

"How can I not be afraid? I don't know you."

"Oh, you know me. You just don't remember me."

"It amounts to the same thing."

"Not quite."

He leaned forward with a suddenness that made her jump. He gave her a look. "Do you want to remember or not?"

"I don't see why you must bully me!" Privately, she thought he and the captain, his father according to Stella, were very much alike.

His eyes narrowed. "Because every time I've tried to talk to you, you've bolted. Maybe I *should* throw you down and force you. Maybe you'd remember my touch more readily than you do my face. That's right, I've touched you, oh, many a time, Jane. I've made love to you. And you let me. You invited me. We were lovers, do you understand?"

No, let it not be true, not a highwayman's woman!

"We're both outcasts. I saved your life when you were on the run. And you saved mine when I was shot by a man I robbed. I saved you again from the flood—but perhaps that doesn't put me ahead, because you didn't think that bridge was safe and I insisted."

Her mind tried to sort through this. "What was I running from?"

He ignored the question. He was leaning forward, his elbows on his knees. He looked at her with narrowed eyes. "Stella told you about me, didn't she? I'm your friend, Jane, your lover. Do you want to remember who you are?"

She licked her lips. Those eyes were too damnably astute. "Stella doesn't know that much about you. She saw you once when she was nine years old. She heard nothing of you from that time until you brought me to Grayson House. She has made up all sorts of fantasies about you—she believes you shot Hart Baywood—"

"I did."

That stopped her. "She thinks you did it to—"

"To keep him from being killed by the captain. Yes. Why else would I do it? Think, Jane? Why else?"

She studied him. "How could you do that? How could you *shoot* somebody?"

"I once shot somebody to save you. Grubneck Nord.

Got him in the shoulder—a meaner wound than I gave Baywood, but then I was in a meaner mood."

She was stunned into silence.

He sat back, his elbow on the tea table, his fist supporting his head. He was looking at her as if trying to figure out what she was thinking.

She looked at the fire. "You never answered my question."

"What were you running from? I'd rather go a little slower than that. Ask me something else."

She swallowed. "You seem to be a man able to inflict hurt without the slightest remorse. And I have been hurt. I have the marks. Did you do that to me?"

His face became a fierce scowl. "No." He got up, kicked the log on the fire, sending up a shower of sparks, then he walked behind her. "I met you not long afterward, though, when the cuts were still fresh."

"Who did it? Why?"

"You must remember that yourself, Jane. It will do no good for me to tell you; it makes you resist." He put his hands on her shoulders and lowered his head. She stiffened.

"The smell of your hair is the same." His hands smoothed down her upper arms. "You're thinner." He leaned further around her, so that his mouth was very near to hers. "I've missed you. Let me kiss you."

"No."

"Yes . . . yes, Jane." His mouth came nearer and nearer.

She wouldn't turn her head. His lips caught the corner of her mouth. They were gentle, undemanding, pleasant. When he saw she wasn't resisting, he stepped around her chair and pulled her up into his arms. His next kiss was more exacting. He opened her mouth and touched her tongue with his own. She felt unwilling to stop him. What was this lassitude?

He stopped himself. Still holding her, he said, "You remember something, don't you? Let me make love to you."

Her limbs felt watery. She needed to sit down. Or lie down. He began to unlace her bodice. She placed her hands over his, but she seemed to have no strength in any of her body to stop him. Somehow she'd known it would come to this. He opened her gown, her chemise. His big fingers were easy with the little ribbons. She was like a puppet with loose strings. He kept one arm around her, to support her. She closed her eyes, knowing he was looking at her. She felt him lower his mouth to her breasts.

She gasped at the sensation of his tugging lips. She should be fighting him, she should be struggling against everything he did to her. But she found it such a sweet comfort. Every tugging caress was a sweet temptation. Like the individual notes of a forgotten song, fragments of memory came back to haunt her. Scenes, smells, a painfully elusive sense of motion and texture. A sense of peace and security. He'd done this to her before. This and more. She was afraid to like it, yet it seemed she had little control over the matter.

She forgot to think. It went on for hours and days and they might have built the pyramids and tired of them and torn them down in the millenniums as he continued to kiss her breasts. When she moaned, she seemed to recall another sound, reedy and high-pitched, a wail, ascending at first like a smoke tendril to the sky, a female cry, though nearly inhuman, gathering force as it rose—with pain!

The pleasure he'd brought her to died off suddenly. She shuddered. In her mind she felt cool air on her bare back, heard the heavy step of a man behind her. Then silence. The upward whir of a cat-o-nine-tails. Then—

She let out a sharp cry.

"What is it?"

She shook her head, not even knowing who was questioning her, unwilling to speak of that memory of pain. A memory so grisly her mind had closed it out.

"Tell me!" The highwayman was looking down into her face from very close above her.

"My back," she said, "he wouldn't stop!" There was pain, echoing and echoing. Tears spilled from her eyes and she sobbed aloud. She remembered those screams, how they had worn her throat raw.

"That's right, Jane."

"Who was it? Who did that to me? You know! *Tell me!*"

"It does no good to tell you," he said again. "I told you I was your friend and you wouldn't believe me."

She didn't believe it now.

The dreamlike recollection of pain lingered, vivid and heavy, drawing her down, causing her to swim in confusion. She heard a voice, saw a wrinkled face. As she grasped at the memory, it disappeared, as always, and was gone.

She hung in the highwayman's arms like a marionette, empty and devoid of sensation. She heard the wind whining outside. "Let me sit down. Please."

He directed her into her chair. And he sat beside her.

He knew her. He knew who she was. He had been her lover. She must trust him. There was no one else. "I'm Jane . . . Fitzpatrick?"

He nodded.

"What do I do?"

"You were a maidservant. You worked for a Mr. Welby."

Who was he? Where? She strained to clutch a memory, to hold it and inspect it and understand it, but she couldn't tear aside that curtain that cloaked her inexplicable past, that insolvable mystery. A maidservant. Mr. Welby.

A memory burst into life: she'd come to hide her pay in her stone cache, and now she was standing on a moorside, the wind whistling in the dry heather. Overhead arched the calm, unobstructed sky. She was going to leave this place soon; she was going to emigrate to Georgia.

She remembered! Not everything, but—"My money!" Memory was followed by realization: "The captain has it."

"You had it in a belt around your waist."

She looked at him keenly. "You're Keith Solomon?"

"Stella must have told you that. The name you know me by is Keith Cutler."

She mused again, demanding to remember. "We were . . ."

"Lovers."

She out her hand to her forehead. "This is so awful, like a curtain hiding half my mind." She calmed herself. "Were you going to America with me?"

His expression hardened. "So you remember that much. No, I'm not."

All right. "I have to get my money from the captain."

"Forget your money, Jane. I have enough to buy your passage—if you're still that intent on Georgia. You're coming with me tonight."

She shook her head.

He said, thrusting the words out one by one with all the strength of his will, "Listen to me. You're wanted by the soldiers. And if you're caught, your life is worth no more than a pebble."

"Why? What did I do?"

396

He said, dry and deceptively calm, "You're not going back to that house and that's that." One side of his mouth quirked, giving him a vaguely sinister expression. "You're just going to have to trust me on this."

An ominous sense of threat, of tension, hung palpably from him. He could force her to go with him. Best to agree. "All right."

He was unconvinced. The fire gleamed in his eyes like two brilliant points of light. "You'll come with me?"

"Stella says I should do what you say."

"And Burne? What does he say you should do?" He reached a hand into her loose bodice and rubbed his bony knuckles over the tender tip of one breast. She shivered under the touch. "You let him kiss you, didn't you?"

He was guessing. She was certain he was only guessing.

"What else did you let him do, Jane? Did he touch you like this? Did he bring this little bud to such a hard peak?"

She leaned forward, pressing her breast into his palm. "I don't remember."

"You sly little slut. If I thought for one minute that you'd let him do the things to you I've done . . ."

"What? Would you shoot him?"

He made a growling noise deep in his chest. "I'm taking you away from here."

"Where is your horse? Outside? Get him." She stood. "I'll cover the fire." She was lacing her chemise. "And put my hair up."

He watched her. He didn't believe her. She stopped and looked at him. "You could tie me up, I suppose."

At last he rose and went to the door. He gave her a final look, and went out.

She didn't bother with her cloak. She followed him to the door. He could be waiting just outside, ready to catch her as she tried to run. She didn't know if going back to Grayson House was sane or insane. She only knew she must risk it. Her money was there, the captain had it, and she must get it back.

She plunged out into the windy darkness. No arms caught her; no large figure barred her way.

Keith brought Eclipse around to the door. He wasn't surprised when he found the summer house empty. Damn her. Damn her to hell. He thought of her hurrying away from him with hunched shoulders and lowered head, butting through the weather, he thought of her with love and anger and with an anxious fear. He could have forced her to come away with him. He should have. He should go after her now, and carry her off kicking and screaming if necessary. He should. He knew he should.

The trees around him bowed and moaned in the wind. He'd felt like this once before, when he'd found the woman of his dreams flinging herself into sure danger out on the moors. When he'd discovered that she wasn't dream-perfect, but that she could be hurt, that she could bleed, and that she could be humanly frightened and driven and foolish. He'd felt this same anger then, this same ruthless desire to leave her to her own fate.

He also remembered how she was when he'd fished her out of the river, her eyes so dead and bleak they were numb to fear and sense. He never wanted to see her like that again. And so he'd let her go, rather than risk driving her deeper into her forgetfulness. She'd remembered a few things tonight. His only hope was that she would remember enough within the next day or so to bring her back to him.

The side door was still unlocked when Jane got back to the house. She needed her money. Where would the captain keep it? Stella would know. Wrestling with all kinds of thoughts, Jane tiptoed along the upstairs gallery to Stella's chamber. She knocked softly. She'd half expected Stella to be waiting for her. But there was no answer. She tried the door, found it unlocked. "Stella?" Her voice was hardly a sigh.

Stella was a huddle of unmoving sheets and bed-clothes in the great curtained bed, obviously sound asleep. Jane moved closer. "Stella." She reached out to shake her.

And discovered that the humanlike shape in the bed was nothing but a rolled quilt and some dresses placed to look as if someone were sleeping there.

Jane backed away. She hugged herself in the chill. There was no sound in the whole house. Stella was gone. To Hart? It didn't matter at the moment. She was gone and Jane was on her own.

Her money. She must get her money. She felt it as strongly as something breathing at her heels.

The logical place for Captain Grayson to keep it was in his desk. She crept down to the library. Outside the windows, the oaks whispered and leaned together like conspirators. She dared light a lamp. Going through the captain's desk drawers one by one, she discovered a flat wooden case. Inside was a pair of long flintlock pistols with ribbed barrels, their butts ornamented with the heads of fauns. A very handsome pair of weapons. Very deadly. They were loaded, ready to fire. No doubt they were the dueling pistols the captain had taken with him when he'd meant to kill Hart.

In her memory she heard the pop of a gun. And a roll of thunder. Lightning. The highwayman on his black horse. Rain. A man had hold of her wrist—but now he let go. He fell backward, shot by the highwayman's pistol.

The silence of the house seemed like spun glass, fine and fragile. She searched on, but found not a guinea of her money. She came across a folded sheet, an engraving, by the looks of it. She opened it.

"The Rose of Midnight."

Chapter Twenty-seven

Burne Grayson Wasn't Keith Cutler

"It's you, isn't it?"

Jane stood straight with a start.

Captain Grayson stood in the library door, his hand still on the knob. He was in his purple dressing gown and nightcap.

She could hardly answer him. The portrait was clenched in her hands. It was all returned to her, like walls falling away. She saw the landscape of her life unimpeded, all in a second. York, that beautiful and ancient city, smelling of mold. Mr. Welby's house. The afternoon shadows cascading through the windows, profoundly slanting, falling. The baron and his paints. Her father, his seamed face, his squinting bloodshot eyes. Herself wandering out on the moors, following one narrow sheep trail after another through the heather, an exile. And Keith. Oh, Keith, with his black hair falling over his forehead.

Murder, dear God, she was wanted for murder.

She made herself look down at the portrait in her hands. "It . . . it looks a little like me."

"Indeed." A moment of gruesome stillness.

"I don't recall—" Her mind floundered desperately.

The captain's eyes were like windows with the blinds drawn. It was as if there were no feelings behind them. "What are you doing in here?" He took in her gown, her loose, wind-tangled hair. "Where have you been?"

Her hand went to her throat. "Just out for some air. I couldn't sleep. I had a nightmare."

"Do you wear Stella's jewels to go out for some air?" He glanced at his desk. "Are you a thief?"

"No! I was only looking for my money. I would like to have it back, please. Now."

He considered her with a balked glare. There was a thick, ugly silence, as though someone had shouted a lot of dirty words. "I think you'd better go to your chamber." He took her arm. There was no sense in fighting him; he was much stronger than she.

He led her upstairs and thrust her into her chamber. "I'll take that necklace."

Jane removed the lapis. She pulled the matching ear bobs from her ears, too. She handed them to him. He closed the door and his steps receded down the gallery. She waited. In a moment she heard them return. What now? But he didn't come in. Instead, she heard the lock turn in the door. She rushed forward, rattled the knob. "Captain!" But he was gone.

She lit a candle. For long moments she just stood by it, remembering, remembering. She paced. She came to the question: what was she to do now? She went to the window. Was Keith down there? She couldn't see him.

She heard it start to rain. The wind blew gusts of it against the house like bucketsful of tossed pebbles. She realized she was shivering. She pulled the coverlet from the bed, intending to wrap herself in it, and found a note on her pillow.

402

Dear Jane,

I don't expect you will come back from your rendezvous, but if you do you will not find me here. Hart's message was in the prayer book. Exodus 13:12. Today is the thirteenth and I'm to meet him at 12 midnight—to make our exodus!

My happiness is marred only by knowing that I may never see you again. If you ever read this note, then I'm afraid you will soon discover how I have wronged you. I hope you can forgive me.

Stella

How had Stella wronged her?

She couldn't concentrate on that right now. She had to get out of here somehow. She went to the window again. It was too high. She couldn't jump.

The chamber was cold, and there would be no logs for the fire until Catherine came up in the morning. Jane stripped off her gown and lay down on the bed with the coverlet wrapped about her. After several hours she fell into a fitful sleep.

Near dawn she suddenly opened her eyes. She listened. Nothing. Nothing. The rain had stopped. There was no sound anywhere. Yet she felt a forewarning, a kind of impression that danger was coming. Coming from many miles away. And it would be there . . . soon.

Burne found out something about you in London. They sent a letter by way of a messenger to York. Whoever they wrote to, he's sure to denounce you.

She sat upright. And stayed that way for a long moment, wide-eyed, listening. But there was nothing. Nothing that could be heard. Or seen. Nothing.

Eventually she sank back against her pillow and pulled the coverlet close under her chin. She forced herself to close her eyes. But she did not sleep again.

It began to rain once more about the time the household stirred. She rose and dressed herself carefully in fresh clothes, in one of Stella's elaborate gowns which had almost become commonplace to her. Today's was autumn orange, a color more flattering to Stella than to Jane. The heavy skirts, stiffly starched, draped over wide panniers. The bodice required tight lacing. Dressing her lush hair into a small coiffure, she studied her reflection in the looking glass. She looked that image straight in the eye. She and that woman would no longer play the bitter pastime of Questions and No Answers.

She placed a flat round cap of white lawn edged with lace over her upswept hair. The streamers fell down her back. She looked exactly what she was not, a lady.

The rain fell, and fell, and fell. She heard the captain's step along the gallery. She knocked on her locked door. "Captain? Please! Let me out."

He did not come near her door, but went downstairs. Catherine came up to light Stella's fire. She didn't come to Jane's room. She must have been told to stay away.

A little later Jane heard Burne's step. He would be going down to his breakfast, drawn by the smell of the morning's fresh bread. Again she went to the door and knocked. "Burne!"

He came along the gallery. "Jane?" He tried the doorknob.

"Your father's locked me in."

A muffled voice from downstairs: "Burne, come down here!"

"Let me out, Burne!"

"Father"—his voice receded—"what's going on?"

The melancholy storm continued. She heard the captain come back up. First he went into Stella's chamber. Jane could almost see him fuming: where is she! I told her not to be late for meals!

Jane braced herself. As she expected, his footsteps soon came to the door. The key clattered in the lock. The door flew back on its hinges. "Where is she?"

Jane hesitated. She was going to have to lie about so many things that she decided it would be best to be honest wherever she could. "Gone," she said. "Eloped with Hart, I would guess."

Another pair of footsteps came behind him. Burne, fully dressed, wearing a coat with a widely flared skirt, a clubbed wig, the club plaited into a queue. His eyebrows were lifted to make half-circles.

The captain rapped out, "Your sister's run off with that fool of a farmer. Order the coach. We'll try to catch up with them."

Burne stayed where he was. "How long have they been gone?"

Jane said, "Since midnight, I think."

"Where did they go?" This from the captain.

"I don't know. She didn't confide in me. I went into her chamber and found what you just found. That was shortly after midnight."

"And you didn't tell me!"

Burne said, "There is very little use in going after them, Father, if they have so much of a start on you."

Despite her own predicament, Jane felt triumphant. Stella had made her escape!

But the captain wanted someone to punish. Glaring at Jane he said, "You helped her."

"I would have helped her. I should have known. She was so radiant yesterday, but I mistook it for . . . I don't know, maybe I thought you had finally driven her mad."

His fists clenched as he started for her. "Why you—"

"Father!" Burne caught his arm.

He continued to glare at Jane. "I found her going through my desk last night like a common thief."

"Is that right, Jane?"

She watched the thought take form in him. Her gladness for Stella was gone, all at once. "I was looking for my money. I want to leave here. He has no right to keep me."

"Where would you go, alone, a lure to every outlaw?"

"She's not going anywhere." The captain's words came quick and harsh. "She found the portrait in my desk. I think she knows who she is." He pushed Burne back into the gallery and started to pull Jane's door shut. The key was in his hand.

"Father, what are you doing?"

"Locking her in. She'll stay here until we receive word from York. I think the wench is a thief—and a trickster—and who knows what else."

Jane's last glimpse of Burne showed him to be dumbfounded.

Noon came and went. Jane knew she was a fool. She should have let Keith take her away. She went to her window again and again. Was he out there somewhere, watching?

The rain no longer beat down so relentlessly. Catherine came with a tray. Burne came with her. "May I come in?" he asked Jane.

There was silence between them as Catherine put down the tray and made up Jane's fire. She left the door open when she went out. Jane eyed the door. Burne said, "Please don't try to leave, Jane. I've promised Father . . . well, please, don't do anything that will cause embarrassment to us both."

He was not so ruthless as his brother. Keith would not have begged her on the basis of civility. He would

406

have dared her to try to escape. She could see now the
light behind his dark eyes that said, Go ahead, try it.
Keith was notoriously dangerous and he found the fact,
not embarrassing, but amusing.

Jane watched Burne for a moment, and decided that
he was very uncertain about what his father was doing.
Perhaps he would set her free. She settled to picking at
her lunch tray. There was a pot of tea. She poured a
cup for Burne. At first there was silence between them,
made deeper by the drip of the soft rainfall from the
eaves and the flickering hiss of the fire.

"This is all turning very ugly," Burne said.

Jane didn't answer.

"I don't know what to think. Why were you going
through Father's desk?"

"I want to leave here."

"Why now, all of a sudden? Does it have anything
to do with Stella?"

Again, she refused to answer.

"Father is determined to ruin the Baywoods, of
course. I'll have to see what I can do to temper that."
He leaned against the mantelpiece wearily. After a moment he added, "Stella was in love once before. Did
she tell you? She was plump and pretty—pretty in her
own way, you know—scarcely past adolescence. He
was a younger son—with no prospects, according to
Father. Henry Hanson, a tall, heavy-boned, moody
fellow. Father sent Stella off to Bath and kept her there
till the boy gave up and placed his affections on someone else. Maybe he never really cared for her, I don't
know. She would have brought him a useful dowry of
six hundred pounds a year, and maybe that was all he
was really interested in."

Burne half closed his eyes to allow his memory to
wander over these events. His face glowed yellow and
orange with the fireglow. "I was at Oxford and hardly

407

realized what was going on. I was pursuing the pleasures of serious drinking at the time. Not that I could have done anything for Stella anyway; I was only sixteen myself. Sixteen and with no other view but to drink my way through Oxford, then go on to lead a comfortable existence.

"But when I came home, Stella was changed. Some of her prettiness was gone, eaten away by melancholy,"

Jane didn't know what to say.

"I hope she'll be all right. Baywood has nothing, even less than Henry Hanson, and Stella was never taught to make do and mend."

"I think she may be more adaptable then you know."

"I'll miss her." He managed a sad smile.

Jane couldn't help but see Keith's features repeated in his, fairer, and stamped all over with the traits of gentility. Stella was right, there was no mistaking that they were brothers, these two, both sons of their disagreeable father.

Outside it suddenly rained hard for a moment, then abruptly stopped.

"What about you, Burne? Have you no desire to escape your father's dominance?"

He gave her a quirky smile. "Have you ever seen my father dominate me?"

She considered, and realized she hadn't.

The logs spit and hissed on the andirons. He said, "Escape to where? To what? I'm not destined for great things or faraway locales. I'm tethered by my need for connection, by my affection for Grayson House. I have no ambition beyond living quietly at home."

She said, "Grayson House is beautiful."

"Yes, it is a beautiful place." He got up and went to stare out the dormer window. The rainclouds were thinning and rending. "But it's not only the beauty. There are certain trees with which I have old alliances, trees I have climbed and fields I have crossed through to get to certain clandestine places. My past is all about me here, fused with the present. What happens today happened yesterday, and will happen again tomorrow, and I need that. I'll marry one day— I'd hoped, Jane . . ."

"Not me, Burne."

He sighed. "You have remembered something."

"Yes, something."

"And you can't tell me?"

"I wish I could."

He didn't hold her gaze. He hadn't the personal force of Keith, who could hold anybody's eye. He said, "Ask yourself, my love, if it was not very heartless to have entranced me."

"I did nothing to entrance you."

"Except be yourself. I almost wish we were butterflies and lived but three days. Three days with you I could fill with more happiness than in fifty common years."

"We're not butterflies and I can't marry you, Burne."

He was quiet for a moment. Then, "Well, I'll find someone else, I suppose. There must always be some provision for the flesh, hmm?" He turned his head to show her his smile, then turned back to the window. "I'll find someone else, and I'll bring her to Grayson House. My children will be born here."

Jane remembered what Stella had told her: Keith had come here once, an anxious boy yearning to be able to say, as Burne did so complacently, that this was his home. And he'd been cast out. How painful that must have been. And while he was beating hemp in prison, Burne was living riotously at Oxford. They'd both received their educations, and now they lived the lives for which they'd been prepared.

"No, I could never leave here," Burne went on. "This is my home. And one day it will be my responsibility. If I 'escaped,' who would take care of it?"

Jane put down her fork, and with her head lowered, said, "You have a brother."

She looked up. Burne had turned. His head was tilted sideways as he considered her. There was no sign of his impish, dimpled smile. He screwed up his eyes and peered at her as though she were in very poor light. "What do you know of my brother?"

In four skips of her heart, she realized it had been a mistake to mention Keith. She poured herself a cup of tea. She stirred cream in, looking past Burne out the window. She groped for words. "Stella told me about him."

He still studied her. It had almost stopped raining again. She dared to say, "What do *you* know of him, Burne?"

"Nothing now. I brought him to Grayson House once—and I have never forgiven myself for it."

The rain erased the snow from the landscape. By early afternoon, the land was decorated by silver wreaths of curling mist. Burne came again to see Jane. His eyes were bruised and accusing. He had a letter in his hand. "This just arrived."

She felt hollow.

"It was brought by the messenger Father sent to York."

She needed to sit down. "May I see it?"

He came into the room, this time closing the door, and handed it to her.

She opened the folded pages and inhaled—gasped

quickly, as if she had been holding her breath. She recognized Mr. Welby's spiky, vertical hand only too well.

"I belive the girl you are harboring is none other than my former maidservant, a young woman of great beauty, known locally (owing to a certain portrait made of her) as 'The Rose of Midnight.' Recently her father came to claim her from her service to me; he needed her help to reestablish himself on his small holding. Jane had saved her earnings during her service to me, and her father wished to use them to better his chances of success on his farm. Jane, however, not only resented leaving her position, but she refused outright to give her father her savings.

I was witness to an unpleasant scene in which she vowed she'd rather see him dead than give him a farthing. I did what I might, the more so because the girl had been a member of my staff for two years and I was fond of her. Perhaps too fond; I fear I was over lenient. Yet that day I spoke to her very firmly, explaining the wickedness in what she'd said. But at that point she seemed fortified against both counsel and prayer. It was then that I realized she had given me a false opinion of her; I did not know the real Jane Fitzpatrick— nor does anyone, I suspect.

To finish this sad tale, her old father was found incinerated among the ruins of their farm cottage the very next day. Jane is wanted for suspicion of his murder.

There was more, an excess of dry detail covering four closely written pages. His report of her was like a snowball rolled down a slope; it grew larger as it rushed

411

along. Her first reaction was a sense of weariness, a desire to give up and just let everything take its course.

"Father has sent for the local soldiery."

She nodded without looking up. This was her own fault. If she'd trusted Keith . . . now she had no one to blame but Jane Fitzpatrick. "I didn't kill him, you know."

"What happened, Jane?"

"He beat me—flogged me. He wanted my money. The cottage was a ruin. As he was starting a fire in the hearth, the thatch caved in on him. I got out barely in time myself. And after what he'd done to me, I was in no condition to help him."

Burne was silent. Jane said, "You must believe me."

He wanted to believe her, she saw that. "I'll see you have the finest barrister. If you're innocent, you have nothing to fear."

"I am innocent, Burne, but I have much to fear. Let me go. Just leave the door unlocked—an accident . . ."

"Surely you'd rather get this all behind you? The law will vindicate you. If you run from it, it will follow you to the ends of England."

"I plan to—"

But she couldn't trust him with that. Burne Grayson wasn't Keith Cutler. He was a fine man, he would make a fine husband, a fine squire. But he could never understand what it was like to not be a Grayson, with all the wealth and security of position that gave him. He could never understand what it was like to be coffled and flogged, to be hunted for the gallows. He could never understand Keith's experience of prison. He'd perhaps visited Newgate with his Oxford friends, or even Bridewell on a whipping day. Jane heard that many of the best-respected people of fashion visited the prisons, and went to hangings. It was a pastime for them, a distraction, an entertainment. Just as many

412

ladies and gentlemen derived amusement in taking a drive on a Sunday afternoon to Bedlam Hospital.

She said only, "They'll hang me."

The day was gathering itself in when next Jane's chamber door was opened. She rose from her chair to see a sergeant of the King's Army. The captain and another soldier, a corporal, stood behind him. She felt nothing but a dull sense of expectation fulfilled. The men moved back as she came out into the gallery. The sergeant looked at her without speaking, comparing her with the copy of her portrait he held in his hands. He had wide mottled lips. He nodded and said, " 'Tis her, all right." He looked her up and down, slowly, as if the hinge of his neck were rusted. "She's tidy as a pin, ain't she? Don't look like a murderess."

The captain was looking at her as if she were some kind of peculiar snake. Burne was nowhere to be seen.

She was taken down to the library where the lamps were lit against the twilight that pressed in on the mullioned windows. The rain had melted the snow over the dark lawn, and tufts of winter grass lay limp under the trees. At first she heard little of what was said between the men; her mind kept drifting; but she knew she must listen. She couldn't let herself wander off from reality anymore.

"Very grave suspicion they have her under," the sergeant was saying. His speech gave away his beginnings in life. Few well-born gentlemen joined in the English army. "As black-hearted a she-devil as has ever been found in the annals of human corruption." He hawked and spat into the captain's fire. "And ye say ye've had her in yer house these past two months and more?"

The captain, seated behind his desk, broke his surly

413

silence to explain himself. "At first she was not right in her head. She was as mad as a sparrow. But I suspected her all along. I have not enjoyed a second's peace of mind. And once I received intelligence of her character . . ." He was staring over the sergeant's shoulder as though square into the heart of Truth.

The sergeant listened with a grave, tense face, but Jane saw a tinge of mockery in the wrinkling of his eyes. "Yer a lucky man, Captain Grayson. 'Tis a sorry business, best passed and done wi'." He looked about him, at the shelves and shelves of books. He reached for one. "Always wanted to meet a gentlemen who wrote books."

The captain sat drumming his fingers on his desk. "No real gentlemen would have authored the books Defoe wrote."

"Defoe?" The sergeant looked at the binding.

"What do we do now?"

At last he put the book back. He gave Jane a glance. She remained safe inside herself. "Well, sir, ye've fulfilled yer duty, and more than yer duty. 'Tis never a matter now for ye or me; 'tis a matter for the crowner and his jury. They have a grand, fierce way wi' evildoers up in the northern parts. After a fair trial, she'll be fairly hanged, I promise ye. It'll be a grand bit o' justice."

Jane stood unmoving, as if locked in a pillory. They were speaking of her as if she were no more than a wolf. An animal. A predator without measure and without mercy. Still she stood quietly. What choice did she have?

It was settled that she would be taken back to York immediately. The sergeant manacled her wrists. Standing close to her, he looked at her hard. She looked directly past him to the caption, who was glowering at her under knotted brows.

She was led past Catherine into the hall. Though the servant woman was in a state of distress, she'd thought enough to get a cloak from Stella's chamber. She handed it to the sergeant, then stepped back quickly and grasped her apron to her mouth. The sergeant frowned, looking at the cloak, then clumsily swung it around his prisoner and tied it at her throat.

He escorted her through the hall toward the front door. And it was there that Jane saw Burne for the first time. He was standing beside the door, wearing a gold coat over soft kid breeches. His face was absolutely flat. Breaking out of her stillness, she said, "Burne, I committed no murder and that's the truth, so help me."

The sergeant tugged at her. "Come along!"

Jane felt very little fear just now, though fear might have been advisable, or apprehension at the least, but it truly broke her heart to think that Burne might believe she had blood on her hands.

She stepped out into the clean air, into the smell of wet branches and drenched earth and evening. The soldiers had arrived by hired coach. The vehicle was drawn up at the foot of the front steps. Holding the door open was a guard, a stocky fellow in a rusty tricorn, wearing a tarpaulin coat with a wide belt around his waist, from which hung a naval cutlass in a worn leather scabbard. His hair was long and straggling, lying on his shoulders. The corporal climbed up to sit with the driver in his box. He had a heavy carbine slung over his shoulder now.

All these people openly gawked at Jane. The sergeant helped her up the mounting steps into the coach and climbed in behind her. The captain stood on the steps of the house and watched as the coachman snapped his whip and the horses started into motion. The coach lurched forward. Soon he would go inside, into

415

his library, and sit behind his big desk and light his curved wooden pipe with a jeweler's precision and delicacy. He would grow old in Grayson House, and grow more irascible and cantankerous than ever.

Jane leaned to peer through the open door into the shadowy hall where Burne remained. She saw him say something to his father, quickly, as though the very words tasted bad and he wanted them out of his mouth.

From the iron gates, she raised remembering eyes to the windows of the house which blazed through the twilight.

The sergeant pulled the window flap closed. It was then that she saw how he was holding back hard on a leer. "Now yer going to be a good girl, ain't ye, Janey? Or I got my methods, see?" His eyes fell down past her face, her shoulders, her breasts, her hips. He licked his wide mottled lips.

She began to feel some of the fear she hadn't felt earlier. Fear at being arrested, at being manacled, at being outside of Grayson House and its protected seclusion. Fear at being a woman in the hands of strange men.

Chapter Twenty-eight

In a Dark Time

The coach was awkward, heavy, unsprung. Inside, the two passengers sat confronting one another. The one comfort Jane had, if she could call it a comfort, was more space than she would enjoy if she were riding elbow-jammed with six people packed into these two seats. Regular stagecoaches took on so many passengers that many had to ride on top, and even wedged themselves into the large wicker basket at the rear which was supposed to hold general cargo. These were days when everyone traveled in groups whenever possible, for safety.

Even without a large company of passengers, Jane soon concluded that a coach was a poor means of conveyance. As the wooden frame jolted along the rutted roads toward York, the only shock absorber was the leather on which the coachwork was mounted.

As the last evening light faded from the sky, she sat as if she'd fallen prey to some spell. Her coiffure came undone because of the bouncing ride, and with her hands manacled, she had no means of repairing it. Wind flapped through the cracked leather windows and caught loose strands of hair and blew them across her face.

Sergeant Conners, for that was her escort's name, eyed her steadily, his heavy body rocking and swaying in the chill isolation they shared. After they'd been on the road for some half an hour, he suddenly said, "Did ye and the fine young gentleman have a time together?"

She gave him the glassiest stare of which she was capable. But as he sat on watching her, she grew edgy. In this fashion the first hours slipped away.

They stopped for supper at a half-timbered roadside inn with narrow windows. With loud clops the team pulled into the courtyard. The corporal, blue-cheeked with cold, opened the coach door and unfolded the mounting steps.

As Jane and the sergeant entered the tap room, her manacles drew every eye. There were several coarse men in breeches and heavy leather shoes, and one young well-to-do man in a cloak. She heard the corporal and the guard in hushed voices telling the patrons who she was. Everyone wanted to have a look at her. And the sergeant let them look their fill.

They were served by a woman in a stained apron. The sergeant wasn't stingy in offering Jane refreshment. However, her appetite, never remarkable, died absolutely under those stares. She shifted on her narrow bench. Though at first everyone spoke in whispers, soon they began to speak freely. Sergeant Conners had no sense of subtlety. When asked who she was and why he was taking her to York, he told the whole story, as he knew it.

"Why'd she do it?"

He shrugged. "I doubt the old man did anything much to deserve it."

Jane was trembling. She felt like a dwarf in a sideshow, like one of the leopards at the London menagerie.

Sergeant Conners was gratified by the crowd's nods and curiosity, by their awe of him. She passed through shame into a deeper valley of despair.

After supper came the rolling, ill-smelling interior of the coach again. The road made a stiff climb, then dropped down. Up again, and down again. They clattered through an ancient town and out of it. Jane didn't know where she was, except that they were traveling north. The sergeant's meal caused him to grow drowsy. His eyelids drooped, they fell shut; he snored. Despite the hardness of her unsprung seat, despite the rattle of the coach, Jane kept falling asleep, too. She fought against that drift into strange impressions and the music of her fleeting dreams, but it was no use.

Until an especially deep pothole rolled her and her jailer both to the sides of the coach. Sergeant Conners clutched his shoulder and cursed. He abruptly opened the door and leaned out. "Here! Ye up there! I thought ye said we was near the Chestnut Inn!" Jane couldn't make out the answer he received. He shouted back, "That's what ye said five miles ago! Tell him to whip up them horses now. I want a bed for the night!"

He pulled the door closed. As he started to heave back into his seat, the coachman obeyed his order. Jane heard the whip (the sound made her flinch), and the coach lurched forward. Sergeant Conners lost his balance. He fell back into his seat and cracked his head against the rear wall. His tricorn was pushed forward over his eyes. For an instant he looked so ridiculous that Jane almost smiled.

He righted his hat and glared at her. Somehow she managed to keep her expression bland. He cleared his throat and hawked onto the straw on the floor of the coach, barely missing the tip of her shoe.

The vehicle's body pitched and rocked. She hardly noticed. She was thinking about Keith. If he had not abandoned her in disgust, now would be a very good time for him to practice his craft in her behalf.

But the danger—she shouldn't wish him to risk his life for her. It wasn't right.

Yet she did wish it. She was that wicked and selfish. If he didn't, and she was delivered to York, there would be no chance at all for her to escape the charge of murder awaiting her. She would be tried by a jury, which was supposed to give her some chance to defend herself. But with Mr. Welby's testimony standing against hers, she knew who they would believe.

She thought back to that scene in his library, when she'd said she'd rather see her father dead than give him a tuppence. It all seemed so long ago that she couldn't even recall what emotions had fueled her fury anymore.

Georgia . . . she daren't even consider Georgia and the new life she'd dreamed of having there, a life in which she and no one else ruled her, in which she and no one else could make her a success or a failure, a life in which she was no one's servant and no one's dependent and no one's drudge.

Wouldn't it be ironic, though, if she were found guilty and given the choice of hanging or transport to the plantations of America? She might be sent to Georgia, where she wanted to go! But as a slave.

The interior of the coach was quite dark, and still no sign of either Keith or the Chestnut Inn. Sergeant Conners, having eaten and napped, now sought to satisfy his third appetite. He suddenly moved from his seat to crowd onto hers. He wrapped his big arms around her and groaned in her ear, "Let's make this miserable trip more entertaining."

His heavy body squeezed her against the leather-

420

paneled wall. Her panniers folded under his weight. She pushed at him with her manacled hands, to little use. He lay against her and started at the laces of her bodice. She heard one of the hoops of her panniers snap. "Let's have a feel o' yer treasures." He cursed her chemise when the lace knotted, but he got his hand down the neck of it, nevertheless, and groped for her breasts. At the same time he plastered his wide mottled lips over hers and smeared a kiss around her mouth and chin. His breath was strong. He clutched and pinched her breasts until she cried out.

He pulled his hand away, but only to put it up her skirt onto her stockinged knee. She felt the pressure of his thick fingers prying her legs open.

"Give in now. Ye're too proud. Do ye think yer too good to be showed to people for what ye are? Ye'll be shown at the gallows. Might as well enjoy all ye can aforehand."

The highwayman's plan was crude; there was no time to conceive of something more elaborate; it would have to do. He sat on his black stallion, dark, in dark clothing, silent and shadowy, behind the broad trunk of a beech tree that grew close by the road. He breathed the coolness of the rain-drenched earth. First he'd followed the coach, at a safe distance, to be sure of the route it was taking. Then he'd come by the shorter horse paths to get ahead of it.

He listened. The night listened. He usually discovered more about the tenor of the guards he meant to hold up, and the habits of the persons inside the coach. He didn't even know if the sergeant carried a weapon. Or if that corporal with the carbine knew how to shoot it. Or if the coachman kept a hidden pistol in his box. But there was no time for caution.

Love, he thought bitterly, it asks you to die for it when at the same time it makes you want to live as you've never wanted to live before.

He heard the rumble of ponderous wheels and the thud of hooves. He pulled his kerchief up over his nose. This was the moment. He spurred his horse from the side of the road into the very middle, and there he took his stand.

For a moment more the pitch black night held only rumors of the thing that was coming, then the lantern-lit coach rounded a curve and came at him like flood-waters breaking over a peaceful bank. He held his horse steady in the on-rolling vehicle's path. One of his pistols was raised in his left hand. His brain blurred and his blood roared through his ears. Tonight there was no thrill, no dark joy. Tonight it all had the quality of a nightmare, because tonight not just his life was at stake, but Jane's as well.

The coachman shouted. He pulled back on his reins and his team lost their rhythm. The lead horses reared a little; all four of them neighed in confusion. The guard on the box gathered himself with panicky effort. He fumbled for the weapon slung over his shoulder. The highwayman found himself looking down the muzzle of an army-issue carbine. The gun fired wildly. He felt a cold dread, such as he'd never felt before, in all his adventures. Darkness edged his vision. He saw the barrel of the carbine point straight at him, saw the flash of sparks, heard the boom. He lunged forward over his horse's neck. The ball grabbed his mask and singed his jaw as it passed.

He righted himself and kept his horse positioned directly before the unstopped team. The coachman was leaning back, hauling on the reins. The highwayman felt the drumming of the hooves coming up from the ground beneath his own horse. His cheek hurt, limning how narrow were his chances of success. He took careful aim at the driver while the guard furiously tried to reload his carbine and the second guard on top of the coach brandished his cutlass. The vehicle came to a stop at last. The horses stamped and whinnied; the lanterns bobbed. The highwayman dropped his reins and trusted his horse to the delicate command of his knees so he could bring out his second pistol. The corporal, seeing two double-barreled weapons pointing at him, stopped trying to load his own. The highwayman bowed, all courtesy, and said, in a cordial tone, "Throw your weapons down, gentlemen, or I'll shoot your driver."

It was always best to threaten the one least capable of defending himself; it made it easier for guards to give up if they could do it in the name of protecting someone else.

The driver was quite helpful in this. With both the highwayman's weapons pointed at him, he looked as if he might faint. "Throw them down, Corporal . . . Mr. Peters . . . for God's sake, throw them down!"

The soldier's mouth pulled together, but he did what he was told. The swordsman behind him followed suit.

Now the highwayman shouted, "You, inside, throw out your weapons—now! Or your driver dies!"

After a short hesitation, he heard, "Ain't got none." There was no way of knowing if the man was telling the truth or not. The highwayman nudged his horse back along the side of the coach. This was the weak moment.

Don't let them see you're afraid. Don't let them know.

Love did this to you.

He stopped by the door of the coach. He felt something trickling down the side of his neck. Blood. From the blazing kiss of that passing ball. The wound burned a little, but he was too busy to bother with it now.

"I have your driver—and your corporal—in my sights, sir. Come out slowly."

The coach door swung open, revealing in the lantern light the shadowed and exhausted faces of the man and woman within. The sergeant's face was a mask of anger as he jumped down onto the road. "Ye'll hang for this, ye brazen-faced rascal!"

It was going to work. It was going to work. Slowly the highwayman's heart stopped trying to leap out of his chest.

"I promise ye, ye'll get no gain robbing this coach."

The highwayman pretended to give that the pause it would deserve if gold were his intent. "I see," he said with impeccable dignity. "And who is that inside with you?"

"Naught but a prisoner I'm transporting. Ha! Did ye think we were carrying gold?."

"It looks to be a woman. Some black-and-midnight hag, no doubt. Hand her out. Let's take a look at the wench."

The sergeant grimly turned and gestured to Jane.

Seeing her wrists manacled like a common criminal's, and then seeing her gown unlaced and how disheveled she looked, he could have shot the sergeant easily, with very little remorse. He said, "Well, well, a handsome woman after all. And not beneath your attentions, I see. What's her crime?"

"Murder."

Keith pretended to study her. "A *very* handsome woman. Since you have no gold, I suppose I must take her for my night's prize. How about it, mistress? I'm sure the sergeant here is a very good fellow and you've been enjoying your journey with him immensely, but I fear he might be intending to hang you at the end of it. Would you prefer to risk me, or him—and a jury of honest yeomen and sheepherders?"

"You, sir," she answered quickly.

He laughed. "Indeed?" He winked at the sergeant. "Either she's extremely brave, or she's found your caresses extremely coarse. Unlock her manacles."

The sergeant fumbled in the half-light. Clearly he was trying to think of some way to foil the plan.

The highwayman prodded gently, "I am a kindly and patient soul, Sergeant, but if you don't hurry up I'm afraid I'm going to have to blow your head off your neck." He eased his stallion near enough so that he could knock the man's hat off with the barrel of one pistol.

The metal cuffs came free of Jane's wrists quickly enough after that. She rubbed the marks they left, made livid by her struggles against her escort's plan of rape.

"Now hand her up to me—but wait! Mistress, if you would be so good, you would make an easier passenger if you removed those ridiculous hip braces."

She was white-faced and wild-eyed, so terrified, in fact, that she forgot her modesty and lifted her autumn orange skirts before all these watching male eyes.

The sergeant's eyes especially followed her hands. The highwayman felt a wash of flame through his body. "Keep your eyes on me, sir! And you on top, turn your backs!"

Jane looked about her, as if she'd forgotten there was anyone else in the world but the highwayman to watch her. She hesitated, then again lifted her skirts. In a moment her hooped panniers fell to the ground. When she stepped out of them, the spread of her skirts was gone. She had to hold up the extra length to keep from tripping on her hems.

The highwayman said, "Now, Sergeant, you may hand her up to me."

She placed herself beside Eclipse so that the sergeant, still at pistol point, could grasp her waist and heave her onto the horse's rump. She locked her arms around the highwayman and murmured for his ears only, "I didn't think you would come in time."

He knew what that meant. The rage he'd held back broke free. He trained both his pistols on the sergeant's chest.

Jane cried, "No, don't!"

"Why not?"

The sergeant, sensing his danger, opened his eyes so wide the whites showed all around.

"Because there's no need! Not now!"

The sergeant's expression was that of the Spartan boy at the precise moment when the fox worked its way to his gall bladder. He and the highwayman exchanged stares. The highwayman said, "I feel a great need."

"Please, don't, don't." Jane's voice was a sob. "Just take me away from here!"

And so for her sake he curbed the violence in him and slid one pistol back into its leather case. "Perhaps we'll meet another time, Sergeant." He gathered his reins.

"Aye," the man struggled to put a little fearlessness back into his tone, "ye can count on it."

The highwayman backed his horse, then turned it and urged it to a sharp canter. In another moment the stallion was galloping into the dark.

A mile from the road, Keith stopped Eclipse abruptly, and jumped off and dragged Jane down. She went into his arms, frantically, and frantically he grabbed her. "Hold me, Keith! Don't let go of me! Don't let them get me!"

"Shh, there's no one to hurt you now. I have you and we're together and no one is going to touch you."

The stars were paling. The two fugitives had ridden all night, following narrow paths and horse trails. Jane's eyes were too heavy to keep open most of the time. The stallion's movement did nothing to help her stay awake anymore. How did Keith keep going? Didn't he feel this aching fatigue?

She rubbed her cheek against his broad back and tightened her arms about his waist. He'd saved her life again, this villain. What was it about him that made him seem more than other men? What was it that bequeathed him such courage, such grace? When had she come to trust his instincts completely and think of him as a hero? Imagine, a highwayman a hero!

She roused when she heard a change in the sound of the road under Eclipse's hooves. They had been on a muddy path, but now the sound was that of the crunch of gravel. Jane straightened and rubbed her face hard with both hands and looked about her. That large dark shadow ahead, that was Grayson House.

"Keith, what are you doing?"

"You want your money back, don't you?" These words, dashing against one another, seemed to strike sparks.

"Not now, it's too dangerous."

"He'll give it back to you—or else."

Eclipse stopped and he swung down. He held his hands up to her.

Whatever he was up to had little to do with her money. This was about Captain Grayson, the man who had shoved a little boy out into the cold on a snowy Christmas Eve. Keith's tone alone gave Jane a piercing sense of the humiliation, the pain, the death of honor he had suffered under the renunciation of his father. She sensed his mood and was afraid.

Eventually she leaned into his hands. She stood silent in his arms for a moment. There was a scratch along Keith's firm jaw, dark with blood. She searched his face—and felt an old habit of tenderness rise up. That hopeless bond they shared closed upon her anew. She was angry to feel it, this love that forced her to act against her instincts.

She recognized the faithfulness in him that had risked death for her again; yet she also recognized that he was about to use her. He could not confront his father for himself, but he could do it for her sake. It was the confrontation, and not her money, which was driving him.

He released her and pulled a pistol from the cases on his horse, and went right to the door and began to bang on it with the heel of his hand. Jane followed, holding her skirts up so that she didn't trip on the hems. On the porch, she automatically reached up to her hair. But it was too much for her. She let it fall again. She was aware of the folds of her dress hanging shapeless about her feet. Had she relaced her bodice? Yes, she was decent.

After five minutes of Keith's knocking, the lock of the door finally began to rattle. He stepped aside, out of sight, pulling his mask up over his nose and the dark gash in his cheek. The door swung open an inch. A sliver of candlelight cut across Jane's face. At a loss, she said the first thing that came to mind, "Hello, Daniel."

"Mistress Jane!" The door opened further. Keith stepped out of the shadows and shouldered it back and pushed himself into the hall. The manservant gave out a little cry. White-faced and red-eyed, he cowered back in his nightshirt and cap. His candleflame flickered.

Behind him was the captain, a candle in his hand, too, and his purple dressing gown over his nightshirt. He also retreated a step from the displayed weapon in Keith's left hand, and gasped as if he had been struck.

Keith said, "I believe you have something that belongs to Miss Fitzpatrick."

The captain stood stunned. Jane wished to God she could run for cover. Her hands were fisted. She couldn't make them unclench. Her heart had been clenched since she'd seen where Keith was taking them. But she loved him, and he needed to do this, and she must help him. Somehow she managed to say, calmly, "As I said before, I'd like to have my money back, if you please, Captain Grayson."

He drew his dressing gown tighter around him and stood at attention, the candle in his hand lighting his gaze to a glitter. Jane felt the touch of that gaze on her face like a flame passing by, too swift to burn.

Keith herded master and servant into the library. He ordered Daniel to make some light. The man stirred the banked fire and threw on two fresh, dry logs. The captain looked at the masked man threatening him with his pistol, then went to his desk. "The girl's purse is in here."

Jane had searched those drawers thoroughly just yesterday—but perhaps there was a secret compartment or a false bottom. She stepped around the desk to watch him.

"Jane—" Keith warned.

Moving much more quickly than she could have expected, the captain grabbed her wrist. He yanked her forward against him, so that the back of her head was pressed into his dressing gown. She could see Keith, but she couldn't get free; the captain held her with one hand that squeezed her throat with frightening power. Too late she realized that in his other hand he had one of his dueling pistols. She felt the tip of its barrel against her temple.

She felt his voice rumble against the back of her head. "Drop your gun!"

In the long, silent pause which followed, she watched Keith's hesitation. "Go," she said, forcing her throat to move against the captain's constricting fingers.

She felt rather than saw him smile his thin and cruel smile. He said, "It is fully cocked, as you can see, and made to discharge at the least quiver of my finger."

"Go—save yourself."

The barrel of the pistol pushed into her temple, warning her to be silent. She winced. Keith stood absolutely motionless before her. She saw that quivering immobility, intense and mute, like a flame where there was no wind. Go, she thought.

"Drop your weapon!" The captain's fingers dug deeper into the sides of her throat; his pistol barrel bruised the delicate skin of her temple.

Still Keith hesitated, until another minute of dead silence elapsed.

"You will let her die?"

Jane felt the white heat of the captain's growing rage. She strained now and again, but these efforts were of no great magnitude. She daren't really struggle.

"Let her go, Father."

The mesmeric spell was broken. The unexpected voice rasped along her taut nerves. Burne. She saw him place himself between Keith and his father. His teeth were bared in what was not intended to be a smile. He came around the desk and his hand grasped the captain's wrist. His deep, husky voice said: "Let her go."

"What are you doing!"

Jane couldn't breathe. The captain's hand was

nearly strangling her. And that barrel tip seemed like a cannon at her head.

"Let her go."

Here was will meeting strong will and finding its match. Burne's hand on Captain Grayson's wrist knotted with power. The captain resisted with all his strength. But whatever force fought in Burne, whatever blaze glowed in his chest, it made him, in the end, the stronger. The pistol lifted away from Jane's temple a quarter of an inch, an inch. Should the captain pull the trigger, however, she would still die, before she could even flinch. She dared not move.

"Burne! You fool!" The captain's voice was choked, forgetting its angry edge in some other emotion—wonder perhaps. Or perhaps simply defeat. In another instant, he gave way. Burne took the pistol from him and at the same time Jane wrenched out of his grasp. She rushed to Keith, to be taken into his arms.

The captain stumbled to the nearest chair. He slumped down and stared at the floor, seemingly broken.

Chapter Twenty-nine

Hangman's Rope, Six Pence an Inch

Burne went to the bookshelves directly behind Captain Grayson's desk. He pulled out *Robinson Crusoe* and half-a-dozen other volumes, revealing a secret cupboard. He opened it and brought out a lady's velvet purse. Jane didn't recognize it. He said, "I believe this is yours." She took it. It was weighted. She slipped her fingers into the satin interior and drew out ten guineas, nine shillings, and four pence.

She glanced at the captain. "This isn't mine."

Burne said, "That's what Stella said she found on you."

She shook her head. "I had a sort of belt, with the coins knotted into it—and over seventy guineas." Odd how she'd been willing to forget her money rather than take the risk of her and Keith's lives, yet now that the risk was taken, she wanted what was hers back as much as ever.

Burne said, "I'm afraid then, Jane, that Stella must have made her escape at your expense. Perhaps she knew you would forgive her."

Jane *couldn't* forgive her. She looked at Burne angrily. But his eyes were on Keith. His tongue flicked across his lips. "You're the highwayman who shot Hart Baywood?"

Keith, still wearing his mask, didn't answer, but only nodded sharply.

"Is Stella safe?"

"I believe so."

The shadow of a shadow crossed Burne's face. "You didn't help her and Baywood elope?"

"I would have if they'd needed help. They didn't."

As Burne stared at him, Keith pulled down his mask. There was that long blood-dark wound along his jaw, too deep to be a simple scratch, Jane saw now; he'd been grazed by the shot the corporal had got off.

He and his brother continued to stare at one another like two strangers who thought they knew each other yet couldn't quite think where their acquaintance had been established. They searched one another's faces to find those small friends from a youth of long ago, two boys who had found and liked one another even before they made the happy discovery that they were brothers.

"Keith." Burne's voice held his grief for all that might have been. In Keith, that sadness had long ago hardened into something else. Temperamentally, they were as different as could be: Burne with his snug, convivial life; and Keith with his insecure and gravely dangerous one. Burne with his reputation for wit—and Keith with *his* reputation. Burne's love for Grayson House which had taken out of him all daring and put in its place the desire to have his future guaranteed. And Keith's desire to kill his love for this same house, a desire which had forced him to boldness, to cunning, and had erected in him the aim to need nothing and no one.

"You." This from Captain Grayson, who also was looking at Keith now with sad recognition.

Daniel stared from the captain to Burne to Keith, his mouth open. Each corner of this triangle was handsome, straight, powerful of frame and fine of feature. Anyone with eyes could see the strong likeness between them. To Jane, however, the shock of that likeness was past, and she had come to see the three as not alike at all. A mere family resemblance, that was the extent of it.

Burne said finally, "You'd better go now. There will be no report of this visit to anyone." Hearing that, Jane thought perhaps not all of Burne's daring was lost.

One of Keith's arms was about her. She felt his magnificent strength. He still held his pistol in his free hand, and kept it ready as he ushered her toward the door. Daniel remained crowded into the corner he'd retreated to earlier, showing all his gums in a mad smile. Captain Grayson remained slouched in his purple robe, round-shouldered, scowling straight ahead at nothing, an aging, discontented, sleepy-eyed squire. As Jane and Keith passed his chair, he looked up at the last instant. Father and son looked into each other's eyes. Jane saw that there was nothing between them, no bond and no desire for a bond.

"Jane." She turned at the door. Burne crossed the room to her. His warm fingers lifted her cool ones; she felt the brush of his courtly kiss. "I'll always regret that I didn't stop them from taking you this morning. I wanted to save you myself—you wouldn't believe the wild ideas and thoughts I had racing through my head. And yet, in the end, I couldn't even tell you good-bye."

"Because you couldn't feel certain that I was not what they said." She tilted her head to study him. "You're not sure even now."

After a moment he said, "I'm not a brave man."

434

He stepped back, relinquishing all his feelings for her, giving her back to Keith. "Good luck," he said, "to you both."

Rooks cawed up out of the naked oaks as Eclipse galloped down the gravel drive. Jane looked back at the bulking shadow that was Grayson House. Part of Keith was in it, some part of his soul—if he had any.

And part of hers as well. She could have loved Burne Grayson. In her mind she could articulate some love for him even now. She could define it: why she loved him, and how. But it seemed that around her heart that wordless warmth and pain that was true passion was all for Keith Soloman, bastard son, Keith Cutler, highwayman.

She turned away from Grayson House, and faced forward again, and trained her eyes on the road ahead. Dawn was glimmering behind her in the east. The sky had cleared. Like the slow sound of a great gong, yellow sunlight swelled over the land. A new day was beginning.

Keith took her to the farm of the Baywood family. Hart's brother recognized Keith by his horse—and his pistols. The family owed him a debt for the life of their eldest son—yet he was a highwayman and their fear of him was palpable.

That being so, it was his money that persuaded them to feel indebted to him and to take in and hide the pair of them. It was an hour past dawn when Mr. Baywood, his cheeks bristling and sagging, showed them where they could bed down in the barn. The broken planks which formed the loft had become separated. Wisps of dry, aromatic hay hung drooping down between them. Jane and Keith climbed up into this hay and made a nest, and with a blanket from the house to cover them, sank into sleep.

Sheltered by Keith's chest and arms, Jane slept most of the day. In the late afternoon, he woke her. "Jane," he whispered, soft as spidersilk. His mouth sought hers. A little confused and disoriented from sleep, she fought the painful emotion that rose in her uncalled and unwanted. He opened her dress and kissed the tips of her breasts until they were as hard as cherry stones. He lifted her skirts and prized open the soft petals of her flesh. With his brutal hands he caressed her tenderly until she almost wept in fearful expectation. At last he rose over her, between her thighs, forcing them far apart, and she was pinned by his crushing weight as he breached her tender entrance.

He went into her like a dagger-thrust and delivered himself of a rush of passion. And through it all, she sobbed in ecstasy.

He closed his eyes again with his hand clasped between her legs, gripping her dark-tressed mound. The relaxation of his grip told her when he fell asleep again. She lay awake looking at the wound along his cheek. It would leave a scar.

As night fell, Mr. Baywood and his dame brought them food and clothing. For Jane there was a faded, rose-colored skirt and bodice, a green shawl, and a full mob to contain her hair. Keith was to dress like a common laborer in rough tunic and breeches. He made a bundle of his jackboots and pistols and black greatcoat. The farmer and his wife kept looking at him. Mr. Baywood's color was better, less pallid, now that -he was about to say goodbye to these awkward guests.

He dared to say, "You're Laurel Solomon's son."

Of course they would have known Keith's mother, who had grown up in this district.

"You look just like Burne," Dame Baywood said.

436

Keith neither claimed nor disclaimed the relationship.

"Stella talked about you once," Dame Baywood went on. "She come to nurse me and help take care of the menfolk when I was sick years back. That's how she and Hart come to know each other. She's a kind bit of a lass. Aye, I'd have perished but for her kindness. But she was that afraid of her father."

"They both were. Wouldn't even tell us where they were going. I wish we knew," Mr. Baywood said in a flat, tired voice. "Do you know, sir?"

Keith said he didn't.

"Hart will send word. And maybe one day, when the captain's gone, they can come back."

Jane's need to leave England was as great as ever. Keith arranged to rent the Baywoods' farm cart. He would leave Eclipse with them until he could return for the horse. Hart's brother said he knew of a place where the animal could be kept out of sight. Jane saw that it was difficult for Keith to part with his faithful stallion, though all he said was, "The horse should be worked."

They left the farm under the merest silver knife-edge of a moon. They traveled in a dead, incredible silence, as if the darkness itself were deaf. Keith kept off the main highway and they met no one, in particular no one who was looking for them. Without a lantern, they bumped over a rough track through fern and bracken.

After a short rest in the morning, they continued. Their road wound through peaceful and wooded dales. There was still no discussion of where they were going. Keith took her toward Bristol slowly, without speaking of it, weaving between towns, northward and southward of the way to avoid any search for a murderess and her highwayman.

She grew weary sitting on the unsprung oxcart's bench. It was a small vehicle, its bed set high over thick

437

wheels. As noon approached, she hardly noted the crossroads ahead, in the middle of which stood a gibbet.

Keith saw it first. He got down to lead the ox lest the scent of the dead man hanging from his rope agitate the beast. Jane saw it now. She looked from it to Keith.

His means of travel and his clothing marked him as a laborer, but she saw the flashing opal ring on the hand that pulled at the animal's bridle. She knew who he was, what he was, how he would end.

Their progress brought them closer to the gibbet. The corpse had been on display for only a day or two and so was not rotted yet. The body had belonged to a young man. It had long black hair. The thick hemp rope held the head at an angle from the drooping shoulders. As they came closer, a boy Jane hadn't seen before darted forward with a knife and a length of rope in his hands, thick hemp rope. He trotted beside the cart shouting, "Hangman's rope, sixpence an inch!"

The dangling man knew nothing of this. Neither did he feel the eyes that passed by his corpse. The breeze stirred his long ebony hair.

Keith snarled at the boy, "Get!" At the same time he yanked on the ox's line. Jane grabbed the cart's bench as the vehicle jerked beneath her. She clutched her shawl about her and tried to keep her eyes turned from the hanging figure, yet she must pass very close by it. No need to hide from the truth: she forced herself to look directly at the gently swinging corpse.

Her high seat put her nearly on a level with the dead face. The felon's features were blue. His eyes were wide open. What color had they been? Had someone loved him? Was there a woman whose breasts he had considered with his hands, a woman he had bound down with his weight and held her and separated her and entered her, a woman into whom he had poured his passions while she lay subdued by naught but a heartbreaking spell from which there was no deliverance?

As the afternoon waned, a chill wind came and swept the sky clean for the oncoming darkness. The road ahead curled up over a hill and disappeared. The ox-cart creaked and groaned over the crest and traveled down the other side into an abandoned village of broken, roofless stone huts. The lurching wheels sank into chuckholes and heaved out of them again. Jane felt as if she'd sat on this narrow bench for weeks.

The only inhabitant of the ghostly hamlet seemed to be a woman who occupied the poorest sort of a cot, built half into a mountainside, of whatever materials had lain to hand—stones, broken timbers, turfs, all sealed together with daub. The frame of a box was inserted as a window, curtained with burlap. The door had been taken from a stable. The top section was open. The upper half of the woman who lived there was framed within this door section as Keith led the ox, the cart, and Jane, up the slope to her.

The woman had the long, thick, pale blond hair of a girl, and like a girl she wore it loose. But her face was a careworn old woman's. Her eyes burned as if with fever. Her clothes were clean, though as ragged as the poorest beggar's, and the form which they covered was emaciated.

Keith muttered to Jane, "What do you think? That she's just a little out of charity with her neighbors?" He gestured to the abandoned cottages of the hamlet.

However odd the situation, night was coming, and it boded a late frost. They needed shelter, a fire, a place to rest.

"May we come in for the night?" he called to the woman. "We can pay for your hospitality."

The woman's feverish eyes stared back at him. Then they moved to Jane. At last she said, "If that's what

439

thou desires.'' She showed no great eagerness. though she opened the lower half of the door.

Keith helped Jane down then drove the cart on behind the hovel. Jane went inside alone.

A turf fire glimmered on the hearth of the single chamber. The warmth it generated was inadequate, considering the drafts coming in between the rough walls. As her eyes became accustomed in the gloom, she registered the extreme squalor. Rags of what were once garments hung from a cord bisecting the room. The bed was a crude board frame with a sackcloth blanket laid over a heap of crushed bracken. Cracked pieces of wood roughly pegged together did service as a stool. A single blackened pot seemed to be the sole kitchen vessel.

She avoided the fanatical, perhaps lunatic, glint in the woman's eyes. She had heard of such destitution, but had never before been inside such a dwelling. She restrained herself from the least display either of surprise or distaste, and sat down on the rough stool.

Outside, Keith staked the ox out to graze for the night within the remains of a church cemetery where long grass grew between the hillocks of the graves. He was struck again by the image he had pushed down all afternoon: the empty look in the colorless eyes of the dead man. The sight had affected him. What had Jane thought? She hadn't said, yet her silence seemed to shout, this is how you will end, Keith Cutler.

He fingered the scab along his cheek. She was changed. She still smiled at him, and kissed him if he insisted. But her eyes seemed to be seeing something else. Not him at all. Jealousy was growing in him like a forbidding cloud. Jealousy not of a man, but of a place: Georgia.

Georgia Colony dominated her now. Her thoughts

were all in the West. It had taken her over. He felt lonely in her presence.

She came out of the hovel as he was getting their blankets out of the cart. She looked calm and lovely, wrapped in Dame Baywood's tattered shawl and mobcap. She said, "There is very little food inside; you should bring in the ham the Baywoods gave us."

She turned, meaning to go back in. He caught her arm and pulled her very near, near enough to see the veins tracing blue under her moon white skin. "Jane, what would you think about marrying me?"

She stared at him for a long moment, and he saw what her answer was going to be before she even spoke. He saw it and his heart hung on every word. At last she said it aloud: "Everything's all wrong, Keith."

He nodded curtly, dropped his hold on her arm, and turned to get the ham out of the cart.

She started back for the hovel. For all her evident calm, she was confused and reeling inside. Her response had come unbidden. Marry him? Hadn't he come this far only out of his sense of responsibility to her? No. There was no use in pretending to herself that his deeds had risen out of pure loyalty, a sense of accountability, mere friendship. He loved her. Yet she had never expected a proposal from him. Even less had she expected that she could decline it. Yet now it was done. Belatedly, she felt the sudden sledgehammer blow of it.

She examined what had gone through her mind in that dreadful instant before she'd said no: that she loved him, too; that she ached with wanting to say Yes!

But he would not be a restful mate. Whenever he took it in his head to run wild, nothing in the world would prevent him.

And finally, he would not go to Georgia. And as her husband, he would not let her go.

441

It was getting dark fast, and she must set her feet with care not to stumble over the scattered remains of a rough stone wall. This place was bleak, full of whispering wind. Before she ducked back into the hovel, she looked westward. A little light lingered there, reflected up above the intervening hills. She imagined that it was reflected up by the ocean. She was close to it now.

She glanced back, but couldn't see Keith for the darkness. Darkness, she thought, was his element.

In the dove gray twilight of morning, Jane first glimpsed the distant line of the sea. She and Keith were both walking in silence, the ox separating them. Their lane plunged down into a dale. When it came up again, there was the water once more.

Nearer at hand lay the wide expanse of the Severn River, clear, reflecting the meringue rims of the clouds with sharp points of light. Ripples licked the long, coarse grass of the bank. From her vantage, Jane could see the river widen and widen into the Bristol Channel, with all the sky over it. Unwitting, she stopped and stared westward with sudden longing.

Keith pulled the ox to a stop in the middle of the rough track and stood watching her. They were both rather stiff and careful with each other today. A profound emotion between two people involved, after all, the power and chance of doing profound hurt. It wouldn't have occurred to her until last night that she could wound Keith Cutler.

Did he know what she was thinking? He knew her better than anyone—but did he understand how her heart had hardened even as her mind had mended? She'd been all in fragments, disintegrated. But then she'd found some strength left entire in her. The

442

strength of her plan. Georgia had been one of the first things she'd remembered. Now she was almost at the end of her long, hard journey, and this glimpse of the sea brought a rush of relief.

She smiled at Keith, suddenly grateful to him for everything. She could never repay him, except perhaps the money he would loan her for her transport to Georgia. She could send that back to him one day. But for risking his life to save hers—how could she ever repay that?

They went down into the gentler grass slopes of the coastal region. Their road took them close by the long Severn. Feeling it was safe, given their disguises, they passed through Glouchester, a bustling market center that had once been the Roman fortified town of Glevum. Jane remembered this from her lessons with Mr. Welby. Amazing what she could remember now! More amazing was how her memories could ever have slipped from her. Though less than a week had passed since her recovery, already she was losing a clear grasp of what it had been like to be a stranger to herself. Soon that period would seem perfectly absurd to her, she wouldn't believe it had happened but had surely been only a dream.

Their way was a curving avenue unfolding views of green fields, rolling downlands, scattered gray barns, with always, always, the shining, widening channel at its heart. Sheep grazed the lush meadows. Cattle rested in the shade. This was a well-farmed area, with thousands of acres of flatland. Stone humpbacked bridges crossed the myriad network of little watercourses. The peace was almost palpable.

They rode through the quaint, steep streets of Stroud, an old town of timbered, black-and-white houses. Though there were inns where hot food could be had, Jane felt a dread of being looked at too closely.

443

She'd come to fear her own face. Hence, they rested the ox and ate a cold dinner by a yew hedge.

They went on a few more miles under an evening sky of pinkish yellow, then slept under the stars on the banks of the Severn, making their bed in the back of the cart.

The sun woke them. Today would take them into Bristol.

Bristol was a great port city, second only to London, an ancient city, deeply soaked in history. It had grown up around its harbor on the River Avon. The Saturday evening streets were full, though a muslin mist was creeping up from the waterside. Everywhere were people, benighted, contentious, passionate, ignorant beings. Gray gulls wheeled and darted overhead, producing raucous noises.

On a better day it might have seemed to Jane a gay, lively place, but in her weary state, it seemed noisy, filthy, evil-smelling, and full of thuglike strangers. The looseness of the morality struck her immediately. She and Keith passed two men singing a ballad of the most scurrilous character. And there seemed to be lewd women enough to furnish a colony of their own.

"The sailors who come in and out all the time draw them, I suppose," Keith said. As he spoke, he touched the livid new scar on his face, a habit he was acquiring.

There were sailors in abundance. The channel was full of great moored fleets, merchant vessels sitting plumply on the soft waves, from Holland, Hamburg, and Norway, from the cold coasts of the New World and the warm waters of the Mediterranean. And besides the merchant sailors, there were squat, barrel-chested local fishermen. Jane spied a Quaker lady going about among them, trying to gently bring a few of them to God, not an easy task, she assumed. The cart passed a bagnio—a steambath and sweating place for gentlemen who needed to recover from their debaucheries. A group of soldiers were staggering toward it now, after what must have been a riotous afternoon.

Jane daren't gawp and stare as much as she'd like to. Keith advised her to remain in the cart with her shawl pulled over her head while he went into an inn. She heard his voice just inside the door: "Bring me the landlord!"

Someone reached up and grasped her wrist. "You look like you need a man, sweetheart." An aging sailor. His face was split by a grin that revealed gaps between his teeth. His open collar showed withered neck flesh.

"Go away." A pair of soldiers strolled by, and with a panicky anxiety, Jane turned her face away from them.

The sailor still had her wrist. "Come now, sweetie, I'm willing to pay. 'Tis a few easy pence for ye, and no trouble, I warrant." He was smiling like an aging conqueror. "Ye'll like what I've got for ye."

"My husband is just inside; you'd better let go of me."

The sailor's withered lips compressed, but then he suddenly let go and shoved off. She saw why. Two fellows of what Captain Grayson would call "the brutal lower population" were beginning to fight out some disagreement on the street. A crowd rapidly gathered and began to lay bets—including a prosperous-looking parson in his robe and bands.

The two burly figures were still slugging it out when Keith came back for Jane. "Why are there so many soldiers wandering about?" she murmured as he helped her down.

He looked up and down the street, as if just now noticing that the town was full of scarlet coats. "They must police the smuggling hereabouts. They probably

445

have no barracks to go to—they're usually billeted in alehouses, and mostly unwelcome everywhere, so they're out on the streets a lot. Come on, let's get you inside."

There was an air of authority on him now. It was very clear that she must depend on him to protect her in this city of soldiers and brazen sailors. He would have to make arrangements for her while she stayed concealed. It was ironic that of the two of them, he was the true criminal, yet because he'd gone about his felonies behind a mask, she was the one more at risk.

Inside the Beadnell Inn, a stout woman in a big apron was on her knees washing the stone floor of the entrance. Keith took Jane past her into the wide, stone parlor where a blazing log fire was launching flames and embers into the broad chimney. The roof beams were dark with smoke. It was a big, steaming-hot room full of food and people and a stew of voices, full of strange eyes who looked at the newcomers. Jane moved closer to Keith for what concealment his shoulder could provide.

He led her up a flight of worn stone stairs to a narrow, timbered passageway on the second floor.

Chapter Thirty

These Would Be Their Last Days Together

Keith leaned out to pull the shutters closed, and the silence of their chamber in the Beadnell Inn left Jane feeling assaulted by the noise she'd suffered on the streets of Bristol. A lamp on a central table lit the room but dimly. She looked at the bed. They had spoken very little during the journey. And they had touched less.

A big-boned manservant came in behind them bearing a pitcher of hot water and a bucket of cold for them to wash off the dust of the road. As soon as he was gone, and before the hot water could lose its steam, Jane peeled off her shawl and bodice, unlaced her chemise and lowered it to her waist. As she washed, Keith came behind her. His hands circled her bare torso. In an instant, she realized how much she'd wanted him to do just that, to touch her intimately, to comfort her. He murmured, "Come here wi' ye, lass." She felt instantly dizzy with longing, and leaned back into his embrace. She turned in his arms, and her head fell back as he lowered his head to lick the warm drops of water from her dripping breasts.

He undressed her. Each garment he unfastened and pulled off felt like a layer of fatigue being pulled away. He laid her on the bed and undressed himself. His muscles shone in the lamplight. He looked down on her and faltered, but not for long: these would be their last days together, the last days and nights of their painful journey.

Still there were no words of any significance between them, just the susurration of their breathing. Jane felt in the caress of his hands the endless number of events they had shared. It was so easy to think, as he kissed her, that he would always be here to love her like this, that he would always be with her. It was hard to believe it would soon be over, that their love would become just another event in her past, something met, experienced, lived through, and finally left behind.

Their bodies moved and turned and locked. She embraced him wildly. His eyes were narrow, as if he were peering into the sun. As a pair of tambourines began to jing-jing-jingle on the street below, he took her.

How did he do it? How did his body dissolve hers into this ecstasy? How did he deliver all of heaven to her closed eyes? He was a highwayman, a thief, a felon, a criminal, and this ability he possessed was surely an unmerited grace.

He took her with an increasingly driven rhythm, demanding more and more, and ultimately claiming all. Time stopped and the world ended in pure beauty.

Afterward, he kissed her once gently, and again, very gently. They slept for an hour, side by side facing one another, spent but still entangled. They woke gradually. Keith's fingers sought the scar of the bullet that had gone through his side, kneading it as if it pained him. He said, "We ought to wed, you know."

The words startled Jane completely awake. She looked at him wonderingly, reproachfully.

448

He himself seemed surprised that he'd brought the subject up again. But the words, now uttered, accumulated substance. "We could buy a little farm, live a simple life. A place with some hop fields and an orchard of apples. I could do some fishing."

She stretched back from him. "And what about me? How would I hide who I am?"

"We could find someplace where you aren't known." He smiled a sword's edge smile. He could be a cordial devil; it was a role he played with skill, a master by experience. He pulled her beneath him and gave her a long, lazy kiss.

She felt a new flare of desire. Oh, she loved him. And she knew he loved her. But she believed it was from their differences, not from any affinities and likenesses, but from the differences that this love between them arose. And it was only a bridge, only a bridge across what divided them. His admission that he loved her did not so much admit more light into their relationship as it showed the extent of the darkness.

With effort, she broke away, and made her voice friendly and logical. "I can't stay in England, Keith. There is no way open to me but one."

"I could keep you here." His voice, so soothing a moment before, suddenly sounded ominous. "I could. What could you do about it? Who could you apply to for aid?" His arms tightened around her, daring her to try to escape him. "Who do you have besides me, Jane?"

She stared at him with all her heart in her eyes. "Why are you saying these things?"

"I mean them." He leaned over her, as poised as a bird—a falcon, an eagle.

She swung her head from side to side on the pillow, a battered, head-against-the-wall movement. "You don't. We both know you don't."

He hovered motionless.

"I'm not afraid of you anymore, Keith."

"I'm glad." Icy light seeped from those dark eyes.

"I can't stay here. There's no place in England where I can hide for long."

Silence.

"But you could go with me to Georgia."

There was no respite from his stare. The mark along his jaw was healing into a scar; it would age his face. A long, long moment passed. Suddenly plaintive, defeated, hurt, he said, "Are you really going then, Jane?"

In the morning, Keith, known to the innkeeper as Mr. Diamond, left the Beadnell Inn after he and "Mistress Diamond" had shared breakfast in their chamber. A cold, disappointing meal. He found it ironic that they were posing as a married couple, a man and a woman who had woven their lives together, just when Jane refused to marry him.

The sunlight in the streets was cold. Soldiers strutted everywhere as if they owned the city. Keith squinted against the brightness of the morning. He had put aside his laborer's clothes in favor of his black jackboots and greatcoat, but he had no fear of being recognized here. He could do all that was needed of tramping around in Jane's behalf. It frustrated her to have to depend upon him—she didn't want to take anything from him—which made him angry. He let loose a curse so vile it surprised even him.

He would have no trouble getting her everything she needed for her fool's voyage. Bristol's shops marketed goods of all kinds, from abroad as well as from England, and Keith had the money for them; he had plenty of money.

England. Home. How could she leave it? And not for a time, not for a month or a year, but forever. She was going to do it, though, that much he'd finally realized. It had taken him a good enough while. All the time he'd been falling ragingly in love with her she'd been bearing her vision in her mind, keeping it before her like a grail. When she'd lost herself with her memory, it had been Georgia she recalled first, even before she'd recalled him.

America! Why, the Americans employed naked colored slaves to wait upon them; they kidnapped Scotsmen, Hollanders, and Welshmen and sold them for slaves, too; they were planning to discard the English language and adopt Hebrew instead. Everyone knew these things. He cursed Jane again, to the blackest perdition. She would drive a saint to murder.

If leaving England—leaving him—to travel across a wilderness of water and stars was what she wanted, fine! He was angry enough that he felt he wanted the separation, too. Why even stay with her until she left? He would, for old time's sake, get her passage and buy her the things she needed—but then he could leave, and with no twinge of conscience. There was no need of them holding each other in the Beadnell's soft, lumpy bed again. He was done with coaxing her to give herself completely to him only to have her take herself back the minute their bodies separated.

And it only got worse the longer it went on.

He shouted in frustration: none of the sound came out of his mouth. It collided upon itself inside his chest and head. He drew himself up, tugged his greatcoat into order, and strode along, looking glassily ahead.

A pair of begrimed children, clad in rags, offered him a handbill. He took it and would have strode on, but the urchins blocked his way. The intensity of their stares was magnified by the rings of dirt around their

451

eyes. He realized what they wanted, and tossed each of them a penny.

The handbill was cheaply printed:

*At the Chapel of the Red Mitre
three streets from King Lane
Marriages performed without interference
by Reverend Mr. Clayton
schooled at Cambridge
and former chaplain to an Earl.*

Keith merely glanced at it before he tossed it away. He knew exactly what kind of reverend this Clayton was—the sort who married a lower-class clientele of sailors, and the occasional young aristocratic couple who wanted to wed without the knowledge of their parents. The more hardened of these scoundrels provided professional husbands who would wed any pregnant girl in a rush, often two or three in a single year. Some would go so far as to marry two lesbians, a bigamist, even victims of force.

Despite Keith's black mood, it took him only half the day to find a ship going to Georgia. Even luckier, the *Andrew Buck* was an American ship, mostly concerned with transporting goods. It had only three cabins for passengers. All this was to the benefit of a woman trying to leave England quietly.

Keith had himself rowed out into the swelling harbor to secure Jane's passage. The story he told Captain James Kimberlee was that a lady friend, Mistress Tomin, had lost her parents and was going to her brother in the colonies. As Keith spoke, he touched the pink shining scar on his jaw.

Captain Kimberlee was more concerned with the man who was waiting to speak to him about shipping ten tons of Parson's Best Beer for the benefit of Georgia's residents. He listened to Keith's story impatiently, doing no more than to insert an occasional word of agreement, and of course to accept the fee for Jane's passage.

This tale of bereavement had the advantage of allowing Jane to wear mourning clothes. The black veils would hide her face when she boarded the ship, and even perhaps protect her from too much notice by the crew during the journey. Though why Keith should care about that, he didn't know. Once she left Bristol, the devil take her! Let every sailor on the ship have his chance to bring that dazed, sensual expression to her beautiful face. Let Captain Kimberlee himself remove all her clothes—everything! and make her lie stripped on his bed while he touched her everywhere. Let him wake in the night and smell her special scent and reach out to find her full breasts and soft thighs available to him.

Keith felt a need to taunt himself in this way. Even though he'd never loved anyone as much as he loved Jane, he needed to believe that he could let her go, that he could even look forward to her going.

What a fool you are, Keith Cutler. Why can you never rest your heart on a possible thing?

He took care to arrange for her to occupy a cabin alone, though it cost the same as for two passengers. He paid the extra, because he knew she would want her privacy. She wouldn't want anyone to see those faint marks on her back, for instance. That would mortify her intensely. Yes, despite the anger and the hurt that kept erupting in him like hot lava, he took care of everything for her with unbelievable thoroughness and accuracy and regard.

This most distasteful business done with, he left Kimberlee's cabin and went up on the white sanded deck. He tried to imagine Jane here. It pained him.

Yet it was a sound ship, as far as he knew anything about ships. He felt the rhythm of its seaworthiness in its pitching, which came up through the deck into the bones of his legs.

As the day ended, he walked along the shore of the channel and looked west where the bright sun was nesting. The gold was veined with gushes of crimson. As the burning ball sank down, it seemed to sizzle until it was quenched by the ocean. The wind off the water grew increasingly crisp. Once Keith would have enjoyed a lonely moment like this, needing nothing else, no one else, to make it complete. Now, he only wished that Jane were here to see it with him.

What was he going to do without her?

What he'd been doing before, of course!

But there was nothing on Earth he wanted to do now, outside of being with her. He loved her. She had opened his eyes to a possibility that had always seemed beyond him: that he could love a woman, that he could want to marry and have a family and make a home for them, to have children and rear them with all the fatherly affection he'd been denied. They say rakish men seldom make gentle fathers, but he would be gentle. He knew he had it in him to be gentle. He was always gentle with Jane.

He'd been walking west along the beach, toward the mouth of the channel. Soon he came to a place where jagged rocks blocked his way. He stooped to pick up a stick of driftwood. He wrote Jane's name upon the strand, but the rising tide came and washed it away.

It had always been her intention only to pass through his life. Yet in doing so she had left him changed. He didn't want to live alone anymore. From the night he'd first seen her, her white cap giving her away in the dark on the road, everything he'd done had centered around her. It had happened so quickly, so intensely,

454

that he was thrown into confusion, even despair, to realize she really did mean to leave him.

How could she do that when she'd made him care, not only about her but about himself, about whether he lived or died? One of the first things Georgie Moraga had taught him back in Bridewell was that the highwayman who cares if he lives or dies usually dies.

An increasingly tense, restless demand spread through him as he stood there watching the tide come up closer and closer to the toes of his jackboots. Maybe he hadn't been bluffing last night. Maybe he really wouldn't let her go. He could take her to Scotland for a few years. Or to France. No one would know her there. He could trick her into it somehow.

Let her go, a voice said. *You have no claim on her.*

He could arrange for that reverend who drummed up business by circulating handbills to marry them. The man would conveniently ignore Jane's unwillingness.

He rejected that idea. It was too ridiculous.

It refused to go away.

But it was too outrageous. Wasn't it?

It kept returning, wheeling in his mind, as sinuous as a circling silver fish. He had a sensation of spinning, blinded by love and daring.

No, it was too inglorious. Too absurd.

Why didn't he have more experience with women? Why did his feelings get involved every time he tried to think what to do? Was it his pride that was suffering? He felt an inner hollowness, and a serious lack of wisdom.

A wave crashed in over the beach, and the water hissed as it dragged itself back to sea. He turned away from the wine dark ocean and started toward the city through the misty blue twilight. He had just over a week until the *Andrew Buck* set sail. In that time, he must make up his mind on some plan. Or prepare himself to lose Jane forever.

A candle cast its light into the trunk that took up much of the space in the small chamber. Jane finished folding into it a walking dress, which was the last of the clothes Keith had purchased for her. She lowered the curved lid on it and all the other things packed away inside: lengths of cloth for future clothes, packets of vegetable seeds for a garden, a few books—as many items as they had been able to think of that she might need in a new and rough world. All bought with the spoils of a highwayman's dark deeds. There was even a purse of coins. He'd gathered from his movements about Bristol that English coinage was scarce and precious in America.

Already sent to the ship was one hundred guineas worth of English commodities. He'd taken care to buy all sorts of implements, ironwork, and utensils such as were necessary for plantations, along with bolts of English cloth goods—stuffs, baize, and wools—all rumored to be valuable in the colonies. Jane could sell them to great advantage, maybe even five times their worth here, giving her the means to start a in modest way of trade, or farming, or whatever else she might choose to do. He'd been generous, her highwayman.

She was due to board the *Andrew Buck* in the morning. This was her last night in England. Her last night with Keith. As she finished packing, she sensed his mind was elsewhere. He was brooding again.

A knock came at the door, and the now familiar big-boned manservant passed in two pints of beer Keith had ordered. She took hers and he held up his own. "To America," he said, leaning with his back to the door, "and a new life."

456

She perched herself gingerly on the tall bed. She felt there were double and shadow messages in his words. He'd been acting very odd these nine days since they'd arrived in Bristol. Very odd indeed. Sometimes he was sunk in a mood so black and dangerous that she daren't even speak to him. Sometimes he was so euphoric that she wondered about his sanity. Then again she sometimes caught him giving her a look of sly cunning. (Though she would never say it, that look was so much like his father's that she almost shivered; she hated to see anything of the peevish, ill-tempered Thomas Grayson in her beloved Keith.) And yet again it might be a look of abject pain that she glimpsed in his face, like grief, a sharp, precise agony.

She lifted her pint of beer. "To America."

He drained his tankard, wiped the wintry smile on his mouth, and sprawled again in his chair. "Tell me once more now, Innocent, how you're going to live once you get there? An unprotected woman among the transports from the London prisons." This was another mood, spiteful and barbed.

She fought back. "You were in a prison."

He nodded agreeably. His teeth were very nearly clenched tight, but he still smiled. "I was. I went in a boy of high ideals and noble intentions, and came out . . ." That clenched smile! "More thieves and rogues are made in prison than by all the leagues and societies of villains in the country. But we aren't talking about me; we're talking about you, about how you intend to live in your New World."

"I don't know, Keith."

"You don't know how you'll live." His matter-of-factness was utterly false.

"I know that it will be an honest life." She wasn't above spite herself when he got like this. "And I know

457

that it can't possibly be any more unpleasant than some of the episodes I've lived through in the recent past."

He pretended to take this in good humor. "What episodes would those be? The ones you spent in my company?" He stared at her with his predator's eyes.

She put her tankard on the table; she'd lost her thirst. "Keith, I don't want to argue, not tonight."

He smiled hugely. "Fine. What do you want to do then, Mistress Diamond?"

They had already dined on bread and a sixpence cut of meat. Keith had regularly passed the waiter an extra farthing so that they were always well served. Nonetheless, she was heartily tired of this room, of the Beadnell Inn, of being a virtual prisoner because of her own face. She'd watched Keith go out each day with envy. From the windows she'd followed him down the street, walking with that deft, definite grace, that keenness of being which defined him, and she'd felt envious of his freedom.

He'd brought in a *Gentleman's Magazine* several days ago, and she'd read everything in it twice. She now felt equipped to say what gentlemen were interested in, and exactly what they felt promoted the comfort of their households—which remedies, which culinary delights, which legal opinions, which political moves. She didn't want to read the *Gentleman's Magazine* again tonight, nor did she want to quarrel. She went to him suddenly, and sank down between his knees, her hands on his strong thighs, and she said, "Can't we just talk?"

"Of course. What shall we talk about?"

This glibness was a slick, hard covering against which she could only slide, without ever penetrating. All at once she was completely downcast. "I wish you would at least try to understand why I'm going."

"I understand completely."

"Then why are you so angry?"

458

He spread his hands in guiltlessness. "I'm not angry. Have I said a single angry word?"

This was maddening. But she must hold on to her patience. "I believe we each have to make the difference in our own lives, for ourselves. Do you understand that?"

He didn't respond right away. He made no move to touch her, as close as she was. He sat gazing at the candleflame that winked and was reflected from the two pewter tankards on the table. His answer, when it came, was not glib; it was suddenly intense—and full of all the anger he had a moment ago denied.

"And what about making a difference for each other? What about the fact that we've stood up for one another, you and I, and lied for one another, and shared our dreams, our secrets? I know everything about you, Jane Fitzpatrick, and I would marry you—but you're going to Georgia! Forgive me if I find it hard to believe you're going to do that, go off by yourself, instead of staying with me—when you know I love you!"

He took her face between his hands and stared deep into her eyes. There was a long minute, full of stars and eras, a waiting pause in time. At last he repeated fiercely, "I love you. I loved you from the moment I beheld you."

He'd never said it outright before. It struck her like a slap, bringing up feelings she hadn't realized she harbored. "If you love me then why are you letting me go alone!"

He stood abruptly, leaving her there on the floor sitting on her heels as he lashed out, "I just might not let you go at all!"

She felt a weight in the pit of her stomach. It took little more than the size of his voice when he was enraged to remind her that he was a man of inordinate strength. And no scruples to speak of. He had the kind of cold nerve it took to do whatever was necessary to make his point.

"Keith, what are you thinking of doing?"

He turned away from her, looked at the door—longingly, she thought. "Nothing."

"You did buy my passage, truly you did, didn't you?"

He stared at her over his shoulder for so long that she thought he wouldn't reply. Then he did. "You have your place on the ship, don't worry about that." But then he laughed, sharp and bitter.

"Then why do I feel you're planning something?"

He only looked at her—with a sort of vacancy in his eyes—then looked away. "I don't know."

"You are, aren't you? You're planning something, Keith. I've trusted you." She rose to her feet. "My life is at stake here. You can't toy with that." She put pleading into her voice, trying desperately to smooth his edgier and more hazardous urges. "I have to get out of England, you know I do. I have no choice. Please tell me what you're thinking of doing."

He answered after a long moment of silence. "I don't know what I'm going to do. Probably see you to the dock and wave goodbye—and seduce the very next woman I meet." He stood with his back to her, his fists clenched. "I'll pick the ugliest one I can find."

She dared to reach out and touch him. It was as if that touch pierced every shield. The moment seemed dream-slow—then blurringly fast as he turned on her. She jumped at the quickness of it. In one swift movement he pulled her into his arms. Arms made of iron. She didn't resist that iron embrace, but pulled his head down and kissed his mouth. They fell into the most racking kisses they had ever exchanged. There was no pleasure about them; rather, they were a torment which neither of them could stop. As they undressed each

460

other, there were more kisses, and broken, futile utterances.

Their bodies were hot against each other. His tongue flicked at the pink points of her breasts. When he lifted her and put her on the bed and parted her legs and kissed her more intimately, she urged him to take her.

He went into her, deeply, with violent jolts that shook her and satisfied her almost immediately.

Yet he held back.

She was content, drifting in that place of suspension between sleep and wakefulness. She felt him kissing her breasts again, nibbling the tiny stone of one nipple, and whispering, "You're so beautiful." He slid further down her body to run his hands between her legs and to kiss her there once more. Though she did not expect a repetition of her pleasure so soon, he roused her and made her cry out with a second climax of delight beneath his hands and tongue. And once more he took her, hard, making a sound of his own with each thrust, half snarl, half moan, and through all her limbs she felt a third scorching consummation.

And still, still, he held back. She thought she'd become accustomed to his appetites and moods. She didn't know this one. It seemed a truly wild landscape.

He suckled her breasts yet again with his very hot, wet mouth. He turned her over and kissed every scar on her back. She suffered the vague unease of that, and shivered at his touch, until he pulled her on top of him.

"Keith—"

"Please—this may be my last hour with you."

Dear God, what were they doing to one another? Love should not cause a man to be driven down into bitterness like this. Love shouldn't hurt as much as her heart was hurting. Pity for them both rose up in her,

461

and tenderness—tenderness flowed through her, a fiery sweetness she could almost taste.

She would be his for this hour. She would behave as if she were his wife, someone who belonged to him. As he urged her downward, as she settled onto him slowly, embedding him inside her, as she felt her breasts gathered by his strong kneading fingers, as she reveled in those unforgettable and ravishing sensations, she granted him the small yielding sounds he caused her to make. They were her gift to him, for what they were worth. They and the whispering song of her hands gliding over his skin, a song that seemed to chant, *We're parting forever. We're parting forever.*

At last his loins bucked upward and they both cried out together and he finally allowed himself to discharge his fiery passion into her—and then it was over. Muscle by muscle, he unknotted. Neither of them could say anything. This was the end, after all, and words were for beginnings.

Chapter Thirty-one

Go, lovely rose—

Edmond Waller: *Song*

Jane winked out like a candle. As swift as that. When she awoke again, it was very early, not yet dawn. The sky was barely beginning to gray into a foggy morning.

Keith was gone. All he had left behind was a note scrawled with the stub of a lead pencil. "Go without looking back."

She put on her mourning costume, a black dress of worsted and a hat with a black veil. At six o'clock, the manservant appeared with a breakfast tray for her. Fifteen minutes later, he and a fellow with a round, red, face came to carry her trunk down to a cart. These things Keith had arranged for her, knowing, without telling her, that he would not be there to escort her himself.

She left the Beadnell Inn. In the predawn fog, she saw nothing of Bristol from her seat next to the red-faced carter but a blue blur. The man's conversation was spectacularly skimpy—nonexistent, in fact. He made sounds with his mouth as though he were ruminating—what Jane termed "chewing his cud." She feared he was a bit simpleminded. Would he really deliver her at the dock?

The blue turned light gray, then a drizzly white. The carter did indeed deliver her at the dock. Here, she found again that all the necessary arrangements had been made for her. She could all but feel Keith's energy in the air.

Except that he wasn't there.

The carter stopped ruminating long enough to give a whistle. Someone whistled back, then shouted, "Ahoy!" Jane saw a sailor in a small boat waving through the fog. He was coming to take her and her trunk out to the *Andrew Buck*. She stepped off the dock into the rocking craft—and she did not look back.

Soon the dock was swallowed in drifting fog behind her. Gradually, out of the tumbling fog ahead, there loomed a seagoing ship. She was handed up to the deck. Through her black veil and the white mist, she saw several dirty, ragged sailors working at this and that. Her trunk was taken below by two of them, but she remained above.

The first thing that struck her about this vessel which would be her home for the next several months was the smell—fish, rum, salt, and the occasional sweaty shirt put in the sun to air.

The captain appeared, his lips crimped into a meager smile as he nodded in her direction, then he disappeared again. He seemed too busy to greet her properly, though he nodded in a harried sort of way.

She stood at the railing, pretending to have no fear, trying to think how she would act if she really were bereaved and going to Georgia to a brother and not simply going off to live among strangers for the rest of her life. For an instant she considered a mad impulse to rush to the nearest sailor and demand to be taken back to the dock. Her jaw muscles trembled slightly.

None of that now. She'd expected to feel this moment of weakness. And here it was. But she would recover.

Still, she couldn't quite bring herself to go below deck yet. Instead, she wandered about looking down ladders and hatchways and through doorways. She kept thinking she heard a baby crying. She watched as another small boat came aside the ship. The sailors hoisted aboard a great hogshead of bread, two large runlets of rum, and a barrel of fine flour. Overhead, the whiteness became blinding. She tipped her head to look up to the top of the mast. It looked to be about a thousand feet high. Near the top was a round basket, the crow's nest.

Another passenger came aboard, a richly dressed merchant, immaculately shaven, carrying a large portmanteau and arriving with a locker with drawers. He bowed to Jane but kept his distance. An officer of the ship appeared. He put his hand to his heart and bowed to Jane, then stood straight as a tin soldier, his buttons glittering even without the sun.

"I am Mr. Pebblewood," he said in a surprisingly nasal voice, "captain's mate." His face was youthful and kindly despite his odd voice. He was tall and blond and had sensitive boyish eyes that tried to pierce her black veils. With that look, Jane's instincts gibbered at her to flee. Sense held her where she was. She was a featureless shape in black, two shadowed eyes, invisible.

Mr. Pebblewood said, "The captain apologizes for not greeting you himself. He's very busy—and rather upset, as I understand it, by a certain turn of events this morning,."

"There's nothing wrong, is there? Nothing that will delay our departure?"

"If it was anything like that he would have told me."

"What about this fog?"

"It will burn off as soon as the sun comes up. Don't worry, Mistress Timons, we'll be going out with the tide."

She didn't want him to know how desperate she was to go. She said, "It's just that I've never sailed before, and now that I've got my courage up, I'd just as soon be off."

"I understand." He began to walk very leisurely forward, tactfully leading her out of the way of two men handling some ropes. "I hope you won't be lonely during the journey. We have only one other lady aboard, a Mistress Lyle, and I fear she won't be much company to you. She has the most choleric baby I've ever seen. They came aboard last night, and the child has not stopped crying for a minute. You'll hear it as soon as you go below."

The merchant now came over. His name was Winston. He was a general importer-exporter, his main business being shipments of general goods to the American plantations in trade for tobacco. His tone and manner were drier than sawdust. He and the captain's mate chatted for a minute or two while Jane pointedly showed she had no interest in joining their discussion. She kept looking up at the mast—a sailor had climbed up into the crow's nest. The men stopped talking and looked up, too. The mast rocked with the boat as it swung at anchor, so that the crow's nest swung back and forth. It gave Jane an odd feeling in the pit of her stomach.

It affected the merchant much more strongly. Suddenly his face turned a poisonous green. "I regret this terribly," he said in a small voice, putting his palm to his forehead, "but I'm going to disgorge my breakfast." And so he did, promptly, all over the deck. Jane barely had time to back away and protect her skirts.

The man was mortified. Mumbling an apology, he disappeared below decks. Mr. Pebblewood didn't seem to know whether to laugh or curse. The sailor he called over to clean up the mess uncorked a flood of horrible vulgarities about "landlubbing peacocks," et cetera. The officer bowed to Jane in embarrassment and left her to herself.

She watched the stringy sailor dab at the sanded deck with his mop. He, in turn, ignored her as though she were invisible. She thanked Keith silently for his idea of the black veil.

She decided that her first impression of the *Andrew Buck* had been accurate: a pile of junk in its last days of decay, manned by a bunch of ruffians. But it was going to take her to Georgia and that was all that mattered.

The sea slapped and sucked at the ghostly shapes of the fishing boats jogging at their moorings nearby. The gold-white sun appeared on the eastern horizon and brightened the air. As the nasal Mr. Pebblewood had promised, the mist began to evaporate.

Activity aboard the ship increased. Jane sensed a change in the current beneath the rolling, creaking ship; the tide was going out. A quickening breeze blew through her formal black skirts. The sails were lifted to the wide, clearing sky. They snapped like great kites taking the wind. The anchor was pulled and the ship began to move, in an oddly gentle way, down the channel. A weakness ran through Jane's body. She thought she would faint.

She looked hard at the landscape sliding by her. As long as she lived she must hold this picture in her memory and in her heart. England. She held back her tears only by reminding herself that England would have devoured all her dreams, possibly even her very life.

As they made their way down the channel, she saw

467

a waterman with his ferry going to Bristol from the opposite shore. A barge with a cargo of provisions passed, and another, loaded perilously deep with coals.

Her first glimpse of the open Atlantic came through a haze of tears. Where the channel joined the turbulence of the ocean, cliffs veered sharply southward. The *Andrew Buck* fought its way forward. The sails creaked and snapped. The laboring ship shuddered fearfully. Jane felt a jerk as the current seized the ship and thrust it forth onto the open, amethyst ocean.

She remembered the night she'd left York. She'd been so certain it would all turn out right. Now she wasn't certain of anything. She'd learned many things about the world, and few of them were reassuring. What if Keith was right? What if Georgia was a nightmare? She felt a tearing inside her, leaving her without a past, without a name, uncoupling her from everything she'd ever known, ever loved. The nose of the ship cut the sea, carrying her away from England, her homeland, the most beautiful place in the world, the true Garden of Eden, the place where she had loved a highwayman.

Keith! That silent untouchable web spun between them was tearing. "I loved you!" she whispered. And despite his last message to her she knew a part of her must always be glancing back to see if he was following.

She had to go below. She was going to cry, and she wanted no one to see her. She made her legs move. It was hard to keep her balance now, with the deck rising and falling on each billow. She made her way across it with her veil down and without turning her head.

Below decks, somehow the smell of saltwater was thicker than in the open air. And the creak of the rigging seemed louder. The narrow passageway was empty. She kept her head down, avoiding the beams overhead. The child's wailing had stopped. Perhaps the movement of the ship had lulled him to sleep. Jane found the narrow door to her cabin and opened it and stepped inside.

And there he was, lounging on the lower of the two narrow bunks, cleaning his pistols. Scattered on the coverlet were extra flints, round bullets, his powder flask, one long rammer. At his feet lay his side-arm sword in its scabbard. She closed her eyes and put her hand out to the close walls for support. She didn't believe what she was seeing. It was too rich, too simple, too fancy, too perfect. For just a moment she had an eerie feeling of not being sure if she was dreaming or awake.

"I've arranged for a penny wedding," he said without prelude, finishing with the pistol in his hand. (He was never fulsome in his greetings.) "Captain Kimberlee isn't happy about it, but he'll do it." His voice was cranky.

"Wh—" She worked her mouth, which was too dry to function. "Why didn't you tell me?"

He tossed the pistol down, swung his feet to the floor, and shrugged. He looked pale with fatigue, there were shadows beneath his eyes making them enormous and dark. Love welled up in her, stronger, needier than she'd ever known it.

He said, "I didn't know myself until nearly dawn. I walked all over town, went into a dozen grog shops and indulged in a saturnalia of drinking into the small hours—though no matter how much I drank, I couldn't really get drunk. I started to leave the city a dozen times—then my legs carried me to the dock and"— another shrug—"here I am." His tone contained a touch of his own surprise beneath the surface petulance.

She desperately schooled herself, compressed her

mind to a pinhead of intense concentration. "This ship is going to Georgia, you know."

He nodded.

"Do you want to go to Georgia?"

He stood slowly, and wobbled a little with the motion of the ship. He caught an overhead beam for balance. "I want you. And I want . . . I guess I want another chance to be the man I'd hoped to be once—before I became the man I am. I don't think I can do that without you, so wherever you're bound to go—and you *were* bound to go, with me or without me, weren't you?"

She considered what he'd said before, about who he'd once hoped to be. "You never told me about yourself. Stella told me about your mother, but I don't know anything about how you grew up, or . . . or what it was like for you in prison." Overhead she heard the scuffing of feet on the sanded wood of the deck.

"Prison." Keith gave a little laugh. It seemed he wouldn't say more, but then, in a cracked whisper, he added, "The walls, Jane . . . they closed me up in there . . . I thought I would go mad."

Tears welled again in her eyes. She threw off her veils and rushed to him. "Oh, Keith!" Her voice was sobbing. She felt as though she had been pulled back from the edge of death.

He took her in his arms and bent his face to her hair. "I don't understand what you want to do in Georgia, I don't understand big, sweeping dreams anymore. I did when I was a boy, but somehow I lost that. Now I just want . . . I just want to *matter*, Jane." He whispered all this quickly, as if the crystal honesty of it were something shameful.

"You've always mattered, Keith."

"I haven't. A person doesn't matter if he's despised, if he despises himself."

"Keith." She felt as though she were caught in something so radiant she couldn't see. "We'll matter to each other. We'll be to one another like no one else could ever be."

"Do you love me?" It was the barest whisper.

"Yes, oh, I do, I love you with all my heart and soul."

"I don't deserve it, you know. But to earn it, to deserve everything you've given me undeserved, to be the man you mistake me for, I think I'd do anything, Jane."

He continued to hold her hard until the ship made an unexpected motion. He set her away from him and she saw that he'd recovered his petulance. His fingers went to her black bodice. Startled by his mood shift, she said, "Shouldn't this wait until after the wedding?"

"Best not. We're still too near to shore, and my courage is not as remarkable as yours. Unless I occupy myself completely, I'm afraid I'll rush up the companionway and throw myself overboard—even though I still don't know how to swim.

"Besides, you look too beautiful. You would be beautiful in sackcloth, which this virtually is—so perfectly correct and more alluring than a doxie's costume."

And so she was taken again by her notorious rogue, her highwayman, such a handsome young fellow, more like a gallant than a common thief. And because of the way he made love to her there on the breast of the swelling sea she opened in a way she had never opened before, and deep in her he touched something she had not even known was there.

They were married that day, though Captain Kimberlee grumbled, first because he'd been required to take on an extra passenger without warning, second because he had so much to do on his first day out from land that a marriage ceremony was an inconvenience, to say the least. Keith was insistent, however. Hence, as the sun sank beneath a ragged embankment of dark clouds and shot out great spokes of red light which fanned the western sky, the deed was done.

Jane retained a strangely clear vision and slowed sense of time all through the short, quiet ceremony that was performed in the officers' quarters with only the nasal-speaking Mr. Pebblewood (called Snuffy by his dark-browed superior) for a witness. When it was over, she wore Keith's opal ring on her left hand.

Captain Kimberlee picked up his quill and felt its tip. Deciding it would do, he dipped it in a jar of ink and wrote out a marriage certificate. Mr. Pebblewood signed it. Then Keith. Jane watched the curiously delicate movements of his big left hand rounded around the moving pen: *Keith Solomon*. She looked at the name in some surprise. Then it was her turn. She wrote: *Jane Solomon*.

As she straightened, Mr. Pebblewood smilingly offered her a tin mug. Keith and the captain already had theirs. "To your health, Mistress Solomon;" he looked at Keith, "and yours, sir."

Expecting tea, Jane tasted rum. The three men seemed glad for her expression; it gave them something to focus on and laugh about, reducing the formality of the occasion to something more comfortable.

The new Mr. and Mistress Solomon, elated and somewhat dazed, stood on the deck of the *Andrew Buck* in the dark of the evening. They were alone but for the working members of the crew. The helmsman stood with his legs spread, clutching the wheel. A sailor tidied an already neatly piled coil of hawsers. Captain Kimberlee and Snuffy Pebblewood liked to play cards at the end of the day. Mrs. Lyle was below in her cabin with her baby, and the merchant was reported to be violently seasick. (Jane had heard him complain through the open door of his cabin to the ship's boy, "I'd just as lief be thrown overboard to drown. It would be a mercy, all things considered.")

She had the feeling she and Keith would be alone during most of the voyage. It gave her a sense of great luxury and fortune. Oh, sooner or later they would have to make some charitable gestures toward their blighted fellow passengers, but not this evening. This evening she was a bride out with her groom under a sky full of filmy clouds behind which shone an expanse of stars all reflected in every moving surface of black, black sea. The *Andrew Buck* seemed beautiful to her now, a gilded vessel at the pleasure of the wind and the waves.

Keith had convinced her that no one aboard had ever seen "The Rose of Midnight." Captain Kimberlee and Mr. Pebblewood's looks at her bared face during the ceremony had made her extremely nervous—but it was the old look, the one she'd known all her life, the one meant for the "beauty" she'd seen (and hardly recognized) in Stella Grayson's pier glass. It was not the look she'd learned to fear, the one that made her feel impaled by her terrible misadventures on the spike of judgment.

She'd put aside her black veil, changed into a rose-and-gray gown, and pinned her braids tight to her head to keep them as neat as possible against the dark fingers of the night breeze.

"Keith, I think we should make a pact to tell no more lies than necessary in the future."

He leaned one arm on the rail and looked down at the water. "Start clean and all that, hmm?" He pretended to shudder. "I don't know if I have the bowels to be really honest. My vices may be too deep-rooted to be weeded out with a light hand."

She was used to his mockery. And she understood it. It was born of a powerful pride that had suffered a lifetime of injustice. But they must both push thoughts of yesterday from their minds. From now on there were only tomorrows, a new world of them. She knew that Keith was a long way from settled in his feelings about leaving England. He'd done it for her; yet she couldn't help but believe that it was the best thing for him. He could start again in the colonies. He would die an old man in his bed, and not violently at the end of a rope. Despite all he said against America, she still believed they were going to a brave new world where the possibilities of progress were countless.

"Do you know what I said to myself when I was out on the moors alone and being stalked by a highwayman?"

He leaned both arms on the rail and smiled out at the ocean, not looking at her. They were wrapped together in the sounds of rushing water and wind, the squeaks of the rigging and the snap of the Union Jack at the stern.

"I kept saying to myself, 'I will not be frightened, I will not be frightened. Just keep on going the direction you have to go—and don't get lost like a dolt.' "

She glanced at him sidelong. His grin was musing. "Do you know what that highwayman said when he saw you, a miserable scrap of a girl—completely lost, by the way—out on the moors? He said, 'Forget it, Cutler. This girl will not be important in your life.' I was determined about that. But next thing I knew, I was shooting a man for your sake." His sidelong glance was impudent. "Actually, not so much for your sake as for mine. I thought shooting Grubneck Nord would impress you.''

She felt his outlaw personality disintegrating, drifting away over the sea like a vapor, leaving a residue that was only Keith Solomon. Still, it was difficult to look at him and not feel a shiver of . . . something. He was not a man who faded into the woodwork, no matter how quiet and unobtrusive he ventured to be. It was his appearance, certainly, but it was something else, too. She'd always felt he was meant for something grand. He had talents and qualities that had never been properly developed. It would be a fine thing to see him become, as he put it, the man he had once hoped to be.

He put his arm about her and she leaned into his side. "We're never going back, Mistress Solomon.''

"Are you very unhappy about that?''

"I was born to be an exile. I still believe civilization is impossible in America and will be so forevermore, but at least I will have you.'' His hand squeezed her waist.

A gust of wind blew a tendril of hair into her eyes. "We're both going to matter there.''

He caught the loose tendril between two fingers and smiled. "You really think so?''

She nodded. A sudden thought intruded. "What about Eclipse?''

His smile faded. "I sent a message to the Baywoods to give him to Burne.''

"That won't make the captain happy.''

For a moment, Keith remained unsmiling. Then he grinned with pure wickedness. "I'm sure it won't.'' He chuckled. "Eclipse, at least, will be admitted into the best society of the place. It'll probably choke the captain every time Burne wins a race to know it was my horse he was riding—the horse that helped me rob many a fine nobleman."

Jane listened to the creak of the deck and the gurgle of the water. "What about the jewels you left buried at your cottage?"

"I told Hart about them the day I shot him."

Jane absorbed that. "You mean . . . why . . . Stella didn't even need my money!"

Keith laughed again. "She didn't know that."

It took her a moment to tamp down her selfishness and settle back into the placid mood she'd enjoyed before. "Do you suppose she and Hart are as happy as we are?"

A sailor moved behind them to put away a bucket of tar. Keith waited until he was out of hearing range to answer. "I hope so. Stella deserves happiness."

Jane pictured her friend's face, earnest and simple and beautiful as the glow of a candle. "Wouldn't it be wonderful if we learned they are emigrating, too?"

"Wonderful? Considering the villainousness of everything colonial? No, I wouldn't wish your America on my gently bred sister, not for a minute. It's enough that I'm condemned to being transported myself."

She wrinkled her nose. "You condemned yourself."

"Hmm!" He gave her a certain look. "But as for Stella, it's not likely we'll ever see her again. Hart probably took her to Scotland."

They watched the sea for several minutes. The *Andrew Buck* rose and fell on the waves. There was the sound of wood creaking on wood. Shyly Jane moved closer to him. "I think I'd like to go below."

He didn't answer for a moment, then he cocked his head so that he could see her face. He was grinning. She blushed. "It isn't *that* surprising," she said. "This is our wedding night, after all."

He threw his head back and laughed: a rarity—and

glorious! They said she was beautiful, but this, this was beauty to stop the heart.

He drew her even closer, and murmured in her ear, "I'd like to have children—if we live through our first encounter with the savage red Indians, that is."

Keith's children. Instinctively she crossed her hands over her abdomen. She had a brief glimmering that there was going to be more to their life together than she could now imagine. Sharper torments. Sharper thrills. They were going to a place where anything could happen, after all. They had a complete new existence ahead of them. Mr. Solomon and his dame were creatures newborn, without a history. What lay before them were the blank pages of an unwritten book. A great book, for she was certain that what they had found is given only once, to those who are very fortunate—and who have the courage to accept it.

Together they turned from the sea and walked side by side toward their marriage bed. Just before they stepped below decks, she looked up at the vast dazzle of the night sky. The moon was just rising, lifting from the black sea like a full-blown rose.

About the Author

NADINE CRENSHAW worked as a medical assistant, an Avon lady, a Fuller Brush man, and a telephone operator before her first novel was published. She is now the author of six historical romances: MOUNTAIN MISTRESS, which was awarded the Romantic Writers of America Golden Heart, CAPTIVE MELODY, EDIN'S EMBRACE, a finalist for the Romance Writers of America RITA Award, SPELLBOUND, and DESTINY AND DESIRE.

Nadine now writes full time and lives in Chico, California with her husband, the youngest of her two children, and a black Persian cat named Lazarus.